The Alexandria Project

*A Tale of Treachery
and
Technology*

Dog Ear Publishing
4010 W. 86th Street, Ste H
Indianapolis, IN 46268
www.dogearpublishing.net

ISBN: 978-1-4575-0928-5

The characters and events in this book are fictitious. Any similarity to real persons, living or dead, is coincidental and not intended by the author. The Alexandria Project, in first draft form, appeared as a serial at The Standards Blog - http://www.consortiuminfo.org/standardsblog.

Printed in the United States of America on acid-free paper.

ConsortiumInfo.org
2012

First Edition

The Alexandria Project

*A Tale of Treachery
and
Technology*

Andrew Updegrove

*To my father, whose humanity and
dedication to others knew no bounds*

Prologue

L ATE IN THE afternoon of a gray day in December, a panel truck pulled up to the gate of a warehouse complex in a run-down section of Richmond, Virginia. Rolling down his window, Jack Davis punched a code into the control box, and the gate clanked slowly out of the way. Once inside, he wheeled the truck around and backed it up against a loading dock as the gate closed behind him.

After unlocking and raising the loading dock door, Davis threw a light switch, revealing long rows of pallets, each stacked eight feet high with boxes of paper plates, cups and towels. He closed and locked the loading dock door, and stamped on the brake release pedal of a hydraulic lifter parked against the wall. Counting to himself, he pushed the lifter along the wall of pallets. When he reached row nineteen, he turned the lifter and maneuvered its long tines under the pallet. Raising it a few inches, he backed up until he could swing the pallet through 180 degrees. Then he pulled it behind him until it was back exactly where it had been before.

Davis had plenty of room to work, because where the pallet in the second row should have been, there was only a large metal plate set in the floor. Near the edge was a small hinged panel, which he unlocked with a key to expose a biometric security pad.

When Davis pressed his thumb against it, he heard a familiar click. Stepping back, he watched as the plate swung slowly upwards, followed by the telescoping ends of a ladder extending up from a deep shaft barely illuminated in red light. Grasping the ladder firmly, Davis descended through twenty feet of reinforced concrete while the door overhead swung silently closed above him. At the bottom, he remembered to don a pair of sunglasses before opening an unlocked door.

As usual, even with this precaution the bright lights in the enormous room beyond nearly blinded him. But soon he could clearly see the endless rows of floor to ceiling metal racks crammed with identical gray boxes. Each box displayed a row of rhythmically blinking lights, and sprouted a bundle of brightly colored wires that ran down into conduits embedded in the floor.

The room hummed purposefully with the sound of thousands of cooling fans, one to a box. Davis felt more than heard the other vibrations that filled the room, generated by the pulse of the thousands of gallons of cooling water that every minute coursed through the collectors lining the walls of the room, absorbing the waste heat that the racks of computer servers threw off. No heat signature would give this facility away from above; once warm, the coolant was directed to the water intake of a nearby power plant, happy to take the pre-heated water from wherever it was that it came from, no questions asked.

Walking along the perimeter of the room, Davis could look down through the open metal grid of the floor at the first of many additional tiers of computer servers. But that always made him a little dizzy, so instead he looked out for the guard he was relieving. No surprise – there he was, heading Davis's way, more than happy to call it a day. When they met, the guard stopped to slip on the coveralls he carried over one arm. Like the semi-automatic pistol the guard wore in a shoulder holster, they were identical to those that Davis also wore.

"What's the weather like?"

"Sucks. Sleet and more of the same predicted till morning."

"Figures. Tomorrow's my day off."

With that, the other man was on his way. In a few minutes he would drive off in the truck Davis had parked outside.

Well, the weather won't be bothering me in here, Davis thought. The room was climate controlled to within a tenth of a degree of a chilly 54 degrees Fahrenheit, and well-insulated by the bomb-proof walls and roof installed above. It had taken two years for a fleet of delivery vans to carry all the dirt and rock away that had been excavated from beneath the warehouse. The same vans had returned with cement, steel, and, eventually, those thousands of servers, accompanied by technicians to set them up. The process had been tedious, yes, but not a single satellite picture had ever shown a trace of the ambitious construction project proceeding underground.

Of course, the effect worked in both directions. With no links to the outside world other than a voice line to his supervisor, the whole bloody world could come to an end and Davis would be none the wiser until after his shift was over.

Davis walked up a flight of steel stairs to the bullet proof, glass-walled security booth attached to the wall overlooking the room. His major challenge for the next twelve hours would be to stand watch in that booth without falling asleep. There'd be hell to pay if he did, because another guard, in another security room far away, would be watching him on a video screen.

The row of video displays in front of Davis allowed him to see every inch of the outside of the warehouse complex. Racked on the wall behind him were a high powered rifle and a shotgun, but it wasn't likely he'd ever need to use them. One flip of the large red switch in front of Davis would flood the server room with enough Halon gas to not only put out a fire, but asphyxiate any intruder careless enough to leave a gas mask at home. Not for the first time, Davis wished that the house where he lived with his wife and their two small children could be as well protected.

But the government didn't put as high a priority on protecting suburban starter homes as it did on safeguarding its most critical computer network facilities. Some storage facilities, like those serving the needs of the Pentagon and the National Security Administration, were located not far away at Fort Meade. Others, like this one, were scattered far and wide, hidden in plain sight but highly secure nonetheless. No way was anyone going to crack this nut. Davis was dead certain of that.

If Davis had been able to electronically monitor what was happening on server A-VI/147 on Level Three, though, his confidence might have taken a hit. True, concrete and steel walls, surveillance cameras and Halon gas were more than adequate to protect the physical well being of his facility against anything short of a direct hit by a "bunker busting" nuclear weapon. But the data on the facility's servers had to rely on virtual defenses – firewalls, security routines and intrusion scanners.

And those defenses hadn't been enough. Someone had gotten inside.

~~0000~~ ~~0001~~ ~~0010~~ ~~0011~~ 0100 ~~0011~~ ~~0010~~ ~~0001~~ ~~0000~~

Meet Frank

THE NEXT MORNING, a morbidly obese Corgi named Lily was sniffing a tree on 16th Street, in the Columbia Heights neighborhood of Washington, D.C. A cold, insistent drizzle fell on her, but Lily didn't care, because Lily was sniffing at her favorite tree. Indeed, the meager processing power of Lily's brain was wholly consumed by sampling the mysterious scents wafting up from the damp earth, for this was also the favorite tree of every other dog in the neighborhood.

Something was nagging at the edge of her senses, though.

"C'mon, Lily! Hurry up!"

Lily turned her head. The annoying distraction was coming from the person at the other end of her leash, someone with stockless feet jammed into worn, black loafers. Above bare ankles, a pair of pajama-clad legs disappeared into a rumpled raincoat. She saw there was an arm holding an umbrella, too, and under the umbrella, a stubbly, forty-something face topped by thinning black hair. Lily decided that the face did not look happy.

"Ah!" she thought. "That would be Frank." Relieved that the distraction could be ignored, Lily returned to the important work at hand.

"*C'mon*, Lily!" the voice said again.

The fact that Frank's face was unhappy was unremarkable. Even in pleasant weather, Frank tended to dwell pointlessly over the minor miseries of his life. Not long ago, those miseries had become much less minor when his mother Doreen entered a retirement home. After helping her move in, Frank took a deep breath and prepared to leave. No use dragging things out, he thought. Transitions are difficult and best dealt with quickly.

Still, it was sad. His mother was standing by the doorway of her new apartment, lower lip a-tremble and Lily held tightly in her arms. It was clear that she was rapidly nearing her emotional limits. Better hurry up.

"Well, Mom," he said, "I guess I'll be leaving now."

Then it happened. With a lunge, Doreen thrust Lily into Frank's arms. He stepped back with surprise into the hallway, too horrified to allow himself to grasp the obvious, while struggling to maintain his grip on the suddenly manic animal.

"The home doesn't allow pets," his mother blurted. "I could never have signed the lease if I hadn't known that Lily would be safe with you. Now don't you worry; I've made you her legal guardian, so it's all set. Now go! Get out of here, before I change my mind."

Frank desperately wanted her to change her mind. But his mother had already slammed the door in his astonished face. He stared blankly at it as the enormity of his plight sank in. Now what? Lily was just three years old, and acknowledged his existence only by barking. He heard his mother sobbing piteously on the other side of the door. He felt like crying, too.

That had been two long, loud months ago. Only recently had he progressed from the denial stage to active mourning.

"*Come on!*" Frank hissed. At last, Lily turned away from her tree. She looked up at him reproachfully, and barked.

"Okay, okay," Frank said, fumbling in his pocket. He held a dog treat up for Lilly to see. "*Okay?*"

Satisfied that her efforts would not go unrewarded, Lily began looking for just the right place to do what finally needed to be done. At last, she squatted, looking blankly ahead. Frank sighed with relief.

A blue plastic bag inverted over his free hand, Frank scooped up Lily's grudging gift. He handed over the treat, jerking back with his fingers barely intact.

"Isn't that just the story of my life?" he thought bleakly as Lily happily consumed her treat. "Every day I give her a cookie, and every day she gives me a bag of shit."

Trudging home through the rain, Frank reflected that his day generally went downhill from there.

—0000—0001—0010—0011— 0100 —0011—0010—0001—0000—

Lily shook herself mightily inside the foyer of Frank's dingy apartment house, wetting what little of Frank was still dry. Satisfied, she planted her substantial hindquarters firmly on the floor, looked up at Frank, and barked. Frank sighed, picked up the still-wet dog, and labored his way up the stairs to his second floor flat.

As he climbed to the top, Frank's rising eyes met a pair of fuzzy pink slippers, a floral house dress, and then a pair of folded arms draped with a bath towel. Just above them, he knew, would be the perpetually hostile face of his across-the-hall neighbor. As that scowling face hove into view, Frank once again noted the uncanny resemblance his neighbor bore to North Korean president Kim Jong-Il. Only with hair curlers.

"'Morning, Mrs. Foomjoy," Frank offered as Lily twisted wildly in his arms. He deposited the dog at her feet.

"Shame on you!" Mrs. Foomjoy barked as she knelt to massage Lily with the bath towel. "Poor, dear wet baby!" she crooned.

"It's raining, Mrs. Foomjoy," Frank observed. "Lily hasn't learned how to use the indoor facilities yet."

"Then why she not wear the lovely rain jacket I give her?" she snorted. "What is *wrong* with you? You don't deserve dog like this!"

Frank couldn't have agreed more. Lily groveled at Mrs. Foomjoy's feet, and then leaned to one side until gravity obligingly rolled her onto her back. The dog gazed up with adoring, goggle eyes as Mrs. Foomjoy rubbed her stomach.

His neighbor grabbed the leash from Frank's hand when she stood up. "I see to welfare of this dog!" she snapped, shutting her door loudly behind her. Frank stood suddenly alone in the poorly lit hallway, a warm, blue plastic pendulum swinging slowly from side to side in his hand. Relieved, he entered his own apartment and quietly shut the door.

Frank hung his dripping raincoat on a hook in the linoleum floored hallway inside. At one time, his apartment's décor might have charitably been described as "Late-Twentieth-Century Divorced Middle-Aged Male." Now the most obvious theme was random clutter. He poured a cup of coffee and sat at the small table in the small kitchen. Before him the large screen of his laptop stared blankly back at him. With resignation, he turned the computer on.

Normally, the sound of a computer booting up would have struck him as cheerful; the imperceptibly soft whir of the cooling fan spinning up to speed; the blinking, blue light that assured him that the device was powering up; the screen phosphorescing into life with a pearly glow. After all, information technology – IT – was not only his profession, but the primary foundation of his existence.

Email was Frank's preferred link to the outside world, providing a social firewall between him and the random messiness of direct human contact. Frank was convinced that digital relations were far safer than their in-person analogue. Electronic communications brought him as close to his fellow man as he usually wished to be. Any more intimate than that, and things were apt to become at best unpredictable, and at worst, well, he'd been *there* all too often before. You never got enough time to think before things started spiraling out of control.

Which brought him back to the night before. Be honest, he mused ruefully. You got what you deserved. Or didn't get what you didn't deserve, to be more precise.

He stared at the keyboard. Should he check his email or shouldn't he? The rational side of his brain said, yes, what's there is there. Deal with it.

But the other side of his brain had a different opinion: "Go back to bed," it whispered urgently, "It's Sunday. You don't have to deal with anything today."

That was true. And who knows what might happen by Monday? There could be a typhoon tonight. Or maybe giant pterodactyls would erupt from a wormhole next to the Lincoln Memorial, scattering screaming tourists towards the safety of nearby Metro stations. That side of his brain was lobbying strongly to take two aspirin, pull the covers back over his head, and let reality take care of itself for another twenty-four hours.

He sighed and made up his mind. Might as well see sooner rather than later what people from his office had posted on line about the night before. A few clicks later and he was at the Facebook page of Mary, the sullen receptionist. Yes, there were pictures from the party. Lots of them. Later would do just fine after all, he decided. He snapped the laptop shut without turning it off.

The sad thing was, for once he had actually been looking forward to the Library of Congress IT Department Holiday party, even bringing his daughter Marla with him, a Georgetown University grad student. He appreciated the great impression she always made on his co-workers. Unlike her dad, Marla was self-assured and sociable. She worked the crowd like a pro, chatting and shaking hands, poised and laughing. How could he feel anything but proud? It was hard not to drink a bit more than usual as he watched her from the security of the bar in the rear of the function room.

More to the point, Frank had been looking forward to making Marla feel proud of her old man as well. Everyone knew that George Marchand, the Director of IT at the LoC, was going to announce his choice to head an important security initiative mandated by the Cybersecurity Subcommittee of the House Committee on Science and Technology. Frank figured he had the spot all sewn up. After all, he was - or at least at one time had been - a recognized cybersecurity innovator; a McArthur Foundation "Genius" Award recipient, no less, in recognition of his widely acclaimed creative work in the early days of computer networking.

So when George stood up and tapped on his glass, Frank sat up straighter. He listened impatiently as his boss welcomed the spouses, thanked the staff for their work that year, and told a joke at his own expense. At last, he began to make the announcement that Frank was waiting for.

And then it happened. One moment Frank was looking sideways to see the reaction on his daughter's face when his name was called, and the next he was hearing someone else's name ring out instead. And not just any name, but Rick Wellesley's – "only out for himself" Rick, a self-satisfied slug of a middle-manager who had never had a creative thought in his life. Someone who had even briefly reported to Frank when he first came to work at the LoC. *Rick Wellesley?* How could this be happening?

But it was. There was Rick, standing and basking in the applause, glancing briefly and triumphantly in Frank's direction. Frank was stunned, his face burning. And then he was angry. Without a word to his daughter, he stood up and marched to the bar, turning his back on the party as George finished his remarks. Knocking back another drink, Frank now felt foolish as well as angry. Everyone was probably looking at him, but he was afraid to turn around and find out. He sulked at the bar until Marla came looking for him.

Sitting now in his kitchen, Frank felt his face grow flush again. After all, everyone had expected the job to go to him. Then, with a wrenching feeling, he had a worse thought – what if no one had expected him to get the job? Maybe he was the only one in the whole damn department who hadn't seen it coming. Maybe everyone had been laughing up their sleeves as they watched him bask in his expected glory, just waiting for his jaw to drop when he realized that he had been skunked by Rick.

Of course that had been the case, he thought wretchedly. He was sure of it.

~~0000 0001 0010 0011~~ 0100 ~~0011 0010 0001 0000~~

And why not? What had he really done in the last twenty years? Sure, he'd become a star at the Massachusetts Institute of Technology – "MIT" to anyone in the know. He'd enrolled at the age of sixteen after skipping two years of middle school. Not that skipping a few grades was unusual at MIT. As an undergraduate, he'd become part of Project Athena, an ambitious effort to create a distributed computing system for the whole university. Of course, the goal for the project's corporate sponsors was to use MIT as a testbed. Later, they hoped to productize the design and make a ton of money.

For some reason, Frank had intuitively locked onto the security challenges that such a system would present. He already had privileges to use MIT's gateway to the government-funded Advanced Research Projects Agency Network – the now-famous "ARPANET" that was the precursor to the Internet. Only select institutions had access to it then, but Frank immediately grasped where Project Athena and the ARPANET together could eventually lead. It hit him between the eyes that this was the start of something big. Linking terminals together around a campus was today's goal, but the next step would be to connect those networks together, using ARPANET technology.

That sounded awesome, but how would you restrict access to any particular data to one person, and not let it be seen by everyone else? MIT was already a hotbed of hackers. If students were going to great lengths now to break into restricted sections of university computers just for fun, what would criminals, or enemy countries, not do to break into classified computers, once someone had linked them all together?

Frank tackled that issue with gusto, if not discipline. He was a big picture guy, and what a big and exciting picture it was! The idea of wide area networks was brand new, and big ideas were needed to make sense of it all; the details could come later. When Frank graduated, he stayed on at MIT, nominally in a PhD program, but for all practical purposes he lived at a terminal in the Project Athena lab, surviving on coffee and code like so many other young computer engineering students back in the day.

Luckily for Frank, he found a mentor – an engineer on loan from one of the sponsoring companies. Surprisingly, the two hit it off, and the older man reined in the younger one enough to keep Frank's ideas from flying off into too many directions at once. He also insisted that Frank get his best ideas recorded in some sort of coherent order. Often they talked until all hours, the older man channeling Frank's enthusiasm and helping him follow his insights down the most productive paths.

Frank never completed his doctorate, but he did finish his Masters thesis – and by anyone's account, it was brilliant. He anticipated just about every security challenge that would arise over the next twenty years as the Internet took off. He also suggested most of the solutions that were later refined and implemented to deal with a massively networked world. Even today, his thesis remained an obligatory foundational reference in just about every new network and Internet security paper that was written.

Frank's thesis also brought him to the notice of the mysterious keepers of the MacArthur Fellows Program – the unknown judges that every year contact a select group of exceptional individuals they have decided, "show exceptional merit and promise for continued and enhanced creative work."

Receiving a MacArthur Fellowship had been the high point of Frank's professional career. But as a practical matter, it also brought an end to it, because the payments of $25,000 every three months for five years gave Frank the freedom to do whatever he wanted to without ever having to acquire the discipline of making his way in the world. It also allowed him to get married.

It was not helpful that what Frank wanted to do usually changed every other week. It wasn't long before his work at Project Athena suffered. He no longer listened to his mentor, and his assigned tasks no longer got done. Instead, he plunged from one question that intrigued him to another, never getting very far along with any of them.

Like many people whose intellectual abilities matured before their social skills, Frank developed an abrupt and assertive manner that helped mask his discomfort around others. That was unfortunate, because his new–found fame encouraged him to become even more obnoxious than ever. Soon, the other guys in the lab were annoyed with his failure to meet his commitments, and also sick of hearing his latest revelations about security – or about any other topic on which he had decided he was now an expert.

Eventually, it was his mentor who took Frank aside and told him that if he didn't shape up, his days in the lab were numbered. Frank didn't take that well. What right did some middle aged, middle-management type with a degree from a state school in the Midwest have to tell a certified Genius anything about anything?

Quite a lot, Frank now reflected, gazing at his closed laptop. Like the immature idiot he was then, he had cleared his things out of the Project Athena lab the same day his mentor had called him out and never returned. Eventually, the MacArthur Fellowship money ran out, and with a wife and young daughter, Frank had to get more serious about working. Or at least he should have. For a while, his thesis and MacArthur reputation carried him from job to job. But when the bottom fell out of the economy, employers received a flood of great résumés for every job they posted.

By then, of course, Frank's résumé was also getting pretty long in the tooth. Frank had no "continued and enhanced creative work" to show for his five years of subsidized, random behavior. He'd never published another paper, and it was others, and not Frank, who turned his thesis ideas into real protocols and products. As the jobs got scarce, reference checks counted a whole lot more, and the feedback about Frank always came back the same: brilliant, arrogant, unfocused, unreliable. That was more charitable than what his soon-to-be ex-wife had to say. But he hadn't listened to her, either.

Frank usually tried not to think much about the years that followed: the start-up that had signed him up as Chief Technical Officer and the VCs that fired him; the time spent without a job at all; the rut he fell into for years after his wife moved out with their daughter, when he said the hell with everything and everybody. That time was a blur of punching the clock in whatever high school, small business or municipal IT department would take him on until he got fired again, then waiting until his unemployment ran out before finding something else he could do in his sleep, until even that became too much to bother with.

Through all that time, though, industry insiders still sought Frank out, so he maintained a low-key consulting business on the side to make sure he could always cover his child support payments. Among the elite in the world of security, Frank still had the reputation of a wizard, able to come up with the kind of insights that would make the most impenetrable problems suddenly transparent. An emailed plea for help describing something dense and dark that had already defied all of the usual solutions would reliably generate a response from Frank an hour or two later, usually beginning, "It strikes me that…" and ending with, "I suggest you try…." Invariably, what Frank suggested worked. But requests for his ongoing assistance went unanswered.

It was his daughter Marla that finally set Frank back on his feet. One Friday when he was once again out of work, he picked her up for their weekend together. But something was wrong; his normally chatty preteen wasn't saying a word. As they walked, she looked down at her feet. Then she looked up as if to ask him a question, only to look down again. After a while, Frank got irritated. "Marla, if there's something you want to ask me, just ask it already!"

But Marla still paused. Finally she said, "Dad, you know I'm in a computer class now, don't you? It's something you have to take in seventh grade."

"Yes," he said, surprised. "So?"

"Well," she said, and stopped. He waited, now curious.

"Well," she started again, "Today we went on a field trip to the computer department of a big company, and we all had to sign in and wear these name tag things. One of the people that worked there gave us a tour, and when she saw my name, she asked if I had a father named Frank, so of course I said yes."

"Uh huh," said Frank, not liking where this was going.

"Well..." Marla paused again, and then the words came rushing out. "She said that she went to school with you and you were the most brilliant person she had ever known and that you'd gotten a big award for being a genius and she wanted to know what you were doing now." Marla stopped abruptly for a long moment. "And I didn't know what to say."

Frank wished this could be all over, and quickly.

But, Marla, of course, needed an answer. "Dad, the guide said you used to be somebody really important."

Frank felt like he was dangling at the end of a rope, turning slowly in the breeze. He looked away, and tried to think what to say. What *could* he say? And then, with all of the disarming innocence of a child, Marla finished for him.

"Dad, she wasn't telling the truth, was she?"

Frank couldn't breathe. His daughter thought so little of him that she had to believe that the guide was thinking of someone else? Or was it that she would be too ashamed of what he had become to be able to deal with the truth? He felt sick.

By then, they were standing in front of the door of his cheap apartment building. The traffic rushed past the garbage cans and trash piled up on the curb, and Frank took it all in. The sights, the smells, his life – they all fit together perfectly, didn't they? Still, he couldn't think of a word to say.

Finally, Marla put her hand on his arm. "It's okay, Dad," she said softly. "Let's go upstairs."

That had been ten years ago. The following Monday he sucked it up and called his old mentor, George Marchand, and asked for a job. George was the head of the IT department at the Library of Congress now, and Frank called him out of the blue to ask if they could get together for coffee.

George had been as gracious as Frank had been uncomfortable. Frank had sent his résumé along by email, for what it was worth, and George cut straight to the chase after the opening pleasantries.

"You know I'll need to bring you in at the bottom, Frank. Can you deal with that?"

Frank was prepared. "Sure, sure, George. I'll be fine with that."

George nodded, brows furrowed. Then he changed the topic. "How's that cute goddaughter of mine these days? I can't even remember the last time I saw Marla."

"She's great," said Frank, suddenly determined; it helped to remember why he was sitting there. "Just great. We get together every weekend. She's in seventh grade now. She's smart as a whip and gets straight As."

They chatted about family for a few more minutes, and then George looked at his watch. They both stood up, and shook hands.

"I won't let you down," Frank said as he looked George in the eye for the first time.

"I know you won't," his new boss said. But Frank could tell he was only being polite.

0000 0001 0010 0011 0100 0011 0010 0001 0000

Sitting in his kitchen, Frank reflected that he'd been as good as his word. But not much better, he made himself admit. Yes, he'd rarely missed a day of work, and no one could say he hadn't earned his paycheck. And yes, he'd earned every promotion he'd been given.

But the promotions had been few, and the last one had been awarded seven years ago. Frank still had tremendous insights into IT architecture, and he remained as interested as ever in new developments in security. His cubicle at the LoC was stacked high with articles covered in scribbled notes, and he read voraciously online as well. For anyone in the office with a thorny problem, Frank was the go-to guy who could always solve it, provided he was allowed to tackle it alone. Sitting at a keyboard, Frank was still The Man – the tougher the problem the better, just bring it on. Three hours, eight hours or twenty hours later, he'd still be turning it over in his mind until suddenly an elegant and creative solution would spring to mind.

Management level work, though, was something else again. Every time George gave him a shot at a long term project with a couple of others to supervise, Frank could never pull it all together.

Half the time, he'd be up in the clouds thinking big thoughts that went beyond the task at hand, and the rest of the time he'd be down in the weeds, diving down rat holes to solve problems that could easily be ignored. The folks he was supposed to be supervising never knew what they would be doing from one day to the next, or what, if anything, Frank did with the work they submitted. Inevitably, George would have to take the project back. It didn't take long before the big projects stopped coming, and Frank settled into the solitary niche where he had stayed ever since.

He wasn't done beating himself up, though. Admit it, he demanded, you were relieved when the projects stopped coming. You've been marking time for years now, and that's all you'll ever do. What right did you have to think George would throw this project your way?

But this had been a *security* project, damn it. That (and the drinks he'd had last night) were what had led him to corner George later on in the cloakroom.

"I'm sorry, Frank," George had said, wrapping his scarf around his neck. "I thought about letting you know ahead of time, and then I didn't. I guess I should have."

"That's not the point, George! Rick can't find his own ass with both hands in a well-lit room. What were you thinking?"

George buttoned his overcoat, and reached for his hat. "Of course Rick can't hold a candle to you when it comes to security, Frank. There's nobody I've ever worked with who has the insight and ideas that you do. And everybody knows nobody covers his butt like Rick."

Frank let his breath out with a rush of exasperation as George settled his hat on his head. "So then why did you pick him?"

George squared off to Frank as he pulled on his gloves, looking him straight in the eye.

"Frank, you may know security, but when it comes to understanding people and how to manage them, you haven't got a clue. Yes, Rick is one hell of a weasel. But you can always rely on a weasel to watch out for himself. That means that if you give him a job to do and tell him his job is on the line, well, by hook or by crook, he'll get it done. And I can't say that about you."

Well, what could Frank say to that? He'd asked George for an explanation and now he'd have to listen to it.

"How many chances have I given you over the years, Frank? I can't remember, can you?" Frank looked away.

"You're twice as smart as I am," George continued. "You should have had my job by now! But that's never going to happen unless you grow up and learn how to perform. If you thought I'd stick my neck out for you with Chairman Steele grandstanding in the House, looking for the next poor bastard to eviscerate in front of the cameras during a public committee meeting, well, you're just delusional. Good night, Frank."

There hadn't been anything Frank could say to that, of course, so he was relieved when George turned and walked away. Furious at himself, Rick and George, in that order, he stalked back to the bar.

Frank decided that was as much of the night before as he was up to reliving; he'd leave the scene with Rick for his next exercise in psychological self-flagellation. It had all escalated so stereotypically anyway; Rick's approach and his smarmy condescension, Frank's insult in response. Okay, enough.

He felt the anger well up again, and with it, a sudden sense of purpose. Screw the jerk; just because Rick got the project didn't mean that Frank couldn't still show him up. After all, Frank had been so sure he had the spot in the bag that he'd already started writing up a proposal with his plan of attack outlined. No way was Rick going to be able to pull this job off; George would realize that soon enough, and then there'd be no one to turn to but Frank.

He snapped open his laptop and punched the keys with fury, rushing through the complicated log-in sequence that would take him into the heart of the LoC's system, where his proposal was archived. Highlighting the file name, he hit the entry key, leaned back, and waited for the proposal to display.

Except it didn't. Frank leaned forward and poked the Enter key again. Still nothing. Perhaps his laptop was frozen. But no - he could still move his cursor.

Then Frank noticed that something on the screen was changing: the background color was warming up, turning reddish, orange and yellow, as if the sun was rising behind it. Now that was different! Frank watched with growing astonishment as the colors began to shimmer, and then coalesced into shapes that might be flames. Yes, flames indeed – but not like a holiday screen-saver image of a log fire – this was a real barn-burner of a conflagration!

Frank wondered what kind of weird virus he'd picked up, and

how. After all, he was an IT security specialist, and if any laptop was protected six ways to Sunday, it was his. So much for whatever he had planned for today; he'd have to wipe his disk and rebuild his system from the ground up.

He was about to shut the laptop down when he saw that the flames were dying away. Now what? An image seemed to be emerging from behind the flames as they subsided. Frank leaned forward; the image became a tall building - maybe some sort of lighthouse? Underneath, there was a line of text, but in characters he couldn't read. Truly, this was like no virus he'd ever seen or even heard of before. He reached for his cell phone and took a picture of the screen just before it suddenly went blank.

Frank was impressed. Whoever had come up with this hack certainly had a sense of style. A weird one, but hey, graphic art of any type wasn't the long suit of most hackers.

Frank got a pad of paper and a pen from his desk and punched up the file directory again, highlighted his proposal, and pressed the Enter key again. This time, he would watch more closely and take notes.

But all that displayed was a three word message: "File not found."

Frank tried again – no luck. He did a search of the entire directory using the title. Nothing. His proposal was gone.

Now he was alarmed. After all, the directory he was staring at was in the innermost sanctum of the Library of Congress computer system, and the LoC was the greatest library in the world. Within its vast holdings were books that could be found almost nowhere else on earth. Recently, the Library had begun digitizing materials, and then destroying the physical copies. If someone had been able to delete files in the most protected part of the Library's computer system, what else might be missing?

Frank raced through a random sampling of sensitive directories, and then let out a sigh of relief; it was hard to tell for sure, but everything seemed intact. He checked the server logs for the Library's indices, holdings and various other resources; everything appeared to be undisturbed, with no unusual reductions in the amount of data stored.

Frank drummed his fingers on the table in the cramped dinette. How to go about figuring this one out? Then he remembered his cell phone, and sent the picture of the screenshot to his laptop. The picture wasn't great, but once he enlarged it he could tell that the characters were Greek. He cropped the image until just the text remained, then ran it through a multi-script OCR program to turn the picture of the Greek characters into text. Finally, he pasted the text into a translator window. No luck – all he got was a "cannot translate" message.

Frank's fingers started drumming again. He reopened the drop down menu of languages in the translator screen and noticed that another language option was "Ancient Greek." He highlighted that choice and hit Enter. This time, the screen blinked.

Frank looked, and then he blinked, too. But the translation still read the same:

> **THANK YOU FOR YOUR**
> **CONTRIBUTION**
> **TO THE ALEXANDRIA PROJECT**

~~0000~~ ~~0001~~ ~~0010~~ ~~0011~~ 0100 ~~0011~~ ~~0010~~ ~~0001~~ ~~0000~~

2

The Plot Thickens

FRANK WONDERED HOW long his phone had been buzzing. He was about to turn it off when he saw that it was Marla. "Hi, kid," he said, "Listen...". But she cut him off.

"Well! So nice of you to pick up. I considered worrying about you for a second, and then figured you'd never really jump out the window – you're only on the second floor, after all, and broken bones don't solve anything. I mean, you're much too logical to miss something like that."

"Marla, I...."

"So how's your big morning-after-the-night-before coming along?"

Frank tried one last time to escape. "Listen, Marla, this just isn't a good time. I'm in the middle of something, and...."

"Right. Fat chance YOU got lucky last night. I'll be right over." She hung up.

Frank looked helplessly at the phone. He started to call her back but then snapped the phone shut. She wouldn't answer anyway.

Turning back to his laptop, he took stock. He had no doubt he'd eventually be able to figure out how the intruder had gained access. The more challenging question was why? All he really knew so far was that a file in the most secure part of a government computer system had been stolen by someone who wanted their theft to be discovered. That, and the fact that whoever was behind the exploit had a snarky sense of humor, or wanted to lead him down the wrong path – or both. No matter how you looked at it, he didn't have a lot to work with.

Frank's fingers drummed on the kitchen table for a full minute, and then he opened the Alexandria Project screenshot again, this time using a photo editing program. But cleaning the image up as much as possible uncovered no new clues. More finger drumming produced no further revelation, either, so for want of anything more productive to do, he deleted the Greek text, typed in the English translation, and stared at the result.

How seriously should he take what had just happened? After all, someone with truly malicious intent would never leave a calling card. Instead, he would do everything he could to avoid detection. So if the cracker wanted his exploits to be known, what exactly was he trying to prove? Perhaps he was just showing off.

That would be troubling enough, though, given how deeply inside the LoC's defenses the intruder had penetrated. What if the files the mysterious cracker had decided should be "contributed" had been really important files? Or files that had just been created, and hadn't yet been backed up to another location?

On a hunch, Frank started typing again. A few new passwords and a number from a different security token than he'd used before, and he was staring at the same directory at the off-site backup center for the Library of Congress. Then he clicked on the Enter key for his security proposal. Nothing. And then the following message appeared:

> *The material you have requested is being cataloged by the Alexandria Project Acquisitions Department*
> *Please try again later*

Frank was impressed; and he had to admit he liked the guy's sense of humor. Whoever had hacked the LoC's system was good – really good. He had not only penetrated the LoC's primary security system, but getting through to the Library's backup site as well, ensuring that whatever had been "contributed" was gone for good. That was truly disturbing. If the intruder could do that with one file, theoretically he could do it with every file on every server available from his point of entry. Frank would have to put some real effort into working this one out.

And then it struck him: why bother?

He smiled slowly and leaned back. All of the tension that had built up inside him began to seep away as he laced his fingers behind his head and stretched his legs out under the table. This was actually rather cool, wasn't it? No, he corrected himself, this was really, *really* cool.

Up until that moment, Frank had been dreading checking his email. Now he opened it with relish.

Yes, there was an email from George waiting for him. Frank grinned wickedly as he read the subject line – in all caps, even: "WHAT IS THE ALEXANDRIA PROJECT?"

"Great question!" Frank banged out happily in reply. "Better get Rick on that right away!" He hit the "send" button with a flourish, staring gleefully at the screen as the message disappeared.

Frank poured himself another cup of coffee and toggled back to the screen with the Alexandria Project logo in translation. He saw it now with a new sense of appreciation. It actually was an awfully good looking image, wasn't it? Very stylish - just right to replace his old screen saver. Amazing how quickly a day could take a turn for the better.

Just then he heard a knock, followed by Marla's key rattling in the door. He got up to usher her in.

"Hey, kid!" he greeted her, smiling broadly. "It's great to see you."

"My, you sound perky," she said, looking at him with curiosity. "I thought after last night's little passion play I'd find you huddled in the corner in a fetal position, moaning softly."

She walked into the kitchen to drop a bag of bagels and fruit on the dinette table, and then went back into the hall to hang up her coat. Returning, she found her father standing behind his laptop with arms crossed and a goofy grin spread across his face.

"So what gives? You haven't looked this happy since Rush Limbaugh got busted for popping pain pills."

Frank just smiled and pointed at his laptop. Marla's expression was quizzical;, but she wasn't about to ask for an explanation if her father hadn't chosen to offer one. She sat down and stared at the screen, searching for clues.

"Okay," She said. "So you've found a new charity you like and that makes you all giggly?" But Frank just raised his eyebrows, so she looked at the screen again, vexed that her father had posed a riddle she couldn't solve.

Finally, she had to give up. "Alright, whoever you are, what have you done with my cranky old man? I'm not saying this isn't a huge improvement, but unless you agree to keep him, you might as well let him go now."

Frank traded his grin for a simple smile and sat down. "Sorry to be so mysterious," he said, pouring her a cup of coffee. "But it's not every day I get to savor something this delicious. And this really is good."

"Fine," she said. "So share."

"Okay, so here's what's up: you've certainly figured out by now that I expected to get the project that George gave to Rick last night. And you've also assumed, I'm sure, that it was a security project, or my nose wouldn't have been so far out of joint." Marla shrugged. Of course, but she didn't want to embarrass her father further by admitting it.

"If so, you're right on target. Now here are two things you don't know: first, the project is an important one: the boys up on the Hill suddenly have their knickers all in a twist about cybersecurity. And it's a damn good thing they do, too, because there are bad guys out the wazoo out there with plenty of reasons to want to stick it to us – North Koreans: Revolutionary Guards from Iran; the big boys in Al-Qaeda, wherever they're hiding out; lots and lots of criminals in Eastern Europe and Russia - who knows who else. And the easiest way to wreak havoc on the only remaining Super Power in the world is via an Internet connection."

"Isn't that a bit of an overstatement, Dad? I mean, with all the money we spend on defense, how could some rogue nation, much less a criminal outfit, manage that?"

"How? Because we haven't done enough to prevent it. It wasn't until last June that the Department of Defense formally acknowledged that cybersecurity needs to be part of national defense at all. That's pretty scary, because if you think about it, our $600 billion annual defense budget makes us more vulnerable, not less so."

"How do you figure that?"

"Because it helps us run everything with computers – all the bombers, all the missiles, all the ground troops – everything. And they're all controlled through the Internet."

"So what? Isn't that why they hire smart guys like you, to set things up so the bad guys can't get in?"

"Sure, the government sets up firewalls and requires people to use passwords and all that, but data still has to get in and out or it isn't useful. The CIA bigwigs at Langley have to suck information in from resources all over the world, and they also have to get instructions back out to their agents in the field. Same with the Department of Defense. All that data is spewing in and out like a giant fire hose – video from predator drones flying over Afghanistan, satellite data from all over the world, battlefield intelligence from spotters in forward positions, and much, much more – gigabytes of it every hour."

Marla looked unconvinced. "Okay, so why is this any different from the old days, when all they had were secure telephones and secret codes for anything that went out by radio? It may be more information now, but aren't the challenges just the same?"

"Yes and no," he admitted, "but the 'yes' bit is by far the smallest part. The first thing to realize is that in the old days, besides paper documents, all you had to worry about were voices and Morse code signals. Both were transmitted using 'analog' technology – electric and electromagnetic pulses. If a bad guy managed to intercept the message, the most he could do was listen and record it to play back later. These days, we send every kind of information imaginable - everything from text to spreadsheets to video to radar images to...you name it. And all that information is transmitted as 'digital' data – just ones and zeroes. Those ones and zeroes can be stored, analyzed, searched, re-purposed- and altered in ways that a voice recording never could."

"So?" Marla asked. "That should just make things a whole lot easier to deal with, shouldn't it? I mean, computers can just encrypt all that information automatically, right? In the old days, I guess the sender had to use code tables and such to encrypt messages one word at a time, and then the receiver would have to do the same thing in reverse. And if someone broke the code and you didn't know it, you were cooked. I remember you telling me how the Brits cracked the Nazi's Enigma machine code and the Germans never figured it out."

"All that's true," Frank said, "but there are some important differences. Back when most information existed only in paper form, it was easy to control how many copies of a top secret document there were, and who had access to them. And you could put them behind walls, locks and guards. Now they're all on servers, and those servers are all linked together, and...."

"Okay, Okay," Marla interrupted. "You've ranted at me about this often enough before."

"Hardly ranting," he said primly. "Simply fulfilling a father's duty to pass along important information to the next generation." She made a face at him. "But to continue: every day, every big enterprise is adding new computers for new employees; swapping out old routers as part of normal maintenance; updating obsolete software and adding new programs. All of that has to be done according to strict protocols, or it introduces points of vulnerability. And when you allow email into your system, bad stuff can come in that way, too – lots of it."

"Okay," Marla admitted. "I've fallen for that stuff once or twice." But her interruption barely slowed him down.

"Every moment, the bad guys are probing our systems for gaps in our defenses. It only takes one vulnerability to allow an intruder to plant some nasty software - "malware" we call it - inside the firewall, and it's usually really difficult for us to find it. Once it's there, the malware can start prowling around. When it finds what the cracker sent it to look for, it opens a "trapdoor" in the firewall and sends that data to whoever planted it in the first place. Or maybe it's been programmed to delete the information so it's no longer available, or perhaps subtly alter it in such a way that while it may seem fine, it's actually no longer trustworthy."

"It all depends on who the bad guy is – a criminal, a spy, or whatever. Imagine he works for, say, Al-Qaeda. The malware he plants just sits there, like a living member of a sleeper cell, just waiting for the right time. You don't know it's there, but it is. One day its clock runs out, or it gets a signal from outside, or maybe it even gets triggered by something inside the firewall it's been waiting for. Then it does something truly destructive, like take down a key system just when it's needed the most – say the national power grid."

Marla broke in. "Okay, okay, I'm impressed. But if this is so dangerous, why don't we hear more about it?"

"But you have, my dear," he replied. "Do any of these names ring a bell? Heartland? T.J.X? Hannaford Brothers?"

"I remember hearing the name Heartland before. Wasn't that the big credit card security breach that was in the news a while back?" Her father nodded. "So I'm guessing the other two were security breaches, too, right?"

"Bingo." Frank nodded again. "In the biggest breaches, ones like those, the credit and debit card information of millions of people gets compromised, and often even by the same guy, a cracker named Albert Gonzalez." Frank pulled Gonzalez's mug shot up on his computer as he spoke and then swiveled his laptop towards her. "There - that's the guy."

"Hmm. Not a bad looking hacker," Marla observed appreciatively, watching her father out of the corner of her eye.

"Cracker!" Frank corrected her. "*Crackers* wear black hats. *Hackers* aren't criminals. Your father is a hacker. But if you insist, I'll call the bad guys 'hackers,' too."

"Whatever," Marla responded emphatically. "Are we getting any closer to the point here?"

"Yes," Frank replied tartly. "And I doubt Gonzalez will look like that by the time he gets out of Federal prison. Anyway, in the data breach you remember, Gonzalez succeeded in planting a virus called a 'sniffer' inside the firewall of an information processing company that sits between the merchants that take in credit card information and the financial institutions that complete the card transactions."

"What a sniffer program does is look for information, and when it finds what it wants, it sends it back to the hacker. All it took was one employee adding a wireless router to the system and forgetting to set the security settings up properly. Probably in no time flat, the automated software Gonzalez was using found the vulnerability, and in went the sniffer. It was two years – and forty million pirated customer records - before Heartland realized it was broadcasting sensitive personal financial data to criminals."

"Okay, so a company goofed up," Marla objected. "I would certainly expect our government to be much more careful."

Her father raised his eyebrows, and Marla paused. "Or maybe not," she admitted.

Frank smiled smugly. "Unfortunately, the federal government is a lot like the credit and debit card system – it's got thousands of locations with computers, countless types of hardware and software products in use (and changing) at any time, and millions of people who might be a little bit lazy or not well enough trained. So every government agency has thousands of points of potential vulnerability. All it takes is one careless moment by one individual, and this time it could be the Department of Defense, or the CIA, or the White House that gets the sniffer – or something more dangerous."

"And it's worse than that," Frank continued, pulling up an article on his laptop from the *New York Times*, describing a recent top brass meeting on how capable the U.S. might be if it had to respond to a cyber attack.

Marla scanned the assessment, reading how the attacker would have all the advantages – no one would be able to pinpoint the country of origin, and it might not even be justifiable under international law for the victim to respond militarily.

"So I'm getting the 'not good' part here loud and clear," Marla acknowledged. "But what does that have to do with you and Rick and the LoC? And what especially does it have to do with that crazy message on your laptop, by the way? Remember your laptop? I believe it's what I saw on your laptop we were actually talking about."

"I'll get to that in just a minute," Frank responded.

Marla groaned and put her head on the table.

Frank made a face this time. "Alright. I'll move on. But just keep this part in focus: for all our wealth and strength, right now any Third World country, or even a terrorist organization, could crash an entire agency – or, for that matter, Wall Street – if they put some smart guys to work on it."

"Fine. I'm appropriately terrified. Now Daddy, please make your little girl feel warm and secure again. You are going to make it all better now, aren't you?"

Frank smiled ruefully. "That's a tall order. But I will tell you what we're trying to do about it, or at least the non-classified details that make their way down to someone at my level."

"The new administration is much more aware of cybersecurity than the old one, thank goodness, and more creative, too. They decided to take a competitive approach to the problem, so they told every single agency and semi-independent department, like the LoC, that it has to come up with its own security plan – and fast. We've only got until February 28 to submit our security proposal to the White House."

"And that's a really good idea. The thought is that if we get fifty different teams competing, we'll come up with a lot more clever ideas than we would if we had just one design team. Even better, we should be able to use several different plans, rather than just one. That way the whole government won't be vulnerable to a single attack across the board, or be as likely to permit a successful exploit in one agency to infect another once it's inside the first one."

Marla interrupted. "And George thinks that Rick is going to be able to pull that off better than you?" She felt offended on her father's behalf.

Frank suddenly looked less cheerful. "Yes, and George may be right. This is one of those projects that requires getting a whole lot of people on the same page. It will take lots of meetings; lots of compromises; lots of cajoling. That's not exactly where I shine. Last night I could have punched George in the nose, but this morning I have to admit everybody else would probably want to punch me within a week if I was in charge."

Marla knew her father was probably right. "Still having trouble with that 'smartest guy in the room' problem, huh?"

"It's not only that," he replied wearily. "Yes, I'd be frustrated when some people couldn't keep up with me. But at the same time, I probably wouldn't focus very well on filling in all the less interesting bits that it takes to make the big picture clear, either. Plus, whoever is in charge is going to have to spend a lot of time grinding away on administrative details, and I get too impatient."

"Couldn't you just get somebody else to do that part?"

"Sure, but there are other issues. Like balancing what's perfect with what's practical, so that overly strict security requirements don't bring everything to a standstill, or require people to do more than you can actually get them to do. To come up with a really good solution, you need to take into account how people really act. Otherwise, they'll just take short cuts that leave security gaps."

"In short, doing something like this takes lots of things I just don't have the patience for. Or for that matter, much talent."

Marla gently changed the subject: "So what about this Alexandria Project thing?"

"Ah yes!" Frank brightened considerably. "It seems that my good friends George and Rick are going to have to face a challenge that's a lot more than either of them bargained for."

0000 0001 0010 0011 0100 0011 0010 0001 0000

3

I just HATE it when that Happens

M ONDAY MORNING FRANK arrived at work early. He scooped up the office copies of the daily newspapers from the pavement outside the staff door of the Library of Congress and noticed that the *Washington Times* was missing. No need to wonder who arrived first today – that would be Rick, the only employee that wouldn't bother to bring a paper in for anyone but himself.

Sure enough, as Frank strode up the half-lit, half-high walls of the LoC's Cube Town, there was Rick, coffee cup in hand. His face lit up as soon as he saw Frank. "Morning, Frank," he called out. "Recovered from your big Saturday night yet?" He raised his coffee cup in a mock toast and leaned casually against his cube so Frank could barely squeeze past.

To Rick's surprise, Frank gave him a hearty welcome as he passed by. "Great to see you, Rick, ol' fella! Only seventy more security-filled days until your big deadline, huh?" Rick's smile evaporated. Frank wondered just how long it would be before Rick showed up at his cube, shame-faced, to ask for help. A week, tops.

Frank's smug smile faded when he snapped on his cubicle lights and saw the note waiting for him: "See me ASAP - George." Suddenly, his smarmy email reply of the day before didn't seem so funny anymore.

George didn't turn around when Frank appeared in the doorway to his office. He was clearly lost in thought, staring at the whiteboard on his wall. Frank realized that his boss had sketched out the LoC's IT system at a high level, noting the particulars of the security defenses that stood between the jungle that was the Internet and the data resources of the LoC.

Frank suddenly thought of the scene in Tracy Kidder's The Soul of a New Machine where Tom West, the legendary Data General project manager, sat alone in an office opening off of a darkened room of computer work and test benches. West's career was on the line. His future depended on whether the "Whiz Kids" he had hired out of college would be able to debug the new computer he'd convinced management to let him design and build. Things weren't looking good at that point, but West knew that all he could do was let things run their course without interfering and hope for the best.

George looked old, Frank thought. George *was* getting old, Frank realized with mild surprise – probably past retirement age, now that he thought of it. And the members of the IT staff at the LoC weren't whiz kids, either. George was probably worried that this project might come to a bad end, making him look bad, too. Well, that wasn't Frank's problem, was it?

Frank was raising his knuckles to tap on the open door when George spoke.

"Hi, Frank," he said, without turning around. "Close the door and have a seat. I'll be with you in a moment."

Frank sat down, wondering for how long George had been aware of his presence. Eventually, George swiveled his chair around. He leaned forward, both elbows on his desk and folded his hands together. He looked Frank straight in the eye as he spoke.

"You know, this isn't a game, Frank. I didn't appreciate your email on Sunday, and if you want to keep working here, that's the last email like that you'll ever send me. Understood?"

Frank was taken aback; this wasn't what he had expected. "Okay, George, no problem. I just wasn't sure what you expected me to say. Who the hell has ever seen something like that before?"

"Like what?" George snapped back.

Now Frank was really confused. "Well, like that fiery screen, and the logo? And what the heck is the Alexandria Project, anyway?"

George didn't say anything, but slid his Blackberry across the desk to Frank.

Frank picked it up and looked at the screen. The email he had answered was open. What was it he was missing? "It's the email you sent to me. What's your point?" Then he noticed something that he'd missed before: the email wasn't addressed to just him, but to "All Personnel" in the LoC.

Frank looked up and saw that George was watching him closely. "Would it surprise you, Frank, to learn that you were the only one who replied to my email message?" Frank said nothing. "And what exactly were you looking for on a weekend in that particular directory, anyway?"

Frank was annoyed rather than flustered. "For Pete's sake, George, I was looking for the draft of the security project outline I'd been working on – that's all."

"Looking for it, or deleting it out of spite? And how about the other files in that directory? Did you want to make it that much more difficult for Rick to get started?"

"What files?" Frank responded, "Are others missing as well?"

"Of course!" George barked. "Two of them. And one of them was Rick's project outline – involuntarily 'contributed' to the Alexandria Project, whatever that is."

Now Frank was alarmed. "Wait a minute, George! Yes, I was ripped at Rick on Saturday night, but no – I'd never pull a stunt like that! And before you say anything, I know that the backup file for my outline is gone, too – probably Rick's as well. But I didn't do that, either. And I also know that it doesn't look like there's anything else missing, or at least not much, if there is. We had almost the same gross storage numbers Sunday morning as we did the night before."

"I know that!" snapped George. "Do you think you're the only guy around here that has a brain? I've already run a complete scan, and there were only three files deleted anywhere in the entire system that night."

George leaned back. "Frank, are you aware that you and I are the only two people in the entire Library of Congress that have access to other people's material in that directory?"

Frank shook his head slowly from side to side.

George gave him a humorless smile. "You should be a bit disappointed in yourself, Frank. Maybe you're not such a security hotshot after all."

Frank couldn't listen any longer. "Can the crap, George! We've known each other for more than twenty years. I know this looks like some kind of silly stunt, but it's not. What would I gain by deleting documents? And hey – I'm no scholar of ancient Greek – I can't even speak a *modern* language other than English. If it wasn't for Google Translate I wouldn't have a clue what that inscription said."

George was looking less certain, so Frank pressed on. "And anyway, how could I come up with something like that screen overnight – with all that fancy flash animation?" Frank was feeling more confident now. He sat back and waited.

"Okay, Frank. Nice points," George said at last. "But this isn't over yet. If you didn't delete those files, then we've got a real problem here. You've got the security clearances to know that the CIA security hotshots use the LoC as a low public-profile testbed to stress test new security protocols before they roll them out in the Pentagon, the White House, and all the other Level 1 security government agencies."

"That means that if someone could hack our files, they could hack anything anywhere." George looked at Frank, but Frank couldn't think what he might be waiting for Frank to say.

"I'm going to have to ask the CIA to check this out," George said at last. "You and I may have known each other for twenty years, but to them, you're nothing. They'll be asking you a lot of questions, and if I were you, I wouldn't get cute with my answers. Do you get it, Frank?"

Frank nodded. "I get it."

"That's all then." George swung back to his whiteboard. Frank stood up to go, but then had a thought.

"George…you said that there were three files deleted in all. What was the last one?"

George replied without turning around. "The last one was own my security folder." Then he did turn around. "I really would watch my step for a while, if I were you."

Frank closed George's door softly and walked back towards his cubicle trying to figure out just how concerned he should be. He barely noticed when Rick jumped up, obviously alarmed, as Frank passed by.

"Hey Frank! *Frank!* Can I check something out with you? I just saw the damnedest thing I've ever seen in my life!"

0000 0001 0010 0011 0100 0011 0010 0001 0000

4

Beware of Greeks bearing Trapdoors

B ACK IN HIS cube, Frank powered up his computer and reflected on what he'd just learned, which was both not much and a lot. Not much in that he still had no idea who was behind the attack or what he was trying to accomplish. But a lot because the only people targeted besides himself were George and Rick, and because only one directory had been affected. That meant that what had hit the Library of Congress was no virus unleashed against websites generally, bent on spreading random mayhem. It was obviously an attack targeted just at their department. And once the hacker had made his way through the LoC firewall, the attack must have been directly controlled rather than automated.

Whoever was behind the exploit also must have known exactly what he was looking for and had figured out where to find it, too. That suggested the intruder had managed to acquire some degree of inside knowledge, or at least that he had been willing and able to spend a lot of time roaming around inside the firewall, figuring out what might be of interest. Frank hoped it was the latter, since the former made it likely that an employee was either directly behind the attack, or had leaked information to whoever was responsible.

Still, it was bad enough if the mysterious visitor had acted without inside help, since that meant there was a hole in the LoC's defenses.

Finding and fixing that flaw wouldn't help now, though, since the attacker would have already created a trapdoor he could use to come and go as he pleased. Maybe as early as tonight he'd open the hatch and start creeping through the servers again. So if it wasn't an inside job, there must be two vulnerabilities to track down and close, rather than only one – the vulnerability the intruder had exploited to get in to begin with, and the custom one he would then have created.

All that was pretty standard stuff. The really weird bit revolved around the animated screen that he and George, and now obviously Rick, had seen when they looked for their security project files. Frank opened the cleaned up, translated screenshot again and gazed at it.

What the hell was the name "Alexandria Project" all about? Did it refer to Alexandria, Virginia? No reason to think so; there must be tens, if not hundreds, of cities and towns with that name. And anyway, why was the message in Greek – *ancient* Greek, no less?

Frank typed "Alexandria Project" into Google to see what would pop up. 44,400 hits. Hmm. He'd need to narrow his search a bit, but how? It looked like he'd need a clue to find a clue using Google. But then he noticed that most of the hits on the screen page referred to projects that involved data. Well, duh! he thought. Frank was no history buff, but even he had heard of the library of Alexandria, and also that it was supposed to have been the greatest repository of knowledge in the ancient world. Apparently, all of the founders of these projects had decided to use the same historical metaphor to identify their activities. That seemed promising. After all, the LoC was the largest collection of printed matter in the modern world. Maybe this was a start.

The only other fact he knew (or thought he knew, anyway) about the Library of Alexandria was that it had been destroyed by fire. Well, that seemed to lock it down – the name on the screen he'd seen, the flames…but what about the Greek letters? Why not hieroglyphics, if he was right in remembering that Alexandria was in Egypt?

Frank moved to Wikipedia, and typed in "Library of Alexandria." The summary confirmed his recollection, but didn't immediately suggest any clues:

The Royal Library of Alexandria, or Ancient Library of Alexandria, in Alexandria, Egypt, was probably the largest, and certainly the most famous, of the libraries of the ancient world. It flourished under the patronage of the Ptolemaic dynasty, and functioned as a major center of scholarship, at least until the time of Rome's conquest of Egypt, and probably for many centuries thereafter. Plutarch (AD 46–120) wrote that during his visit to Alexandria in 48 BC, Julius Caesar might

have accidentally burned the library when he set fire to his own ships to
frustrate Achillas' attempt to limit his ability to communicate by sea....

Okay, so he could understand if the intruder had used Latin instead
of hieroglyphics, but he still didn't get Greek. Frank tried "Alexandria"
next, and there he found what he was looking for:

...In ancient times, Alexandria was one of the most famous cities in the
world. It was founded around a small pharaonic town c. 331 BC by
Alexander the Great....Alexandria was known because of its lighthouse
(Pharos), one of the Seven Wonders of the Ancient World; its library
(the largest library in the ancient world); and the Catacombs of Kom el
Shoqafa, one of the Seven Wonders of the Middle Ages....

So that explained the language issue. Frank recalled that Alexander
the Great was Greek, well Macedonian, but close enough – so he would
have spoken Greek. The Alexandria entry also confirmed that the tall
building on the screen probably was a lighthouse, as he had suspected. Now Frank was getting somewhere – assuming that he wasn't
being led down the garden path just the way the intruder intended.

Frank kept reading, learning that the king that built the library
wasn't just another Egyptian pharaoh, but the founder of the Greek lin-
eage of monarchs that took control of Egypt after Alexander died.
Apparently, Frank read, it hadn't taken long for his generals to start
fighting over the late conqueror's empire. Ptolemy, one of his most
trusted generals, had been content to vie for less than the entire known
world, and lucky enough to secure Egypt as his own. Unlike some of
the other generals, he also lived long enough - another forty years - to
consolidate his position, and pass his new kingdom on to his descen-
dants. They ruled until Rome eventually moved in and took over the
whole neighborhood.

Frank reflected for awhile on what he had just learned. He could be
pretty sure now that it was the Library of Alexandria that was being
alluded to on the contribution screen. But how to make use of that
knowledge? Were the clues meant to lead him on, or astray? If the latter, he hoped the intruder might have been too clever by half. After all,
Frank now knew a little bit about how the hacker's mind worked, and
what kinds of things he knew that interested him. Maybe more, if Frank
set his mind to it.

He drummed his fingers for awhile. Well. Clearly he wasn't going to
solve a mystery like this all in one morning. Time to think about getting some work done. He started to turn off his computer, and then

stopped himself, calling up first the translated, and then the original images of the Project's calling card. He saved both to a thumb drive, dropped it into his pocket, and then deleted both images from his laptop. Then he set his hard drive up to defragment. Over the next couple of hours most of his hard drive should overwrite itself. A real pro would still be able to reconstruct the image, but any less skillful person tampering with his computer would never know it had ever been there.

To his surprise, Frank realized that half the morning had already passed while he was noodling around the Web. When he opened his email, he found that George had sent another message to all staff. Once again, the subject line was, "What is the Alexandria Project?" (this time, with only initial capital letters). It read as follows:

Everybody,

I've received some interesting guesses in response to my weekend email question, but none of you got it right. So here it is: the Alexandria Project is what I've decided to call the security project we're undertaking between now and the end of February.

As you may know, the Library of Alexandria was the greatest library of the ancient world – until it was destroyed by fire. Today, the LoC is the greatest library of the modern world, and we're increasingly moving towards a digital, rather than a paper world. We can't any more allow the LoC's digital holdings to be compromised by hackers than we can allow the books in our stacks to be destroyed by fire.

Our new code name captures the importance of this project, and I'm expecting all of you to cooperate fully with Rick and his team as we push forward.

George

Nice cover, thought Frank. With one message, George had explained away the weekend email trap that Frank had blundered into. If more files disappeared and others saw the same "contribution" screen, George could pass it off as some kind of test without people becoming concerned. George had probably sold that line to Rick already.

Not for nothing, you're the boss, Frank thought appreciatively. Tom West would be proud.

0000 0001 0010 0011 0100 0011 0010 0001 0000

5

So How do Ya like them iBalls?

FRANK FIDGETED NEXT to the cheese and crackers, looking helplessly for his daughter in the crowd. He hated social events with a passion, and especially having to speak to people he didn't know. He was sure that every sentence he uttered came across as a brainless non-sequitur.

But fair was fair. Marla was finishing up an internship with a local high tech company, and at the last minute, her date had come down with the flu. She had kept him company at the Library of Congress holiday party the weekend before, and this time it was his turn.

"Please, Dad," she'd said over the phone, "There's this guy at work that's been hitting on me all week. It'll do you good to get out of your crummy apartment, and how can you turn down a request to protect your little girl?"

How could he indeed, he had thought at the time. But now, all he wanted to say was, "Where the hell are you?" But be fair, he told himself as he nursed his Dos Equis. Marla had started looking pretty green around the gills on the way over and had disappeared into the Ladies' Room almost immediately after they arrived. Likely enough she was coming down with the flu, too. Wasn't everyone?

Frank sighed again. He held his beer in one hand and drummed his fingers quietly against the wall behind his back with the other. Across the room, someone was making an entrance. Oh joy, Frank thought. That must be iBalls.com's CEO.

Frank snorted. iBalls! What a lame concept! He thought he'd seen everything during the madness of the Internet bubble years – companies formed to sell dog food over the Internet; year-old start-ups raising $100 million investment rounds; companies going public without a dollar in sales. He had assumed it would be decades before the high tech industry saw that type of insanity again.

But no - things seemed to be heating up all over again, and maybe worse. Now that Twitter had re-legitimated the no-revenues business model, the venture capitalists were charging back in, hoping to raise mega-funds once again that were far too big to invest intelligently. Too big, that is, unless they started fire-hosing money down the gullets of companies with nonsensical business plans again, just like before.

Frank gave a short, humorless laugh. That was just the right metaphor, wasn't it? VCs were like French farmers - force-feeding the goose until its liver turns to pure fat, then selling off the bird before it dies of the farmer's own absurd excess. Pâté de foie gras start-ups! Frank felt pleased with himself. The metaphor summarized the inanity of venture capital just perfectly.

Of course, it had been pretty bloody for everybody who'd had their face in the trough after the bubble burst in 2000. Somehow, though, the VCs got away scott free, in public, at least. As Enron flamed out and Arthur Anderson collapsed, and even as Congressional subcommittees were humiliating Wall Street bankers before CSPAN-TV cameras, the VCs simply melted back into the shadows and rode it out. Everyone seemed to forget that it was the VCs that had tied these laughably inappropriate companies up with shiny red bows to begin with.

Of course, no one spoke up who really knew what a huge part VCs had played in the pump-and-dump charade that had driven the NAS-DAQ index to such absurd heights. Say you were an investor. You'd made money with VCs in the past, hadn't you? And the best funds were hard to get into, right? So if you wanted to get into the next fund, best to keep mum, so as not to offend.

Well, how about if you were a high tech lawyer or accountant? You still needed the VCs' business, didn't you? And if you were an entrepreneur, well, it's not like you wanted to go back to work for IBM. So everyone just kept their mouth shut while the ugliness unwound behind the scenes. The VC funding scene should have gotten back on a healthy foundation after that, Frank thought. But that could only happen if the

VCs had returned to the rules of the old days, when a $200 million fund was a big one, and there were plenty of deals to go around.

But that wasn't good enough now, and the reason was obvious. If you could get 2% a year of a $100 million fund as a management fee, why not get 2% of a $400 million fund? Or how about 2% of $800 million? Hell, why not make it 2% of an even $1 billion? Some VCs did.

Maybe things never would have gotten so crazy if Netscape Communications Corporation hadn't been such a big hit, Frank thought. But only seventeen months after being founded in April of 1994, Netscape went public in one of the most successful IPOs of all time. There was just one problem: unlike Apple Computer, which had raised more money in its IPO than any company since Ford Motors, Netscape was only just starting to produce revenues. Still, the stock ran up from $28 to $75 on the opening day. After that, everyone wanted to play the VC game. That's what allowed the funds to balloon in size.

Soon it wasn't unusual for a fund targeted at start-up companies to raise $600 million, $900 million, even a billion dollars – and then even more. In a rational universe, these new megafunds would have hired more people and made more investments. But what sense would that make? Then the VCs would have to split the profits with more partners. And gosh knows, they were too smart for that. Better to stick with twenty-five investments per fund and drive their portfolio companies to hire one hundred employees the first year - even buy Super Bowl ads if they couldn't spend their VC money fast enough to justify an IPO before the bubble burst, just as everyone knew it eventually must.

And now we've got "iBalls!" Frank though in disgust. By now, his no-longer covert finger drumming was beginning to turn heads.

Just then, someone tapped a glass held high in the air. It was iBalls.com's twenty-something CEO, Chad Derwent.

"Quiet, everybody, quiet!" Chad called. "Welcome to the iBalls.com holiday party – I'm delighted you could all make it. It's been a great year for the Company, and next year we're going to knock the old iBall right out of the park!" People began to quiet down.

"I've got two really big pieces of news for you tonight," Chad continued. That made everyone shut up, because a rumor had been circulating that everyone wanted to be true.

"The first is that we filed our S-1 Registration Statement with the Securities and Exchange Commission today! That's right, everybody, we're going public!" A collective cheer erupted among the lower level employees. Senior management, already in on the good news, smiled smugly. Chad waited for the hoots to die down, and when they didn't he started tapping his glass once more, but to no avail. Every employee in the room had stock options, from the receptionist up to the most senior members of management. Frank groaned at the utter, recurring absurdity of it all.

Finally, Chad succeeded in shushing the crowd. "And now for my second announcement: we've got a very special guest tonight. I'm sure all of you have heard of Josh Peabody – one of the founders of TrashTalk LP – the very coolest VC fund in Silicon Valley. No one's got a better nose for a hot company than Josh - without him, there'd be no MyPuppies.com site to help you find names for pets that go great with the names of your kids (or, hey, even the other way around!). Or any MyFace.com, where you can find a future spouse who looks as much like you as possible (how can you help but fall in love?). Who else do you know that thinks like that?" Frank's blood pressure was rising dangerously.

"Anyway, when Josh offered us a term sheet, we knew the rest was going to be easy. It took us a long time to convince him to let us keep the name "iBalls" instead of, "My...," " well, you can guess "My What", but...." Laughter drowned him out.

Frank already knew the rest through Marla. Josh's fund persuaded iBalls.com to take $50 million in exchange for 60% of the company's stock, but who cared how much stock the Company had to give up? It would be smooth sailing with a Triple-A tier fund like TrashTalk backing the Company.

"And here he is now! Let's give a bit, warm iBalls.com welcome to *Josh Peabody!*"

The crowd began to split like the Red Sea to let Peabody stride through, shaking his clasped hands over his head like a victorious boxer. This being the Beltway, everyone was dressed fairly conservatively, but Josh was resplendently Silicon Valley, wearing a tailored sports jacket, black shirt, pressed jeans, hand-tooled boots and a haircut that John Edwards would have envied.

After he shook hands with Chad, it became clear that the great VC would grace the crowd with a few words of his boundless wisdom. Josh wasn't very tall, so he hopped up on a chair so everyone could see and hear him.

"Let's hear it for *you*, iBallers!" he shouted, and everybody cheered happily; those that had taken greatest advantage of the open bar pumped the air with their fists.

"Settle down, settle down," Josh laughed, but he was happy to wait them out. "You know, I just can't tell you how psyched we all are back on Sand Hill Road about iBalls.com. iBalls! It's got to be the greatest, purest concept I've ever seen. Within one minute of Chad and Sanjay starting their pitch, I turned and whispered to my partner, "We've got to get this deal!"'"

Everyone cheered again. "No really, people, I mean it! I mean, in the early days of the Web, it was all about eyeballs – getting people to visit your site. The hell with revenues – if you could get the eyeballs, you knew – you just *knew* – that somehow the dollars would follow. And they did! Netscape ended up having to give their browser away, but how much did AOL pay to snap them up? $4.2 billion, that's how much! How about Google? Sergey and Larry didn't have a clue how they'd make any money for years, and now their stock is over the moon! And hey, how many of you use Twitter?" The response indicated that a great many indulged in the occasional tweet.

Josh paused for effect, and the crowd grew quiet. "So just how do you beat that? Where do you go after Google, YouTube, Facebook, and Twitter? None of them had revenues until they'd blown through a fortune, and look at them now. How do you top that?"

"With iBalls, that's how!" he shouted. "It took a couple of geniuses like Chad and Sanjay here to get that Web 3.0 isn't going to be about traffic at all – it's not going to be about getting potential customers to you – it's going to be about you going to them! We've all heard the phrase "virtual company" before, but no one had ever thought of making a virtual company totally virtual! How can you be more "all about your customer" than to exist only at their websites? Now that's true genius!"

"So no surprise where iBalls can be found today: as of this morning, there were over *1.5 billion* iBalls out there! By this time next year, Chad tells me there should be an iBall on over 10% of the Web pages in the entire world! And every day, it costs the Company less and less to put an iBall on a Web page. That's because our unique, patented reverse auction process drives our price down farther and farther as more and more website owners reverse-bid their way in."

"So it's no wonder that today it's almost impossible to surf the Web without seeing one of our iBalls winking back at you, no matter where you go. In just one year, the iBall has become the single most recognizable new brand in the on-line world. One day soon, we'll come up with a way to monetize this amazing, amazing asset. So let's hear it for Chad and Sanjay – and, of course, for *TrashTalk!*" The crowd obediently gave it up.

Marla had told Frank that paying tens of millions of dollars to people all over the world to put a stupid logo on their sites hadn't been what Chad and Sanjay had originally had in mind at all. Instead, they intended to offer an array of free, fun animations and other "widgets" that people would want to put up at their websites for visitors to enjoy; the iBall was just one of hundreds of animated graphics they had in mind. Anyone could download them and do whatever they wanted with them – even delete them any time they chose. All Chad and Sanjay wanted in return was the ability to pull back a modest amount of anonymized click information from as wide an array of websites as possible, using their widgets to gather the data. With that kind of information in hand, they could spot usage trends and sell Web analysis to customers for a profit.

Of course, that would have been far too tame for Josh Peabody and the other cowboys at TrashTalk. And then there was the problem that Chad and Sanjay only wanted to raise $500,000 – after all, getting your programming done in India was cheap. After that, their business plan called for relying on viral, word of mouth marketing to spread the news. If all went as planned, they could then raise of a million dollars or so to build on the buzz and move out into the broader marketplace. With any luck, they'd still own most of the stock and be able to sell the Company before the competition moved in. Making $20 or $30 million wouldn't get their faces on the cover of *Wired* magazine, but it wasn't an unreasonable target. And it would be enough to produce a great return for all concerned within a few years' time.

Indeed, until they connected with TrashTalk, everything had been going according to plan, only better. They got the first $500,000 from a local angel group for about 15% of the Company's stock, and completed the programming off shore on time and within budget. They had a real stroke of luck when a buddy of Sanjay's came out with a killer iPhone app, and as a favor, included a feature that automatically added an iBall to the phone of everyone the app downloader called. Soon, iBall's were popping up and winking at mobile phone users everywhere, and everyone wanted to know just what those iBalls were all about.

That was when the guys at TrashTalk noticed. They invited Chad and Sanjay out to Menlo Park to present their business plan. They even sent a charter jet back East to pick them up at a private airstrip outside Washington. Chad and Sanjay were understandably impressed, and almost before they knew what hit them, their company had $50 million in its bank account, and TrashTalk had 60% of its stock. Oh - and the Company had a new business plan, too.

That had been one of the conditions to TrashTalk's investment. While Chad and Sanjay were still in the Valley, Josh had pitched

41

the reverse auction idea – why wait for viral marketing to take the Company to a paltry $20 or $30 million valuation? Why not conquer the world in record time - go for an IPO at a billion dollar market cap in 18 months? After all, the TrashTalk fund had $900 million to put to work, so Josh couldn't waste his time and his investors' money with any Company that couldn't soak up its fair share of cash. TrashTalk money was for big boys, not kids who didn't have the vision and the *cajones* to swing for the fences.

Who could blame Chad and Sanjay for being blown away? Only a year before they'd been roommates in college, and now a famous venture capitalist was telling them they were geniuses. Soon they *were* being profiled in *Wired* Magazine – not long after, Chad appeared on *The Daily Show*, and how cool was *that?*

Frank thought he was going to puke. He remembered Josh from his MIT days, although he was sure that Peabody wouldn't remember him. Back then, and for quite a while thereafter, Josh had been nothing special. But then he'd been lucky enough to be in the right start-up at the right time. It got snapped up by a big company in 1997, and for cash – a whole lot of cash. All of a sudden, Josh was a rock star. A few months after the sale, the old-line VCs who had funded his venture invited him to join them as a partner with hands-on Internet start-up experience. Josh's company had been the one home run in their current fund, and they wanted to have someone with Internet credibility on the team as they went out to raise a new fund.

Josh turned out to have the golden touch. Before the bubble burst, he brought the fund into some of the only late bubble-era companies that managed to sell for a tidy profit after the crash. But by 2003, he was tired of being under someone else's wing, so he contacted a couple of up-and-coming young Turks at other West Coast VC funds and suggested they go out on their own. The smart money liked what they were pitched, and lo and behold – TrashTalk LP was born.

All of this could be learned from the extremely complimentary Wikipedia profile that Frank was sure Josh had paid someone to write. About the only detail it contained that didn't scream money and success was the fact that Josh was gonzo over cats.

Venture capital and cats…. Just as the Big Man from Silicon Valley appeared at the cheese and cracker table, Frank remembered a sardonic idea he'd had years before. On impulse, he shot out his hand.

"What a pleasure it is to meet you, Mr. Peabody. I mean, what a *privilege* it is to meet you in the flesh – I've heard *so much* about you."

Josh gave a half-polite smile, and tried to side step his way past Frank to the food. But Frank matched him side-step for side-step.

"Say, let me get you a drink while you fill your plate," Frank said. "What will it be?"

"Scotch and soda, thanks," Josh said with resignation, realizing he'd been snagged for at least a minute or two. Frank gave the order to the bartender, and turned back to Josh. "Say, I've got an idea that I've always thought could be a real money maker. Let me take just a minute of your time to tell you about it." Josh hoped the bartender would hurry; he'd been buttonholed this way too often in the past.

"You know, I heard what you said about volume now, revenues later, but I think having a revenue stream can still come in pretty handy – in fact, I believe that in difficult times like these, you really need two – and three revenue streams would be even better."

Josh's drink was ready now, but Frank was too quick for him. He grabbed it from the bartender and held on tight while Josh dropped his arm, itching to make his escape.

"So here's the idea – I don't need you to sign a non-disclosure agreement, do I? No? Great! It's all about cats."

With that, Frank thrust the drink into Josh's hand. Against his will, the VC found himself wavering between the desire to flee, and curiosity over what kind of cat-centric business plan this oddball might have in mind.

"So here's the idea – the first revenue stream, that is. Everybody loves kittens, right? I mean, they're cute, they're playful – who can help loving a kitten, even if they don't really like cats? But hey – everybody knows what happens with kittens. Before you know it, they grow up to be fat, snotty blobs of fat, and what do you have then? Just an arrogant, furry doorstop, that's what!"

Josh was turning desperately away when Frank stopped him in his tracks. "So I asked myself, what if you could invent a perpetual kitten?"

Josh's love for dollars got the better of him, and he turned around again. "And, uh, did you figure out how to do that?"

"Yes – sort of, anyway. Here's how: we breed a line of genetically identical cats, just like they do with lab mice. Each one will be black, with cute little white mitten paws – maybe even six toes, for people that go in for that sort of thing – and we call every one of them "Fred" so they'll always answer to the same name."

Frank paused for effect, and then hit Josh with the clincher: "And instead of selling them to people, we rent them."

"Rent them?" Josh asked blankly. "Why rent them?"

"Because that's how you get a perpetual kitten, of course. Once your energetic, darling little Fred starts showing symptoms of morphing into a door step with a bad attitude, you trade it in for a new Fred, and Presto! You've realized the magic of the perpetual kitten! It's really just like pet cloning, except much easier and cheaper - instead of paying a fortune to clone your kitty at the back end, you breed an endless supply of identical ones at the front end."

Against his will, Josh found himself listening more closely. "That's an interesting idea, in a totally weird kind of way. But you said there were three revenue streams?"

"Absolutely!" Frank suddenly looked at him suspiciously. "Say – are you sure I don't need you to sign an NDA? No? Well, you are a VC after all, so I guess I can trust you. We'll need the customers to sign NDAs, though, and that brings us to the second revenue stream."

Frank looked to his right and then to his left to be sure no one could hear him, and then leaned closer to Josh. "Here's the second revenue opportunity," he said in a conspiratorial whisper. "So now we've got all of these superannuated Freds, right? But what can we do with them? They cost money to feed, and you couldn't get much from someone who wanted to grind them up for fertilizer."

Josh stepped back involuntarily, but Frank followed him.

"Luckily, though, there's always a big demand at medical laboratories for cats for experiments, and it turns out they pay pretty good money if you can provide the pedigree of your pussies."

A look of vague horror began to spread across Josh's face. He tried to take another step back, but found that his back was already up against the wall.

"Don't worry, don't worry," Frank laughed, pulling him back with an arm around his shoulders. "We won't really have to sell the kitties to the nasty doctors - or at least not too many of them, anyway - mostly, that's just a story we tell people when they come back for a Fred exchange."

"You see, when the customer asks what's going to happen to ol' Fred after they turn him in, that's when you casually mention the cat lab – and how cool is that? I mean, how often do you get to use a word like "vivisection" as part of a marketing pitch? Anyway, when the customer hears that, they'll almost never want to give poor Fred up to the guys with the scalpels."

Josh waited, aghast. What could possibly come next?

"And that's when you tell the customer about the lease buy-out option. It might have been cheap to rent-a-Fred to begin with, but if you don't turn him back in, it'll cost you a bundle!"

Frank stopped abruptly, beaming with triumph.

"So what do you think?"

But Josh was already edging sideways in shock, bumping into some-one and spilling his still-full drink down his shirt.

"Hey, wait a minute," Frank called, "I haven't even had a chance to tell you about my other idea – you see, you pair the parents of thirty-something couples who won't give their folks grandkids with single par-ents that never get a weekend of peace to themselves." But Josh had finally succeeded in escaping into the crowd.

Frank was still chuckling to himself when Marla, looking pale, found him.

"Sorry to leave you alone so long, Dad, I know how much you hate events like this. Did I see you actually talking to someone?"

"Yes indeed," Frank said. "And this time around, I think you would have been proud of me."

0000 0001 0010 0011 0100 0011 0010 0001 0000

6

The Perils of Profiles

W HILE FRANK WAS enjoying himself spear phishing venture capitalists, back at the Library of Congress files were flashing out of view like fireflies on a summer's eve. One by one, documents important and banal, short and long, wafted silently off into the digital darkness to points unknown, leaving only Alexandria Project contribution screen code in their place.

Thus it was that at 10 on Friday morning, Frank's office phone buzzed, and he heard the inevitably bored voice of the receptionist. "Your turn. Conference Room Two."

Frank logged off his computer and stood up with a thoughtful look on his face. Just enough time for a little self-coaching as he walked down the hallway. Stay cool, he thought. Stay calm. You don't have anything to worry about, so just tell the news.

That sounded good, but then again being interrogated – okay, interviewed – by a CIA agent wasn't something he recalled reading in his job description. And it didn't help that the interview sheet at the front desk included the names of only three other IT department staff, or that he was unable to figure out why their names appeared and others' didn't. Maybe those that did were just a cover for including him? Or maybe the counterintuitive choices were intended to confuse him and put him off balance? Anything was possible. Hell, this was the CIA, for Pete's sake.

And while we're at it, he thought, why were these interviews being conducted by the CIA at all, and not the FBI? Nobody knew at this point whether the attacks were coming from home or abroad, but the LoC was in the U.S, so shouldn't this be the FBI's turf?

Then there was the fact that nobody else being interviewed had any reason to be nervous. The little chats in conference room two were being passed off as just another part of the LoC security project. Per George's latest email memo, the recent file grabs were part of stress-testing the system, and the contribution screens were simply intended to dramatize the importance of the task at hand. Likely enough, only Frank suspected that these interviews were deadly serious. So while others might be expecting a half hour break from the tedium of their jobs, he had to worry whether any slip up would put him on a watch list.

The door was ajar when Frank reached the conference room. He paused to collect himself, and then rapped on the door frame before walking in.

Seated at the table inside was a man in his late twenties. Frank took in the expensively styled haircut, silk tie, and gratuitous suspenders. The CIA, it seemed, had sent over someone who had watched too many spy movies for his own good.

Frank had expected either some bored, bureaucrat type, or someone genuinely intimidating. Anyway, someone older and more experienced. Instead, he was going to be quizzed by this fancy-pants kid. As he walked into the room, Frank smiled at the young man's self-important demeanor. Nothing that a stalled career, a big mortgage, and a weight problem wouldn't cure in a few years, Frank thought. This would be a cake walk.

"Have a seat," the young man said without rising. "Mind if I record our conversation?'"

"That's a rhetorical question, I assume?" Frank responded, realizing he was off-script already.

"Actually, yes. Thanks for your permission." The agent didn't bother to look up as he cued up the recorder.

Frank flushed as he settled into his chair. "And you are?" he asked.

"Agent Cummings," the young man replied in a distracted voice as he typed Frank's name into the recorder. "Cybersecurity Investigations Unit."

The agent pointed to the microphone in the middle of the table. "Okay, let's get started. Please state your name and department."

"Frank Adversego. Cybersecurity Snafus Unit." Cummings looked up sharply. Frank smiled.

"Cute," Cummings replied. "But that's not your full name, is it? So let's try that again."

"Okay, Frank Joseph Adversego. Library of Congress IT Support Staff."

Cummings paused and leaned back in his chair. "Okay, Mr. Adversego. One last try. Please state your full name, with no omissions this time."

Frank was caught off balance by that one. As far as he knew, his full name didn't appear anywhere in his employment file.

"Frank Joseph Adversego, Junior," Frank stated evenly, but his eyes showed his surprise.

Cummings looked pleased with himself. "Don't be shocked, Mr. Adversego. We are the CIA, after all."

"After all, you are," Frank smiled back.

Cummings leaned back and looked Frank in the eye. "Doesn't your dad mind you dropping the 'Jr.'?"

"If you know I've got my father's name," Frank shot back, "then you know I haven't seen the bastard since I was twelve." He reached into his pocket and pulled out the thumb drive with the Alexandria Project screen shot on it. He began tapping it on his knee so he wouldn't unconsciously start drumming his fingers on the table.

"That's right, Mr. Adversego, as a matter of fact I do know that. Skipped out on you and your mother without warning, I believe. You have my *most sincere* sympathy. So maybe we can pick up some speed now, yes?"

An hour later, Frank was no longer angry. Just bored. Instead of continuing with pointed questions, Cummings had simply plowed through what appeared to be an endless series of questions, probably put together by some poor junior staffer confined to a windowless cell deep in the bowels of CIA Headquarters.

Frank sincerely hoped that staff person was the erstwhile Agent Cummings, who increasingly impressed Frank as a self-important prig without nearly enough mental horsepower to justify his ample self-regard. Frank had never liked company-man types to begin with, and being stuck in a conference room for an hour with a real Company man was testing his patience. Frank was playing with the thumb drive on the table now to amuse himself at the CIA agent's unknowing expense.

Still, it was a relief to be responding to questions that were such easy lobs. Half were clearly intended to catch Frank giving answers that were inconsistent with facts in his personnel file or with questions asked earlier in the hour, while the rest seemed intended to nail down what his usual work day was like – what kinds of tasks he performed, what types of directories he needed to access, and so on. If this was Cummings's big chance to play a real, grown-up Secret Agent Man he wasn't making much of the opportunity.

Finally, Cummings paused and began shuffling through his notes." So what do you think of the LoC's security architecture?" he asked in an off-hand way.

Frank was sneaking a look at his BlackBerry and glanced up. "What do you mean?"

Cummings continued his shuffling. "That's up to you. It's an open-ended question."

Frank paused. Was this just another random question, or a trick one? What did Cummings expect him to say?

"Well, I guess it's okay," he replied.

"Okay? That's pretty non-specific."

"I guess you could say that. Or you could say that it's an open-ended answer." Frank smiled sweetly.

Cummings smiled back. "Okay. Let's try this one then. Does the LoC's architecture meet the standards of a MacArthur Genius Award winner?"

Frank wasn't going to let Cummings get him off balance this time. "My, my. Didn't you ever learn you can catch more flies with sugar than vinegar, Cummings? By the way, do you have a first name? Oh – I got it – it's 'Agent.' Say – do you mind if I call you 'Agent'? It's fine with me if you want to call me 'Frank.'"

Cummings stared at Frank for awhile, weighing his options. "Carl," he said finally, putting his notes down and folding his arms. "So now – *Frank* – how about telling me what you really think of the LoC's security architecture?"

Frank nodded his head up and down happily. "Well, *Carl*, I'm glad we're finally getting to know each other better. I'd think it would be tiring calling people "Mr." and "Ms." all day, not to mention being "Agented" back in response. It must be bad enough having to ask those same dead-end questions over and over."

Frank paused. Carl glared.

Frank decided he'd made his point, and figured it would be foolish to overdo it. So he quit smiling before he began talking again. "Seriously, though, it's not bad, for a big shop like this. Of course, any outfit this large can only do so well. But it's pretty good."

"What do you say, "It can only do so well"?"

"Well, like most places, we go by the book, and everybody everywhere uses pretty much the same book, figuratively speaking, so the bad guys always know what they're up against. That might be more or less okay, but everybody makes mistakes, and we do too. Because everyone uses the same book, naturally those mistakes are pretty predictable as well. So all the bad guys have to do is wait for us to screw up in one of those predictable places, and they're in the door."

Carl starting taking notes again. "Why's that? How do they know when you've made a mistake?"

Frank looked at Carl carefully for a second, and then started to feel more charitable towards him; he decided this kid really didn't know much about IT, and here they'd gone and stuck him in the Cybersecurity Investigations Unit.

Frank continued in a more conversational tone of voice. "They don't have to know when, just which mistakes are likely to occur. Here's an example. You can't just set up a network, make sure it's secure, and then forget about it. We've got employees coming and going all the time, so that means we're shutting down old and setting up new computers constantly. Every time, we've got to get everything right, or we might leave a hole in our defenses."

"We're upgrading software all the time, too – not everything at once, but bit by bit, because that spreads the cost and labor out, and because new products and new versions of old products don't all come out at the same time. Finally, all the hardware has a purchase date, and it all gets cycled out on a fixed schedule for reliability, budget, and obsolescence reasons. Once again, every time we change out something, we have to be sure that all of the security controls on the new gear are set up again the right way, or we've blown it. Unfortunately, it's a whole lot easier to forget to do something than it is to realize it."

"That still doesn't tell me how a hacker knows when or where there's an opportunity to strike."

"Like I said, they don't need to 'know' when there's an opportunity. They just need to know what an opportunity looks like. Then they can design a 'bot' – an automatic robot program that can recognize the opportunity – that hammers away every nanosecond at our firewall, waiting for a momentary lapse. All it takes is for a port to be left unguarded for even a moment, or some other minor glitch – and the bad guy slips inside. Funny, I was just explaining all of this to my daughter the other day."

To Frank's surprise, Cummings looked suddenly uncomfortable. "So then why do everything the same way?" Cummings responded quickly.

"Ah, there's the rub. Because firewalls aren't like physical walls. Back at Langley, everybody probably has to pass through just one or two gates to access the grounds, and I'm sure those gates are manned night and day, whenever they're open. And you've certainly got regular and infrared cameras watching the perimeter all the time, and motion detectors besides, and probably more spooky stuff, too, that I've never heard of. People are easy to detect in a half a dozen ways, so I'm sure you'd know in a heartbeat if a bad guy even tried to get in."

"Of course, people that want to come in through the gate have to show identification, and for other parts of your facility, they must have to do more than that – you probably use biometric scanners, for example. And all that data can be checked against all kinds of databases before you let them go farther. Once you do let them in, I expect you don't let them out of your sight unless they work there. Maybe not even then; I wouldn't be surprised. And after the U.S. Anthrax attacks back in 2001, every piece of your mail must be scanned, and zapped with radiation, too."

"Of course," Cummings interrupted. "But what does that have to do with cybersecurity? You can't put physical walls in front of data, and you can't have a guard checking every email that's sent to reach one of your employees."

"Of course not. But you can very much use exactly the same means in a metaphorical and technical sense – by designing virtual walls and gates, by automatically requesting and checking security credentials against databases, and by scanning attachments and links in email before they're allowed to be opened."

Cummings wasn't interrupting, so Frank continued.

"Still, though, you can't 'see' a computer program, and that does make it harder to keep things secure. And remember, I also said that everyone's firewalls are getting hammered all the time. So returning to the physical world, think what your guards, cameras and motion detectors would be up against if instead of looking at wide, floodlit lawns outside your perimeter, there were thousands of people milling up against your fences day and night? How many guys would you need to keep sitting at computer monitors then, trying to figure out which were gardeners and which ones were enemy agents, especially if they're all carrying garden shears?"

"But we've all got anti-virus software," Cummings objected. "To use your metaphor, isn't that supposed to be able to tell the gardeners from the spies?"

"Yes and no. There *are* lots of people trying 24/7 to pick out the bad guys from the gardeners – but when they do figure that out, it's almost always after some – or maybe a whole lot – of systems have already been compromised. So while there are public lists of viruses, worms, and Trojans – we lump them all together and call them "malware" - somebody had to identify each one as bad stuff before they could put it on the list. If you're in charge of security, you've got to keep checking that list all the time. And there may or may not yet be a fix you can download to protect yourself from everything on it."

"Oh yes – and there's this other big difference between the physical and the digital world. Unlike Langley, where I expect you only welcome in a limited number of carefully pre-cleared visitors a day, there's this thingy they call the Internet. And oh boy, how we all love the Internet! We want data to be coming in and going out all the time, every day, day and night. So instead of being able to just check people at the Langley gate, it's like we've got all four Metro lines going right through the CIA cafeteria."

Frank was on a roll now, galloping away on his favorite hobbyhorse. "But wait – it gets worse. At least over at the CIA you're a bunch of spooks, and you only talk about spooky stuff to other card-carrying spooks. I'm sure you compartmentalize information up and down the chain and keep things locked down tight. And I expect you've got at least one computer system that isn't connected to the Internet at all, or anything else that is."

"Okay! There's your answer!" Carl interjected. "Just limit Internet access to just a few people, and cut off all the rest. Instead of having a small network that's disconnected from the Internet and a big one that is connected, do it the other way around." He looked pleased with himself.

"Theoretically, you could. But unfortunately, we're all addicted to access – right up to the top brass, even though we know we probably shouldn't be, at least until we get this cybersecurity problem nailed. We're like kids in a candy store – we want to have the goodies *now* and worry about the cavities later, even though deep down inside we know we might lose all our teeth."

Frank noticed that Carl was starting to look bored, so he tried a more graphic illustration.

"Let's use the Pentagon as an example – how's that for a place that needs to worry about cybersecurity? But no, they're into "network centric operations" now, big time. That means they want everything, everywhere, accessible on one big network to anyone with the right clearance. They want to link everyone from a grunt on a mountain trail in Afghanistan to the Chairman of the Joint Chiefs of Staff - and from a road side sensor to a missile silo, too. And until they replace it, everything's hooked into the same Internet we use at home, so *technically* every hacker might be able to figure out a way to see and read everything the military can."

"Yeah, but they can't, right?" Cummings said, doing a bad job of hiding a yawn. "Otherwise, we wouldn't keep doing what we do."

"Oh no?" Frank replied, annoyed. "Did you see the story the other day about the Taliban intercepting the video from Predator and Reaper drones in Afghanistan, because the Army didn't think a bunch of terrorists would be sophisticated enough to worry about? It turns out all Al-Qaeda had to do was buy some off-the-shelf software to hack their way in. And now the military says it won't be able to encrypt the video until at least 2014. How's that for a case of candy and cavities?"

"So what do you do?" Cummings asked, checking his watch. Now Frank was getting annoyed. This guy just wasn't getting it.

"Well, to stop that, we have to add an administrative layer to be sure that only the right people can see the right information. That means you have to identify and categorize all the data, and then assign a security level to it and access categories, and so on, and then you also have to credential everyone on the network with the appropriate rights to the appropriate data. But wait – you're not done yet – because then you also have to supervise the matching of credentials with the exchange of only the right data. And did I mention you also have to figure out whether someone logging on is really who they say they are?"

Frank paused. Cummings looked up, as if he hadn't been paying attention. Frank leaned forward and began to speak more emphatically.

"Well, we do. So at the same time that you're making it *technically* possible for everyone to have access to everything, you're also trying to set all of these security conditions so that each person – out of millions of people with some degree of access – can see only what they're meant to see. Of course, you want to be sure that they can't change anything they're not supposed to change, either, because that would be even worse. And remember: there are no armed guards at the security gates checking who gets through the firewall – just computer protocols and programs, all on autopilot. It's all just software."

"What's wrong with protocols and programs?" Carl asked.

"Nothing, up to a point." Frank replied. "For most commercial purposes, they're good enough. Matter of fact, there's a point at which you don't want to make them better, because the cost becomes prohibitive, or it slows things down too much. At that point, businesses just try and keep them more or less up to date, and plug the gaps with insurance instead of security."

"So economically 'good enough' security is what we've gotten used to. Think about your credit cards – if someone steals your card and uses it, you don't worry about it. The card company has a computer program that detects the over-use and shuts it down quickly. Yes, the bank may have already lost some money, but that's built into their profit margin, so the customer doesn't realize that he's had to pay a thing. Yes, identity theft is a bigger deal for the person who's hit, but it hasn't happened to enough people – yet to get Congress to intervene."

"So what's wrong with that?" Cummings asked. "That makes perfect sense to me. Why pay for more protection than you need? Credit card costs are already too high."

"What's wrong with that is that a lot of things, like national security, aren't like credit card information. Say we're talking instead about the Pentagon, or a nuclear power plant, or a Presidential election. You can't buy enough insurance to cover the consequence of someone hacking a missile silo, or a nuclear reactor. And insurance couldn't compensate at all for corrupting the servers tabulating a swing state election, could it?"

Cummings leaned back and folded his arms. "Well, I'm not buying it. I can't believe the Pentagon, the President and everyone else is just looking the other way while we go to hell in a cybersecurity hand basket. You must be overstating the problem."

Frank snorted. "Haven't you been listening? We haven't even begun to address cyber-security. What we need to do is get creative – come up with ways to trick the bad guys while still letting the data get through that we want to get through. But instead, we just keep trying to build stronger virtual walls, and forget that we still can't *see* the bad guys, or even all the chinks in the walls."

Cummings had long ago quit taking notes. He sat there quietly, letting Frank run on as he picked up speed.

"When you get down to it, as long as we keep doing things the way we're doing them now, we're just kidding ourselves thinking we've got any cybersecurity at all. It's like Homeland Security, which is a total joke, only worse. And how can you be worse than Homeland Security? It's now almost ten years since 9/11, and we're still only scanning half the baggage that goes into the holds of passenger planes!"

"But it is worse, because if the worst happened, you might not even know your system has been compromised. So it can keep right on happening! The whole damn things a fraud, really – it's the electronic equivalent of the Emperor's new clothes. Except this time, instead of a little kid asking an awkward question, it could be a terrorist, or North Korea, and they're not going to tell anyone. If something doesn't happen to make us wake up soon, it could be a very big bang that finally does!"

Frank paused for effect, and then stopped short. What happened to just answering questions and telling the news?

Cummings looked pleased. "Thanks, Frank," he said pleasantly. "That was extremely helpful. I confess that I don't know as much about computer systems as I wish I did; that was very educational."

Frank looked at Cummings warily; he'd said a lot more than he needed or wanted to.

"So, are we done? I've got a stack of work on my desk that isn't getting done on its own."

"Almost done. There's just one last thing you could help me with. I haven't asked the others about this, but since you seem to understand the hacker mentality so well, you might be able to provide some useful insights. Back at the office some of our folks have been putting together a profile of whoever might be behind this *Alexandria Project* exploit. Mind if I show it to you?"

Frank sat up straighter; this was the first time Cummings had been upfront about the *Alexandria Project* being a serious matter. Frank realized that he still had the thumb drive in his hand, and jammed it into his pocket.

"Okay, sure."

Cummings pulled a sheet of paper out of his briefcase and slid it across the table. Frank gingerly pulled it the rest of the way across and began to read:

Case File: CSIU –LoC - CXFG - 7

Suspect Profile

Date: December 15, 2011

Event analysis: Exploits do not appear to be economically motivated, and are clearly meant to be discovered. Person responsible is therefore trying to make one or more points. Possibilities include the inadequacy of LoC security and/or its security staff. Because the exploit is ongoing, the person responsible is demonstrating, and likely reveling in, his self-perceived superiority over those that he knows are trying to track him down.

Identity:

- Gender: Male

- Age: 35 – 50

- Occupation: On staff IT professional

Psychological profile: Suspect will have a very high IQ, be well-educated, and creative. He will have a history of rebellion and lack of respect for authority, and be overly impressed with his own talents. He will have a low opinion of those who he thinks are incapable of thinking outside the box, including his superiors and his co-workers, and will not conform well to normal job expectations. He will likely have held many jobs, and few for very long. Suspect's personality will have rendered him socially isolated at a young age, and a loner throughout adulthood. He will have formed few close connections with his co-workers.

Motivation: Suspect resents his lack of traditional success, and particularly the successes of those he believes are his intellectual inferiors. He is likely to be obsessed with security issues, and convinced that only he truly understands the danger they present. He will also believe his vindictive attacks are heroic acts that only he can perform. The attacks have likely been triggered by a specific act or event that offended suspect's sense of self worth (e.g., the promotion of a co-worker).

Reviewed by: GLM, CRC, FHR

Frank was careful not to appear concerned when he glanced up, but Cummings was looking at him with a faint smile.

"So what do you think, Frank? Does that profile hold water? Does it sound like anyone we should be checking out?"

Frank felt clammy inside his clothes. "I can understand how this might make sense to you," he said finally.

"Good!" Cummings said, turning the recorder off with a click. "That's very helpful, coming from someone with your, how should I phrase it – ah yes – your background and skills."

Frank sat stock still, trying to remember every word he'd said during his ten-minute tirade.

"I've got just one last question, then. Will you be home this evening?" Frank nodded, surprised.

"Good." Agent Cummings said, snapping his briefcase shut. "I'll stop by around 7:00 PM to pick up your passport."

~~0000~~ ~~0001~~ ~~0010~~ ~~0011~~ 0100 ~~0011~~ ~~0010~~ ~~0001~~ ~~0000~~

7

What a Difference a Day (and a Decision Tree) Makes

F RANK STRUGGLED TO organize his thoughts as he left the fiasco of an "interview" he'd just endured. Time to be logical, not emotional, or he just might find himself in jail. Yes, that's what he'd need to do.

Though the thought of jail was unsettling, the concept of logic was comforting. His current situation wasn't really different from any other challenge he dealt with at work, he told himself. All he had to do was break the problem up into a set of questions, and then answer them, right? The answers generated by his "decision tree," (in programming parlance), would tell him what to do.

So what question should he start off with, he asked himself as he sat down in his cubicle. Well, the first logic "gate" appeared to be whether Cummings really thought Frank was the culprit. Frank took out a pad of paper, turned it sideways, and wrote "Am I under suspicion?" on the left. Then he added two lines, one slanting up and one slanting down to the right of his question. Next to the "up" line he wrote "no," and "yes" next to the down line.

If the answer to this first question was no, then Frank would have already reached the end of his decision tree, and could relax. But if the answer was yes, then he had more work to do. Frank weighed the possibility that Carl was jerking everyone around, and not just him. Negative, Frank decided. Everyone else thought the disappearing documents were part of a test, not a real exploit, and George would want Carl to keep it that way.

So that means I'm in trouble, Frank told himself. See? I'm making progress already, he added wryly.

He forced himself to focus. What should the next question be? He decided it should be whether he should do something to influence the outcome, or not. He added two more slanted lines. "No" meant just getting back to work. That, and trying harder not to do anything stupid.

But what would "yes" mean?

Frank settled back in his chair and sorted through the few alternatives he could imagine. The only one that seemed to make any sense was for him to figure out who was actually stealing documents from the Library of Congress and turn that person in. So he added "Find hacker?" and two more slanted "yes/no" lines. Now what?

He decided that there were actually two parts to that question – was it likely enough that he might catch the hacker to make it worth the effort, and was there any reason not to try? He thought enough of his own abilities to opt for "yes" on the first part, and turned to the second – would launching a personal crusade to catch the hacker be a smart move, or another dumb one? After all, why not just let the powers-that-be muddle through?

Frank decided that question had an easy answer, and that the answer was "no" – because the powers-that-be were a bunch of bungling chowder heads when it came to security. Look at how often the government had been hacked already, and how infrequently it had gotten to the bottom of it. All they did was look more and more foolish each time it happened. Why would the CIA be any more successful this time than before?

Frank looked up from his notes and stared at the ceiling. Was that the end of the decision tree, or was there another critical question he hadn't thought of yet?

Maybe. How important was it that he find the hacker? And how much time did he have to do so?

Okay, he thought, let's assume that the Feds don't catch the hacker, and that things just keep getting worse. Chairman Steele's Cybersecurity subcommittee was already out for blood, based on other security breaches that were in the news. There would be hell to pay if an agency had to admit at a public hearing that it had not only been hacked, but that it was *still* being hacked by someone leaving animated calling cards behind. And this at the same time it was supposed to be proposing a plan to make itself hack-proof!

Okay, but so what? So what if the CIA *never* catches the wily Alexandrians? If he just kept his nose clean, what can they do to him? Hell, it had taken the FBI years to find someone it could credibly charge with responsibility for the post-9/11 anthrax scare!

Frank suddenly remembered that the authorities investigating that case hadn't taken long at all to leak the name of a suspect - who later turned out to be innocent. Frank turned to his laptop and found the guy's name in a few key strokes: Dr. Steven Hatfill.

How convenient that had been, he reflected cynically. The public was screaming for the FBI to catch the culprit, but the case was turning out to be almost impossible to solve. Leaking the name of a "person of interest" was a neat way to take the heat off, because the media could be relied upon to take it from there. And so they had - the newspapers and cable shows pounced on the poor S.O.B like the packs of jackals some of them were, making the researcher's life hell. Hatfill had to spend a fortune in court before he was finally exonerated – seven years later.

Frank was beginning to feel queasy. He returned to his decision tree and added another question to his chart: Was scapegoating by the Feds standard operational procedure in tough cases or not? If no, then his problem wasn't urgent. But if yes, then he was not only in danger, but time might be short. He Googled "terrorist scapegoat" and waited for the hits to display.

3,250,000. That wasn't good.

The search reminded him of another situation that had been in the news years ago, involving the guard who found a pipe bomb at the Atlanta, Georgia Summer Olympics and came to regret it. Frank typed "Atlanta pipe bomb guard" into the Wikipedia search window, and there he was – Richard Jewell. Frank clicked on the link and read:

> ...*Early news reports lauded Jewell as a hero, for helping to evacuate the area after he spotted the suspicious package. Three days later, The Atlanta Journal-Constitution revealed that the FBI was treating him as a possible suspect, based largely on a "lone bomber" criminal profile.*

Ouch! The mention of criminal profiling hit pretty close to home.

For the next several weeks, the news media publicly dissected Jewell, Frank read. It sifted through every detail it could uncover about his past to see how well it mapped to the "lone bomber" profile developed by the FBI. Conveniently, that had been leaked to the press as well. Many in the media rushed to portray Jewell as a failed law enforcement officer who had likely planted the bomb so he could find it and be a hero. Two of the bombing victims even filed lawsuits against Jewell on the basis of this reporting alone.

Now that was *really* great, Frank thought. Maybe Agent Carl had used the Jewell profile as a starting point for what even Frank was starting to think of as his own psychological portrait.

He sat back. The playbook seemed clear enough: if you can't catch the right guy quick, any convenient dolt will do if they match any halfway credible profile. Next, leak his name to the press – or hey, why not a House Subcommittee – and relax. They'll take it from there.

Frank tried to tell himself he was being paranoid. But if this was paranoia, how to explain all the "guilty man found innocent" stories that were flooding the newspapers these days, now that DNA testing was so cheap? Just about every single case involved the victim of a tough, very public case and a lazy prosecutor. Only a lab test had eventually cleared those who had been falsely accused, in many cases after they had spent years, or even decades, languishing in prison..

Except there weren't any DNA tests to clear you if you were accused of stealing computer files. Matter of fact, there really wasn't *any* way to exonerate you, Frank realized – except by catching the real culprit.

"For Pete's sake, Frank, will you *stop* with the drumming!"

Frank looked up in surprise, and then down at his hands, catching them in mid-beat. He grabbed the edge of his desktop to make his digits behave.

"Sorry, Mitch," he called over the top of the cubical wall.

Okay, he told himself. This is ridiculous. I'm panicking for no reason. Cummings is probably just your average self-absorbed secret agent wannabe making himself feel important. Get a grip on yourself and get back to work.

It was then that Frank noticed an almost imperceptible green flicker at the top of his laptop screen. As always, his laptop was turned on and sitting next to his desktop computer. He stared at the laptop and waited. Sure enough, there it was again. Someone was watching him using the video camera on his own computer!

Frank's eyes widened. When could his laptop have been compromised? Just about anytime, he realized. It was always lying out on his desk at work, and as often as not, even when he was at home he was logged on to the LoC system. It could have happened while he was trading jibes with Carl – or days ago. Maybe even before he had deleted the Alexandria Project screen shot and then immediately defragmented his hard drive.

Frank's head began to spin. What else had been placed on his computer? A keystroke logger recording every letter he typed? Did Cummings know every website Frank had visited over the past week? And what kinds of sites *had* he been visiting?

All kinds, Frank realized. Notorious cracker sites. Security sites. Hell, he'd just now been looking up famous terrorist attacks on the Wikipedia. Anyone who needed a scapegoat could ignore 99% of the sites he'd visited in the last week and tie the rest as tight as you please back into that stupid, lame, profile.

For the second time that day, Frank broke out in a cold sweat. Whoever was attacking the LoC site was damned good. He'd left no tracks at all, other than those he'd meant to be found. Frank doubted the CIA would get to the bottom of the hack quickly, if ever. And Congressman Steele's subcommittee meetings would resume in a week.

Well, that brought him to the bottom of the decision tree, didn't it? Yes, Frank decided, it certainly had. He took the thumb drive with the Alexandria Project screen saver on it out of his pocket and idly contemplated it. Then, on a whim, he took off the chain with the St. Christopher's medal he'd worn out of habit since he was a child. Opening the chain, he slipped the thumb drive on next to the medal. He might not be religious, he reflected, but he sure could use all the good luck he could get. Then he stood up and put on his coat.

"So – did you drum yourself out of here, Frank?" Mitch asked as he walked by.

Frank gave a dry laugh. "Yeah, Mitch. I guess that's a pretty good way of putting it."

0000 0001 0010 0011 0100 0011 0010 0001 0000

8

Face Off with Fearless Fosdick

TO FRANK'S DISGUST, it was love at first sight for Lilly when Carl Cummings arrived to relieve Frank of his passport. But Frank's chagrin turned to glee when he realized that the CIA agent was terrified of dogs. Frank stepped out into the hall to better appreciate Carl's frantic and ineffective efforts to fend off the obese corgi's surprisingly energetic advances.

Predictably, Mrs. Foomjoy popped like a jack-in-the-box out of her door across the hall to see what the ruckus was all about. Frank thought she looked magnificent in her full regalia of house dress, fuzzy pink slippers, and curlers. He watched with new respect as she lit into Cummings for his lack of appreciation for canine affection. At last, she snatched Lily up, and then, as suddenly as she had appeared, Frank's apparition of a neighbor vanished behind her energetically slammed door.

Carl turned wide-eyed to Frank, a helpless look on his face. But Frank simply smiled and tucked his passport in the agent's jacket pocket. "Sorry for my bad manners, Carl. Next time I'll introduce you." He closed the door in the bewildered agent's face.

Chuckling, Frank walked back up his apartment hallway. Once he had decided a few hours ago to fight back, his spirits had immediately begun to improve. Ever since, his mental wheels had been spinning with mounting excitement as he scoped out his next moves.

Frank took the first one on his way home, stopping at a convenience store to buy a six-pack of Heineken, two cans of soup, a quart of orange juice – and two disposable cell phones, each loaded with $100 of pre-paid time. While hardly complete, his plans were already beginning to take shape.

With Carl's visit behind him, Frank could return to those plans. But as he put his groceries away, he heard his doorbell ring and a key rattle in the lock of his apartment door. Moments later, Marla arrived breathlessly in the kitchen. Still wearing her coat, she threw herself down in a chair by the table.

"Tell me – please *TELL* me - that Carl Cummings wasn't here to visit you?" Marla demanded. "It's just a coincidence he was walking out of this building, right?"

Frank was both amused and shocked. "You know not-so-special agent Cummings?"

"Oh – my – God, yes. What was he doing here?"

"Picking up my passport, as it happens. Today he informed me in so many words that I'm Numero Uno on the CIA's suspect list. He made it clear that he'd be keeping a close eye on me."

"You! Whatever for?"

"Well, it seems like the Feds are still very much in the profile business, and the profile they've come up with fits me like a glove."

"That's crazy. You're the last person on earth likely to pull off something like this. And even if they thought you were responsible, what can they do without anything to tie you to the security breaches?"

"Well, for starters they can take my passport – that's what Carl stopped by for. I probably should have made him get a court order first, but it seemed smarter to not make a fuss and just give it up. And speaking of court orders, I expect he could also get a friendly judge to approve a wiretap on my phone. Or a microphone in my kitchen, for that matter. Want to take a walk? It's a lovely evening for a walk, isn't it?""

Marla began to object, and then got the point. "Sure. Just lovely."

Neither of them spoke as Frank locked his apartment door. A few moments later they were walking up 16th Street towards the Starbucks on the corner

"Dad, do you really think this is serious?"

"I don't rightly know, kid. On the one hand, there's nothing I'm aware of to link me to what's going on. But on the other hand, George's cover story isn't going to stand up if any more files disappear. When that happens, everyone at the LoC will be looking for the culprit. Worse yet, next week George will be testifying - under oath - in front of Congressman Steele's subcommittee. What happens if George gets asked the wrong question, and has to admit that the Library of Congress is being hacked right now, and he has no idea by whom?"

"Well, what does happen? And whatever happens, why does that become your problem?"

"Because the FBI and the CIA don't enjoy looking like a bunch of donkeys, even if some of their people do exhibit a strong family resemblance. They'll need a fall guy, and at the moment I'm afraid I may be the most conveniently located candidate for the job. All they need to buy some breathing room is to have someone like Carl provide a reporter with a tip from, 'a source who requested anonymity because he was not authorized to speak.'"

"Dad, that's ridiculous! What kind of person would carry out an order like that?"

Frank opened the coffee shop door and held it for his daughter. "So what's your opinion of Carl Cummings?"

Marla's mouth opened and shut twice. Then she walked past Frank, and kept on walking until she reached the last table in the back of the coffee shop.

Frank smiled to himself and bought a couple of lattes to give Marla a chance to digest the news. Rejoining her, he took a seat across the table from his daughter and raised his eyebrows.

"So?"

Marla held her cup in both hands, and paused before she spoke. "Carl Cummings is a jerk."

Frank looked up at the ceiling. "You know, that's not the most insightful conclusion you've ever shared with me. As a matter of fact, I'd already reached pretty much the same conclusion through my own finely tuned powers of observation."

Marla frowned but said nothing.

"So let me try again. How did you come to know Fearless Fosdick?"

"Fearless who?"

"Later. Now give."

Marla put down her coffee and took a deep breath. "So, it's like this. My first year at George Washington I took a big lecture course with a couple hundred other freshman, and Carl was the grad school teaching assistant assigned to my discussion section. I was stuck with the cretin for a whole semester."

"Okay, so two hours a week with a cretin may be annoying, but it's not exactly waterboarding. As I recall, you decided your first roommate was a cretin, too, and now you're the best of friends. So why such a negative reaction?"

Marla squirmed and then gave up. "Alright, so maybe I went out with Carl a few times."

Frank suppressed a smile with difficulty. "With... Carl. Okay. So if he's such a cretin, and you only went out with him a few times, how come you weren't surprised to learn he's now a CIA agent?"

Marla gave him a pitying glance. "Dad, everyone – well, everyone who doesn't already have a foot in the grave – has a Facebook page."

Suddenly, the words came tumbling out. "It was really low rent of him. Professors and teachers aren't supposed to date students – there's, like, even a policy against it. You know I didn't date much in high school, and he is pretty good looking. And he knew how to dress. All the girls in my section thought he was, like, totally hot."

Frank wrinkled his nose. "Don't say 'like' all the time like that."

Marla ignored him. "So when he took an interest in me, I was flattered. Soon, we started going out pretty heavy."

Frank decided that the conversation had reached a Too Much Information inflection point and cut her off. "I'm assuming it didn't end well."

"Hah! Let's just say that to top it off, he gave me a C on my final exam."

Frank winced. Neither of them said anything for a minute.

"So who's Fearless Fosdick?" Marla asked at last.

Frank turned on his BlackBerry, glad for the change of topic. "Fosdick was the creation of Al Capp, a brilliant cartoonist with a strip called Li'L Abner that ran for more than forty years, beginning during the Depression. It was filled with oddball characters with outrageous names like Moonbeam McSwine, Senator Jack S. Phogbound, and Appassionata Von Climax. The strip was still running when I was a kid, and I loved it."

"Capp lampooned everyone, and everything. One of the things he spoofed unmercifully was another comic called Dick Tracy, a drama strip that ran for almost exactly the same time period under its original author, Chester Gould (somebody else does it now – badly). Tracy was always pursuing equally bizarre evildoers with names like Flattop Jones, Pruneface, and The Mole. Each had a face to match."

"Gould's Tracy was supposed to be the all-American, straight-shooter type (literally) – tough, smart, and invincible. Capp created

Fosdick, of course, to be the same, but exaggerated the same characteristics outrageously. He pulled it off by creating another strip within the Li'l Abner series, and made Fosdick Li'l Abner's "Ideel." Abner would rush to the post box every day to read Fosdick's latest exploits. Here – read this from Wikipedia – it's how Capp described his own character:

> *Fearless is without doubt the world's most idiotic detective. He shoots people for their own good, is pure beyond imagining, and is fanatically loyal to a police department which exploits, starves and periodically fires him.*

"Sound like anyone you might know?"

Marla laughed.

"Here – let me find you a picture."

Frank took back the BlackBerry and hunted up an image of Fosdick. He handed the device back to Marla.

"My God!" Marla almost shrieked. Serious-looking people with laptops stared their way in annoyance. Embarrassed, she leaned forward and whispered, "Take away the little mustache, and that's him!"

"So now you know what I'm concerned about. I'm afraid that your buddy Fearless may get a lot of heat from upstairs if he doesn't produce results. And if he can't produce results, well, maybe a little diversion might be the next best thing."

Marla was serious now. "So what are you going to do, Dad?"

Frank tried to speak more gently now. "Marla, if things get too tense, I may decide I need to go away for awhile. If that happens, you won't be able to call me on my cell phone, or email me, either. We'd have to assume that you're the first person the CIA would tap in an effort to trace me back through you. Can you deal with that?"

Marla looked at him with concern, not knowing if he was serious. She realized he was, and wondered whether she should try to argue him out of doing something she worried could backfire badly.

"But Dad, if you run, they'll be sure it's you."

"I know. But I think the best way I can clear myself is by finding whoever is behind what's going on. There's a lot more I can do if I'm not under surveillance...websites I'd need to visit and people I'd need to be in touch with that would otherwise make me look even more suspicious. And I don't have any confidence that the CIA is going to catch these guys on its own."

Marla looked down at her latte. It was untouched, and now cold.

"Okay, Dad. I trust you. And yes, I'll be able to deal with it if you decide you have to…drop out of sight." Then she tried to lighten up the mood. "Have you thought of an alias yet?"

"As a matter of fact, yes. What do you think of 'Carter Columbo'?"

Marla rolled her eyes. "Okay, I've seen your thrift store raincoat often enough to get the 'Columbo' part. But where did 'Carter' come from?"

"Obviously you don't read enough spy thrillers. Haven't you noticed there's invariably a government employee named 'Carter'?"

Marla managed a wan smile, but didn't offer a response. There didn't seem to be much else to talk about, so he gave Marla's hand a squeeze, and stood up.

Neither of them spoke as they left the Starbucks and walked back to Frank's flat. Marla waited until they were in front of the apartment building before she asked, "Dad, if you really do take off, will there be any way we can keep in touch?"

Frank smiled. "Yes, I think so, kid. But you'll just have to wait for a little bird to tell you how."

$$0000 \quad 0001 \quad 0010 \quad 0011 \quad 0100 \quad 0011 \quad 0010 \quad 0001 \quad 0000$$

9

You've Got Mail!

ARRIVING AT WORK on Monday, Frank found a Post-it® note on his monitor bearing just three words: *See me – George*. That wasn't good. It looked like another week was going to get off to an interesting start. The question was, how?

Frank took his time walking down the hall. He'd had enough unexpected developments already, and wasn't looking forward to any new ones. But the distance was short, and it wasn't long before he arrived at George's office. Marchand saw him immediately, and motioned for him to sit down. Then he slid a sheet of paper to the edge of his desk.

"This arrived in Saturday's mail. Read it where it lies. I don't want your fingerprints on it."

Frank recognized the logo at the top of the letter immediately: a tall, ancient-looking building that might be a lighthouse. Startled, he looked up at George.

"Read it."

Frank pulled his chair closer and did as he was told.

THE ALEXANDRIA PROJECT

December 11, 2011

Dear Mr. Marchand,

Allow me to apologize for any inconvenience my organization's little demonstration may have caused to you and your staff. Also, be assured that your materials will be quite safe with us.

We hope that your recent contributions to The Alexandria Project have made real to you a matter for which someone with your responsibilities should have the utmost concern: the headlong rush of government towards complete reliance upon the Internet, notwithstanding the increasing number of cyberattacks being launched by enemies of the state.

You should also note with alarm the government's intent to replace all paper-based systems with electronic archives. As this process accelerates across the public and private sectors, the day is not far distant when our enemies will be able to eradicate the knowledge upon which our very lives depend.

When Julius Caesar set the blaze that destroyed the Library of Alexandria, and with it, the accumulated wisdom of the ancients, at least he could plead accident rather than intent. Above all other government offices, yours should know better, and hence our selection of the Library of Congress as the starting point for our campaign to force a return to sanity.

Please know that the reach of our capabilities extends to every one of the Federal Agencies – and to all commercial, academic, and non-profit enterprises as well. Lest you doubt the truth of this statement, you will find that at 6:00 AM on Monday, December 20, the master security plans of the Department of Defense, White House, Library of Congress, MIT and Google will be contributed to The Alexandria Project. We will read them with interest, deficient as they are.

> Widespread contributions from other leading academic, media, and commercial contributors may only be avoided if the administration publicly announces an immediate halt to further transitions of government systems to digitized archives. We look forward to that announcement, with full supporting details, in the very near future.
>
> Very truly yours,
>
> ZENODOTUS

Frank looked up, and George nodded. "Six o'clock, on the dot. You should see my email inbox. So what do you think?"

"Where do I start? First of all, what's he talking about, saying that the LoC is starting a 'destruction policy'?"

"Ah, that's an interesting clue, isn't it? You'd have to be very highly placed in the LoC to know about that, so whoever "Zenodotus" really is, he's got access to inside information. Needless to say, that's troubling."

"As you know, the LoC's funding comes out of the Congressional budget. With the economy in the tank and the deficit soaring, the legislators need to show they're willing to share the pain. That said, of course they don't want to cut their own staff or perks, so they've told everyone else they have to double down on their own reductions. We've got to figure out how to lop 10% off our budget every year for the next five years, and as it happens, one of the easiest ways to do that is to digitize and pulp books as fast as we can."

"But how much money can that really save?"

"Much more than you'd expect. We already add new material exclusively in electronic form, and if we start getting rid of the old stuff, we can cancel the new storage facility we were going to build out at Fort Meade, cut down on the curatorial staff, mothball parts of our current facilities – the list goes on and on. Hosting servers is a whole lot cheaper than hosting books, and we can show increased public access benefits by throwing more and more material on line. We can make it look like a win–win proposition."

Frank was mildly shocked. "We'd really do that? Start pulping millions of books?" He was as digital as the next IT guy, but like most LoC employees, he'd become fond of the aura of the millions of books, maps, music, and more that surrounded him at work. Personally, he thought that the Alexandria Project folks had a pretty good point. Not that this was the time to admit it.

"You said the letter arrived by mail. Where was it postmarked?"

"Alexandria, Virginia. But who knows whether the post box was just down the street from the author, or whether he drove five hundred miles to post it there. As you'll recall from the anthrax scare, if you want to remain anonymous, there's no better way to communicate than through the good old U.S. mail."

Frank tried a different tack. "Okay, so let's talk about the author. What do you make of "Zenodotus"?"

"That part's easy. Turns out he was a Greek grammarian, literary critic, Homeric scholar – and the first head librarian of the Library of Alexandria. So the story line holds true."

"Yeah," Frank countered, "But what if the whole thing is simply a cover for something else? How disruptive would it be if every agency's IT department is thrown into chaos? And what happens to every other legislative priority if Congress has to drop everything to save the country from a 'cybersecurity crisis'?"

Frank stopped abruptly at that point. George guessed why." So does this make you look more, or less, suspicious?"

Why deny it? Frank thought.

"I admit the thought did just cross my mind."

"I'm thinking it doesn't help you, Frank. On the one hand, you shouldn't know about the pulping program yet – that won't be announced until next week. But on the other, if you've been sneaking around every directory on the servers, why wouldn't you have stumbled on this?"

Frank said nothing. Instead, he looked down at the letter again, trying to commit as much of it to memory as he could. Then he leaned back.

"Why did you share this with me, George? Does Cummings know you intended to tip me on this?"

"Cummings doesn't know this letter exists - not yet. I only got here a half hour before you did, but I happened to flip through the weekend mail before getting down to business."

"He'll be pissed."

"He'll get over it. If he finds out, I'll tell him I wanted to watch you read the letter and see how you reacted."

Frank looked up sharply. He wondered which way the conversation was about to turn.

"So what would you tell him?"

"I'd tell him you looked genuinely surprised," George said evenly. Then he leaned forward and continued, more softly, "Don't worry, Frank. I don't think you have anything to do with this. You and I have known each other for quite a long time – I'm even the godfather of your daughter, in case you'd forgotten."

Frank breathed a silent sigh of relief, but George wasn't done yet.

"I know you can be a bull-headed idiot, Frank. And more often than not, you're your own worst enemy to boot. But I don't think you're a big enough moron to pull a stunt like this."

Frank gave half a smile. "I'm not sure 'thanks' is the appropriate reply to a statement like that, but I will acknowledge a sense of relief."

"I wouldn't go that far, Frank. When you compare this letter to the little rant I understand you committed to Carl Cummings' audio recorder, it doesn't look good. As soon as you leave this room, I'll naturally have to call the CIA and turn this letter over to them. After that, all hell's going to break loose. This isn't just an annoying little problem here at the LoC anymore. This is about to turn into a public relations disaster for the administration."

There was no denying that, Frank realized. It looked like he might have less time to prepare than he had been counting on.

George continued. "The CIA will obviously be able to keep the lid on this with the DoD and the White House. I don't know how they'll deal with the folks at MIT and Google – maybe they'll just leave them in the dark for now, or maybe they'll be upfront and ask them to play ball. Either way, I don't see a major university and a public corporation calling in the press over something like this if the CIA gives them a gold plated excuse not to. But if Zenodotus & Co. start snapping up documents here, there and everywhere,

this will hit the front pages – fast. Come to think of it, I bet the next letters will go to the *New York Times*, CBN and - God help the President - Fox News, each of which will have just had their security plans "contributed." Now, won't that just be fun?"

"So just exactly how screwed do you think I am, George? After all, there's not really anything at all to connect me with this."

"I can't answer that, Frank. You're right; there's no smoking gun pointed directly at you. But the genie is out of the bottle now. There's not much I'm going to be able to do to help. We both know that if the CIA decides that it needs to have at least one "person of interest" in their sights so they look like they're doing their job, it's likely to be you, for lack of a better volunteer."

Frank let that one hang in the air for a moment, and then stood up. "Well. I guess that's that, then. I appreciate all you've done for me, George – I really do. Thanks for letting me know about the letter, too. The more I know, the more I can defend myself. Or at least it helps me think I can."

Frank was at his boss's door when George spoke again.

"Frank – one last thing."

What now? Frank thought.

"Let me know by the end of the day what explanation you want to use for your absence, because as of 5:00 PM Friday, you're on paid administrative leave."

0000 0001 0010 0011 0100 0011 0010 0001 0000

10

Good Boy, Carl!

"GOOD *MORNING* AGENT Cummings!" The normally sullen receptionist smiled brightly at the handsome young agent. As an afterthought, she added, "Oh! I almost forgot. Mr. Marchand would like to speak to you."

"That's nice. I'll get around to it."

"Oh, but he said *right away* – just as soon as you arrive! He's in that conference room right there." Mary pointed at the door to her right.

Carl gave a nonchalant smile and walked on. Who was George Marchand to be telling a CIA agent what to do?

Ten minutes later, coffee cup in hand, Carl strolled past Mary again. Rewarding her with a wink, he opened the conference room door without knocking and stepped inside.

To his surprise, he saw his boss sitting next to George, and next to him, the head of the CIA's cybersecurity division, Michael Armstrong. Carl got a much bigger surprise a few moments late when he heard Armstrong call George "sir."

Ignored by those in the room, Carl slipped quietly into an empty chair at the end of the table. He decided it was time he started listening very carefully to what George had to say.

"So that's the news on the political front. Mike, give me an update on the attacker profile that we believe in. Dave, you play devil's advocate."

"Unfortunately, sir, we really don't have a profile. There's no end of possibilities for who we could be up against, once you assume this whole Alexandria story is a pile of crap."

Carl's boss interrupted him. "So let's stop right there. Why should we assume it's a pile of crap?'"

"It was an attack after our last meeting that sealed it. What's important is that this time, they took "litmus test" files we had planted as bait, and we confirmed they were able to decrypt the files almost immediately. We know the encryption algorithm has been compromised before, so now we only use it when we want to pass false information along to bad guys – or, as in this case, when we want to know whether we're up against the pros, or just amateurs without access to supercomputers. Conclusion: this isn't any bunch of cranks – or any disgruntled employee, either – that we're dealing with."

"So if the Alexandria story isn't genuine, why are they playing around with us?" Dave countered. "Why don't they just do whatever it is they really want to do and skip the theatrics?"

Mike shrugged. "Well, it may be that they need to test their techniques further to be sure they'll work before they pull the trigger on what they're really up to. Or maybe they still haven't figured out how to get to what they really want. Either way, they might have figured we'd detect them before long, so why not come up with a ruse to confuse us?"

"Okay, let's say that's conceivable. But if it's not really about book pulping, why are they hacking the Library of Congress?"

Mike pointed to George. "The same reason Mr. Marchand's cover is to be the head of the IT there. Since the LoC is the secret testbed for security systems for the entire government, if they can crack the most secure servers he's got, they can get to anything in any agency. They'll even be able to do that next year, after we roll out the new wave of security the LOC is testing now."

Dave jabbed a finger at him. "But choosing the LoC could have been just dumb luck. How can you tell it wasn't?"

"We can't," George interrupted. "But we also can't risk assuming it was. Keep going, Mike."

Dave sat back, and Mike continued. "So let's agree to assume that the whole Alexandria story is just a cover to throw us off track. If that's the case, the letter Mr. Marchand got this morning is brilliant, because now we have to treat the Alexandria Project like a real danger – whether it's a sham or not. Any day now, the lid will blow off if they decide to swipe a file and someone calls the papers – hell, if they decide to start swiping files *from* the papers! MIT and Google have agreed to keep quiet for now, but we can't play whack-a-mole with every damn server owner in the country."

George spoke up again. "Agreed. Let's move on. So now that we've decided we're not looking for a bunch of Internet-Luddites, who should be on the suspect list?"

Mike shrugged. "Where do I start? The Russians have been saber-rattling against us ever since the President announced he supports inviting the last of the former eastern bloc countries to join NATO."

"Meanwhile, the Koreans have their hair in a knot because the President is saber-rattling against *them*. They've been firing off missiles every other day this week to show how tough they are."

"Of course the Iranians hate us recreationally to begin with, but since we planted the Stuxnet worm in President Ahmadinejad's beloved nuclear centrifuges, his position has been shaky. If he doesn't figure out a way to make us look bad again, Ayatollah Khamenei may throw him out of the boat to protect himself."

"Next, there's China. They're pissed at us over all the cybersecurity things we're pissed at them about, because we've been public in our criticism of them. They prefer to discuss these things discretely behind the scenes. Maybe they figure that if we're going to hammer them for harboring cybercriminals anyway, they might as well get something out of it." Mike paused.

"And then there's the French." Everybody in the room except Carl rolled his eyes.

"Let's not even talk about the French," George interjected.

"Good call, sir. So to sum up, we've got plenty of eligible suspects, but nothing to lead us to focus on one over the others. And it sounds like we're just as much in the dark on the technical side, too."

"That's not quite true, Mike," George replied. "We do know they can get past our firewalls at will, even while we're scanning our system in real time and can't find a single unauthorized port. That means that even if they installed a trapdoor to begin with, they're no longer using it. "So they must be able to fool our system into thinking they're an authorized visitor."

"We also know that we can't catch them when they enter, or track them once they're in. My best guess is that they penetrate the firewall during a time of heavy traffic, and then change their identity every few seconds once they're inside. That way they don't leave any bread-crumbs for us to follow. They probably visit us regularly to update the code that steals the files, or maybe they delete it and plant it again somewhere else, and then log out – all within a minute or two of gaining access. Hours later, the new code executes, and bang! – we've been had again."

The CIA men absorbed that for a moment. Then Mike spoke up.

"So how about your golden boy – what is it, Frank? Has he come up with anything yet?"

At the mention of Frank's name, Carl sat up abruptly, spilling most of his still-steaming coffee into his lap.

Noticing his presence for the first time, the others turned to watch Carl thrash wildly away at himself under the table.

Suppressing a smile, George decided to cut the young man a break. "Perhaps I owe you an apology, Carl. Actually, Frank isn't a suspect at all. Never has been. But he is a security genius. If anyone I have on staff is going to figure out what's going on here, it's him – but only if he really drills down on it. And that's not Frank's strength. Thanks to you, he's rather more motivated to get to the bottom of this than he would be if I'd simply told him to start digging."

Flustered, Carl forgot his junior status. "So you played me as a stooge to set him up?"

"Actually, Carl, I set him up more than you did. You see, the weekend Frank's file disappeared wasn't really the first time the Alexandria folks struck. We'd already been losing files for two weeks, and had no idea who was hitting us. So I recorded the contribution message, removed Frank's file myself, and left the message for him to find. Your part came later, and you played it perfectly – just as we had hoped. We couldn't be more pleased."

Carl looked uncertain, but had regained sufficient self control to know that we would be smart to keep his mouth shut.

George turned back to the other men and continued, "Instead of attending to his assigned duties, Frank has been knocking himself hunting for the Alexandria Project ever since Carl interviewed him. Starting next week, he'll be able to do that full time without guilt, because I've told him I've got no choice but to put him on administrative leave."

Carl was thinking rapidly, trying to calculate whether he'd been made to look stupid or not. He didn't like the way his math was coming out. This meeting had been just one surprise after another. What, he wondered, could possibly happen next?

George obligingly supplied the answer. "Which brings me to the reason I asked you to step in, Carl. Now that you know what's really going on, it's time you were reassigned."

Okay, that was a surprise, Carl thought. To what?

But George wasn't in any hurry to satisfy Carl's curiosity." Among security people that matter – here and abroad – Frank is very well known. He's a go-to guy for everyone who is anyone in cybersecurity, and he can go anywhere online and be in touch with anyone he wants to."

"Whoever is really behind the Alexandria Project must already know that, and will take it for granted that Frank is playing a key role in trying to hunt them down. We need to assume they will be willing to do anything necessary to prevent him from doing that."

George paused, and looked Carl in the eye. "Do you understand?"

Carl nodded, adding "Yes, sir" in response to a sharp glance from his boss.

"Good. Therefore, when you walk out of this room, your new full-time assignment will be to protect Frank Adversego, without him knowing it, and without allowing him to guess that he's no longer a suspect."

Carl was stunned. A project like that was below his meager, but hard won, pay grade. But what could he say?

"One more thing," George added. "As you know from Frank's file, he has a daughter in town named Marla. The next best way for the bad guys to get to Frank would be to get to her. So the second part of your job is to do everything necessary to protect Marla. We'll make sure you have the resources you'll need to protect both of them."

George waited for a reply, but Carl only stared back at him blankly, looking as if he might be ill at any moment.

Losing patience, George spoke again. "Good. Then this would be an excellent time for you to get started, don't you think?"

Carl realized that, "Yes, sir," was the only available response. So he stood up, yes sir'ed George, and left the room, ears burning and holding his empty coffee cup in his hand.

Mary, of course, had been lying in wait for him, looking forward to his re-emergence from the conference room. "Did you have a good meeting, Agent Cummings?" she asked brightly.

For a moment, Carl tried to regain his composure, and then gave it up. Saying nothing, he set his coffee cup on her desk, took his coat from the closet, and left her sitting, puzzled, at her desk.

0000 0001 0010 0011 0100 0011 0010 0001 0000

11

Have I got an App for You!

WHILE CIA AGENT Carl Cummings was being brought to heel by George Marchand, Frank was sitting at his kitchen table, tapping away at the cramped keyboard of a cheap netbook connected to a neighbor's unsecured WiFi network. Even this was risky, he reminded himself, so this brief session would have to be his last until he moved on.

A few keystrokes more and he had logged on to the bank account of the Pangloss Game Company. Mentally crossing his fingers, he clicked on the link for an account that read "iBallZapper." When the new view displayed, the number that immediately caught his eye was in the balance column, and that number was $147,396.78. A slow smile of victory spread across Frank's face as he hit the refresh button. The number jumped upward by another $38.42. His plan was unfolding nicely.

Just ten days before, though, he had been sitting in the same chair wondering how he could possibly afford to execute the strategy that was taking shape in his mind. No matter how he looked at it, he needed something he didn't have: money. And he needed a lot of it, too.

That was a problem. Frank was fiercely, if perversely, proud of his relative penury. His father had skipped out on the family while Frank was still in secondary school, and if Frank hadn't scored a great scholarship, he never would have made it out of Brooklyn. Even so, he'd had to work at one part time job or another from the time he was fourteen until he graduated from college. He had been determined that Marla would never have to do the same. Since his salary at the Library of Congress was modest, that meant living in a pretty crummy part of town. Still, he could look forward to a pension when he retired as a civil servant – and more importantly, Marla would graduate from college and grad school unburdened by debt.

But now that wasn't good enough. He had never anticipated suddenly needing a lot of cash. Hell, he didn't even own a car, much less a house he could borrow against. And what he was planning now would require more money than he could run up on any reasonable number of credit cards, much less repay after the dust had settled.

Frank's fingers drummed so hard on his table he finally became aware he was causing himself pain. But what was he to do? Where does an IT guy go when he needs big money to fund a project? Frank didn't have any well-off friends or family to borrow from, and he sure as hell wasn't going to be able to get money from some venture capitalist.

Or could he? Frank stood up abruptly and grabbed his coat, making sure that one of his cheap pre-paid phones was in the pocket. With Lilly yapping angrily at his ankles, he threw his coat on and left the apartment in a rush, shutting the door in the outraged animal's face.

A minute later, he was walking rapidly to nowhere in particular in wet, falling snow, his hands shoved deep into his pockets and his mind spinning at top speed. The pieces of the plan cascaded into place almost effortlessly, and after a half hour of walking, he opened the phone to call an old MIT classmate, Archie Pangloss. Archie had kept loosely in touch with Frank over the years so he could tap him for free security advice as the need arose. Now it was payback time, and Frank was betting that the irrepressible Archie would love his idea instantly.

Luckily for Frank, Archie was available and took the call.

"Hey, Frank! What's with the unlisted number? I almost didn't pick it up."

"Sorry about that. My phone's dead so I picked up a cheapo at a convenience store to hold me over till tomorrow. But listen – here's why I called. I've got what I think is a great idea for a new mobile game app, and I'm hoping you'll publish it for me."

Frank described the game in detail. As expected, Archie ate it up.

"Awesome concept, Frank! Any time you want to hang it up at the Library, there's a concept design job waiting for you at the Pangloss Game Company. If this goes viral we'll own the number one spot at Apple's App Store until the fun's over – and we're very good at getting the word out. For this one, we'll go all out. How soon can you get the code to me?"

Frank paused. He wasn't a game developer by training, and he was banking on mostly bolting together a bunch of open source software he was thinking should already be out there on the Web.

What the hell, he thought, and took the plunge. "Well, as a matter of fact, I am in kind of a hurry to see this launched. If you can do the graphics by the end of next week, I'll get the backend to you at the same time. Then we do the integration over the weekend, and with any luck we go to market on Monday. What do you say?"

"No sweat. The graphics will be the easy part. This is a lot closer to Pong than Grand Theft Auto. We can re-skin some basic point and shoot stuff we use all the time. Even with just a week to work with, we can come up with some fun animations and sound effects."

Frank breathed a sigh of relief. "Great. Now here's the thing, Archie. I'm, uh, having a little trouble with my ex-wife, and this would just be a really bad time for a lot of money to start coming into my bank account. You've been there, so you know what I mean, right? So how about we split the profits 50 – 50, and you deposit my half in a sub-account at your bank. You can just send me an ATM card and wire instructions, and if I need any cash over the next few months I can just tap into the sub-account that way."

"And hey - don't give me any credits on the app, or name me in the copyright notice, either. My ex's lawyer is a sneaky bastard, and for all I know, he's got a private investigator keeping an eye on me. What do you say?"

"As far as I'm concerned, what happens in Frank Land stays in Frank Land. If you want me to get all the fame and glory for designing a killer app, well, I can deal with that. As long as we get the financial stuff straightened out before tax time, I'm cool."

"Excellent! Archie, tell me honestly, though. Do you really think this game will be successful? I'm kind of in a spot financially."

"No question about it, Frank. How could it be otherwise in this best of all possible game worlds?"

Archie's perpetually upbeat attitude usually irritated Frank, but this time he was grateful for the encouragement. He had a hell of a lot of work to do, and only a week to do it in. And he had no Plan B.

0000 0001 0010 0011 0100 0011 0010 0001 0000

The Monday that the Pangloss Game Company launched *iBallZapper!* Frank's app immediately leaped into the record books of massive, multi-player on line gaming. True to his word, Archie unleashed his flaks on the Web, and they instantly blanketed the social media landscape with rave reviews. In no time, the rave Tweets were flying thick and fast. After that, the game sold itself, since it was as easy to play as it was competitive. And the biggest daily and weekly winners could make real prize money to boot.

The concept of *iBallZapper!* was as simple as you could get: just download the app, sign in, and then go hunt and kill yourself some iBalls – and iBalls were everywhere. Once you found one, all you had to do was place your cursor on it and click, thereby sending it spiraling into an awesome, swirling black hole. It was fun, too, because you could choose from a long list of sound effects to accompany each horrified iBall as it disappeared into the maw of the cosmic abyss. Soon, startled passengers on subways and buses everywhere were surrounded by a cacophony of strange sounds, from the Wilhelm scream to Meg Ryan's fake orgasm in *When Harry Met Sally*. Those introduced to the game by sadistic friends got RickRolled. But whatever the soundtrack, every time another iBall winked out of existence, the player racked up more points.

And there was no end of potential players, because the app ran on all the major mobile phones – not just the iPhone, but also the Android in all its many flavors. Anyone could download the app for free. Frank and Archie could afford to give *iBallZapper!* away, because they were making the big using another piece of software: the *iBall Resurrection Engine*, a widget they provided – again free – to the owner of any website that hosted iBalls. Just one click and the engine would automatically download and install itself.

And who wouldn't want to download the Engine? For every two iBalls that disappeared from a site, the Engine would resurrect one – in turn triggering a new payment by iBalls.com to the Website owner. So while the game continued to became more competitive as the number of remaining iBalls decreased, site owners cashed in big-time on iBall payments, as well as on increased ad revenues from the hoards of iBall Zappers prowling the Web for more virtual prey.

Of course, while the iBall Replacement Engine was free, The Pangloss Game Company took a small piece of the action every time it replaced an iBall. Site owners couldn't care less, because the Engine did all the work while iBalls.com's money flowed in.

And flow it did, as word spread far and wide, at home and abroad. *Ka-Ching!*

0000 0001 0010 0011 0100 0011 0010 0001 0000

iBalls.com founders Chad Derwent and Sanjay Shah fidgeted nervously in the posh reception area of TrashTalk LLP's offices in the heart of Silicon Valley. They were waiting for Josh Peabody, the venture capital rock star who had brought TrashTalk – and $50 million of its money – into iBalls.com. Surely, each thought, Peabody would be able to help them figure a way out of this mess. Money was literally fire hosing out of the company's bank account, and at a faster rate by the minute. It seemed like the whole world had gone *iBallZapper!* mad.

"We've got to just shut it down," Sanjay said for the tenth time that morning. "We won't be able to last out the week otherwise. don't care what anybody says, we've got to throw the switch *now*."

"We can't just shut it down. Remember that stupid click wrap license the lawyers made us use? Have you ever read it?"

"Of course I haven't read it! It's a frigging clickwrap license! Nobody reads a clickwrap license! It's just something you have to get past before you can do what you want."

"Yeah, well I read it this morning. It says that we can terminate the service anytime we want to – on ten days notice."

"Well, screw it! We'll just have a malfunction then. Hell, the way things are going, they ought to expect our servers to crash!"

Both of them swung their heads in unison as they heard the unmistakable sound of The Wilhelm behind them. The receptionist was clearly not attending to her day job.

"I could cry," Sanjay moaned in a convincing voice. "It's all crashing down around us. We should never have let that idiot Peabody persuade us to give up our original business plan."

Just then, the great VC himself swung in through the glass doors of TrashTalk's offices, a travel bag slung over one shoulder. He noticed them almost immediately.

"Hey guys! Great to see you. C'mon down this way and we'll find out what's on your mind. Cappuccino? No? Well, give me a few minutes while I get myself set up for the day." Sanjay looked at his partner incredulously as they followed Peabody down the hall.

Josh ushered Chad and Sanjay into a conference room and went off to the kitchen. Sanjay was becoming more frantic by the minute. "What's on our *minds*? He's crazy. He's completely out of touch with reality."

Chad was just as thrown by Peabody's demeanor, but he tried not to show it. Wasn't it TrashTalk's money that was flying out the door? He pushed Sanjay down into a chair. "Take it easy. He's got to be just as concerned as we are. I'm sure he's just putting on a brave face for his staff. Once we're alone with him we can come up with a strategy to buy some time and figure a way out of this."

They sat in silence until Josh finally waltzed in.

"So what do you think, guys? Would you have ever *dreamed* you could get publicity like this? I had my assistant put this little video montage together just for you – and now here you are! How cool is that?" This time, Chad couldn't help himself. He moaned softly in harmony with his partner.

Peabody turned on the projector and leaned back to enjoy the show. Chad and Sanjay watched in growing horror as video clip followed clip from CCBN, CBN, and Bloomberg. One after another, the financial pundits wondered what the deal was with iBalls.com. Had the start-up been hacked? Was it all a gimmick, with some kind of surprise ending yet to come? Nobody could figure out what was really going on. The video ended with Glenn Beck raging against this rampant assault on capitalism, obviously launched by the Chinese or the liberals – most likely Chinese *Nazi* Liberals!

Josh clapped and whooped. "Did you see that! Glenn Beck! By tonight, you'll have people that have never used a computer before zapping iBalls!"

Sanjay could contain himself no longer. "You're stark raving mad! We'll have to pull the public offering! We'll be bankrupt by the end of the week!"

"Guys, guys, you just don't get it, do you? The whole *world* is watching this unfold. In my entire career I've never seen a phenom like this. You couldn't get publicity like this even if I was willing to give you another one million dollars."

Josh clicked the projector off. "Which, by the way, I'm not."

Chad looked alarmed. "So what are we supposed to do?"

Josh shrugged his shoulders and tried to look sympathetic, an expression that didn't come naturally to him. "Ah, now that's a tough one, isn't it? I checked with our lawyers, and they couldn't recommend a way to put a stop to the run on the bank. If you shut down the servers, there'd be a dozen lawyers filing class action suits by sundown, representing all of the sites that already have iBall contracts. The legal guys tell me you'd lose for sure. So it looks like it really doesn't make much difference whether you claim the servers crashed, or just let this run its course – the end result will be the same. Naturally, what you actually do is your decision."

Chad looked sideways at Sanjay, wondering whether he was leaning more towards hysteria or bloodshed.

Chad tried to sound confident and business-like, but his voice came out squeaky. "Josh, what's with this "you" stuff all of a sudden? It's always been "we" before. And I have to say, you're acting pretty blasé with $50 million of TrashTalk's money flying out the door." Chad hoped he sounded more like a player than he felt.

"Ah, well, you know, it's really okay – but I do appreciate your asking. As you guys know, we never let the grass grow under our feet here at TrashTalk. We're always coming up with new ideas – new angles – new *innovations*. So of course, when the real estate bubble burst, we got to thinking. What happens now to all those smart guys that came up with credit swaps and derivatives to begin with? Nobody in their right mind is going to let them loose to sell that kind of junk on the public markets again...". He stopped short, and then continued more thoughtfully, scribbling a note to himself, "At least, not for a few years, anyway."

Looking up, he continued. "So where was I? Oh right! So we got to thinking – why not hire some of these guys up cheap and launch a start-up to sell derivatives to venture capital fund investors? That way, investors could hedge their bets. If one of our investments makes money, that's great. But if it turns out to be a loser, they just collect on the derivative they bought to insure against the loss. Then they can give us even *more* money to invest for them! And then we thought – why stop there? Why not set it up so we and our investors could even make a profit on a washout? Insurance companies won't usually won't pay you back more than you lost, but if we give them a few percent of our investment fund, well, everyone can be a winner. It would be like a perpetual motion money machine!"

Chad was feeling desperate. "That's exactly what it would be like, and just as impossible! And even if you could get people to buy into such a stupid idea, how will that help you get out of this fiasco? You're going to look like a total idiot when we go under! Who would ever let you in the door again?"

Josh tried to look hurt. "Chad! *Chad!* I thought we'd gotten to know each other better than that! I'm really and truly hurt. I can't believe you'd even think that Josh Peabody would ever let himself look like an idiot."

"Here – this will make the whole situation a lot clearer."

Josh flicked the projector on again. The screen lit up with what looked like a sound stage, with lighting and makeup people bustling around like ants. Chad realized with a shock that the person in center stage getting his makeup adjusted was none other than Josh. And the set he was standing on was that of the hit primetime CCBN show called MadMoney.

Josh leaned back with evident delight. "You'll love this! This is so awesome even I can't even believe it. Jim Cramer is dedicating a *whole show* to our concept! This is going to run tonight!"

With that, the camera swung to an onstage video monitor blaring the lead-in trailer that introduced MadMoney every night. When it swung back, there was Jim Cramer, shirtsleeves rolled up in trademark fashion. His face filling the camera, Cramer launched into his usual choppy, introductory shtick.

... other people want to make friends – I'm - into - MAKING - MONEY! Unless you keep UP with the MARKET, you'll - get - HAMMERED. You've got to INNOVATE to STAY AHEAD!

That's why I'm dedicating this show tonight to an AWESOME new market play invented by an AWESOME market PLAYER. My guest tonight is legendary Silicon Valley venture capitalist JOSH PEABODY, of TRASHTALK!

Josh clapped. "Isn't this guy just the greatest? I can't get enough of him!"

Cramer and Josh shook hands, and Cramer started speaking again.

So tell us Josh, what's this new market strategy all about?

I'll do better than that, Jim. Let's watch the numbers play out in real time so you can really get the feel of it.

That sounds GREAT Josh! So what are we seeing on that monitor over there?

That one is showing the action on the new secondary market we've set up to trade in VC fund derivative securities. With these securities, VC investors can't lose. Not only that, every average Joe in America can become their own VC, too, and all without any risk! What we're watching is trading in derivatives we sold a few months ago to protect our valued investors in case any of our investments doesn't turn out quite as we hoped.

Wow, Josh, that trading is really ACTIVE! It looks like there's LOTS of BUYING and SELLING going on! What's causing all that volatility?

[Laughing] Well, any of your viewers that are into online gaming will really enjoy this.

The camera swung around to another monitor. On it was a number in dollars. The number was spinning rapidly like a gas pump in reverse selling $10 a gallon gasoline.

Huh! That number's dropping like a STONE, Josh! Tell the audience what they're looking at there!

That [pausing for dramatic effect] is the bank account of one of our portfolio companies – an outfit called iBalls.com.

Sanjay let out a shriek of animal rage and tried to leap over the table. But Josh was ready for him, and made it to the door with time to spare. Chad heard the door locking from the outside, leaving him in shock, and Sanjay sobbing in helpless frustration, spread-eagled on the conference room table.

With that, the camera swungBack in Washington, D.C., Frank couldn't help himself. He logged on one more time using his neighbor's WiFi network, and headed straight to his *iBallZapper!* account: now it read $342,852.58.

Funny, isn't it, he mused, sending one more iBall to its doom so he could hear Meg Ryan's convincingly sincere climax one more time. And all these years I thought that venture capital was just for losers.

~~0000~~ ~~0001~~ ~~0010~~ ~~0011~~ 0100 ~~0011~~ ~~0010~~ ~~0001~~ ~~0000~~

12

Now You See Me
(and Now You Don't!)

F RANK HAD BEEN leaning back in his cubicle chair for two hours now, feet up on his desktop. From that angle, he could keep an eye on Carl Cumming's temporary office down the corridor. But the agent refused to show his face. The guy must have the bladder of a camel, Frank thought. Wouldn't he ever need to relieve himself?

Finally, Cummings emerged. Frank leaned forward nonchalantly, still tapping away on his laptop. But once the agent had passed behind him, Frank leaned backward again to see where Cummings would go.

Good. Cummings was headed for the reception area door - and now he was through it. Frank waited for a minute to pass, then grabbed his coat, his laptop, and his more-than-usually full backpack. He idled slowly up the corridor, waiting for the agent to return.

When he finally saw Cummings through the glass of the reception area, Frank walked the last few steps to the front desk. As expected, Cummings noticed that Frank was on his way out the door. Pretending that a headline had caught his eye, the agent picked a newspaper up from the reception area table within easy earshot. Perfect again.

Frank stopped in front of Mary's desk and waited until she irritably glanced up from the celebrity magazine that was commanding her full attention.

"What?" she snapped.

"I'll be back in a couple hours, Mary. I vowed last year I'd never leave my Christmas shopping until the last minute again."

"Good for you," she grunted, eyes already back on her magazine.

Frank pointed to his back pack. "Especially when I realize I should return half the stuff I bought already." Mary ignored him. Smiling to himself, Frank walked out into the hallway.

Someone else was now standing in front of Mary's desk. She looked up in annoyance, and then broke into a broad smile instead. This time it was that good looking young CIA agent.

"Oh! Hello! What can I *do* for you, Agent Cummings?"

"I'm off to a meeting, Mary. If anyone calls, it'll probably be a couple of hours before I'm back."

"Why of course, Agent Cummings. A couple of hours. I'll be *sure* to let them know." Mary made a show of writing this down. But when she looked up again, he was gone.

Once in the hallway, Cummings popped his earpiece in and punched the speed dial on his cell phone.

"IT Rat is leaving the building. Tail him and report back. I'll provide support. Confirm."

"Tail IT Rat and report back; you'll support."

Cummings was feeling crapulous as he strode down the hallway. "You'll have the resources you need," Marchand had promised. Resources, indeed! Here he was relying on some kid straight out of school. He'd be lucky if Bert Tyro even managed to spot Frank leaving the building.

Cummings took the elevator to the lobby level. As he marched out, Agent Tyro's voice crackled in his earpiece.

"IT Rat just caught a cab."

Cummings left the LoC lobby and walked across the broad pavement to the cab stand, listening carefully.

"Following IT Rat West on Independence."

Cummings eased himself slowly into a taxi.

"North on 3rd."

The cab driver waited for instructions, but Carl wasn't yet sure where to go. The driver turned to look over his shoulder, and Carl stalled for time. "What department stores are nearby?"

"Well, we got your Filene's, and your Macy's. Neiman Marcus. Marshall's, you name it. This ain't East Podunk."

"West on Pennsylvania Ave," came the voice in his ear.

Carl took a guess. "Okay, Macy's – that's on G Street, right?"

"Last time I checked, yeah."

The cab driver saw his fare scowling in the rear view mirror, and wheeled away from the curb without further comment. If he can't take a joke, well, the hell with him.

Before they reached the department store, Agent Tyro confirmed Carl's guess. Not long after, Cummings was sitting in a "hubby" chair in the jewelry and perform department on the first floor of Macy's. Hiding behind the front section of the *Washington Post*, his mood grew blacker by the minute as Tyro's youthful voice passed on the mundane details of Frank's miserable shopping expedition. For this, Carl had given up a better paying career in the private sector?

Frank, it seemed, was running up his charge card on the third floor, half-filling two shopping bags with the kind of innocuous items a middle-aged man without much imagination might buy for relatives he rarely saw.

Agent Tyro grew increasingly bored; even worried that someone might think he was shoplifting as he loitered around the floor. He fingered the badge in his pocket, just in case someone approached him. Seeing Frank looking lost in the housewares section, Tyro debated making a wisecrack to Cummings. Nope; bad bet. Tyro might be a newbie, but he'd already figured out that Cummings' sense of humor had been surgically removed at birth.

Meanwhile, Frank had enlisted the help of a floor walker. He was following her from one department to another, walking back and forth past the elevator bank. How about a Sweater? No? Maybe a quilt? *No?* Then surely this nice afghan over here would be just right? Huh. Well….

Tyro rolled his eyes as the sales assistant and her indecisive poodle of a shopper headed off across the floor again. The agent glanced down and scrolled through his email. Nothing interesting there, either.

Tyro looked up, and saw that the floor walker was looking around with a surprised look on her face.

He jerked to attention. Frank had vanished! He must have ducked into an elevator this time as they walked past. *Damn!*

Tyro reported in to Cummings in an agitated voice as he all but ran towards the elevators. "IT Rat headed up by elevator. I'll take the fourth floor; you take the fifth." Then his cellphone cut out as the elevator doors shut behind him.

Cummings stood up and headed towards the elevator bank on the first floor, but ignored Tyro's request. With both of them hopping in and out of elevators, Frank could easily elude them. With a disgusted look on his face, he stood twenty feet back from the wall where he could get a clear view of the floor indicator lights as they flashed on and off and the main entrance as well.

But which of the elevators was Frank on? Damn it, there were four elevators, and the building had eight floors!

Thirty seconds after stepping into the elevator, Frank stepped briskly out onto the fourth floor and immediately ducked through the adjacent fire door and into the stairwell beyond. He raced down to the basement level landing, and then worked as quickly as possible.

Into one of the shopping bags went the contents of the other. Over the railing it went, down towards the utility sub-basement. He listened for it to hit. Good. Out of the backpack and onto Frank's head went a wig and dark glasses. Then he pulled out and donned a woman's reversible raincoat. Last of all he stuffed his backpack and the coat he had been wearing into the second shopping bag and raced back up to the first floor landing.

A moment later, Frank opened the stairwell door and walked out as a reasonable facsimile of his elderly mother. A few steps later and he had walked past Carl Cummings and onto the street. And now he was just one more anonymous shopper riding the escalator down into the Metro Center subway station.

Long before Cummings and Tyro faced up to the fact that they'd been snookered, Frank was boarding a Glenmont train for another short ride. By the time Cummings was banging on the security guard's office door to commandeer the video tapes of Macy's stairwells and exits, Frank was walking into Union Station, Washington's Amtrak terminal. And as Carl was steeling himself to report to headquarters that Frank had given him the slip, his quarry was leaving a train station restroom, wearing a sweatshirt with the hood pulled up and his eyes cast down.

At one point, the Amtrak station security video tapes Cummings later reviewed revealed a nondescript, possibly middle-aged, presumably homeless man shambling across the concourse, a garbage bag slung over his shoulder. In it were all of the belongings the figure had to his name, at least for now.

That was the last blurry image that Cummings saw that might arguably have been Frank, as he wearily screened tape after tape from bus stations, terminals and other exit points. It hardly mattered, though, because he knew that by now Frank was long gone.

The question, of course, was where?

0000 0001 0010 0011 0100 0011 0010 0001 0000

13

Welcome to Las Vegas!

TWO AND A half days after dropping off the map in Washington, Frank staggered off a Greyhound bus in Las Vegas, Nevada. Though tired and dirty, he felt remarkably energized. It was time to get down to work! But first, he had to find his next ride.

With his knapsack slung over one shoulder, Frank scanned the bus terminal for anyone that might be Earl Jenkins. He had assembled a mental picture of the kind of man that would post an ad in *Millennial Survivalist and Assault Rifle Monthly*, and assumed it would be easy to pick him out of a crowd. Problem was, just about everyone hanging around in the Las Vegas bus station looked like they might be a charter subscriber. Now what?

"Mr. Columbo?"

Frank turned to find a tired looking, forty-ish woman in jeans, flannel shirt and hiking boots. "Yes, that's me."

"Thought it might be," she said, looking at his North Face coat. "My Pappy asked me to meet you here. He don't get down to Vegas much, so he figured he'd hit the craps tables some before heading out again. Hope you don't mind too much if we have to go hunt him up."

After two and a half days without a shower or a decent meal, Frank actually did mind too much. But there wasn't much he could do about it, so he shrugged and said, "Please call me Carter."

"Ida May Jukes is my name, but just plain Ida works right well."

Frank followed Ida May Jukes as she walked out of the bus station and swung herself up into an old pickup truck. Frank did the same as she started up the ancient heap. Soon they were heading south on Main Street.

Frank had never been to Vegas before. Once they merged onto the Strip, his tired eyes widened as they passed bastardized versions of the Eiffel Tower, New York City skyline (complete with a roller coaster he didn't recall noticing in the original version), a castle with multicolored turret roofs reminiscent of an enormous PlayMobil® toy set, a Sphinx, and a huge black pyramid ("At night it's got some kinda laser thing com'in out of it!" Ida explained). She took a right off the Strip just after the pyramid, and then a left into a huge parking garage.

"Pappy likes to start at Mandalay Bay. He thinks the dice runs best there. But if they ain't break'n right, he moves up the Strip to the Excalibur. Their tables is pretty good, too, and they got great burgers. Food's a whole lot cheaper, too."

Frank decided no response was required to that, so he simply followed Ida as she headed for a flight of stairs. Soon, they were walking along an indoor promenade between randomly themed restaurants, with facades decorated with everything from naked torsos to a twenty-five-foot tall headless, pigeon-stained statue of Lenin. Frank seemed to be the only one in the throng who found the scenery to be a tad unusual.

He found the casino floor to be even more bizarre. Heavily made up, spike-heeled teenaged girls who had seemingly been inflated into their skin tight prom dresses strutted their way between the tables. Frank assumed they must be oblivious to the crowds of slovenly people wearing t-shirts and shorts, clutching oversized drinks in one hand and equally large cups of slot machine tokens in the other, who were clearly not as convinced of the glamour of the setting. Pudgy, bored-looking waitresses wearing ill-fitting short red dresses carried over-priced drinks away from the bar, and garbage back to the kitchen. A fleet of new, spot-lit Chevrolets completed the scene, turning slowly like mirrored disco balls above the din of the gaming tables on tall pedestals, sales prices attached.

So this is Las Vegas, Frank thought. Well, yee-ha.

After a few minutes of wandering about, Ida concluded that the dice wasn't running right for Pappy at the Mandalay, so they made their way to the Excalibur, which turned out to be the gargantuan PlayMobil castle. Ida led them on a circuitous route that wound indoors along underground passages and outside over pedestrian bridges spanning ten lanes of traffic.

Frank continued to marvel as they passed a kaleidoscope of tattoo parlors, ice cream shops, lingerie stores, and enormous ads for a variety of entertainments the existence of which Frank had until then never suspected. Not able to help himself, he stopped to stare at a series of large, blue, sloshing tubes from which downward-facing heads extended ("Full-body water massage," Ida informed him helpfully).

They continued, and finally Ida stopped and pointed to a wiry, gray-haired man in an unbuttoned wool shirt worn untucked over a t-shirt and old jeans. He was sitting alone at a small table in an underground food court. "That there's Pappy."

Earl Jenkins looked up when they reached his table. As predicted, he was holding the remnants of a burger in both hands.

"This here's Mr. Columbo, Pappy."

"Shit," Earl responded by way of acknowledgment. "I couldn't get them damn dice to break right for me no-how."

Frank was pretty sure this didn't require him to say, "Pleased to meet you," so he just stood there.

"Pappy, I reck'n Mr. Columbo would like to see the truck, now."

Frank nodded hopefully, and Earl dropped what was left of his lunch. He stood up and wiped both hands on the seat of his jeans before offering one to Frank.

"Pleased to meet you, Columbo. You bring cash, like you promised?"

"Yes, indeed. Can I see the truck now? I'd like to get on my way before dark."

With confirmation that he'd be paid in the manner least likely to attract the meddlesome attention of the IRS, Earl warmed up appreciably. Instantly, his persona morphed from casino mark to Las Vegas hustler.

"You betcha, Columbo. And oh, she's a dandy! She don't have the sparkle she did when she rolled outta the factory, but then again, neither does you or me, heh?" Earl gave Frank a poke in the ribs, and favored him with a grin that revealed more good humor than teeth.

"Anyway's, she's still dependable as can be. Runs as good on free, used vegetable oil from a fast food joint as she does on diesel, and she's got enough clearance you can just about walk under her. Four-wheel drive and ten-ply tires, too. What she can't drive 'round, she just drives over, pretty as you please!"

Frank had learned all this from the ad, and was counting on it being true, too. Now that he had succeeded in dropping out of sight, he was planning on staying that way.

Earl was on the same wavelength. "AND, she's loaded like noth'n you ever saw when it comes to get'n off the grid and say'n 'Kiss my butt!' to the rest of the world. If what yer look'n for, as you say, is to get some serious write'n done without nobody to bother you, well, she's just the ticket!"

On their way back to the parking garage, Earl told Frank how he had come to own such a wondrous vehicle. He allowed as how Frank must have already guessed Earl wasn't nobody's fool. No surprise then that when that Y2K computer plot came along to take down the world, they weren't going to catch Earl Jenkins with his pants down, no sir! He'd read all about how there would be food riots and worse, so he sold his machine shop back in Tennessee and bought himself a stripped down MountainTamer Expedition Vehicle – just the truck bed with the shell on top, and then fitted it out himself. He added extra fuel and water tanks, a water purification system, and "more solar panels and gun racks than you ever did see in one place, much less on one set o' wheels."

Frank couldn't help asking, "So what did you do when Y2K came and went and the world didn't end?"

"Oh, I didn't care 'bout that too much. I figured that was just the wake-up call I needed to get ready for the real thing when it did come 'round. You look like a clever guy, so you must listen to Rush Limbaugh and Glenn Beck same as me. They really opened my eyes, sure to goodness."

"You just wait – I don't know exactly what it's gonna be or when, but it's a com'in – make no mistake! Maybe it'll be some kind of bio attack to the water supply, or maybe we can't stop them damn Liberals from socialize'n the bejeebers outta the whole blessed country. Or maybe some of them there cyber-terror fellas everyone's talk'n about brings down the whole house of cards. You just wait and see if I'm not right!"

Hearing that last example, Frank had to admit that maybe Earl wasn't completely extraterrestrial after all.

"Anyway, I been keep'n this here rig up to date ever since. She's got satellite TV, satellite broadband Internet, and more juice in her batteries from them solar cell panels than you could use if you was to host a Tea Party rally, speakers 'n all."

With that, they stepped out into the bright glare of a surface lot, and behold - there was Earl Jenkins' four-wheel drive wonder. Frank had to admit, it was a sight to see.

On the back end, Earl had added a top-to-bottom rack system on which a dozen ten gallon water and gas tanks were tied down. Above the front of the shell he had mounted a tractor trailer-scale wind deflector, and behind that a multi-layer sandwich of metal and glass that Frank assumed must be the solar panels. Behind that was a nest of antennae and dishes that obviously made up the telecommunications array. Frank winced when he read the bumper stickers.

"Now you just get yourself ready to see someth'n you ain't never seen before," piped Earl, cackling with glee. Frank couldn't imagine what might come next, given that he was already looking at something he had never imagined, let alone seen, before.

"Alrighty, Mission Control, stand by to deploy!" With that Earl withdrew what looked like a TV remote from his pocket, and began pushing buttons. Motors started to grind and whir, and creaking noises filled the air. The solar sandwich quivered.

With a final groan, the panels lurched into action, first opening side-to-side, like the top of a cardboard box, and then unfolding again and again lengthwise in two directions until the array was at least twenty-five feet wide. Earl punched a few more buttons, and the array pivoted on top of the truck until it was pointed at the sun, tilting at the same time until it was at right angles to the sun's rays.

Earl watched Frank's open-mouthed amazement with obvious satisfaction. "Hell, Columbo, you ain't seen noth'n yet. Behold, the *Solar Avenger* in all her glory!"

Without waiting for Frank's reaction, Earl hopped into the cab of the truck, and turned on the engine. Then he turned the wheel hard over, and slowly crept in a circle around Ida and Frank. As he did, the array stayed locked on the sun like a paparazzi on Brangelina. Frank felt like he was being orbited by the International Space Station.

The circle complete, Earl hopped out, slammed the door and strode back until he was facing Frank, arms crossed. Behind him, the solar array whirred, creaked and groaned itself back into the stowed position. A smile of pride nearly split Earl's stubbly face in two.

Frank reached into his pocket and took out a thick envelope. With complete honesty, he said, "Mr. Jenkins, that is one piece of work, and no mistake."

"You ain't just whistl'n Dixie, Columbo! And don't you worry, I got all them boxes of stuff you sent ahead stacked inside. All twelve of them, just like you said. Say, for a writer, you sure do work with a lot of electronical stuff."

"Oh, I do a lot of research – lots and lots of research," Frank said hurriedly. "And you know the junk they sell these days – if I want to get away, I better bring back up equipment, right?" Frank figured this was a good time to flash his cash, and handed over the envelope. Earl snatched it out of his hand.

"No question 'bout that. It's all crap these days!" Earl cackled as he slowly counted the sixty hundred dollar bills he shook out of the envelope. Then he counted them a second time before finally handing the keys and remote to Frank.

"Well, Columbo, you just have yourself a peach of a time out there in the boonies. I'll see you right back hear in a couple months, just like we agreed."

As Frank climbed into the cab, Earl asked, "Say, where you figur'n on goin', anyways?"

Frank stopped, half in and half out of the truck. This wasn't a question he was normally willing to answer to anybody. But a thought had just struck him. He climbed back down and took out his wallet. Then he carefully removed an old black-and-white picture, much creased and faded. In it, a child sat on a man's shoulders. Both were smiling, and above them soared tall, ram-rod straight trees with heavily veined bark.

"Maybe you can help me with that. Do you know where I can find trees like these?"

Earl took a quick glance and handed the picture back.

"Hell! You might's well ask me where you might *not* find trees like that." He pointed across Las Vegas Boulevard. "All you got to do is head north for about as long as you feel like, and then turn yourself east or west – it don't make a diff'rence, so just take your pick. Nevada's noth'n but big, wide valleys and long mountain ridges – wave after wave of 'em, one after t' other, each one run'n north-north east to south-south west. You cross any one o' them suckers, and when you get up to 'bout 8,000 feet, all you'll find up there is them trees – Ponderosa pines, we call 'em."

Frank stuck out his hand to Earl. "Thanks very much, Mr. Jenkins. That's just what I needed to know."

His course now clear, Frank climbed into the cab, put the truck into gear, and set out on the next stage of his plan. It was time he went and found himself some o' them there cyber-terror fellas.

0000 0001 0010 0011 0100 0011 0010 0001 0000

14

Desperately Seeking Adversego

IT WAS ONLY 8:00 AM, but Carl was already having a bad day as he emailed back and forth with his detailer at the CIA.

Who can you give me today?

>Bert Tyro

Again? Can't you do better?

>You want to tail a student?

Right

>On campus?

Right

>So who do you want, Uncle Jack?

Okay, Okay. Who else you got?

>Ernie Cazou

Cazou! The target will trip over him while he's tying his shoelaces

This was pathetic. But what could he do? Carl started typing again.

Hell. Give me Bert

>Too late; just gave him to Phil. You got Ernie till 8:00 AM. Out

Carl fumed as he tapped out his orders to Ernie Cazou, sending him Marla's address and instructing him to report anything unusual. Then he turned to the boring reality of his own day.

Sad to say, he now had only two responsibilities: protecting Marla without her knowledge, which was the ho-hum job he'd just assigned to Ernie, and protecting Frank, whose whereabouts were unknown. The FBI had issued a nationwide alert a week ago, but that didn't excuse Carl from doing his best to locate him as well. Not that he had anything else to occupy his time anyway.

Marla, of course, might know where her father was, but Carl's orders were to keep her in the dark. She obviously wasn't going to tell the CIA where her father was anyway, and certainly not to him. Carl uneasily considered the likelihood that Marla still despised him. Given the total lack of ambiguity on that subject she had conveyed during their last conversation years ago, this seemed like a pretty safe bet. So the obvious line of attack was to covertly track Marla, and hope to intercept a message between father and daughter without either being any the wiser.

Nominally, that would be illegal, because the CIA was barred by law from eavesdropping on U.S. citizens. But the FBI was not so constrained, and it hadn't been very hard for someone his boss knew at the Bureau to get a judge to approve taps on Marla's phone and Internet account "for protective purposes." After that, getting direct access to the tap had been easier than it was supposed to be, and what the judge didn't know wouldn't hurt him – or hopefully Carl, either.

That had been the simple part. The hard part was figuring out how someone as savvy about security as Frank would go about communicating with Marla, if he contacted her at all?

How indeed? Carl would just have to be as observant as possible as he prepared to spend the better part of another boring day shadowing Marla's activities on the Internet.

0000 0001 0010 0011 0100 0011 0010 0001 0000

It was a sunny day on the Georgetown campus, so Marla set her coffee on one of the tables that lined the windows in Leavey Center. She took care to sit with her back to the window as she opened her iMac and connected to the campus WiFi network.

Feeling rather voyeuristic, Carl watched on his computer as Marla scanned the headlines at the *New York Times* website, skimmed her email, and then checked out a few Facebook pages. Next, she opened her Twitter page.

Carl had no reason to know it, but Marla's previously meager Twitter account had become remarkably active since she learned that her father might have to skip town. Every day she had started following a few more people. Many of those people obligingly began following her as well. Her Twitter page now displayed a bewildering and constantly expanding array of messages from rock bands, political figures, friends, environmentalists and whomever.

A Twitter alert the day before, for example, had informed Marla that someone named bieberfan457 was now following her. Sure enough, as she scrolled down through the endless column of today's blindingly inane Tweets, a message from bieberfan457 caught her eye: it read:

>*bieberfanXYX OMG! If only!!!!! http://bit.ly/CXAacb OMG!*

The OMG!s beginning and ending the Tweet were just what her father had instructed her to look for before he left, but she forced herself to ignore the message for now. Instead, she scrolled to the end of the page, and then returned to the top and began randomly clicking on links and reading what she found as she moved down the page. Eventually she was back at the OMG! Tweet and clicked its embedded link.

Marla suppressed a smile when she found herself reading the top item in a thread at the Celebrity News message board of Oprah Winfrey's website. That message read:

Who thinks JUSTIN BIEBER should be on the Oprah Show?

>*I do!!*

Marla was surprised that her wonkish father had any idea who Justin Bieber even was, but the display of his trademark (i.e., warped) sense of humor made her feel closer to him. Not being into 'tweener-pop', Marla barely knew who Bieber was, either, but she appreciated the fact that mimicking adolescent Web comments would make it easier for her father to code a message without being obvious.

Just as expected, she found a comment from bieberfan457 towards the end of the page. It read as follows:

13.   Re: JUSTIN BIEBER Dec. 21, 2011 7:32 AM In response to:
homey20

>Oh, that would be SO TOTALLY COOL! He's got to know he'd get
an AWESOME reception.. OMG! Very upbeat greetings from every
true lover! Really, my TOTAL, most FANTASTIC feelings! WOW!!

>I can't wait!

>PS: NO! He's not GAY!!

Casually, Marla opened a spiral bound pad of paper and turned to
the last sheet of paper, just above the hard plastic cover, so that the pressure of her pen wouldn't leave any impression on the pages
beneath. Writing quickly, she wrote down the first letter of each word
between the doubled period after "reception" and the double exclama-
tion point after "WOW": OVUGFETLRMTMFW. She also scribbled
down the word "NO" after the "PS:"

Marla closed the Oprah page and went back to randomly clicking
links at the Twitter site for a few minutes before closing it down. Setting her laptop aside, she picked the pad of paper up again and created
a chart that looked like this:

```
A  B  C  D  E  F  G  H  I  J  K  L  M  N  O  P  Q  R  S  T  U  V  W  X  Y  Z
1  2  3  4  5  6  7  8  9 10 11 12 13 14 15 16 17 18 19 20 21 22 23 24 25 26
26 25 24 23 22 21 20 19 18 17 16 15 14 13 12 11 10  9  8  7  6  5  4  3  2  1
```

Then she compared the letters she had copied down from the message
to those in the chart. The first letter in the series was "O," which was
directly above the number 15 in the first line of numbers in the chart. And
the number in the second line was 12. That meant that "O" was to 15 as 12
was to the real letter in the message. And the letter directly above 12 in the
first line of numbers was L. Hardly the most sophisticated encoding
scheme, but then again no one would know which message board comment
contained the encoded message to begin with.

It took only a couple of minutes for Marla to convert each of the first
letters from her father's Bieber comment into other letters. Now her pad
looked like this:

```
A  B  C  D  E  F  G  H  I  J  K  L  M  N  O  P  Q  R  S  T  U  V  W  X  Y  Z
1  2  3  4  5  6  7  8  9 10 11 12 13 14 15 16 17 18 19 20 21 22 23 24 25 26
26 25 24 23 22 21 20 19 18 17 16 15 14 13 12 11 10  9  8  7  6  5  4  3  2  1
```

```
O  V  U  G  F  E  T  L  R  M  T  M  F  W
L  E  F  T  L  V  G  O  I  N  G  N  L  D
```

Marla leaned back in her chair and sipped her coffee. The first part of the message was easy, because she knew from her father's last encrypted message that he had been headed for Las Vegas. That meant the first part of the message read:

Left LV

Good; hopefully that meant the first important step in his plan had gone as planned. The next word was clearly "going," and she knew the last two letters stood for "Love, Dad." That left only the letter "N," which must stand for north. But what in the world was north of Las Vegas?

It would be too risky to open an online map of Nevada to find out, but the campus book store was in the same building. Later on she should be able to flip through an atlas without anyone being able to tell what she was looking at.

All she had to do now was remember that the word "NO" had appeared after the "PS" in the message; she was getting the hang of this pretty well. When she saw the same word at the beginning and the end of some future Tweet she'd know her father had something to tell her once again. While Ernie loitered in the hallway outside the restroom, she tore up the chart and flushed it down the toilet.

After Marla had disconnected her iMac from the Georgetown WiFi network, Carl Cummings snapped his own laptop shut. Leaning back, he shook his head in disappointment. Justin Bieber and Oprah Winfrey – my God!

How could a person of his sophistication ever have been attracted to a girl like that?

0000 0001 0010 0011 0100 0011 0010 0001 0000

15

The Alexandria Project Makes the Evening News

R ICHARD RYAN STOOD center stage in the CBN Nightly News studio. As always, he was impeccably dressed and at ease in a conservative business suit. He shared a last quiet joke with the intern straightening his tie, and then on cue turned to the camera to pre-record the lead-in to the evening's broadcast. As usual, he read the day's headlines from the teleprompter with a serious expression. Then, with a warm smile, he alluded to the "Making a Difference" segment that would close the broadcast before concluding with one of his signature phrases: "Nightly News begins *now*."

That chore accomplished, Ryan strolled over to the expansive news desk from which he would orchestrate the rest of the evening's show. He settled in as the big digital clock on the wall counted down to the 00:00 display that meant it was Air Time.

Ryan could hear the theme music playing that would provide the bridge between the reading of the headlines he had just recorded and the live portion of the show. Even now, seven years after succeeding Tom Brokaw as anchor and editor of CBN's nightly news show, he still listened with satisfaction as a taped voice intoned, *"From CBN World Headquarters in Los Angeles, this is CBN Nightly News – with Richard*

Ryan." All across America, some ten million faithful viewers settled into their couches to watch the leading evening network news show.

As the last bar of music faded at 00:42 on the now forward counting timer, Ryan looked directly into the camera, ready to read the lead story of the day. Right on schedule, his script started to scroll down the teleprompter, and Ryan began to read in an appropriately earnest voice.

> *Good evening. We begin tonight with the shocking news that the U.S. Government is hiding a threat of global collapse from the American people.*

Anyone paying close attention at home might have noticed that Ryan hadn't mentioned this story in the lead-in just a few moments before. They might also now be noticing the furrowing brows on the news anchor's face as he continued to speak, less confidently than before:

> *The danger I refer to is the imminent threat that our government, the military and the financial sector - indeed, all of modern society - will be taken down in one dramatic attack by cyber-terrorists or an enemy nation. It could happen as soon as tomorrow.*

What the hell was going on here, the normally unflappable Ryan wondered. Had someone higher up in the network jumped the script at the last minute to avoid being scooped by NBC, CBS, or God help us, Fox News? Why hadn't someone at least slipped him a note, damn it?

Ryan struggled to prevent his growing anger from affecting his voice. But he was also distracted by the video monitor next to the teleprompter that allowed him to see what viewers at home were seeing on their TV screens. It looked like a Greek Temple being destroyed by fire. What was *that* all about?

But the teleprompter scrolled inexorably on, and all the camera-imprisoned news anchor could do was to keep on reading.

> *In a dramatic move to expose this threat, a cyber-action group called the Alexandria Project announced today that it will radically step up the rate of contributions it will accept from the White House, governmental agencies, major corporations, universities, and news media, beginning with this broadcast - right now.*

With that, the teleprompter went blank. Taken aback, he looked to his stage director, who was staring in bewilderment at the live show monitor. Ryan followed his gaze, and saw that the burning temple had been replaced by an image of a tall building – perhaps some sort of ancient lighthouse. Below it a message glowed in letters that seemed to be etched in flames:

> **THANK YOU FOR YOUR**
> **CONTRIBUTION**
> **TO THE ALEXANDRIA PROJECT**

Faced with nothing but a blank teleprompter and a video he could neither control nor understand, Ryan used the only line he could remember from his vanished script. Staring straight into a camera that no longer mattered, he said, "We'll be right back."

0000 0001 0010 0011 0100 0011 0010 0001 0000

All across the country, some twenty million other Americans were watching the news anchors on all of the other network and cable news shows each struggling in their own way through the same experience. Only on the oxymoronic Fox News cable channel did the anchor continue to read from his appointed script, asking his audience to decide for themselves whether they thought it was just a coincidence that "Obama" and "Islam" each had five letters.

Apparently, the Alexandria Project was only interested in archiving shows that reported actual news.

0000 0001 0010 0011 0100 0011 0010 0001 0000

George Marchand had no use for what passed for television news reporting. He was therefore not immediately aware that the Alexandria Project had made good on its promise to take its campaign for cybersecurity, whether real or diversionary, to the public. But at 6:03 both his desk and cell phones began ringing simultaneously. As he paused to decide which to answer first, he noticed that new email messages with "urgent" icons were popping up on his computer screen like crocuses on the first warm day of spring.

Whatever was up, it didn't look good.

0000 0001 0010 0011 0100 0011 0010 0001 0000

By 8:00 PM that evening, a furious Carl Cummings was standing in a cold drizzle across the street from an elegant townhouse in Georgetown. With Bert and Ernie and just about every other resource – except Carl - suddenly assigned to tracking down those behind the Alexandria Project, Carl had no choice but to tail Marla in person. According to Bert's last log entry, Marla had disappeared an hour ago into this tastefully restored colonial residence with a well-dressed, thirty-ish gentleman. Only a single muted light filtered through the closed curtains of an upstairs room. And then that light winked out.

Carl stepped further back into the shadows. He hoped for more reasons than he was prepared to admit that Marla and her "friend" would momentarily reemerge onto the street. Ten minutes later, he was still waiting.

Carl cursed under his breath and turned up the collar of his coat as the rain turned to sleet. It was going to be a long night.

0000 0001 0010 0011 0100 0011 0010 0001 0000

Most of a continent away, Frank was driving down an endlessly dark two lane road in Nevada. As suggested by Earl Jenkins, he had headed north on his way to nowhere in particular in search of Ponderosa pines and a secluded place to crack code. But a couple hours out of Vegas, he had begun to think that his first hot meal in three days might taste a lot better coming from someone else's kitchen than from one of cans he'd laid in stock for his wilderness mission.

But what the map called Ash Springs turned out to be not much more than a fork in the road, and the next dot on the map to the north that looked any larger (though not by much) was 150 miles ahead. So with the sun setting, Frank turned west on Route 375, hoping that Rachel, Nevada might do better by him, at least to the extent of providing a decent cheeseburger. Had he been looking up instead of down at his map as he accelerated out of his turn, he would have noticed a roadside sign that announced that he was now venturing down "America's Extraterrestrial Highway."

It was well after dark when Frank began braking into Rachel, Nevada. Motoring through what passed for town in second gear, he saw only the lights of a scattering of houses set well back from the road. Not until he was halfway through what little there was to Rachel did he spy anything promising ahead. Downshifting again, he read a sign that informed him he had found a motel, bar and restaurant. As he turned into the parking lot, he couldn't help noticing what appeared to be a flying saucer hanging from the boom of an oversized 1940s vintage tow truck.

Frank switched off the engine and walked across the tumbleweed-dotted parking lot. With more curiosity than hope for a decent meal, he opened the door of what the sign had improbably proclaimed to be the Little A'Le'Inn.

~~0000~~ ~~0001~~ ~~0010~~ ~~0011~~ 0100 ~~0011~~ ~~0010~~ ~~0001~~ ~~0000~~

16

You Want Aliens With That?

WIIEN FRANK STEPPED out of the dark, moonless night of the Nevada desert into the bright light inside, he entered the entirety of Rachel's commercial district. Part of the cluttered room was filled with a pool table and counters covered with t-shirts and other paraphernalia, but along one wall ran a counter punctuated by the backsides of a couple of patrons sitting on stools; a few more folks sat at tables. Behind that counter stood a waitress of substantial proportions, a cash register, and a modest assembly of liquor bottles that apparently constituted the bar component of the Little A'Le'Inn. That took care of the predictable part of the room. Then there was the rest.

Despite the odd spelling, there couldn't be much doubt over the meaning of the café's name. Hung on pegboards, sitting on shelves, and hanging from the ceiling was an impressively random collection of just about anything you might (or might not) imagine could be associated with an extraterrestrial theme.

Frank added his own backside to the lineup at the counter and studied the array of memorabilia covering the wall behind the counter – alien posters, alien postcards, alien pens, alien coffee cups, and dozens of busts of aliens of every shape, configuration, and size. Despite the bizarre range of material, there appeared to be consensus among most interpreters on two central facts: aliens are green, and they have large, black, slanted eyes.

As Frank surveyed the clutter on the wall, he noticed a small mirror, and in the mirror, the eyes of the man sitting next to him. He realized that those eyes were staring back at him intently over the brim of the man's beer mug.

"Howdy. What'll it be?"

Frank smiled at the grey-haired, matronly waitress. He looked down and scanned the short menu she slid across the counter. When in Rome, he thought.

"How about the Alien burger – medium, with Swiss. What's on tap?"

"Bud, Bud Light. In bottles we got Miller, Coors, and Corona."

"Corona sounds right; thanks."

Frank felt out of place. According to the sign his headlights had picked out at the edge of town, Rachel boasted all of 98 inhabitants, assuming everyone was home for the evening. That meant about five per cent of the citizenry had decided to have a night on the town. He looked around for something to stare at to feel less like a bump on a log, and spotted Anderson Cooper's familiar face peering out from a small TV screen on a shelf in the corner of the bar. Even with the sound turned off, that would do.

A moment later, the camera zoomed in on a monitor behind Cooper. On it, a familiar phrase glowed red, as if lit by flames.

Frank sat bolt upright, staring at the message.

"How 'bout that, eh?" a voice next to him said.

Frank, eyes still wide in shock, turned to see that the voice belonged to the man that had been examining him in the mirror. He was old, Frank saw, but he could only guess how old. Clearly, he'd spent many years in the harsh weather of the high desert; his skin was lined and leathery, and his hair and stubbly chin were grey and grizzled.

Frank was still grappling with the implications of the Alexandria Project going public, and simply nodded.

"Bart Thatcher," his seat mate said. "Pleased to meet you."

"Carter Columbo," Frank replied, shaking the hardened hand held out to him. He imagined he saw a look of amusement flicker across Thatcher's eyes when Frank offered his alias, but concluded the circumstances were making him paranoid.

"Yup. Looks to me like we got ourselves a little problem here," the old man continued. "Not that I'm surprised. Been expecting it for awhile now, myself."

Frank hadn't listened to the radio on his drive up from Las Vegas, preferring to focus on his still-evolving plans. Now he desperately wanted to get back to his truck and find out what had happened. For the moment, though, he figured he'd be safer changing the subject.

"What's with all the little green men?"

Thatcher smiled. "If you don't know, I guess you're just passing through. Fact is, that's the reason most folks from away come here at all. You ever heard of Area 51?" Frank shook his head no.

"Well, now. Guess I got to start back aways then. Y'see, just a few miles south of here is this ultra-secret test area for new military planes and weaponry. Some folks would tell you it's a secret place for a whole lot more, too. The government doesn't even admit it exists, but you just try and get there. You won't get very far."

"So how does anyone know about it then?"

"Oh, that ain't too difficult. We see stuff from time to time that we're not supposed to. Lights that move too fast and go in ways they shouldn't. Sounds you never heard before. And we know there's a mighty big complex back behind those mountains you see to the south. Time was when you could hike up to this one spot and look down and see all these buildings and runways. Nighttime come, and you could sometimes catch yourself a real show."

"Then, back in 1995, the Air Force boys took that spot away from the Bureau of Land Management. Once they did, they moved their surveillance cameras and motion detectors back this side of the ridge, and you couldn't go there no more. But we'd all seen it by then."

"Not that you really have to go there to see things anyways. Why, one day some new kind of jet plane augered straight down into Route 375, right here in the center of town – pilot punched out just in time, and parachuted in down the road. In no time, they'd picked him up and Rachel was a-crawling with Air Force folks, contractors and armed guards. By the same time the next day you were lucky to find a stray rivet in your yard."

"Sounds like you've got some interesting neighbors. But what does that have to do with aliens?"

"Well, that's a good question. Maybe you remember the U-2 spy plane? Well, we pretty much know they tested that here, and that takes us back aways, don't it? The SR-117 Blackbird, too."

"Then there's those new radar stealthy planes – the fighter and the bomber that you've seen in the news? B-1 and B-2? We seen them years before anyone else did – back before anything that looked like that was supposed to exist. Let me tell you, when you see something like that come whooshing over a rise out of nowhere and pass two hundred feet over your head, it makes an impression that sticks with you."

"But now let's say you try and find out what it is you just saw? Who you going to ask? Not the folks at Area 51, because you can't get in there, and anyway it doesn't exist. Hard to get a phone number for something that don't exist, isn't it? So some folks start to wonder whether it's really the military that's there at all. Maybe it's somebody else. Or maybe it's both of them. Maybe you heard about the Roswell Incident?"

"That's the one where people think the government covered up a UFO crash, right?"

"Bingo. Well, some folks think they brought the debris from that crash over to study in Area 51. Maybe they brought back an alien corpse, too. Maybe they even brought back a live one."

"You don't really believe that, do you?"

Thatcher chuckled. "Me? No, not me. But enough folks do to keep this place open, and sell a lot of t-shirts and trinkets, besides. Yeah, we get some live ones here, you bet'cha. Me, I'm just grateful I don't have to drive all the way to Vegas to get me a burger. Bad enough I gotta drive sixty miles to get a tank of gas. How'd you like that burger, anyway?"

Frank realized for the first time that it was actually pretty good. Throughout the conversation, he'd been more than distracted, watching the silent TV out of the corner of his eye as the picture switched from network to network, each time showing the same sequence: a news anchor speaking; a burning temple; and then the familiar contribution screen. Holy hell – they must have hacked all three networks, and GNN besides. How long could it be before the whole world was after him?

Frank was suddenly anxious to get moving. "Pretty good. Say, I'm looking to spend some time writing – I've got a camper outside – and I don't know Nevada. Where's a good place to get away from it all and not be bothered?"

Thatcher smiled. "Well, you're sitt'n there. But if this ain't lonely enough for you, just about anywhere else in Nevada should fit your order. Over 90% of the land is public – BLM, National Forest, state. Nobody's living on it but ranchers, and it's a long piece between them. Other than the couple highways we've got, all you'll find is gravel roads and Jeep tracks. I hope you got good tires, and recommend you keep a good eye on 'em, too.

Frank, the city boy, felt lost. The idea of not having a destination was something he was having a hard time processing.

"Got it. So how about if I wanted to be someplace where I could still drive into a town to get food and gas now and again, but where no one was likely to stumble on me? Someplace I could settle into for awhile and just let my mind run? Maybe someplace that looks like this?"

Frank pulled the picture of the boy on his father's shoulders under the tall trees out of his wallet again, and passed it over.

Thatcher squinted at the picture and gave it a long look. He handed it back to Frank, and then walked across the room and pulled a map off a display rack by the door. Returning, he spread it on the counter and pointed to a small circle two thirds of the way up the state. "This here's Eureka – it's an old mining town that's lost its mines. Closest thing to a landlocked island you'll ever find. More than a hundred miles in any direction to the next town, and not a whole lot in any of 'em when you get there. It don't amount to much, but it's got everything you're going to need."

"Now look here." Thatcher put an X on a pass on the top of one of the long mountain ridges that striated the map of Nevada. "What you want to do is take this here road out of Eureka and follow it till you see a sign that says Petroglyph State Park. You go past that sign another two miles, and then you look for a dirt road heading north – it'll have a cattle grate, not a gate – in the fence." Thatcher wrote the directions on the map as he spoke.

"You just follow that road for as long as you can, and you'll see you rise up out of the valley and head through pinyon and juniper – them's short trees - for a good long ways. Eight, maybe ten miles. Ignore any tracks that head off to either side; shouldn't be hard; you'll be able to tell which road's yours, 'cause all the others'll be more faint. Once you're up a few thousand feet, the Ponderosa pines will take over, and your road will start to sort of dribble out right in the middle of 'em. You'll have yourself as fine a view to the west as you'll ever want to see. Nothing but forever, and no one to keep you company but the wild horses. There's a good spring of water there, too. I've been there now and again when I needed to get my head straight, and I expect it's just what you're looking for."

The old man folded up the map and held it up in the air. "Pat, time for me to settle up. Add this here map onto my tab, and add my buddy's meal to it, too."

Frank started to protest, but Thatcher ignored him as the waitress handed him the bill. Thatcher left a few bills on the counter for a tip, and the two men walked out into the still of the night. Frank couldn't help but look up, hoping to see something mysterious flash across the sky. But only the countless stars sparkled above.

"That your rig?"

"Yes – I rented it from a guy that put a lot of effort into customizing it."

"Well now, that there sure is a sight to behold, and no mistake." Thatcher chuckled. "You best park that contraption outta sight if you head into Eureka, and walk the rest of the way. Otherwise, you'll be the talk of half of Nevada."

Frank looked at the truck uncomfortably and realized that Thatcher was right.

"That sounds like good advice. Thanks for that – and for dinner."

"My pleasure. Don't get many new folks to chat with up here at this time of year." Thatcher looked him up and down and then held out his hand one more time. "Good luck with that writing," he said, a twinkle in his eye, and then walked around the corner of the bar and into the night.

0000 0001 0010 0011 0100 0011 0010 0001 0000

17

A Geek Grows in Brooklyn

AS SUGGESTED, FRANK headed north towards Eureka. A full moon began to rise, illuminating the arrow straight gravel road that extended ahead. The bright light of the moon also revealed the ramparts of mountain ridges on either side bounding the broad valley between. Frank drove onward down the well-graded road, unconsciously accelerating to over seventy miles an hour. Soon he felt lost in space and time, suspended as he was between the moon above and the silvery landscape beneath, flying endlessly onwards towards the shimmering vanishing point where road and mountains converged in the far distance.

Frank's eyes eventually wandered down to the speedometer, and his foot flew to the brake. He gave his head a shake, and turned on the radio, hoping to catch the news. But the numbers on the dial cycled endlessly when he pressed the search button as the radio failed to find a hint of a signal.

He turned the radio off and tried instead to focus his mind on the implications of what he had seen on the TV screen earlier that evening. But he was too distracted by something he couldn't put his finger on as he stared at the moon-washed valley ahead. Finally, he pulled to the side of the road, and killed the engine and the headlights. Immediately his world was consumed by moonlight and silence.

Frank let his mind run free. And then, for the second time that night, he slid the well-worn picture out his wallet. He held it in his hand, and watched it come alive in the light of a curious moon.

0000 0001 0010 0011 0100 0011 0010 0001 0000

The most that Frank ever shared about his pre-college past was that he had enjoyed a "storybook childhood." Then he would change the subject, because the clichéd line was a private joke at his own expense. Yes, the story was a common one, but the plot was straight out of Grimm's Fairy Tales.

As Frank understood it, it all began in the early '60s, when Frank Adversego, Sr., dashingly good looking in his Corporal's uniform, was mustered out of the army and returned to his neighborhood in Brooklyn, New York. Fit, tanned, and cocky, he seemed exotic and worldly to the girls he'd known. Especially in comparison to the other local guys, who had all taken jobs straight out of high school.

This hadn't, after all, been a time and place where first generation kids went to college. It was a get-a-job-and-get-married neighborhood. A job where you helped your immigrant parents sell pizza from a store front or stock shelves in a corner grocery.

If you were lucky, you had an uncle in a union who could set you up as an apprentice to a plumber or a carpenter. Or maybe you could score really big, and get a job as a fireman or a cop – then you'd be set for your whole working life, with a pension to follow. Most of Frank's friends hadn't been that lucky. The local guys all had menial jobs now, and more than one kid. And the local girls were all the mothers of those kids.

And then there was Doreen Nolan. She had always been stubborn and wild. And she was still single, though not for want of offers to change that. Doreen wanted out of the neighborhood in a big way, and knew that no local guy was going to abet her escape. So far she was only a sales clerk in a department store, but the store was downtown, and on Fifth Avenue, to boot. Still living at home, she could afford to dress for downtown. You could catch the eye of the right sort of guy downtown if you were pretty enough – and Doreen was.

She didn't feel bound by any of the other rules of the neighborhood, either. Although she lived on the Irish side of the main street, that didn't stop her from talking to the Italian kid that had left a nobody and came back a handsome soldier with a swagger in his step and a knowing look in his eye. When he asked her out for a date, she said yes.

The next few months passed rapidly. Frank, Sr. had saved most of his pay while in the service, and he applied to Fordham University and Hunter College – NYU and Columbia, even – on the GI Bill. They'd told him in the Army that he'd scored way up there on his IQ test, and Frank had big plans. That gave him and Doreen something in common.

Weekends they lived it up downtown, dancing, taking in the latest movies and spending Frank's savings. Doreen played up to Frank as someone more sophisticated than the rest of the neighborhood girls, and he played up to Doreen as someone with possibilities. Together they masqueraded before their friends as an attractive young couple with money to spend and great expectations for their future. Frank even got into NYU.

But as they sweated through an unusually hot city summer, Frank and Doreen began to realize that they didn't really have much in common besides the desire to feel superior to their high school friends. Worse, Doreen realized that Frank's idea of family life was having a wife that waited on her husband hand and foot, just like his mother. And Frank realized that Doreen really did have a mind and plans of her own.

By then, of course, it was too late, because by August they found out they had one more thing common: Doreen was pregnant.

Things happened all too predictably after that. There was a wedding in the neighborhood Catholic church followed by a reception in a VFW hall. And instead of a ticket out of Brooklyn for Doreen, there was a walk-up apartment down the street from the one she had grown up in. They tried to put up a good front, but by now they both knew the game was over.

With rent to pay, Frank's hopes for full-time college, followed by a fancy career, evaporated. Instead, he found a job in a garage where a cousin worked. As a kid, he had always been tinkering, and in the Army he'd trained as a mechanic. What he couldn't get to run was barely worth scrap, so it didn't take long for his boss to notice. He got his first raise within a few months.

That didn't help much on the home front, though. Back then, nobody wanted to see a pregnant woman behind a counter in a fancy store – or really any place else, either. So not long after they were married, Doreen had to give Manhattan up. Now there was nothing to do but sit around the cramped apartment, sometimes crying, and stare out the window at the drab streets she had so much wanted to leave behind. Or she could visit with her sisters, sitting with their crying babies in their cramped apartments. No Saturday nights out now. Not on a single income and a baby on the way.

When Frank, Jr. arrived, things were already tense. Maybe they could have found a way to share their disappointments and move on, but Frank wasn't a talker, and Doreen wasn't about to stand in for his mother when he came home from work. It was all too easy to find fault and bicker, when both felt cheated and trapped. Before Frank, Jr. turned one, his father was staying out late most nights, taking night school classes or having a few beers down the street with the boys from work. On weekends, while Frank crammed for school, Doreen would be at her mother's with the baby. That was better than the other alternatives, which seemed to have narrowed down to silence and yelling.

It was the sort of marriage you could have found behind the doors of a dozen apartments in their neighborhood, or indeed in any other working class neighborhood in the Five Boroughs. But, oh my, they sometimes thought to themselves - it had all happened so fast. No surprise that Frank was destined to remain an only child.

Frank, Jr. learned early that it was safer to keep to himself at home than to step into the line of fire. He well remembered the shock of the first time he saw a friend's mother give her husband a real kiss when he came home from work. Where did *that* come from? After that, he was painfully aware of signs of affection, not only between the parents of his friends, but between his friends and their sisters and brothers as well. Life at home seemed colder than ever.

As Frank grew older, his home life became more complicated. Year's later, reading a news story about the Balkan war, it occurred to him that he had been like some ineffectual U.N. peacekeeper, sent to a God forsaken hole where he lacked the authority to make a difference but presented a convenient target of opportunity if he didn't watch his step. All he could do was watch while the locals undermined each other in the light of day, and garroted each other in the dark of night. Neither of his parents took any prisoners – except Frank.

The time honored solution would have been to find a life of stickball and running wild in the streets. Sadly, Frank found that while he was bright, he was anything but athletic. He hated being the last pick whenever a crowd of kids chose up sides for a game, so he dropped out of the street crowd.

By default, school and a few organized activities became his world. Joining the chess club and math team, of course, branded him indelibly with nerdhood, so eventually he decided to flaunt his prowess in math and science class in revenge. It didn't endear him to anyone, but on the other hand, no one was going out of their way to be endeared to by him, anyway.

And it did make him feel superior to his classmates - like father, like son. Moreover, he didn't have to be a real genius to realize that the best way to get the hell away from home and school was to skip as many grades as he could, get a college scholarship, and leave Brooklyn for good. Happily, the one thing both parents agreed on was the importance of getting a fancy college education for Frank, Jr.

That might have been the whole story. But unfortunately it wasn't. Frank never knew what the last straw might have been, but one day he came home from a weekend Boy Scout Jamboree and tossed his backpack on the floor.

"Hi, Mom," he called from the kitchen. "What's for dinner?"

She didn't answer, so he stepped into the darkened living room. There she was, sitting in her usual chair and gazing out the window.

"Mom?" he said softly.

But she was lost in thought. Frank suddenly felt frightened by her furrowed face, half hidden in shadow and half dimly illuminated by the fading light that penetrated the old-fashioned lace curtains in the window. She seemed to be balancing a question of great weight, her head nodding slightly, sometimes back and forth, and sometimes up and down.

Frank felt torn between the need to hear her speak and a sudden fear of what she might say. Then her forehead relaxed. An odd look, perhaps of triumph, spread across the ghostly half of her face he could still see.

" . . . Mom?"

Finally aware of his presence, his mother switched on the table lamp at her elbow, and then turned to look at him.

"Frank," she said in a quiet but determined voice, "Your father has left us. And he won't be coming back."

That was all the explanation he would ever get.

-0000- 0001- 0010- 0011- 0100 -0011- 0010- 0001- 0000-

18

May the Force be with You

JUST AS BART Thatcher promised, Frank saw nothing but forever when he looked to the west – forever made up of wave after
wave of ever more purple mountains that culminated in a final sharply
defined silhouette spread against the horizon. From high above, where
the branches of the stately Ponderosa pines he had been seeking almost
touched, the squawks of scrub jays filtered down, accompanied by the
dappling light of the afternoon sun. It was the perfect setting to enjoy
life in a state of nature, but for the computer sitting in Frank's lap.

Sadly, Frank was oblivious to the stunning view before him, now
that he was focusing non-stop on cracking the secrets of the Alexandria
Project. His goals were clear: figure out how those behind the Project
penetrated their targets; devise technical defenses capable of stopping
them; and – most importantly – figure out who they were and what they
were up to. But it wasn't going well.

The first goal hadn't taken long to accomplish. Predictably, any target important enough to be interesting to the Project was big enough
to have had plenty of weaknesses that any determined hacker could discover. Frank concluded that instead of using a single, innovative tech-
nique, the Projecteers generally employed a variety of fairly standard
methods to exploit garden variety flaws in the defenses of their victims.

That realization made the second challenge more intimidating – particularly since he had no idea what the ultimate goal of the Project might be. If the bad guys in fact were only trying to demonstrate the vulnerability of essential systems, well, there wasn't going to be much he could do about that. There were simply too many poorly defended targets of opportunity to shield, and too much work required to insulate them. But if the random attacks were intended instead as camouflage for a much more targeted and nefarious objective, how could he stop that attack unless he knew what the target was?

Frank concluded that he had no choice but to abandon defense as a strategy and go on the offense, which meant tracking down the Alexandria Project back to its source. But how? Not only could the individuals behind it be anywhere, but they were certainly smart enough to direct their attacks through routers scattered all over the world. And indeed, it seemed as if they had attacked from a different point of departure every time.

So it was that a very frustrated Frank Adversego was sitting in a folding chair in the outback of Nevada, poking around the dark corners of the Internet in hopes of picking up the trail of his quarry in the places where

hackers were most likely to hang out. During the first day he nosed around the sites where millions of pieces of valuable personal financial information traded hands on a regular basis like so many hog futures. But he couldn't find any indication that the Project might have a financial motive.

For several days after that, he scoured the Web for any buzz connecting the Chinese, the Russians, the North Koreans – any nation at all – to the Alexandria Project. Once again he came up dry – there was nary a rumor to be found that seemed credible enough to follow up.

Today he was trying something riskier – visiting sites that might be linked to terrorists. Frank knew the CIA would be monitoring these same sites very closely. Some of them were doubtless decoys set up by the agency itself to identify people susceptible to recruitment by the real bad guys.

Anyone might browse into one of these sites and swiftly move on without attracting too much attention. But if Frank followed a link from any of these sites to another of the same ilk, he'd be sticking his head up high enough to attract the wrong sort of attention. To prevent that, he'd loaded software that would establish a new IP address for his laptop each time he switched to a new site, making him appear to be a different visitor every time.

By late afternoon he was frustrated. After four days perched in his mountain aerie probing the Web, he had nothing of value to show for it. Feeling cranky, he slipped the thumb drive off the chain around his neck and plugged it into his laptop. For the hundredth time he watched the vivid visuals of move through their enigmatic cycle, and for the hundredth time, he failed to notice anything new of interest.

It was no use. As the sun settled onto the horizon, he grudgingly admitted that he had no choice but to play his last card.

He would have to contact Yoda.

~~0000~~ ~~0001~~ ~~0010~~ ~~0011~~ 0100 ~~0011~~ ~~0010~~ ~~0001~~ ~~0000~~

Frank had first encountered Yoda many years before, back when he was still living off his MacArthur grant. In those days, only serious computer users and not many of them with academic, scientific or government credentials could get on line. There were no graphical user interfaces, either. All you saw were ghostly white letters marching across small monochrome computer monitors as members of arcane user groups posed questions and received answers in discussions that barely hinted at the vast, virtual world of interaction that lay ahead.

Out of the ether of one such discussion a curious, recursive voice responded one day to a question Frank had posted when he ran out of inspiration in the middle of a particularly difficult project. After describing the situation at a Usenet bulletin board, he watched as the following message appeared:

>*Maybe the answer you know already.*

What the hell was that supposed to mean, Frank wondered? Not very imaginatively (or tactfully) he responded:

What the hell is that supposed to mean?

A response followed immediately:

>*Maybe in the way is your nose. If your nose you move, the answer you may see before you.*

That was all there was to the message, other than the name of the sender - someone improbably calling himself "Yoda." Puzzled, Frank went back to read his original question. To his surprises, he saw a dimension of the problem that should have been clear to him from the beginning. He typed a response to Yoda's message:

You're right - I should have seen that myself. Thanks!

But there was no reply.

Not often, but ever since, Frank had returned to the same discussion group, still hosted on a UNIX server by someone who likely had forgotten it still existed. For years now it hadn't been used by anyone but Frank and his mysterious mentor with the inverted prose style.

No matter how long it might be between visits, whenever Frank returned, Yoda was always there, as enigmatic, omniscient – and frustrating - as ever. Long ago Frank had given up trying to draw Yoda out on his identity, which was clearly impossible. Yoda only answered security related questions, and then only obliquely. Frank invariably felt like he was consulting a Magic Eight Ball or Ouija Board - only it wasn't much fun.

Yoda was so gnomic that Frank sometimes wondered whether a developer had created him as a program capable of passing the Turing Test. If so, it was a damn good program, because Yoda's infuriatingly obscure responses always helped Frank unsnarl whatever rat's nest he was trying to unravel.

So it was with as much weariness as hope that Frank logged in to the ancient user group, keeping his mental fingers crossed that no one from Washington was monitoring it. He typed:

Yoda, I have a problem.

Amazingly, it was only a few minutes before an answer began to scroll across his screen.

> *Long has it been, Frank. What is your problem?*

It's a tough one. If you follow the news, you must know about the Alexandria Project.

> *Follow the news I do not. But know of the Alexandria Project, I do.*

Frank's heart skipped a beat.

You do? Do you know who they are?

> *A strange question is that you ask. Who am I? Who are you? Who is anyone? What is "who?"*

Frank took a deep breath and made himself slow down. Then he began to type a long explanation of what he knew, and what it was he was trying to accomplish. Finally, he ended with a question.

So you see I need help figuring out two things: how do I protect sites from the Alexandria Project, and how do I find out who is behind the Project itself?

Frank realized he had typed several pages of text. He wondered how much Yoda might know about the Project already. But nothing appeared on Frank's screen for a long time. He drummed his fingers on his knee as he waited impatiently.

At last, Yoda's response began appearing on his screen.

> Two problems you pose not one. Explore the second you must first, because solve it first you must.

Frank was mildly disappointed. He'd already concluded that much on his own.

Okay – thanks. So how do I find those behind the Alexandria Project?

> Consider the lobster.

What? This was a pretty odd answer, even considering the source. Frank looked up, and noticed that a spectacular sunset was unfolding before him. He took a deep breath and tried to assume the Zen-like frame of mind that might help him divine the insights that Yoda might be sharing. Then he began typing once again.

There is much of interest in the lobster. But what about the lobster should I consider? His senses? His taste? His ability to shed his shell?

> Before a lobster you can consider, a lobster you must have.
You mean I must find a lobster?

> The fisherman does not the lobster find; the lobster finds the fisherman.

That was true, Frank mused intently. A lobsterman sets traps, and then the lobsters crawl into them. Yoda must be suggesting that Frank should set a trap that would attract the Alexandria Project to him.

Frank hadn't considered setting up a fake target site – a "honeypot" in security lingo - because he had already witnessed the attacks the Project had made on the Library of Congress. Did Yoda think that there was more to learn by further observation?

You mean I should set up a honeypot?

> *Decide that you must for yourself.*

Let's say I do. And let's say those behind the Alexandria Project take the bait. What then?

> *Consider the spy.*

First lobsters, and now spies! Frank mulled that one over for awhile, trying to open his mind up to all possibilities. The Alexandria Project intruders were at least a lot more like spies than lobsters, so this felt like progress. Still, he couldn't make out where Yoda was going. He'd have to try to see if he could nudge Yoda into giving him another clue.

That made Frank nervous. This had already been a long exchange for Yoda, and Frank was worried that he might lose interest and drop off at any moment. But all Frank could think to type was:

Okay. I don't know what they are really up to, but they are certainly acting like spies along the way.

Frank waited but got no response. Desperate, he added:

And, like spies, we don't want them there.

>*Never?*

Frank let out an audible "Huh!" That was an interesting reply. When might a spy be welcome?

He leaned back and stared vacantly into the growing darkness that one. Well, if you could turn a spy against its master, he could become your servant instead of your enemy. And even without turning a spy, you might be able to feed him disinformation, and mislead his master. Maybe that was what Yoda had in mind.

You can sometimes feed a spy false information. Is that what you mean?

> *What does "mean" mean?*

125

Frank groaned and tried another tack.

Let's say I'm following what you have in mind. If I am, how could misleading the intruder help me in this situation?

>For yourself, decide that you must.

Much as he might hope otherwise, Yoda was, as usual, unwilling to do Frank's work for him. Frank knew from long and painful experience that he had gotten as much of Yoda as he could on this question, so he set his laptop aside and began pacing rapidly back and forth across his clearing, lost in thought. The lobster part was clear; if he could fake a complex IT environment and bait it with the right type of information, he could watch the intruders in action. Perhaps he could even mislead them. But the people – whoever they were – at the Alexandria Project didn't have to send spies to do their work. They were able to penetrate sites from afar. So how could he turn an intruder against itself?

Frank stopped in mid-stride. Well, maybe he wouldn't have to turn the intruders themselves. He knew that they were planting malware at the sites they attacked. He should be able to find that software and alter it. If he did, he might be able to make it return false information – or even plant software of his own on the Project's own network. Perhaps he could "turn the spy" after all, with the Alexandria Project being none the wiser. But how would that help him achieve his goal?

Frank sat down and began typing again.

If I can lure the Project crackers into my honeypot, I can watch what they do until I can imitate them. Then I can remove whatever robots or other malware they plant and respond just as that software would respond – except nothing malicious would be happening. Is that what you have in mind?

>"In mind" have I nothing. A collection of synapses is a mind, or so they say. If right they are, that is all have I "in mind."

Frank could afford to smile this time at Yoda's coy reply, because now he had the beginnings of a plan. But that plan would still only get him half way home, so he started typing again.

I think I'm okay on that part now - thanks. But I'm not sure how this will help me find the Alexandria Project itself.

> Follow the iBalls you must.

Frank stared at his computer in utter astonishment. Why in the world was Yoda bringing up iBalls? Did he know that Frank was involved with them? If so, how in the world had he made the connection? Cautiously, Frank typed:

iBalls?

> *iBalls I say, and iBalls I mean. Follow the iBalls, you must.*

Frank was still taken aback, and simply typed:

How?

>*The force will be with you if the crowd you let be your source.*

Enigmatic as it was, Frank appreciated that this was as direct as Yoda had ever been with him. But the meaning of Yoda's advice still evaded him. *Tantalized, he tried one more time.*

I hear you Yoda, but I don't yet understand you. How can I use iBalls to find the Alexandria Project?

But Yoda's patience – or his willingness to do Frank's work for him - had reached an end. He signed off with this final cryptic line:

> *Get by you will - if an island you are not.*

~~0000~~ ~~0001~~ ~~0010~~ ~~0011~~ 0100 ~~0011~~ ~~0010~~ ~~0001~~ ~~0000~~

19

More than One Can Play that Game

GEORGE MARCHAND SAT uneasily at the witness table in the hearing room. On a raised platform before him stretched a long, wooden rampart bristling with microphones. Entrenched impregnably behind that rampart sat all but one of the members of the Inquisition also known as the Congressional Subcommittee on Cybersecurity.

Crouching like a pack of hyenas on the floor between the subcommittee and the witness tables were dozens of photographers, polishing their lenses in anticipation of the kill. To George's right, a bored looking C-SPAN video engineer peered at him with mild curiosity from beside his camera, waiting for the fun to begin. They reminded George of vultures waiting impatiently for a dying wildebeest to get on with it, already.

George glanced at his watch with resignation. It was almost 10:00 AM, and therefore time for today's orgy of Congressional ego gratification and wrathful citizenry appeasement to begin. George hoped his introductory role in the hearing would be brief.

Precisely at 10:00, Congressman Titus Steele, the Chairman of the Subcommittee, made his entrance through the single door that penetrated the wall behind the Subcommittee platform. Taking the center chair, he rapped a gavel decisively three times, and stated, "This hearing will come to order."

Aging but still forceful, "Tight-Ass" Steele was an elder statesman with little patience for anyone that didn't know how the game was played. George noted uncomfortably that the Congressman was looking more irascible than usual, which was saying a great deal. Ever since

Steele's party had lost control of the House, he had been smarting over his loss of influence. And today, it was George's misfortune to be the warm-up act for the blood sport that lay ahead. As little as he looked forward to his own supporting role in the inquest, he was grateful that the tenderizing of the Directors of the CIA and FBI was scheduled as the main event.

Steele paused for only a moment for the hubbub to die away, and then launched into his opening remarks, peering over his spectacles at the standing-room only crowd of journalists and spectators packed into the hearing room.

"This morning I learned that we have been attacked yet again by those calling themselves "The Alexandria Project." This time, the perpetrators had the temerity to seize control of the computer systems of *American Idol*, the Home Shopping Channel, and Disney World – in short, they are assaulting the very foundations of our culture and society."

"Needless to say, the members of this Committee demand that these attacks must stop! Immediately!"

"Now the purpose of today's hearing is to find out for the American people why those responsible for protecting this great nation from its enemies have not already brought these brazen Internet vandals to justice."

"Call the first witness."

Steele glowered at George as the Sergeant-at-Arms rose to read from his list: "George Marchand, Chief Information Officer, The Library of Congress."

The light on the base of George's microphone had barely turned red when Chairman Steele barked out his first question.

"Mr. Marchand, I understand that the Library of Congress was the first Federal office to be attacked by this Alexandria Project. Is that correct?"

George leaned forward as all eyes and cameras swiveled in his direction. "Yes, sir. That is my understanding as well, sir."

"When was that?"

"We believe that it was the evening of November 29th of this year."

"And when did you discover the attack?"

"The next day, sir."

"What was the nature of the attack?"

"A single file had been deleted in my personal security directory. When I tried to open it, the "contribution" screen that everyone has seen by now on the news came up instead of the file."

"I see. What did you do then?"

"While the file deleted wasn't particularly important, the directory it had been removed from was sensitive. For this reason, I personally performed an internal investigation of the intrusion using our established protocols in an effort to determine how the attackers had gained entry."

"And were you successful?"

"No sir, I was not. After I finished my investigation, I completed our standard incident report so that if the intrusion was repeated we could pick up where I had left off."

"Is that all you did?"

"Yes, sir."

"And why is that?"

"Like every major enterprise user of information technology, we're under constant attack by all manner of intruders. This intrusion was novel, because of the screen, but otherwise unremarkable."

"So you didn't report this attack to anyone in the CIA or FBI?"

George moved uneasily in his chair. He *was* the CIA, but he could hardly reveal that in an open hearing room.

"No, sir. There are no inter-agency protocols in place at this time that require any departmental head to report garden variety cyber attacks to any central government security agency."

"Are you trying to tell me that when an agency of this great nation is attacked by an unknown enemy that someone in your position doesn't contact the CIA and FBI so they can get to the bottom of it?"

"I'm afraid that's right, sir. Allowing me to do that would require Congressional action."

George decided to take a chance and throw his boss a lifeline in advance of his testimony. Taking a deep breath, he continued, "As a matter of fact, the Inter-Agency CIO Council has been recommending to your Committee for some time that a rapid response unit be set up within Homeland Security that we could report...."

"MR. MARCHAND!"

George stopped in mid-sentence and waited.

Glowering, Steele hunched forward and chose his words carefully. "Mr. Marchand, I believe that I'm the person asking the questions here, and I don't recall asking what you or any other government employee may have recommended. Am I correct?"

"Yes, sir, that's correct, sir, but I thought that it would help solve this problem if...."

At that, Steele began gaveling aggressively. "The witness will approach the Committee table!"

Startled, George stood up and walked slowly forward. Steele glared at the C-SPAN engineer, who obediently turned the camera away and began scanning the audience.

George reached the wall of the Subcommittee's fortress, and stared up into the outraged face of the Chairman. Steele flipped the switch on his microphone to the off position.

Leaning towards George, Steele spat his words out quietly but forcefully. "Mr. Marchand, I don't believe you really understand what a *televised* Congressional hearing is all about. Well, I'm going to do you a favor and tell you before I resume my questioning."

George knew exactly what a televised Congressional hearing was all about, but wisely decided to keep that knowledge to himself.

"A Congressional hearing is about allowing those on this side of the dais to express outrage and condemnation about things that we should have prevented but didn't so that no one holds us responsible. In doing so, we are free to humiliate those on your side of the dais to our hearts content and for as long as we wish if it will help us get re-elected. Do I make myself perfectly clear, Mr. Marchand?"

"Abundantly, sir."

"Good! Now as originally planned, you were not the focus of this hearing. But I can change that in a heartbeat if I wish, and you should know that I am only one heartbeat away from making that decision. Now is *that* clear?"

George nodded affirmatively.

"Good! In that case, I would recommend that you listen to my questions very carefully from now on, and answer them in exactly the way that you can tell I want you to answer them. Do that, and I'll move on quickly to the next witness. Do you understand your role in this hearing *now*, Mr. Marchand?"

George nodded his assent again. Steele flipped his microphone back to the on position as George gratefully returned to his seat.

"Now Mr. Marchand, at what point did you dutifully report this incident like a good civil servant to the CIA and FBI, and why do you think it took them so long to do anything – *anything at all* – to protect the American people from this terrible menace?"

0000 0001 0010 0011 0100 0011 0010 0001 0000

Ever since Frank's email exchange with Yoda he had been working night and day on the honeypot he hoped would attract the Alexandria

Project. But now that it was done, all he could do was wait and hope that those he sought would take the bait.

But would they? After all, there were millions of potential targets in the world, and Frank had no way to know how the Project was selecting its targets. If they were choosing their victims one by one, then Frank's strategy was statistically doomed to fail. He was betting, though, that this was no longer the case. Now that the Project was publicly humiliating multiple system owners on a regular basis, everyone was scrambling to beef up their defenses as quickly and completely as possible.

Frank doubted the Project could be penetrating this many targets unless they were deploying a "botnet" of thousands of personal computers hijacked without the knowledge of their owners. Using these "zombie" computers, the Project could robotically storm computer systems throughout the Web and find those with weak defenses. They could then pick and choose their targets from among the vulnerable and humiliate those with the highest public profiles for maximum effect.

But still, the Internet was a very big place indeed. How long might it take a botnet to discover his trap? Or perhaps he hadn't done a good enough job creating the illusion of an enterprise-level system to match the profile used to generate the botnet's target list.

Frank realized that he was pacing back and forth inside the cramped confines of the *Solar Avenger* and sat down. That was worse, so he began busying himself rigging up an alarm system that would allow him to venture outside and not miss an attack when it occurred. First he connected the scanning programs he'd loaded on the honeypot to a sound generator, and then set the generator to react only to the type of input that represented the type of file-probing intrusion he had monitored back at the Library of Congress – the tip-off that an Alexandria Project bot was testing the honeypot's defenses. Finally, he connected his computer to the camper's sound system. That way he could pace around outside in a progressively more hyper-caffeinated state while listening for the tell-tale sound that would signal success. On a whim, he disconnected the sound generator, and linked the program to a series of music files instead. Might as well announce good news with good music.

For the rest of the day, Frank spent his time trying to refine the next steps of his plan. But with no assurance that he could act on any of those next steps he found it difficult to concentrate. It was not until late afternoon that he was startled by a loud voice erupting from the Avenger's speakers:

"Give me an F!"

Frank dashed madly back into the camper as Country Joe MacDonald and the assembled multitude at Woodstock rapturously completed the Fish Cheer. Jumping in front of the computer screen, Frank pulled up the intrusion report and watched as it completed.

Good! The scanners hadn't identified the attack to any known malware. That meant that this might be the real thing. The next question was whether the Project – if it was the Project – had taken one of the files they needed to remove for the rest of his plan to work.

Frank called up the honeypot's text file directory, and then opened the menu of the directory holding the decoy security architecture files he had doctored. He clicked on the first file and it opened without a problem. So also with the second. And the third. And the fourth.

There was only one file left. He held his breath as he clicked on it. At first, nothing happened. Then, a familiar, warm glow began to suffuse the screen.

Scrub jays shot off in all directions from the pines over head in response to Frank's whoops of joy and relief.

0000 0001 0010 0011 0100 0011 0010 0001 0000

For once, Frank was relaxing. With his back turned to everything man-made, he sat in a folding chair with a cold beer in hand and watched the colors of yet another magnificent sunset imperceptibly morph and fade into a soft, rosy glow.

For perhaps the first time in his life, he felt truly at peace. Maybe it was the huge separation he felt between the world he had left and this far away Eden, suspended between the still, mountain-shadowed valley stretching away below and the equally vast and darkening sky above. Or perhaps he had simply never been able to empty his mind sufficiently to allow the stillness of a beautiful evening to wholly connect with his city-bred senses.

Whatever the reason, Frank found himself following a very different line of thought than he had ever considered before. Perhaps he was crazy to be immersing himself in this Alexandria Project madness. The iBalls revenues were still rolling in, and if he could design one successful game app anonymously, why not another? What would be so wrong with making an offer to Jenkins for the *Solar Avenger* that the old man couldn't refuse, and then spend the next year up here just contemplating his navel?

As the sprinkling of stars emerging overhead became a numberless multitude, Frank was well on his way to persuading himself, at least for tonight, to do just that.

Suddenly, the stillness and his beatific reverie were shattered by a discordant, soaring shriek – somehow, Jimi Hendrix had just launched into his interpretation of the Star Spangled Banner here in Frank's Nevada aerie. But Frank's startled annoyance turned quickly to confusion as he realized what was happening: a second, different intruder was attacking the honeypot.

0000 0001 0010 0011 0100 0011 0010 0001 0000

20

The iBalls Shall Rise Again

iBALLS.COM CEO Chad Derwent sat alone in his office in Silicon Valley. Outside his open door, rows of empty, silent cubicles stretched from one end of the office floor to the other.

For the last several minutes he had been staring down at the stack of papers on his desk, paralyzed by the title of the one on top: "Petition for Liquidation in Bankruptcy."

Chad couldn't bring himself to look at the rest of the documents, but he couldn't bear to look up, either, because he knew what he would see - the big picture on his wall where Sanjay and he were posed with their first half-dozen employees. Everyone was smiling, because iBalls.com had just gone live on the Web. Back then, he'd never supposed it could ever end like this.

But it had, and there was nothing to be done about it. Nothing to be done but pick up his pen and begin to sign the grim documents in the big stack of paper, one by one.

The phone rang. Chad looked at it in surprise. When was the last time *that* had happened? As soon as it became clear that iBalls.com could not survive, the stench of failure had descended upon him, and even his email had dwindled to a trickle. Was it his mother?

With a sigh, he put down his pen and pressed the speakerphone button.

"Chad here."

"Good morning, Mr. Derwent. My name is Carter Columbo. I don't believe that we have ever met, but my client would like to discuss a possible investment in iBalls.com."

Chad gaped in astonishment. Was this guy insane?

"Is your client Nigerian? Don't you guys usually send me email?"

"You have a fine sense of humor, Mr. Derwent. I can appreciate that under iBalls.com's current circumstances that an offer of investment might seem a little unusual. Still, my client's interest is real, and he would like to make you a proposition that could save your company."

For the first time in a week, Chad felt a spark of hope. After the disastrous meeting with Josh Peabody, he had sent cancellation notices to all of iBalls.com's existing customers, and pulled the page that allowed new companies to sign up to download iBalls. But the passage of the ten day notice period required under iBalls.com's customer license agreement had been excruciating. Hour by hour, he had watched the company's bank account plummet. Despite letting all of the employees go and terminating every other obligation that could be broken, iBalls.com's bank account now stood at $106.42 – and its outstanding payables topped $600,000.

"And who exactly might your client be?"

There was a long silence. Then, the formerly confident caller said sheepishly, "If I tell you, do you promise not to hang up?"

Chad's small spark of hope winked out. Still, what have I got to lose, Chad thought.

"Sure. Hit me."

Another pause. "The Pangloss Game Company."

Chad thought he must be hallucinating. He was pretty sure that what he remembered about his meeting with Josh Peabody had really happened. But he was having trouble believing that he was now sitting here in iBalls.com's deserted offices taking a call from the game developer that had destroyed his company.

"...Mr. Derwent?"

Chad stared at the phone.

"Mr. Derwent? Are you still there?"

"Yeah, yeah, I'm still here. You know, though, it's the funniest thing. I was pretty sure there I heard you say that the company that drove my company into the ground like a tent peg now wants to make an investment to save it."

"That's right, Mr. Derwent. I did. Now, what I'd like to say...."

Chad cut him off. "You are from Nigeria, aren't you?"

His caller sighed. "Mr. Derwent, of course this is all rather awkward. Indeed, my client feels badly about the events of the last two weeks. But as you can appreciate, if there are no more iBalls, then there can't any more *iBallZapper!* games. Right now, the buzz for iBalls is huge, but a few months from now, everyone will have forgotten about them. So my client is genuinely interested in helping you get your company back on its feet rather than waiting to buy your assets out of bankruptcy. That is, if you're willing to assist it in launching another game pronto."

Chad looked at the stack of unsigned bankruptcy papers, and then at the picture on the wall. For the second time during this strange call, he thought: Well, what do I have to lose?

"Okay. I'm listening."

0000 0001 0010 0011 0100 0011 0010 0001 0000

"Jack Posner here to see you, Josh."

"Okay, Lynne. Bring him down to my office."

Josh Peabody swiveled his desk chair and looked out over Sand Hill Road moodily. Jack Posner was iBalls.com's outside counsel.

Josh wasn't used to finding himself in a position like this. And in fact, his lawyer had advised him not to meet with Jack. Better to let iBalls.com file for bankruptcy without any input from its controlling stockholder, TrashTalk's attorney had said, given that you'll profit so handsomely from its failure. Of course, his lawyer also warned him that iBalls.com's founders might try to sue him personally for being a director of iBalls.com while secretly betting against the company. Typical big firm legal advice – technically accurate, ridiculously expensive, and totally useless.

So Josh decided to ignore his attorney and meet with Jack anyway. After all, he'd sent business to Jack before, and if Jack knew what was good for him, he'd want to stay on Josh's good side for the future. Josh figured it would be smarter to make that point in person than in an email that might look…awkward in the wrong setting. Like in front of a jury.

There was a knock at the door. As Josh swiveled back, he put on his best salesman's face and stood up.

"Jack! Great to see you, old man." Josh strode forward, extending his hand. "How's your golf game doing these days?"

"Not bad. Funny you should mention that - my firm's sponsoring a benefit tournament down in Carmel next month – $5,000 per player. Maybe you'd like to join my foursome?"

"Absolutely! You've got a deal. Just ask Lynne on your way out to put it in my calendar. Tell her I said to move anything else to fit it in."

Might as well lay it on, Josh thought, pulling a personal check from his desk drawer. He filled it out and signed it with a flourish.

Josh motioned Jack towards one of the two couches in the corner of his office. Sitting down next to him, Josh tucked the check in the lawyer's jacket pocket.

"So what brings you here today? Have a new start-up you want me to take a look at?"

Jack offered him a small smile. As if Josh didn't know why he was there. "Actually, no, Josh. I want to discuss iBalls.com with you."

"Sure, sure. Anything I can do to help with the shut down, just ask."

"Good. As you know, I have to act in the best interests of all iBalls.com stockholders, and TrashTalk LLP is only one of them, so please keep that in mind. As you always say, business is business, so don't shoot the messenger."

"Of course," Josh replied evenly. "That's why I'm always so confident recommending you to new companies we invest in." He watched Jack carefully to see if he would take the bait.

Jack smiled again and then continued. "Don't think I don't appreciate it, Josh. Anyway, yesterday I got a call from Chad Derwent saying he wanted to talk about bringing a lawsuit against you and each of your Board appointees for breach of your fiduciary duties as directors."

Josh started to object, but Jack raised his hand and kept talking.

"Hold on, hold on! You and I go way back, so of course, I pointed out to him that such a suit would be very expensive to prosecute, and that its outcome would be uncertain. But Chad insisted that he could no longer work with you or your appointees on the board – I believe he used the word "cronies," actually. He said that if a lawsuit wasn't the answer, than I had to come up with another way to get rid of you."

"So here's what I suggested. If you and the other TrashTalk directors resign, and if TrashTalk gives up the special rights it holds under the investment documents, Chad and Sanjay will execute a full and final release of you, TrashTalk and the other directors."

Jack took two copies of a document out of his briefcase and handed them to Josh. "I volunteered to put together a brief Surrender of Rights and Mutual Release Agreement for him, and here it is. You'll see it's already signed by all of the management stockholders."

Jack started to hand the documents over, and then paused. "I almost forgot. Chad and Sanjay requested that I ask you one last time whether you would consider investing more money in iBalls.com?"

That was an easy one. "Absolutely not. Not on any terms they could possibly offer me."

"That's what I assumed, so I also added in a waiver of TrashTalk's future investment rights, and pre-approval of any investment that they might be able to bring in."

Josh pretended to skim the brief agreement while mentally reviewing the situation. iBalls.com was doomed – no two ways about that. There wasn't a fool big enough to invest in that smoldering train wreck. All Josh had to do was wait for the bankruptcy filing he knew Chad planned to file to become final, and he could cash in the policy brokered by TrashTalk's new VC derivatives start-up. If he was no longer a director, he couldn't personally be tainted by any actions Chad and Sanjay took as the ship went down, and the release would protect him against liability for anything that had already happened. What wasn't to like about this unexpected development?

The fact that it was all too easy, Josh told himself. He looked hard at Jack. "I have to say, I'm a bit surprised you were able to get Chad and Sanjay to take your suggestion, given how bitter they seem to be. How did you persuade them to sign this?"

"Easy. I reminded them what a small place Silicon Valley is, and I pointed out to them how foolish it would be for them to burn their bridges to no purpose. They didn't like it, but they got it."

That was true, Josh told himself. You couldn't take revenge to the bank. And that was his favorite destination in the whole world. He made up his mind.

"Well, of course, the iBalls.com story has been a great disappointment for us here at TrashTalk. We put a very large sum of money behind Chad and Sanjay and now that money's all gone. Still, we believe in supporting our management teams even when they make bad business decisions, so no hard feelings from our side."

You miserable toad, Jack thought. He'd read Chad and Sanjay's original business plan, and knew how and why it had changed.

Josh continued, "I'm disappointed to hear that Chad and Sanjay are having a hard time looking at things the same way, but if they think they can do a better job back on their own, so be it." Josh signed both copies of the agreement, and handed one to Jack. He placed the other carefully in a drawer, and stood up, signaling the meeting was over.

"I appreciate your helping Chad and Sanjay take a more professional approach in this difficult situation. Young entrepreneurs need someone older to remind them that business is business."

"Business is business," Jack concurred, smiling. He turned to leave.

Josh was beginning to feel like his old, brash self again as he stood in the hallway, arms crossed, watching Jack walk away. Life should always be this simple. On impulse, he called down the hallway, "Hey – be sure to tell Chad and Sanjay I wish them luck, will you?"

Jack turned and gave him a broad smile. "I'll do that. You know, Josh, if I were you, I wouldn't be too quick to count those guys out."

0000 0001 0010 0011 0100 0011 0010 0001 0000

"All systems go."

Frank smiled to himself as he read the three word email from Archie. The events of the past week had been profoundly satisfying. Archie was delighted to have a new game to launch, now that the original supply of iBalls was running out. He was even more delighted that Frank was willing to bail out iBalls.com on his own without asking his partner to chip in. Even Chad and Sanjay were pumped, once they understood that Frank was willing to underwrite their original iBalls.com business plan as well as pay off the current bills.

Frank's new plan was straightforward, at least the part that he was willing to share with Archie and the iBalls.com team. iBalls.com wouldn't pay people to download iBalls anymore. From now on, site owners would have to pay to get them. They would also have to give permission to iBalls.com to gather and aggregate data about who was visiting their sites. The owners would be happy to buy in, though, because millions of iBall fans were just waiting for the new game to begin. What easier way was there to attract thousands of new visitors to your site?

Chad and Sanjay were delighted. The coding needed to launch the new wave of iBalls was trivial, and they wouldn't have to pay a dime for marketing. The Pangloss Game Company would take care of that, so for the first time in its history, iBalls.com would actually be turning a profit.

The game that Frank had devised to drive the new wave of iBall downloads – and accomplish his real goal - was called the "Lotto iBalls Challenge," and the concept was simple. For the first week, anyone could download as many iBalls as they wanted to display at their site, at a minimum bid of $1.00 apiece. There would be no reverse auction this time, though. The longer a site waited to buy in, the higher the price might rise as the limited number of iBalls available sold out. Once they were gone, the game players could begin hunting them down.

And hunt them they would, because the contest would be like a lottery, with the big prizes going to those who captured the code of the iBalls with the winning numbers. The more iBalls you hunted down, the more money you stood to win.

That was the elegant part of Frank's plan, although it was Yoda who had provided the inspiration. Frank had puzzled for days over the last clue his mysterious mentor had shared with him:

> *The force will be with you if your crowd you let be your source.*

And then it hit him – "crowd sourcing" was what Yoda had been nudging him towards – using the thousands of free volunteers the Internet could deliver to help him in his quest. Frank had come to realize that he might never be able to track the Project back to its lair on his own. But why even try if he could get the Project to do the job for him? All he had to do was trick the Project's malware into unknowingly carrying an iBall back to its master the next time it snatched a file from the new honeypot he would set up for the purpose. Then he could use the thousands of avid iBall gamers to find that iBall for him. With that many ingenious hackers on the hunt, he was confident that every last iBall would be found and captured eventually. Just like the Project, the most determined gamers would even construct robots to hunt and kill thousands of iBalls automatically rather than locate and zap them individually. And with so much money up for grabs, the game would attract the type of contestants that wouldn't let firewalls stand in their way, either.

So, unbeknownst to Chad and Sanjay as they prepared to push the new iBall download pages live, or to Archie as he readied the new game marketing campaign, Frank was finalizing the files that he would place in his trap once the game was well advanced. Those files would include embedded code that would simulate an iBall without displaying one. After all, he hardly expected the Alexandria Project to maintain a public website. But the Project would need to have a computer or server on which its own programs and data were stored. That's where the iBall from Frank's honeypot would end up, and also where the internet connection would be located by which it could be found by a determined contestant's robot.

Could the gamers really find every iBall? Well, just the year before DARPA, the same agency that had funded the initial creation of the Internet, had used a game to trigger the development of a wave of innovative, social media-based search strategies. All the agency had to do was offer a prize and wait. By adopting a crowd sourcing approach, it could study what had worked best after the contest was done, thereby saving millions of dollars of development fees and gaining access to many more strategies to pursue than it ever would have managed on its own.

Like the Lotto iBalls Challenge, DARPA's contest had also been simple: the agency promised a prize to the first team to report the locations of ten red weather balloons the agency briefly displayed thousands of miles apart around the country at the start of the competition. The winning team, from MIT, nailed all ten locations in under nine hours. DARPA had offered only $40,000 in its contest, but that modest amount (plus the glory of beating everyone else) had been sufficient to set off a frenzy of activity. Frank was betting that by promising a prize of $1,000,000 to whoever found and captured *The Big iBall*, at least one of the teams would find and bring home the one that he was counting on the Alexandria Project to remove from his honeypot.

That iBall would be different from all the others, though. Even though it wouldn't display a visual image, it would still "look" like an iBall to a Bot. More significantly, it would have location-based capabilities that would allow it to determine where it had been removed to as well. Once its code was captured by a gamer and returned to The Pangloss Game Company, it could also be identified immediately as being different from all the other iBalls being turned in. Frank would be looking for it, and when it came in he'd know at last where The Alexandria Project – and hopefully the second mystery intruder as well – could be found.

But first he would have to wait. It was going to be a very long week.

0000 0001 0010 0011 0100 0011 0010 0001 0000

Josh was feeling good. TrashTalk was getting close to launching a new $1 billion fund, and he was looking forward to the new influx of management fees it would generate. They were really pushing the envelope this time, and planned to ask the limited partners to let management pay itself an extra percent of the fund assets on the management fee - that meant another $10 million a year, most of which Josh and his two full partners would split up after sharing a few crumbs with their junior partners. Cashing in the $65 million insurance policy on iBalls.com would provide the kind of proof of their exalted status that should seal the deal.

Josh punched the button on his buzzing phone with a flourish. "W'sup, Lynne?"

"A reporter from The Register, Josh. Want me to tell her you're tied up?"

"That's okay, Lynne. Go ahead and put her through." Josh felt like gloating to someone - even a reporter.

"Josh Peabody."

"Hi, Josh. Lydia Sparrowhawk. Any comment on this morning's press release from iBalls.com announcing their relaunch and the cramdown of TrashTalk's investment?"

"I beg your pardon?" Josh was thunderstruck. He desperately typed "iBalls.com" into Google News. Sure enough, there was a press release from his portfolio company - jointly issued with The Pangloss Game Company.

"Gosh, Lydia, I beg your pardon. Somebody just handed me an urgent message. Gotta go!"

Josh read the press release with mounting horror:

Pangloss Game Company joins Forces with iBalls.com to Create World-Class Gaming Partnership

iBalls.com recapitalized as gamers anticipate new blockbuster game

Palo Alto, California - The Pangloss Game Company (TPGC), the world's leading provider of prize-based game apps, and iBalls.com, the leading provider of down-loadable, graphics-based market data collection software, today announced they have entered into a strategic partnership that will set the stage for a new level of on-line gaming. Under the partnership, TPGC has acquired 85% of iBalls.com in the form of a new class of super-priority preferred stock. As a result of the investment and the adoption of a new incentive plan for management, former controlling stockholder TrashTalk LLP's ownership will be reduced to 0.001% of the Company.

TPGC and iBalls.com also announced the launch of an innovative new global contest called the *Lotto iBalls Challenge®*, featuring a $1 million prize for the lucky gamer that captures *The Big iBall®*.

"We're unbelievably excited here at iBalls.com," said iBalls.com CEO Chad Derwent. "Unlike Josh Peabody and TrashTalk, TPGC truly gets the future of the Internet. And with the unlimited financing that TPGC brings to the table, our long-term success is assured."

Josh quit reading as his blood ran cold. TrashTalk had just been crammed down so hard its $50 million stake was now worth almost – but critically, not quite - nothing.

Josh quickly dialed up the CEO of VC/Derivatives, Inc., the TrashTalk portfolio company he was counting on to bail him out on the iBalls.com investment.

"Hey, Jeremy, Josh Peabody. How you doing?"

"Great, Josh. What's new?"

"Oh, nothing, really. Just checking in. But hey, since you mention it, somebody just asked me how the terms would work if we cash in on one of your VC policies. If we ever had a big write down, we could just call you up and get paid, right?"

"That doesn't sound right to me, Josh. But Jack Posner happens to be right here in the conference room with me, and he wrote the claims language. Let me put him on."

Jack Posner! That was iBalls.com's attorney, too. Josh struggled to make his voice sound normal, but he could already feel the noose tightening around his neck. "Hey Jack, small world. I'd forgotten I lined you up with VC/Derivatives. So to repeat my question to Jeremy, all we have to do is show VC/Derivatives the basis for a write down and they'll pay up, right?"

"Of course not, Josh," Jack replied in a patient voice. "We'd never do such a poor job of writing a policy for a start-up you invested in. The company that you buy insurance on would have to declare bankruptcy and be liquidated first. Otherwise, how would you know that you would end up losing anything? As long as a company's still alive, it could turn out to be the next Google some day."

Jack heard a faint gurgling sound from Josh's end. He could have left it at that, but hey, life was short.

"Bummer about iBalls.com and The Pangloss Game Company, huh Josh?"

Silence. Should he give the knife a final twist? After all, this couldn't be happening to a nicer guy. And he certainly wasn't ever going to get another referral from Peabody anyway.

"I guess it's just like you always say, though. Business is business."

0000 0001 0010 0011 0100 0011 0010 0001 0000

21

Does the Dear Leader have a Rocket in his Pocket, or is he Just Happy to See Us?

THE PRESIDENT OF the United States was treating himself to an early breakfast of bacon and eggs. And why not? If a Commander-in-Chief couldn't ignore his personal physician's orders on his seventieth birthday, why bother to have the job at all?

"Ready, Mr. President?"

"Go for it, Harry."

Adlai Stevenson Harrison was the President's Director of National Intelligence. He was also one of his oldest and best friends, and one of the few advisors the President invited to visit him in the family's private quarters upstairs at the White House.

The President put on his reading glasses as Harrison handed him the Daily Brief he had completed a half hour earlier.

"Hmm. I see you've moved Korea to the top of the list. What's new since yesterday? Have they gone and sunk another South Korean boat?"

"No, nothing that dramatic. But we're worried that this time the North might push the envelope a lot farther than usual."

"Because?" The President sampled his eggs with appreciation.

"We're receiving reports that last year's crop failures were far worse than previously thought. The winter's less than half over, and we estimate that famine conditions will prevail over more than 75% of the country by February. With Kim Jong-Il looking more frail each time he pops up, we're beginning to worry that the inner circle may decide they need a more dramatic international crisis than usual to distract the population."

The President put down his fork and sat back with his coffee.

"'May decide?' According to the DB you handed me, Jong-Il is saying he's going to turn Washington instead of Seattle into a "Sea of Fire" if we back the South on that last sinking. What's the latest on their missile program?"

"The truth is, there are some new developments we're watching closely. You'll recall that the North tried to launch a satellite back in April of 2009. They used a three stage missile, and at least the third stage failed. The payload hit the ocean about 1300 miles down range. Of course, back home the regime claimed the launch was a complete success."

"That launch used a Taepodong-2 missile. Armed with a full-size warhead, it could have hit Alaska if all had gone according to plan. With a warhead half that size, we expect they could have hit one of our west coast cities. In today's speech, Jong-Il claims they're ready to not just test, but also to deploy a new version of the Taepodong - one that could hit the east coast."

"What do our folks think about that?"

"Well, the Taepodong-1 test back in 1998 blew up a few seconds after launch. The Taepodong-2 got off at least one stage, and maybe two, with good success. So they've learned a lot along the way. And their friends the Iranians have been doing very well with their missile program. We know that North Korea has sold nuclear secrets and equipment to the Iranians before, so it's not a reach to think the North may have swapped nuclear technology to Iran in exchange for help with their missile program."

"But have we seen such a missile?"

Harrison felt uncomfortable. He wished he'd delivered the next piece of information in yesterday's Daily Brief.

"As of yesterday, our satellite images were telling us the North is preparing their two most sophisticated launch pads for use. We couldn't from those images what they may be planning on sending up, but today's pictures may tell us more."

146

"So you're telling me the North Koreans may be able to hit us anywhere in the U.S. if this new missile works. What about a nuclear warhead, though? Both their first nuclear tests fizzled, right?"

"That's what we've always concluded. According to our seismic data, the yields were pretty low. But the devices clearly worked, and that's the concerning part. Once you've succeeded in refining fuel to the point of sustaining fission and demonstrated the ability to trigger that process, the rest is all details – and those details are a lot more available than we'd like to think. We've got to assume that they bought every piece of Pakistani information A. Q. Kahn was willing to sell. And also that there wasn't any information the bastard wasn't willing to sell."

"I see." The President thought he knew where this was going, and he didn't like the destination.

"The other possibility is that the tests didn't fizzle at all. We know the North hasn't been able to produce much weapons-grade fuel from the reactor they have – maybe enough for six one kiloton bombs, tops. With the two tests we've monitored, they've therefore used up at least a third of their total stockpile of enriched uranium. They can't afford to run more tests without losing the strategic value they gained by demonstrating that they've got a nuclear capability.

"But what if those weren't proof of technology tests after all? And what if they were only half kiloton bombs? If so, what we detected might have been completely successful tests of smaller, more lightweight warheads. If that's the case, they've demonstrated twice in a row that they can make a missile-deliverable warhead of dangerous size that works."

Outside, it was starting to snow. Harrison wondered whether the President was aware of it as he stared out the window, tapping his teaspoon quietly on the tablecloth. Finally, the President asked, "What do we calculate the odds are of that being the case?"

"Well, Mr. President, as you know, there's no country where we have less reliable intelligence to work with than North Korea. That means that just about everything we do have is by way of inference and conjecture, and not based on direct intelligence. So we'd be kidding ourselves if we even tried to come up with anything like a percentage estimate."

The President turned and looked at him, slightly annoyed. "Okay, let me rephrase my question. When I walk into the Oval Office today, do I, or do I not have to take their wretched 'Dear Leader's' threat seriously?"

Harrison had expected this question, and for the last twelve hours had struggled with what he would say in response. After North Korea had followed its first missile test with a second only a month later, Harrison had divided his analysts into two teams: one to argue on the data for a credible nuclear threat, and one to contend that the North's technology wasn't yet capable of delivering a nuclear warhead to the U.S. He'd spent half of last night reading and re-reading the resulting position papers. When he finally went to bed he still hadn't reached a conclusion.

Harrison saw that it was snowing heavily now. The spectral branches of the bare trees on the White House lawn were tossing in the wind. Looking into the dark turbulence of the world outside, Harrison decided he had been resisting a conclusion he was not yet willing to accept. Not for the first time, he was grateful that his friend sat behind the desk in the Oval Office and not himself.

"I'm sorry, Henry. I think that you have to assume that we've got a real problem on our hands."

The President tapped his teaspoon on the tablecloth a few more times, and then set it down neatly next to his plate. Harrison noticed that most of his eggs and bacon were uneaten.

"Well, that's that, then," his boss said quietly. He pushed a button on the phone on the table and a voice instantly answered.

"Yes, Mr. President?"

"Virginia, what times today can you open up for me without the press wondering what's going on?"

There was a pause. "10 to 10:45, and 1:30 – 3:00, Mr. President."

"Good. I'll want a one-hour meeting of the National Security Council this afternoon. Do what you need to do to clear everyone's schedule as much as possible. And I want to have that meeting somewhere where we won't attract too much attention. Can you do that?"

"I'm sure we can work that out, Mr. President. I expect that many of the Council members are out of town, so we'll need to video conference them in."

"That's great, Virginia. Thanks."

He was reaching for the speakerphone button when Virginia spoke up again.

"Happy birthday, Mr. President!"

The President turned to give his old friend a tired smile before he replied. "Yes, Virginia. Happy birthday to me."

0000 0001 0010 0011 0100 0011 0010 0001 0000

Carl Cummings was on a tear. Much too loudly, he was talking over his cell phone to his detailer back at headquarters.

"Look, damn it, this is the second time in ten days you haven't been able to give me anybody."

"C'mon, Carl, what do you expect me to do? I can't work miracles here."

Carl clutched the phone to his ear as he stared out at the street. "Do you know where I am? I'm standing behind a tree in Georgetown half a block from Saxby's, that's where I am. I'm getting covered in snow and I'm stamping my feet to stay warm and kids with backpacks are giving me weird looks like I'm some kind of pervert they should report to the campus cops. I've had about all of this I can take."

With that, the detailer decided he'd already had more than he could take. His voice switched from conciliatory to cold.

"Listen Cummings, let me give you some friendly advice. Pull out your ID and look at your hire date. You've got five years with the Company, maybe. And in case you've been too busy admiring yourself in the mirror to read the papers, we've got a couple of wars on and more hotspots popping up all the time. Some people around here have real work to do, got it? So why don't you just quit whining and get back to tailing your mark?"

Carl was about to unleash an appropriately responsive blast into his phone, but as he turned back towards the street he found himself abruptly frozen in place with his mouth open. Not three feet in front of him stood Marla Adversego, with her arms crossed and a look on her face that would stop a bull in full charge.

Carl shut and opened his mouth twice without uttering a sound, and then swallowed.

"Gotta go," he said into his phone.

Marla dropped her arms to her side as Carl stuffed his phone in his coat pocket. He noticed that her hands were rolled up into fists. Involuntarily, he took a step backwards.

Marla stepped right up to him again and hissed into his face, "You're following me, aren't you?"

Carl tried to think fast, but found that his brain was temporarily out of order.

He gave up. "Yeah. Yes. Yes I guess I am."

Marla stared at him for what seemed to him like a full minute.

"Okay, then follow me!" She turned on her heel, and walked off at a rapid pace towards the Georgetown campus.

Carl stood still for a moment, dumbfounded. Then he cursed to himself. Damn it – what choice did he have? Following her was his assignment.

For a couple of blocks, he followed a hundred feet behind Marla, feeling like an idiot. How far behind someone who's not supposed to know you're following them but does anyway do you walk?

Finally, the absurdity of the situation became too much for him. Half running, he struggled to catch up to Marla. When he got close, he called ahead, "Look, I'm sorry. This isn't like you think it is."

Marla whirled around.

"*Oh really?* And exactly what do you think I think it is?"

Carl found that he was tongue-tied again. What actually *did* he think she thought it was?

She jumped in. "You think I think you're following me because you're interested in me? Is that it? It is, isn't it? You know what? You're *pathetic!*"

She spun around and walked off once again, more briskly than before.

Carl stood stock still for a moment, and then began chasing her again, angry and bewildered at the same time. *Was* that what he had been thinking she was thinking?

He called ahead again. "Alright, *alright* – I don't know what you think this looks like. But please – stop for a minute and let me explain."

They were standing in the middle of the Georgetown quad now. It was too early for many students to have ventured out, so they were alone in the falling snow. Finally, Marla stopped, crossed her arms once again, and stared ahead without looking at him.

"Look, I know that your father isn't behind what's going on. I didn't know that at first, but I do know that now."

Marla turned around with a furious look on her face.

"Then why the hell hasn't anyone told me he's in the clear so I can tell him? What's the *matter* with you people? Do you even know what you're doing?"

Carl felt helpless, and then made some quick decisions. "I'm sorry. I can't tell you why no one's talked to you. All I can tell you is that we assume that whoever is behind the Alexandria Project must know about your father's reputation in security. If that's so, then we also have to assume they'd assume we're using your father to help catch the hackers."

Marla still looked hostile, but she was listening carefully now.

"Marla, everybody knows your Dad is the best there is. Whatever the game is that's going on here, we've got to assume that the bad guys are playing for keeps. That means that they'll do anything to get to your father and stop him from discovering who they are."

"So why *are* you following me?"

Carl looked briefly around them, and then said more softly, "Marla, I just said that they would do anything to get to your father."

Well, that made sense, didn't it? She probably was at risk, and Carl had probably been following her for weeks now. Marla suddenly felt off balance rather than angry; ten minutes ago she had been a grad student with a backpack walking to class at Georgetown, and now she was a pawn in a national crisis with a 24-hour CIA detail covering her. She needed time to think.

Distracted, Marla wondered what time it was, and turned to look towards the clock tower on the side of the quad. But it had dissolved into the falling snow. She wondered whether it was snowing where her father was, too. She could see only one of the trees dotting the quad, barely visible in the near distance; everything else was a grey void out of which ghostly, individual snowflakes swirled into view before disappearing once again. She noted with surprise that each flake looked darker, and not lighter, than the silent backdrop of the storm.

She realized that Carl was staring at her, and forced herself snap back.

"Okay," she said, once more in command. "Give me everything you've got." Then she turned and started walking again. But this time, she moved more slowly, allowing Carl to walk at her side.

0000 0001 0010 0011 0100 0011 0010 0001 0000

It was indeed snowing in Nevada, too. Unable to sleep, Frank was pacing back and forth in his clearing, waiting for dawn and for someone to take his bait of doctored iBalls. The snow was drifting, and he wondered whether he'd be able to get out of his mountain hideaway if he wanted or needed to. He'd had to fold up most of the solar panels, too, fearing they might collapse under the weight of the deepening snow. If it stayed cloudy, he'd need to use the *Avenger's* gas-powered back-up generator to keep everything running.

Lost in thought, he didn't notice how deeply the snow was building up around the path he was trampling in the snow. In the background, he could hear a muffled heartbeat, steady at seventy-two beats per minute, floating through the falling snow like the very life force of the wilderness that surrounded him.

No surprise, there. With little to relieve the anxiety of waiting to see if his master plan would work, he had returned to playing with his electronic toys. One diversion he had dreamed up was to program in a new

151

sound every day to confirm that his monitoring software was functioning properly, and another to alert him when the Alexandria Project eventually (he hoped) breached the defenses of his new honeypot.

But day after day, the alarm failed to sound. A metronome had borne witness to the first twenty-four hours of "no activity" signals from his intrusion alert software, as had full days of Pachelbel's *Canon in D Major*, the waves at Malibu, and the sounds of termites devouring a stump, pirated from an old National Geographic documentary. Frank had been up in the mountains for weeks now, and things were becoming a bit surreal even without the termites.

He couldn't help wondering if this whole enterprise wasn't a ridiculous farce. As usual, he'd been confident that he'd come up with a foolproof plan when he first thought of it. Also as usual, he was consumed with self-doubt once his strategy was not immediately validated. As he paced, he reviewed his plan over and over, questioning every assumption upon which it was based.

Abruptly, he realized how cold he felt. How long had he been walking in the clearing? To his surprise, he realized that the snow was now over a foot deep.

Frank hugged himself and shivered. He looked around the clearing for a sight of anything in the mad, dark swirl of snow, but there was nothing identifiable to be seen. The only sensations he could detect, besides the piercing cold, were the wind-driven needles of snowflakes striking his face, and the throbbing heartbeat that he felt more than heard emanating from the all-weather speakers of the camper. Just like that night when he had driven north on the endless road that disappeared into the distance of the moonlit, desert night, he felt lost in space and time. Only tonight, he felt suspended in a void of nothingness as well.

And then something changed. What was it? He tried to stop shivering, the better to concentrate on what it might be.

That was it – the heartbeats were beginning to distort. Frank unconsciously put his hand to his chest as he realized that his monitoring software was going into atrial fibrillation.

In the muffling embrace of the snow, Frank could no longer tell where the sound was coming from. He turned to his right, and then to his left, confused and listening as hard as he could. Suddenly, all was silent. Realizing the absurdity of the thought even as he had it, he wondered whether he should call 911?

He whirled around. Were the heartbeats beginning again? Or was that the sound of muffled drums?

And then, one by one, the slow, austere sound of horns swirled around him like the snowflakes – the pure, soaring opening notes of Aaron Copland's Fanfare for the Common Man.

Laughing like a madman, Frank floundered through the deepening snow in what he hoped was the direction of the *Solar Avenger*.

The Alexandria Project had taken his bait.

0000 0001 0010 0011 0100 0011 0010 0001 0000

22

What a Difference a Dong Makes!

GEORGE MARCHAND WAS ordering a mixed selection of donuts at The Bakers Dozen, a coffee shop in a small town outside the Beltway. Paying for his purchase, he asked the teenager if they had a restroom. "In the back," she said, counting out his change without looking up.

George strolled through the seating area and walked through an open door. Ignoring the two restroom entrances he found there, he began to climb a flight of stairs that rose, turned a corner, and dead-ended at a closed door.

When he arrived at the top, George saw that this door had neither a lock nor a doorknob. He slid his fingers along the right side of the door frame until he felt a recessed area. Pushing against it, he felt the door trim unlatch. George lifted it open on hidden hinges and looked for the security device that would allow him to open the door. There it was – a metal plate at head-height, painted the same color as the wood but for a small, black circle in the middle. He positioned himself so that his right eye aligned with the circle, and a light flickered on, scanning the retina of his eye. With that, the light winked out and door swung open to reveal a modest-sized room containing nothing but an inexpensive conference room table and chairs. He saw that there was another door in each of the other walls. Sitting around the table, one to a side, were two men and a women, each about his own age. One of the them was the Director of the CIA.

"How come I always have to buy the donuts?" George asked to no one in particular as he closed the door behind him.

"I guess you're just lucky, George. You want me to pick up some dry cleaning for you on my way upstairs next time?" one of the men said.

George took a seat next across from the Director, and nodded to his two co-leaders on the Alexandria Project investigation. Each of them, he knew, had entered the building through a different street level commercial establishment.

"Sure, thanks. Anyway, what's with the face-to-face meeting?"

George hadn't been to this particular room in a while, but it was typical of the dozen or so discreet locations the CIA maintained in the D.C. None of them were fancy, but all were highly secure and conveniently located for ready use when the brass wanted to hold meetings with field operatives without jeopardizing their covers. It was easy to concentrate there as well – none of their Blackberries would work with all of the shielding in the walls.

The Director replied, "Actually, this isn't a face-to-face meeting at all. For the record, this is just a social get together. It's been much too long since we've had a chance to enjoy each others' company and shoot the breeze, don't you think? No need to enter this in your logbooks."

George raised his eyebrows and said nothing as he passed the box of donuts around. This was different.

The Director peered into the donut box and settled on one with cinnamon sugar.

"You know, this is my favorite secure meeting room. Best donuts anywhere. And it's always someone else's treat."

"Anyway, I had an interesting meeting over at Homeland Security yesterday. We covered a lot of ground, and finally got around to the Alexandria Project investigation. Of course our good friends from the FBI were there as well."

Ah, George thought. Now he knew what the topic was. The House Cybersecurity Subcommittee hearing had been an ugly exercise for all concerned. Chairman Steele's strategy had been to pit the CIA and the FBI against each other. One of them, he claimed, must be asleep at the switch, so which one was it? With each question, Steele had turned up the heat, trying to goad each witness into revealing some detail that would provide him with an opening to attack the other.

The CIA Director had declined to play the Chairman's game at first, but his opposite number at the FBI had willingly played ball. Ever since 9/11, the FBI had felt like its domestic turf was being invaded from all sides. Subjecting itself to the authority of the new Department of Homeland Security had been bad enough. But sharing responsibility for domestic cybersecurity with the CIA had really put a burr under the FBI's saddle.

Without ever accusing the CIA of anything in particular, the FBI Director implied that every point of weakness and responsibility on the cybersecurity front clearly lay on the CIA's side of the equation. And after all, how could the FBI protect America if it didn't own the entire project?

Relations between the two agencies hadn't benefited from the hearing, George knew. He listened with interest to hear what the CIA Director had to say.

"It was quite an interesting meeting. Now that I think of it, you might say we picked up right where we left off at the end of the Steele hearing. If I didn't know that we were all on the same team, I might have even gotten the impression the FBI sees this whole Alexandria Project investigation as their big chance to kick our butts out of the country - and then take our passports away so we can't come back."

The Director let that sink in for a moment as he dunked his donut in his coffee and took a bite.

"So you might want to keep your wits about you till this situation is resolved. You might even want to look over your shoulder now and then to see if our valued allies over at FBI headquarters are keeping an eye on you as closely as they're keeping an eye out for the bad guys. It may be that they're watching us even more closely."

George and the others exchanged sidelong glances.

The Director finished his donut and wiped his hands on a napkin. "You know, we really ought to do this more often. It seems like we never have time to enjoy each others' company anymore. And I really do enjoy a good donut now and then."

The Director stood up and smiled, and the others followed his lead. A moment later, four doors closed silently and the room was empty once more.

0000 0001 0010 0011 0100 0011 0010 0001 0000

Marla Adversego, it seemed, needed a book to read and was having trouble making up her mind. It looked like a good mystery novel might do the trick, but nothing seemed to be just right. Even after fifteen minutes at Amazon.com she still hadn't found a book that quite made the grade, no matter how many "people who bought this book also bought" links she clicked on and reader reviews she read. Finally she seemed to have found just what she was looking for in one reader review, and stared at the screen intently while scribbling a few notes on a pad of paper.

Almost as an afterthought, she punched a few more keys, and bought David Baldacci's latest thriller to give credibility to her time online.

A few minutes later, Marla picked up her phone, dialed a local number, and waited for the "Hello?" at the other end.

"Coffee?"

There was a pause, and then a surprised voice said, "Sure. Where?"

Marla gave an address. "See you in a half an hour."

0000 0001 0010 0011 0100 0011 0010 0001 0000

President Rawlings looked across the broad cabinet table somberly. How old was this particular piece of furniture, he wondered? How many presidents had sat exactly where he did today to decide whether to take a step closer to war? Could he decide as wisely? He grasped the edge of the table with both hands, as if to draw wisdom and strength from its smooth, solid weight.

But if the table had any wisdom to offer, it wasn't sharing any today. So the President cleared his throat and the subdued chatter around the table rapidly subsided.

"Good morning. You all know the topic of today's meeting, so let's get started. General Hayes, please give us the aerial surveillance update."

Brigadier General Fletcher Hayes had never attended a National Security Council meeting before, and he was determined not to show it. More of an academic than a field officer, he was as conscious as the President of the historical precedents for the presentation he was about to give. Who, he wondered, had delivered the aerial recon review to President Kennedy in this same room at the beginning of the Cuban Missile Crisis?

Hayes rose from his seat, and nodded to the four subordinates that were standing next to the empty easels placed in the corners of the room. Each assistant placed a four by six foot satellite photo on his or her easel.

Hayes began to speak. "The picture you see was taken at 1200 local time today by one of our satellites over North Korea. What you are looking at is Launch Pad 10 at the North's main military launch facility. As you can see, there is a missile in position next to the gantry, and the area is clear of any supporting vehicles. From this we conclude that the missile is ready to go, except for fueling. In other words, it can become fully operational within approximately twelve hours of an order to initiate the launch sequence."

On signal, the assistants placed a nearly identical picture on the easels.

"And this is a photo of a missile in a similar state of readiness on Launch Pad 12. The question is, what sort of missiles are we looking at?"

The General motioned once more to his assistants, and this time they placed a large diagram on the easels that displayed a series of increasingly larger rockets, together with a map with concentric circles centering on North Korea.

"Here you see the four largest known missiles in the arsenal of the North, from smallest to largest – the Scud C Upgrade, the Nodong, both in yellow, and the Taepodong 1 and Taepodong 2 – the two missiles in blue. The map in the upper right shows the presumed range of each launch vehicle. As you will note, the largest circle shows that the range of the Taepodong-2 missile, carrying a conventional nuclear warhead, would reach Alaska. With a lighter payload, we assume it could reach the Pacific Northwest.

"Now let's return to our surveillance photos." The General nodded to his assistants, and a new blow-up appeared on the easels.

"What you see on the left half of this display is Launch Pad 10 once again, but this time the photo was taken later on the same day, at 1645 local time – just before sunset. The picture you see on the right hand side was also taken just before sunset, but this picture was taken on April 4, 2012. The missile in this picture is the Taepodong-2 missile the North launched with partial success the next day.

"Now if you open the folder in front of each of you, you will find a diagram with the outlines of two multi-stage missiles, with the larger of the two superimposed over the smaller. These outlines were created to the same scale, and were produced by measuring the shadows that you see on the pictures on the easel after compensating for the change of seasons."

"As you can tell from the scale on the left side of the diagram, the larger of the two missiles is about 20% taller than the smaller one. If you look carefully at the silhouettes, you will see that this difference results entirely from the extension of the second stage. The third stage appears to be unchanged, with no increase in the size of either the delivery or the payload sections."

"Finally, you will note that the silhouette of the first stage of the larger missile is much broader, by reason of the addition of a booster rocket on each side of the main launch vehicle."

"Our assumption is, therefore, that what we see on the launch pads now are indeed the Taepodong-3 missiles that Kim Jong-Il claimed a week ago he intended to target at the U.S."

The General paused. "Are there any questions so far?"

The room was silent. Then the President spoke.

"General Hayes, do we believe that any of the components of the larger rocket are new?"

"Excellent question, sir. Unfortunately, for all practical purposes the answer is 'no.' The first and third stages appear to be identical to those of the Taepodong-2, while the larger second stage is also the same as the one used with the Taepodong-2, except with larger fuel and oxygen tanks made possible by the added thrust supplied by the booster rockets added to the launch configuration. Increasing the size of those components presents no new engineering challenges of any significance. And the size and shape of the booster rockets is an exact match to the solid fuel rockets the North has been successfully launching for years."

"Have they successfully launched mixed solid and liquid fuel configurations before?"

"Yes, sir, they have."

"Thank you General. Please proceed."

Hayes nodded to his assistants.

"What you see superimposed over this map of North America are arcs that represent the ranges that we believe a missile of the size of the Taepodong-3 would have, based upon differing payload weights."

The Council members peered especially intently at this map. The first arc approximately followed the line of the Rockies, while the second took in Chicago, St. Louis, Dallas, and Houston. The third arc included the entire United States, except for the bottom third of Florida.

"More specifically, these arcs relate to payloads equivalent to 4,000, 3,000, and 2,000 pounds in weight."

The President spoke up again. "And how did you select those weights, General? Are they arbitrary, or do they have particular significance?"

The General chose his words carefully. "Mr. President, we were using a variety of educated guesses when we chose the weights for this particular purpose. Essentially, they represent a range of assumptions based upon the level of sophistication that the North Koreans may have achieved in the design of their nuclear weaponry as it correlates to weapon weight and force. If that sophistication is high, then the current weight of their nuclear warheads may be as much as half that of a crude device."

"Depending upon which of those assumptions proves to be accurate, the arcs therefore represent the current capability of the North to deliver a 1 kiloton nuclear warhead to the continental U.S., assuming that their delivery vehicle operates to full design potential."

"One last question, General. Have your people formed any opinion on the probable weight of the payload the third stage of these rockets is intended to carry, based on the available volume of the third stage?"

"Yes, Mr. President, they have."

"And that opinion is?"

"Between 1800 and 2100 pounds, sir."

"Thank you very much, General. I'm sure we'll be inviting you to join us again soon."

0000 0001 0010 0011 0100 0011 0010 0001 0000

Carl Cummings saw Marla sitting in the window of the coffee shop in Alexandria, Virginia where she had asked him to meet her. He paused at the counter to buy a cup for himself, and then joined her. Ever since their walk in the snow on the Georgetown campus, Carl had been finding his bachelor flat especially depressing. All of his good friends were married now, and his evening options had narrowed to not much more than channel surfing. Was this meeting intended for business reasons, or, dare he hope it, for getting re-acquainted?

One look at Marla as she glanced up to greet him answered that question.

"Ah, there you are," she said. "Have a seat."

Carl did as he was told. "Any luck?" he asked.

Marla looked around discretely and then in a low voice said *"Yes!"*

Carl stirred his coffee and considered his next question. He now knew from Marla that Frank and she were indeed communicating online, but he knew better than to ask how. He could tell that Marla was still of two minds over whether she could rely on him completely, and Carl was unsure how to gain her full trust.

"How much luck?" he asked quietly.

"We've got a location."

Carl tried not to show surprise; there were people not far away. "That's excellent. Where?"

Marla did not reply immediately. Instead, she stared out the window uneasily. Frank had decided to gamble on letting her work with Carl up to a point, but he clearly still had his doubts. The responsibility of being right about Carl therefore weighed heavily on Marla's shoulders.

Still, what choice did she have? They needed to catch the Alexandria Project operatives before Frank could consider himself in the clear. But while cyber sleuthing was up Frank's alley, physically catching potential terrorists was not. Anyway, so long as Frank stayed in hiding, what did they have to lose?

Best to go ahead and take the plunge then. Marla set her coffee cup down and pointed across the street with her chin. Carl looked through the window at the storefront he saw there. A sign over its door read "Alexandria Antiquarian Bookstore."

"Where?" Carl asked, confused.

This time, Marla pointed unmistakably at the store front with one finger.

"There."

0000 0001 0010 0011 0100 0011 0010 0001 0000

23

Fancy Meeting You Here!

"*THERE?* THAT DUSTY old bookstore? That's where you think the Alexandria Project that's trying to take down all of western civilization is based?"

"Yes, "that dusty old bookstore"! And don't talk so loud!" Marla snapped. "My father's certain that's where the attacks are coming from. We're in Alexandria, right? So it all ties together. And in case you've forgotten, the first gripe the Alexandria Project mentioned in the letter they sent George Marchand was about the Library of Congress pulping books, so why not a bunch of book fanatics?" Marla gave him a hostile look as she blew her nose, and Carl noticed for the first time that she had a bad cold.

"Okay, okay. It's just not what I had expected. But don't worry, I'll take it from here."

""*I'll* take it from here?" What's that supposed to mean?" Marla was more than annoyed now.

Carl looked surprised. "You know, I'll report in to headquarters. We'll comb the store without the owners knowing anything, and if we can find the right evidence, we'll arrest them."

"Right." Marla said. "Now you're using the right pronoun. That's just what *we'll* do – you, headquarters – and *me*."

Carl looked as alarmed as he felt. "Now, Marla, come on – this is highly technical work, and dangerous, too! You can't expect to be part of it."

But Carl was now talking to the back of a newspaper, so he stopped. Okay, if that's the way she wanted it, that's how she could have it. He grabbed his coat and started to get up. He'd just to get a search warrant and….

Carl stood next to the table for a moment. Now exactly how would he get that search warrant? As of now, he didn't know diddley squat what he might find in the Alexandria Antiquarian Bookstore. As a matter of fact, he didn't have anything at all to tell the judge other than what he had just heard, and Marla could deny that if she wanted to.

Carl suppressed his annoyance with difficulty. He cleared his throat and then started speaking again, this time with a note of pleading in his voice. "Now please, Marla, let's just be reasonable here…."

0000 0001 0010 0011 0100 0011 0010 0001 0000

Half an hour later, Carl was sitting in his car, dialing George Marchand. Marla had declined to be reasonable.

"George, Carl. Good news, bad news time here. The good news is that Marla just gave me the location that Frank thinks the Alexandria Project's operating out of. It's an old book store in Alexandria."

"How sure is Frank?"

"She says he's dead certain, but she wouldn't say how he knows. Anyway, it looks like it should be an easy place to check out. If we can get a warrant this afternoon, we could even get in there tonight – it closes at 1700, and it looks like the store takes up the whole building. No apartments or offices upstairs."

"So what's the problem? That's why Homeland Security's got its own judge on call, 24/7. Get down there with Marla and have her swear out an affidavit and let's get cooking."

"Well, now, that takes us to the bad news. Marla says she's not going to sign an affidavit unless I let her go into the building with us. She says she doesn't trust us yet. She says she's worried that we'll just disappear the Alexandria Project guys and Frank won't have any proof that someone else was responsible for what's going on. She wants to be a witness to whatever we find so we can't leave her father out to dry."

George thought for a moment. Marla was his goddaughter, and she might believe him if he came clean with her. But that would mean revealing his other life with the CIA to her. He took a deep breath.

"Okay. So here's what we're going to do."

0000 0001 0010 0011 0100 0011 0010 0001 0000

At 4:45 that afternoon, a man in coveralls with "Able Locksmiths" embroidered across his back was sitting at the same table in the same coffee shop in which Carl and Marla had been arguing that morning. He took his time finishing his coffee as he watched the sales clerk through the plate glass window of the Alexandria Antiquarian Bookstore across the street. At last, two people were lined up at the cash register. Picking up the bag of tools by his feet, he left the coffee shop and walked quickly across the street.

Entering the bookstore, he interrupted the clerk with an apologetic smile. "Pardon me, ma'am. Where's the lock with the problem?"

"Excuse me? What lock?"

"Back door lock. The one that's sticking."

The clerk looked confused. "There's only one back door. It's through the curtain in the back and down a few stairs."

"Thanks – have it fixed for you in a jiffy."

He walked away before she could reply. Once past the curtain, he knelt by the back door and examined its ancient lock carefully, looking for name of the manufacturer. Finding it, he pulled an enormous ring of master keys out of his tool bag, and riffled through them till he found the right section of skeleton keys. He selected one and tried it; no luck; another; no luck.

On his third try, the lock opened easily. To be on the safe side, he tried it from the outside as well. Perfect..

He stretched a rubber sleeve over the key to mark it, and stood up. A minute later, he was walking past the clerk as she counted out the cash register for the day.

"I wish every repair was that easy," he said cheerfully to the clerk, giving her a warm smile. "Couple shots of powdered graphite, and she was as good as new."

"Do we owe you anything?"

"Nah, I had another job just up the street, so my travel time's already covered. No charge – this'll be my good deed for the day."

And with that, he was gone.

0000 0001 0010 0011 0100 0011 0010 0001 0000

Half a world away in Pyongyang, Kim Jong-Il, Supreme Commander of the People's Army and Chairman of the National Defense Commission of North Korea, was presiding over a strategy session with the top civil and military leaders of his government. He looked tired and detached as the ranking commander of the Korean Peoples Army, General Chan Bach Choy, finished his presentation.

"We can begin fueling the missiles the moment you give the order, Dear Leader. Just over eleven hours later they can be on their way – of course, only on your command."

"And the troops, General? When will they be fully deployed?"

"As you know, 85% of the People's Army, about 1,000,000 troops, are always deployed along the Demilitarized Zone. We've added another 50,000, but we've also been moving random companies closer to the DMZ to create uncertainty as to how many additional troops have been deployed and what we have in mind. This has forced the South to keep repositioning its forces defensively in response, keeping their leadership off balance. In addition, all leaves have been canceled beginning yesterday. Our forces will therefore increase daily as those already on leave return."

The General looked at the Dear Leader confidently. "Of course we have also activated and begun moving 2,000,000 of the Red Guards into position just behind the regular troops."

Kim Jong-Il looked back in surprise. He inclined his one good hand slightly so that the General would pause, and then beckoned Kim Lang-Dong, the President of the Supreme People's Assembly to his side. "Did I order the Red Guard into position?" he asked in a hoarse whisper. "I don't recall authorizing that."

"Of course you did, sir. At our meeting last week. And I must say that it was one of your most brilliant decisions. Never before in one of our manufactured crises have we called the Red Guard to the DMZ. Your daring took our breath away, and the West has reacted just as we hoped. Never before have they taken us so seriously...."

Kim Jong-Il leaned back into his seat in confusion. He knew that his memory had become unreliable since his stroke the year before, and that he needed to rely on those around him for support. But lately his understanding of important matters seemed to be more frequently inaccurate or incomplete, and that concerned him. Hesitantly, he gestured to the General to continue.

"The Red Guards will be fully positioned by Friday. We will then be ready to conduct the missile tests when you give the word."

Jong-Il sat up in his chair and stared at the general, who paused. After a moment, Jong-Il gestured to him to approach as well.

The Dear Leader felt confused; was he forgetting what the entire plan was all about? Hadn't the intention been simply to scare the West by letting their spy satellites see the refueling begin? Wouldn't that, plus the deployment of extra regular troops to the DMZ, be sufficient to finally bring the U.S. unilaterally to the bargaining table at last?

Bach Choy was now standing before him. "Tests, General?" Jong-Il whispered to him.

"Of course, Dear Leader. Just as you described in your private instructions to me ten days ago. Is the time not ripe for me to reveal your master strategy to the others, sir?"

Kim Jong-Il felt concerned. What could he say? He nodded slightly and strained to make sense of what he would hear once the General had resumed his place at the rostrum.

"We must test the Taepodong III before we know that we can credibly threaten the West with our nuclear weapons. We must also know whether America's anti-nuclear defenses can truly destroy our rockets mid-flight or not. Their Joint Chiefs claim they can, but their own civilian experts say they can't."

"Of course, we will not really allow our missiles to pass a point in flight at which the U.S. might retaliate in kind. But that point is beyond the line at which the American's anti-missile interceptors will destroy our missiles if they are capable of doing so. And it is also past the point in the flight plan at which the third stage of our missiles will fire, so we will be able to perform the full test."

General Bach Choy extended a congratulatory arm towards Jong-Il.

"Your idea, Dear Leader, of destroying our own missiles just before the point of retaliation is a stroke of pure genius. If our missiles fail, or if the enemy destroys one or both of them, we can still claim to our people that we destroyed them after having proven their capabilities, and we can use the test results to perfect our designs."

"But if even one of our missiles is destroyed by us, then Washington will know fear. And the Yankees will have no choice but to come to the bargaining table."

The Dear Leader nodded. Now he understood everything. It was a good plan indeed. One of his best plans ever.

0000 0001 0010 0011 0100 0011 0010 0001 0000

Frank was sitting in a folding chair in his clearing, enjoying an unexpectedly warm midday sun. The ground was bare – all of the snows of the recent blizzard had been swept away by the fierce rains that followed a few days later. Like the weather, Frank's plans were once again in a lull, with nothing technical let to do. He was desperate to hear from Marla whether or not the Alexandria Project culprits had been flushed out and captured.

Too wired to work, and with no real work to do anyway, Frank sat in the sun. He hoped that the sound of the scrub jays, the sun, and the mild breezes would relax him.

It wasn't working. He forced himself to sit there, grimly determined to make himself relax, or bore himself to death trying. Steadfastly, he looked out over the valley until a far away sparkle of light on the mountain ridge to the south caught his eye. That was strange; he had followed the Jeep track up in that direction once when he was lost in thought, trying to work out a particularly difficult issue. Eventually, the track had faded into not much more than a livestock path. He couldn't remember encountering anything at all in that direction – no collapsed cabin with broken glass windows to catch the sun; not even a discarded beer can.

A minute later, he saw a flash of light again. This time it seemed slightly closer. Without thinking much about it, he shifted his chair so that he could watch more comfortably. No longer tense, he watched, fascinated, as the flashes of reflected sunlight appeared and disappeared, ever so slowly creeping along the mountainside and heading generally in his direction. He remembered that he had seen a pair of binoculars hanging inside the truck, and went to fetch them.

Settling back into his folding chair, he rested his elbows on its arms and searched the rocky slope where the light had last appeared. To his surprise, he saw what looked like a Jeep laboriously picking its way across the slope, its fenders rocking up and down and from side to side as the driver eased the vehicle across the uneven terrain.

Frank cradled the binoculars in his lap. What might this be all about? He hadn't seen a soul in more than a month. Could whoever this was be looking for him, and if so, why?

Frank felt suddenly self conscious. He realized that his clearing was a mess. Beer cans, water bottles, and random bits of camping equipment were scattered everywhere. He began tidying up. If he was going to have company, he might as well not look like a total slob.

Then he returned to his chair to watch and wait.

0000 0001 0010 0011 0100 0011 0010 0001 0000

Carl and Marla parked their car on a side street a half a block from the Alexandria Antiquarian Book Store and walked towards the alley that ran behind it. Just as they reached it, a man stepped out to meet them.

"George! What are you doing here?"

Carl tried to look innocent. "Sorry, Marla – I guess I forgot to mention this part of the plan to you." Actually, it had been simple payback. He wanted to regain some measure of control over the situation and was determined to keep Marla in the dark as much as he possibly could. "We needed someone in a hurry to hack whatever systems we might find here, and since no IT expert has more experience dealing with the Alexandria Project than George, we thought we'd see whether we could enlist his help. Luckily for us, he said yes."

Marla nodded to George and blew her nose. "Okay. Now what?"

Carl looked up and down the street. "Just keep chatting while I find the right door and unlock it. When I wave, walk naturally up the alley until you reach me."

Carl waited until the main street at the end of the block was empty of pedestrians, and then strode off into the shadows of the alley.

"How are you, George? I haven't seen you since that wonderful Christmas party."

George looked uncomfortable. "Fine, Marla, just fine." Now what should he say? "I hope you don't mind my asking, but how's your father?"

Now it was Marla who wasn't sure how to reply. What would her father want her to say? With relief, she saw a dark shape step out of the shadows down the alley and wave to them. "Let's go," she said and began walking.

Three buildings down, they found Carl with his hand on the knob of a door. He held his index finger to his lips, and then silently swung the door open. As they entered, he turned on a pen-sized flashlight that cast a pale red circle of light on the threshold of the entrance. Then he closed the door behind them.

The three stood silently just inside as Carl cast his light in every direction. Finally, he pointed his flashlight at a door in the corner of the room and whispered, "We've already had someone check out the rest of the first floor today, posing as a customer. Unless there's something in the attic, whatever's here to find must be down the stairs behind that door. Follow me and test every step as you go."

Carl crossed the darkened room, opened the door, and began to descend slowly and gingerly, placing his weight gradually on each stair tread as he crept downward, holding his flashlight in one hand and sliding the other along the wall to steady him. After a few steps, he stopped and listened, turning to face the other two, a question on his face.

Marla strained to hear; yes, she heard something as well – muffled voices, almost certainly. She nodded affirmatively. More carefully than ever, they eased their way downwards until they reached a closed door.

They could all clearly hear voices now, but it was difficult to catch more than the occasional word with certainty. Carl knelt down and set his flashlight on a step, taking care not to allow its light to shine under the door. Then he took a slim package from his coat pocket, opened it, and removed a device the size of an iPod. Silently, he unwound the two wires wrapped around it. At the end of one was a suction cup, which he licked and pressed against the door. Then he pressed the bud at the end of the other wire into his ear, and moved a switch on the tiny recording device.

What he heard was both bizarre as well as much better than any data he might have hoped to lift off the computer server had come to find. He listened intently, watching the sound meter on the recorder.

"What is your conclusion, then, Callimachus?"

"The public cannot be expected to put up with these cyber attacks much longer. With each wave, they become more furious and distrustful. Some are starting to withdraw their money from banks, fearing that their accounts may be falsified and their money disappear. If the attacks continue much longer, the entire financial system will be in danger of collapse."

"And you, Aristarchus?"

"I agree. A few more well-publicized attacks, and entire segments of commerce will begin shutting down as people realize how vulnerable they are when computerized systems are compromised. Oil, food, and gasoline supplies have already been disrupted. Soon, airlines will begin canceling flights for lack of traffic because people are growing afraid to fly; hospitals will empty out because patients will worry that their medical records may have been altered without their doctors' knowledge. When elections are held this fall, voters won't trust the results."

Then a voice asked, "Zenodotus, what shall we do?"

There was a pause. Then a tired voice said, "Who would have imagined how dramatically and quickly our most dire claims would be proven? The plan we put in motion a few short months ago has succeeded beyond our wildest dreams. Who could have expected what has happened?"

And that's a wrap, Carl thought as he disengaged the microphone and confirmed that the recorder had worked properly. Excellent! Time to get back to the street as quickly and quietly as possible and call in the boys with the body armor to arrest the culprits, whoever they might be. All the three of them needed to do now was watch the doors from the outside in case the meeting ended too soon.

But as Carl turned around to motion the others upstairs, he saw that Marla's face was bizarrely contorted. And one of her hands was rolled up in a fist, pressed against her lips. Carl's eyes widened as he wondered what the hell was wrong with her.

Then the reality of the impending disaster hit him. He threw up his hands in a silent gesture of "Stop!" just as Marla unleashed an explosive sneeze.

All three of them froze and listened. There was a sudden silence on the other side of the door.

Damn! No choice now! Carl spun around, drawing his Beretta from his shoulder holster at the same time as he slammed his other shoulder against the door. Bursting through, he hit the floor in a shooter's crouch. *"Freeze!"* he bellowed, in the loudest and most threatening voice he could muster. Blinded by the sudden light of the room, he gripped his gun in both hands, jerking it from side to side in order to cover however many people might be in the room he was struggling to see. Behind him, George and Marla crouched on the bottom-most stairs.

As it happened, Carl could hardly have asked for a more obedient audience to obey his command. Still blinking, he realized that six startled, elderly men were seated around a table. Two wore beards. Four wore tweed jackets. All wore expressions of shock and awe. In front of each was a small stemmed glass, and in the middle of the table stood a crystal decanter containing a brown liquid.

A man with the voice of Zenodotus was the first to collect himself. "I presume you'll be reading us our Miranda whatevers now?"

Carl could not yet speak. Which was just as well, as CIA agents didn't have authority to read Miranda rights anyway.

Zenodotus continued helpfully. "Perhaps a glass of sherry, then?"

With that, Carl recovered his wits, and sternly instructed them, "Everyone put your hands on the table where I can see them."

Twelve hands were immediately placed on the table. Each dignified gentleman laced his fingers together and sat straight up in his chair. Carl felt like he was addressing a Sunday school class.

The man they called Zenodotus sighed. "Why don't you all just have a seat and make yourselves comfortable? Clearly, we have a bit of explaining to do, and then you can take us to wherever it is that you should. To tell the truth, it will be quite a relief to all of us if you would."

0000 0001 0010 0011 0100 0011 0010 0001 0000

Frank was actually relaxing, fascinated by the slow approach of the tiny, distant vehicle as it worked its way around boulders, across depressions, and finally onto the Jeep track he had explored a few weeks before.

170

Although he was the polar opposite of a social animal, Frank had been in isolation for a long time. He was also very out of touch, he realized. Not once had he used the satellite dish to pull in a TV or radio signal, and the only online news he'd pulled up related to the Alexandria Project. For all he knew, the world had ended and he and the mystery driver were the last men alive.

Eventually, the vehicle reached the treeline and disappeared. Perhaps a little news from the outside wouldn't be a bad thing to hear, Frank thought. He set out a second chair, and a cooler with a six-pack of beer on ice in between. Why not? he thought, and opened one up to help pass the time.

Not long afterward, he heard the distant growl of an engine in low gear, and soon he glimpsed a vehicle as it lurched into view between the Ponderosa pines. It was an ancient, boxy car with a high wheel base, a spare tire mounted on the front hood, and a tubular roof rack the length of the four-door body. At last, the odd vehicle wheeled into Frank's clearing and came to a halt.

It seemed only polite to stand up, so Frank did. When the driver swung open the door and stepped out, Frank saw to his surprise that it was the desert rat he had met at the Little A'Le'Inn.

"Howdy," the old man said as he walked in a jerky fashion across the clearing. "Ah me! These old bones just don't handle a rough ride like they used to."

Frank motioned to one of the folding chairs. "Have a seat, then. Beer?"

"Don't mind if I do; don't mind if I do." With another loud, "Ah me!" he settled into the chair.

Frank opened the cooler, and handed him a cold one. "What brings you up here?"

"Well, I reckoned that if I sent a city boy like you way the hell up here, p'raps I ought to come check in on ya once't to be sure the bears hadn't et ya up. Here's to ya!"

The old man took a long pull on his bottle. "Ah me!" he said once again, this time smacking his lips loudly. "Yup! That hit the spot." Then he looked around the clearing. "But it looks like you're doing okay up here, so I guess I was worrying about nuth'n. Glad to see it. Hate to have had somethin' unfortunate on my conscience. It's got enough to keep it busy already." He gave Frank a grin and said, "Here's to ya!" again.

Quite a character, Frank thought to himself. Straight out of central casting for a Western movie. "That's some car you have there. What is it?"

"Land Rover – '58. Back from when they could go anywhere, do anything. Not like them bogus sedans that set ya back a fortune that they're push'n out now. Huh! Bought it in '69 used and I've kept it on the road ever since. Noth'n else like it. Body's aluminum – lasts forever, if'n you don't wrap it around a tree. I hoisted her up and put a new chassis under her in '93. Hope that one lasts longer than I do." He grinned at Frank again.

"Well, you certainly know how to drive it. I've been watching you work your way over that ridge and down here for the last two hours. Why didn't you just come up the way I did?"

"Well, you know, I remembered as how you didn't want any company up here, and if I'd a laid a new set of tire tracks up from the road down below, it'd kind of advertise that someone's up here, now wouldn't it? Anyway's, it's a nice day for a Sunday drive, now ain't it?"

Some Sunday drive, Frank thought, as he realized he didn't have the foggiest notion whether it was Sunday or not.

"Well, I guess," was all he could think of to say as he began to worry: why should the old man have gone so far out of his way to protect Frank's privacy? He couldn't think of a good reason.

"So I see ya found yourself a real nice place to settle in under them trees you was a-look'n for." He paused, and gave Frank another sideways look. "Say, what is it about them pines, anyway, that speaks to ya?"

Frank shifted uncomfortably in his chair. "Well, you see, I was somewhere out here before, a long, long time ago. Coming from back East, I'd never seen country like this before. And those trees, so tall and straight and set out at a distance from each other like it was some kind of well-tended park just seemed, well, sort of majestic, I guess."

Frank turned his head and pointed to a stand of shorter trees. "And I remember trees like those over there, too, the ones with the light gray bark and the fluttery leaves."

"Aspens," the old man said quietly, watching Frank closely as he picked up speed.

"And I remember the bright sunshine and the clear, crisp air and the endless, blue, blue sky out here – it was like everything was in a Kodachrome picture. I'd never seen anything like that before. Once I got back home, I never saw anything like it again." Frank stopped abruptly, lost in memories.

The old man sat for a little while, and then asked gently. "Out here alone, was ya?"

Frank watched the setting sun, mesmerized by the sudden flood of memories he'd been suppressing ever since he had arrived. "No, no, not at all. I was just eleven, you see. I was out here with my dad. It was in the summer and the garage he'd been working at had gone out of business, so one day he just said, "Let's you and me go see the U.S.A." And that's what we did. Just him and me, we loaded up this old Jeep he had – he was a hell of a mechanic – with a bunch of camping gear, and off we went."

"We drove non-stop till we hit the Mississippi, me sleeping half the time in the back seat and him driving all the time in the front. Once we crossed the big river, he gave this big sigh of relief. He'd woken me up just a few minutes before so I wouldn't miss the river as we crossed it, and when we reached the other side, he broke into this big grin, and said, "At last I can breathe again!""

Frank had forgotten that moment until just now. I wonder what he meant by that, he wondered?

The old man rolled his beer bottle slowly between his weathered hands and didn't look up. "You still get together with him when you can?"

"Hah!" Frank spat the word out. "I wouldn't walk across the street to get together with my dad – assuming he's still alive. That fall, the one after we went out West, he skipped out on my mother and me and I never saw or heard from him again. Left us high and dry. No warning. Just like that."

There was silence for awhile as the sunset dimmed before them. Finally, the old man said quietly, "Not meaning to pry or nuth'n, ya know, but why you figure he did that?"

"How the hell should I know? My mom never talked about it. One day I just came home and she said, "Your father's gone." That was it. Just "Your father's gone," and I couldn't get another word out of her." Frank shook his head, staring at the sunset, his brow furrowed.

For a full five minutes the two sat in their chairs in the gathering darkness, each alone with his thoughts. Finally, Frank spoke. "You know, I lied to you a little while ago. I *would* walk across the street to see that bastard again, but just to ask him one, simple question – ask him why he walked out on us." Frank stopped and choked up a bit, "Why he walked out on *me*."

The old man looked down at his beer bottle again, and then turned his gaze up to the now dark sky. He found the Big Dipper, and then followed the pointer stars. There it was – the North Star. Was that really the way he should go, he wondered?

Finally, he made his decision and lowered his gaze. He pulled his wallet out of the pocket of his jeans, and slowly slid something out of it. He gave it a brief, fond look in the dim light shining out of the truck behind them, and then he gently placed the dog-eared, black and white picture on Frank's knee. Frank reached out to pick it up, and then stared at it in wonder. In the picture, a child sat on a man's shoulders. Both were smiling, and above them soared tall, ram-rod straight trees with heavily veined bark.

The old man abruptly looked away, and cleared his throat. Then Frank heard a long forgotten, but now much older voice, say with a pronounced Brooklyn accent, "Well, son, I guess now you've got your chance."

0000 0001 0010 0011 0100 0011 0010 0001 0000

24

Sarin? You Thought I Said Sarin?

GENERAL CHAN BACH Choy, ranking officer of the People's Army of North Korea, was walking across a broad plaza at the side of the President of the Supreme People's Assembly. They had just left a meeting with the Dear Leader, and had only a few minutes to converse without being overheard by their aides, or by those in the listening rooms that monitored the microphones that were everywhere.

General Bach Choy knew that they were not completely safe from surveillance even here. Certainly some member of the Secret Police was filming them from a hidden location using a telescopic lens, so that another agent could try to read their lips. The General therefore walked with his head owed and his hands clasped behind his back. Being at the top of the chain of command in the paranoid, otherworld of North Korea meant you were always being spied on by everyone else in the inner circle. And, of course, you were spying on them as well.

President Kim Lang-Dong spoke first.

"Are you sure that you can destroy both Washington and New York, General?"

"There can be no doubt." The General smiled to himself. He had made no effort to bring the President more deeply into his plan than necessary. No need for the President to know about 'Mrs. Foomjoy' or any of the other flowers in the General's garden of espionage that had bloomed so successfully.

The President would have liked to question him more closely, but there was so little time. And in any event, the most important part of the plan was not to destroy these cities, but to depose the much despised clan of Kim Jong-Il for good.

"And the rest of the plan – that is in place as well?"

"Most of that will take care of itself. Just before the missiles are fired, Jong-Il and his three sons will take their places in their private bunker. He doesn't trust them more than he does anyone else, and especially the oldest one, Kim Jong-Nam, now that everyone knows the youngest son has been anointed as his father's successor."

"Excellent. But how do you know we can trust the oldest one?"

"You needn't worry. I am quite convinced he cannot wait to perform his appointed function. He secretly loathes his father, and he doesn't trust Kim Jong-un, the new heir apparent, for even a moment. Why should he? Only one faction can take power when Jong-il is dead. It would be so sad if some unfortunate accident were to befall him, so that one of the other available sons could be propped up in his place. The only question is which son will get rid of which brothers as soon as Kim Jong-Il is in his grave – so why wait?"

The President nodded. The logic was as sound to him as it must be to the three sons.

"What will be the means of the final step?"

"The oldest son will be wearing a wrist watch with a vial of Sarin hidden inside. When Jong-Il and the sons are sealed in the bunker and receive news that the attack has been launched, he will push one of the buttons on the watch, and the liquid will vaporize. There will be more than enough gas to kill everyone in the room within minutes."

The President stopped and stared at him. "But General...why would he do such a thing if he, too, would die?"

"Because we have given him a second present as well. That one is a gelatin capsule that he will slip discretely into his mouth before releasing the Sarin. He will rely on the capsule containing atropine and pralixidome, the two antidotes for Sarin contamination, to protect him while he watches his brothers and father writhe and die."

The President was confused. "But General, what then?"

The General smiled. "Mr. President, just because he *relies* on the capsule to contain the antidotes does not mean the capsule will in fact *contain* them. But he will be convinced that he is safe, and that is the important part."

The President's mouth opened with a silent *Ah!* of appreciation as they continued their slow walk toward their waiting limousines.

"It was easy to arrange a little demonstration to convince Kim Jong-Il's son of the efficacy of the antidote, although it was not so enjoyable for one of the mice involved. We prepared a sealed chamber with two compartments, each with a mouse and a feeding bowl. But only the food in one bowl had been treated with the antidotes."

"We allowed Jong-Nam to press the button that admitted the Sarin to the chamber, generating a most theatrical hiss. Within seconds, one mouse was dying a horrible death, while the other simply sat and groomed itself. You should read a description sometime of the ways in which the body reacts to the administration of Sarin. It really is a most unpleasant way to die. But it does provide a most convincing display."

"And he was comforted?"

"Oh yes, quite – he seemed to enjoy the demonstration immediately. I'm afraid he must not be very fond of his family at all. And conveniently for us, the Number One Son is hardly the brightest star in the heavens."

The President smiled. He admired the simple elegance of the plan. He also appreciated the fact that the General had laid it out in such detail while the President had asked only leading questions. He fingered the recorder in his pocket, and was reassured by the warmth generated by its battery. If anything went wrong now, he could easily betray the General, using the recording as proof of his treason and of the President's own loyalty.

The General interrupted his thoughts. "And what will you do to make sure that the plan is successful?"

The President instantly became more guarded. "Have no worries. I have committed my role to memory, and rehearsed it many times."

The General smiled. "I am sure you have, my friend. But we must leave nothing to chance. Now tell me – what is the first thing that you will do?

Lang-Dong could not avoid answering. "Ah yes. Well, on the signal,... "

"What signal?"

"The signal I receive from you. "

"Please be precise. We must be sure that there is no confusion."

He must not arouse the General's suspicion. But it hardly mattered. The President could edit his own recording later.

"The call from you stating that the Dear Leader and his sons have gone to their bunker."

"And what will you understand that to mean?"

"I will understand that to mean... that the Dear Leader and his sons have, ah, that they have gone to their final rest."

"Then what?"

"I will call an emergency meeting of the Executive Committee and reveal to them that the Dear Leader and his sons have been killed in a vicious and unprovoked attack by the United States. I will read to them the proclamation that I will say the Dear Leader had prepared against such a terrible eventuality, appointing you and me as the new leadership, with full powers to direct all civil and military functions."

"What else?"

"I will also inform the Committee members that immediately outside are heavily armed members of your personal guard, who will stay at their sides for the indefinite future for their personal protection against possible enemies of the State. After I inform them of that fact, I will be pleased to accept their personal pledges of support, and their incriminating signatures on the proclamation testifying to their total allegiance to the new regime."

"Good. And then?"

"You will join me shortly thereafter, and we will jointly release the proclamation on state television, as well as the fact that our troops are pouring across the Demilitarized Zone on their way to an assured victory reuniting the Motherland."

"Exactly. I am glad that you are very clear on your part."

With that, they reached the limousines.

"Our conversation will have been well noted," the General said, shaking the President's hand. "We must not speak again until after the proclamation has been read."

The General motioned to two corporals standing at attention beside his car. With a smile to the President, the General removed a slim object from his breast pocket. It was about the same size and shape as the recorder the President had been fingering in his own pocket. The General handed his device to one of the corporals.

"Take good care of this until I ask for it," he said. The corporal threw a sharp salute, and retreated to the other side of the limousine.

At a nod from the General, the second corporal approached, carrying a valise in one hand, and a strange device in the other, connected to the valise with a coiled wire. It looked like a gun, but instead of a barrel there was what seemed to be a small radio antenna dish. The corporal patted down the President, and then aimed the strange device at the pocket that held the digital recorder.

The President felt a creeping sense of horror possess him as the General swung himself into his car and rolled down the window.

Lang-dam tried to sound unconcerned. "What was that all about?"

"Microwaves. Who knows, some enemy of the State might have planted a device on you - of course without your knowledge - and recorded our conversation. Later, the scoundrel would doubtless fabricate a situation where he would jostle you, and remove the device without your realizing his sleight of hand. But no matter - the microwave gun will have destroyed the memory chip in any such device."

The President stood frozen in place. The tables had turned so swiftly! The General could betray him now at any time, if he wished. A sudden horror gripped him: should that happen, there could be no doubt that the President would die an extremely slow and agonizing death on the order of the Dear Leader. perhaps even through the administration of Sarin gas.

"Farewell, my friend." The General said with a pleasant smile. "You have no idea what a relief it is to have someone to rely on so completely. After the conversation we have just had, I believe I can trust you with my life." The General tapped the brim of his hat with the tip of his swagger stick, and then the limousine was gone, leaving the President of the Supreme People's Assembly of North Korea standing forlornly by the side of the road. Forlorn, but more committed than ever to the plan they had just discussed.

0000 0001 0010 0011 0100 0011 0010 0001 0000

Frank was sitting alone by a dying campfire, the first he had lit in his clearing in the wilderness. He and his father, now snoring inside a sleeping bag spread on the ground not far away, had sat next to the flames through hours of conversation. Frank wasn't yet sure what he should and shouldn't feel after harboring so much animosity for so long. Doubtless, that would take time to work out.

Even so, he already realized that much of the pain he had converted into disdain had apparently not been his father's fault at all. Assuming, of course, that he could believe everything he had just heard - how his dad's lieutenant in the Army had joined the FBI on his return to the States, and later recruited Frank's father to act as a plant in a mob sting operation. How that project had gone terribly wrong, forcing his father to flee New York City and enter a protection program far away. And how he had not been allowed to communicate with Frank or his mother for a year thereafter, for their own protection.

Frank could easily believe that his mother might have refused to take his father back after that. She was a strong-willed woman, and it had been abundantly clear to Frank, even as a child, that no warmth existed between his parents. He could even believe, as his father had said, that she had insisted that his dad agree to never contact his son again. Frank knew that Doreen Adversego had never played for anything but keeps.

Watching the embers die, Frank wondered what it must have been like for his father, suddenly whisked away to a nowhere location in the Southwest, especially after he learned that he had no home to return to.

Luckily, the FBI had offered Frank, Sr. a job, and during his year out of sight he learned all about computers, codes and security while the mess was cleaned up back East. He found that he had a natural affinity for computers. He had already fallen in love with the Southwest during his summer trip with Frank, so with nothing to take him away, he simply stayed out west, with a new name, a new identity, and a new career as a full-time FBI security specialist.

Frank was grappling with mixed feelings over another part of the tale he had just heard. The "anonymous donor" that had funded his full scholarship was no longer anonymous. So that scholarship was no longer much to be proud of.

That really shouldn't be much of a surprise, he forced himself to admit. Yes, he had ranked first in his class in the math and science courses that captured his interest. But he'd barely passed any of the others. He'd been lucky to squeak into MIT at all, much less get a free ride through college besides. His father may have promised not to contact Frank, but luckily for Frank that hadn't kept him from keeping a watchful eye over his son from afar through all the intervening years.

And then there had been that last surprise at the end of the evening, as his father was preparing to leave the circle of firelight and get himself some sleep. Frank was self-conscious and embarrassed, recalling the harsh words he'd unleashed about his father earlier in the evening before he knew to whom he was speaking. Still, reconnecting with his father would take time. He might as well be upfront about that, he decided, as they said shook hands and said goodnight.

"I hope you'll understand if I don't yet feel comfortable calling you 'Dad' for awhile."

"That's okay, Frank. I'm out of practice calling anyone 'son.'"

Then his father smiled and put a hand on Frank's shoulder. "If easier it should come to you, just 'Yoda' may you call me.'"

0000 0001 0010 0011 0100 0011 0010 0001 0000

Marla and Carl were meeting in the coffee house in Alexandria, once again seated at an isolated table. Across the street, the antiquarian bookstore was dark. A sign in the window said "Closed Until Further Notice."

"Unfortunately," Carl was saying, "their story checks out. Our preliminary review of everything we've found – hard drives, email, server logs, you name it – indicates that the old guys were never responsible for successfully hacking anything other than the Library of Congress."

"It seems the guys we caught had hired someone else – no surprise – to do the hacking. But then he went rogue on them, and started hacking everything in sight, still using their silly Alexandria Project calling card when he did. They'd never met him face to face, or even spoken to him by telephone, so there wasn't a damn thing they could do about it. One day he was working for them, and the next their emails to him just started bouncing."

"We also found the botnet they had paid him to set up, by the way. It was still randomly hammering away at networks, probably to give the hacker some camouflage in case we got wise. But unfortunately it's not the one he's using now."

"The old guys were willing to piggyback on the mayhem their runaway hacker was producing for awhile, but it didn't take long before they realized that what they'd started had gotten way out of control. I think they were genuinely relieved when we came bursting in."

"Well, so what?" Marla replied. "Can't you just arrest whoever was working with them? They must be responsible for all the other attacks, right?"

"Maybe. But then again, maybe not. I expect your father would have a better idea about that than I would. Maybe it's time you allowed us to speak with him directly?" Carl purposefully stirred his coffee without looking up.

Marla fired back. "Maybe. But then again maybe not - trust you, that is. Anyway, I can't believe that you guys can't figure that out on your own. It's clear those elderly librarian types didn't do the high tech part of this on their own. Who do they say was working for them?"

"They don't really know, believe it or not. They say that they never met the guy face to face, or even talked to him on the phone. Everything was always handled by email."

"So how did they find him?"

Carl gave a short bark of laughter. "On Craig's List! Can you believe it? The guy who picked the code name Zenodotus said, "Isn't that where you find everything these days?""

181

"That's ridiculous."

"Is it? Have you been on Craig's List lately?

Marla ignored him.

"Anyway, the old guys probably thought they were being very clever and secretive, using only email and their silly, ancient Library of Alexandria librarian names. But we don't really know who they connected with – not yet, anyway. Maybe they did enough fumbling around on the Internet that they attracted attention from real bad guys, who then pointed them to a fake ad so it would look more innocent."

"What we don't know is whether the guy they hired just fell in love with their Alexandria shtick and took off on his own, or whether there's something more serious going on. If the latter is the case, then we've got a big problem on our hands."

"Silly me," Marla replied. "I was under the assumption we already had a big problem."

Carl looked unhappy and stirred his coffee for a moment. Then he leaned closer, and continued, "The problem is, one of the Alexandria Project guys is a Community Representative on the Advisory Board of the LoC, and he had enough access to be dangerous. He provided his ID and password to the mystery man they hired. Turns out Advisors have deeper access than he realized – and maybe deeper than George realized as well. That got the hacker off to an easy start, because now he could find the system's weaknesses from the inside."

"But that doesn't explain how they broke into so many other agencies so easily. How did they pull that off?"

Carl paused again. He looked around and leaned forward still further, lowering his voice until Marla could barely hear him. "Look, Marla, I've already told you a lot more than I should. But I expect that it may be important for your dad to know this, so I'm going to share something with you that's *really* secret. You've got to understand that this goes to no one, ever, other than Frank."

Marla nodded, uncomfortable at being so close to Carl.

"The LoC isn't just a sleepy department of a government agency. It's also used as what they call a "testbed" – a place where the IT guys and security guys can roll out new technology. That way, they can test the hell out of it in a real-world setting before they deploy it across highly sensitive areas of the government, like the Pentagon and White House."

"The idea has always been that no one was likely to try too hard to hack the computers of the LoC, so it would be a safe place to work the bugs out of new systems without laying too much on the line. At the same time, it's still a big, complex enterprise processing huge amounts of data. And it connects with Congress and other agencies, so its IT policies, architecture and interfaces have to be the same as those of every other agency in a lot of respects. So once the security wizards get things just right at the LoC, they figure they're safe to install everywhere else."

"Unfortunately, that's exactly what the security guys were up to, right before this mess blew up. Everybody at the LoC - like your father – was supposed to think that they were competing to produce a new security upgrade. In fact, the one they had been using for the past six months had just been pushed out across all the agencies."

"So you mean once the bad guys figured out how to crack the LoC they could crack the Pentagon?"

"Bingo. And Homeland Security and the White House and everything else besides. Because they're all now running the same security protocols, over the same architecture, as the LoC."

"But what about all the private companies and universities they broke into as well? They weren't all using exactly the same security systems, were they?"

"Well, no, that's right. But nobody goes out and invents a whole new way of creating security, and that was true for the LoC as well. Everyone uses pretty much the same concepts, building blocks and strategies, and then refines them from there in ways that they hope will keep them one step ahead of the hackers. So while some parts of the LoC's upgraded security infrastructure were different from what was there before, they weren't necessarily that different from what outside security experts are designing and selling to their customers."

"We figure the bad guys just used robots to hammer away at the millions of eligible targets out there, and then made use of the ones that they could get into the same way they were able to hack the LoC."

"So we're back to where we started?"

"Yes. That's pretty much the size of it."

Marla avoided his gaze, and looked instead at the darkened book store across the street.

"So how about it, Marla? Isn't there anything else your father could tell us to help us out? We've hit a brick wall here."

Marla didn't like the position she was finding herself in at all. She already knew that her father had made another big discovery. He had also indicated that he didn't want to share it yet, or maybe even at all, if he didn't have to. But after the raid on the bookstore, it really did seem to her that they should be able to trust the CIA. Clearly, the agents couldn't have learned anything that could tie the antiquarians to Frank. So there shouldn't be anything left to fear from the CIA, right?

Marla made her decision, and excused herself from the table, leaving Carl with a puzzled look on his face.

Once inside the rest room, Marla pulled her phone out of her purse, and pushed a speed dial button. She wrote down the numbers that displayed on a piece of paper. Then she hit a second button, and copied those numbers below the first. Finally, she subtracted the second set from the first, and then dialed the resulting number. She immediately pushed the exit button before the call could ring at the other end. Then she threw away the paper with the number on it, and returned to the table.

Without saying a word to Carl, Marla highlighted the number she had just entered, and then hit the "send" button.

0000 0001 0010 0011 0100 0011 0010 0001 0000

Frank was sleeping like a baby, more warm and secure than he had felt since he was a child. But there was something bothering him; an almost familiar sound that he couldn't quite place. Why wouldn't it go away?

Then his eyes snapped open like a Jack-in-the-Box: it was the sound of the satellite phone he had bought in case of emergencies! And the only person who had the number was Marla! He jumped out of bed and began throwing dirty laundry in the air as he searched for the phone.

Finally, he found it. "Marla! Hi! What's wrong?"

Marla caught her breath at the sound of her father's voice; she should have realized he'd assume the worst when he heard his emergency phone ring.

"Nothing Dad – nothing! I'm sorry, I didn't mean to alarm you. I just needed to tell you what we've found out and ask for your help."

"Thank God you're okay! Go ahead." Frank slumped into a chair, shaking from head to foot.

"We caught the guys at the location you sent us to – but they turned out to be just a bunch of antique book dealers. Yeah – that's right – book dealers! Tweed jackets and the whole bit. It turns out they're only behind the LoC attacks and none of the other incidents. They hired somebody else to do the hacking, and they don't know who he is; they only communicated by email. And it looks like he isn't using their computers, so we're stuck and we need your help."

Marla had a sudden thought. "Was this the only location you ever found? Could there have been another one you located somewhere along the way?"

184

Frank was still feeling weak and rattled. Of course there had been a second intruder – he'd known that now for a long time. And yes, he'd found a second location through the iBall crowd sourcing gambit. But could he afford to tell anyone where the second location was until he could check it out for himself?

Carl watched as Marla's eyebrows shot up. "Dad, that's impossible! How could that be? Yes, of course I believe you – we'll check it out. And yes, we can get off the phone now."

Carl looked at her anxiously. "Well? Where is it? What's so strange about where it is?"

0000 0001 0010 0011 0100 0011 0010 0001 0000

Across town, an FBI agent took off his earphones with a smile. He punched a few buttons on the console in front of him and waited for the readout. Perfect – he'd been able to get an exact fix. He put his headset on again and called his supervisor.

"All good things come to those that wait, Boss. We've got Adversego."

0000 0001 0010 0011 0100 0011 0010 0001 0000

25

The Bacon and Eggs will get you Every Time

CIA DIRECTOR JOHN Foster Baldwin pressed a button on his intercom.

"Yes, Gwen?"

"Mr. McInnerney for you, sir."

The Director gave an inward groan, and then told his assistant to put the call through. What the hell could he want? Baldwin hadn't spoken to FBI Director Francis X. McInnerney since the two of them had been mauled by Congressman Steele weeks ago. And why would he want to? McInnerney had done everything he could to deflect Steele's wrath towards the CIA. And with some success, too. Whatever McInnerney might be calling for, Baldwin doubted he'd like it.

"Hi, Francis. To what do I owe the this rare honor of a personal call?"

Baldwin heard McInnerney chuckle. "Don't worry, John, no honor intended. Just following the rules by promptly informing a partner in Homeland Security about an important development."

"How diligent of you to do so." Well, now he knew the category in which this would not be a welcome call. McInnerney was calling to gloat over an FBI breakthrough in some matter of joint responsibility.

"Yes indeed, I wanted you to be the first to know that we've cracked the Alexandria Project wide open."

Damn, Baldwin thought. If that was true, the CIA would have to share the glory of its own recent discovery with the FBI. If only Marchand had been able to move in a few days sooner.

"Congratulations," Baldwin said in as non-congratulatory a tone as possible. "What is it that you've come across?"

"We've found the mole that was working in the Library of Congress, and we expect to have him in custody by the end of the day."

"Is that so? And how have you tied him to the exploits?"

"Glad you asked, because that's the most interesting part. Now that all the Homeland Security agencies use the same database, we were able to read the write-ups your boys put together about this guy. And apparently we found more of interest in them than your own folks were able to."

"Really."

"Yes, really. It was all there for your analysts to see. This guy Adversego has the motive, the profile, the opportunity and the skills to pull the whole thing off. And then he drops off the face of the earth, after giving your boys the slip using the kind of tactics you'd find in a Grade B movie."

Baldwin had no idea what the FBI Director was talking about, but he didn't like what he was hearing. All he knew – or feared he knew, at this point – was that George Marchand's team had captured those responsible for at least the Library of Congress attacks. What could it be that McInnerney's boys had discovered?

But the FBI Director had more good news to share.

"The only hard part to figure out is why your guy Marchand hushed the whole thing up. Now isn't that an interesting question?"

"Actually, Fran, I'm sure that it's not nearly as interesting a question as you may think...."

But McInnerney cut him off.

"Save it for Congressman Steele, John. Right now I've got a few other calls to make. And the first one will be to him." The line went dead.

Baldwin pushed back from his desk and tried to digest the implications of what he had just heard. What if the FBI was about to arrest someone the CIA knew about and could have hauled in themselves?

Baldwin pulled Marchand's full field report out of a file, and this time read more than the Executive Summary. According to Marchand, the CIA had been led to the Alexandria Project by someone named

Frank Adversego, an employee of the Library of Congress who had initially been led to believe that he was personally under suspicion, and had skipped town as a result. Moreover the CIA's information was obtained second hand through his daughter, and Adversego's current location was still unknown.

Marchand also reported that the members of the Project were not capable of launching the attacks themselves. No progress had yet been made in determining who had assisted them, but Marchand assigned a high probability to the likelihood that the same parties were behind the scores of copycat attacks that were still continuing.

Baldwin set the report aside and thought hard. What would he be thinking if he was McInnerney and had read the same information?

That line of reasoning led him quickly to an unsettling thought. From what he could tell from Marchand's report, this guy Adversego had fingered the booksellers without explaining how he knew who they were. Perhaps Adversego really was the hacker behind the operation. Maybe he had turned in the booksellers to deflect the CIA's attention from himself?

Yes, Baldwin concluded, that's exactly what McInnerney would think. Worse, that's what he would report to Congressman Steele, whether the facts supported that conclusion or not. Worst of all, if the FBI could catch Adversego and impound his computer equipment, how would the CIA be able to refute McInnerney's claims?

The answer, he realized with concern, was that it couldn't. The FBI would not only claim credit for breaking the case, but it would also say the CIA was either incompetent or protecting the culprit. No, that wasn't quite fair to McInnerney, Baldwin realized. The FBI Director would say that the CIA was incompetent *and* protecting the culprit.

The Baldwin was beginning to feel extremely uneasy. For all he knew, Adversego really was guilty. Perhaps Marchand's trust in him was misplaced, and the CIA was about to be hung out to dry.

Baldwin reached a decision. He couldn't let the FBI capture Frank Adversego. And George Marchand had to be kept out of the loop, or he might tip Adversego off.

He glanced at the clock on his desk. This would require quick and decisive action.

~~0000~~ ~~0001~~ ~~0010~~ ~~0011~~ 0100 ~~0011~~ ~~0010~~ ~~0001~~ ~~0000~~

Marla unlocked the door to Frank's apartment, and motioned Carl and George in ahead of her.

"Let's sit in the kitchen. It's the only semi-habitable part of my father's apartment."

George looked around the room and decided not to comment on Marla's definition of habitability. "So your father says the real hacker is located somewhere in this building, huh?"

"Yes, but that's as close as he can get to telling where they are. We'll have to take it from here."

"How about it George," Carl asked. "What's our next step?"

George shook his head from side to side slowly. "That's not going to be easy. This building has four floors, and there are twenty-four mail-boxes in the lobby downstairs. I can't set up monitors in one location and scan every apartment. And whoever we're looking for isn't going to have a room full of servers in their living room – all the serious equip-ment will be far away. So it's not like we can scan for unusual electro-magnetic activity, or listen for extra air conditioners chilling a data room. We'll have to actually intercept data that we can identify as sus-picious."

"So what does that mean? That we've got to get a court order and tap every apartment in the whole damn building?"

"Actually, it could be worse than that. For all we know, whoever we're looking for may be across the street. Maybe they're just tapping into someone's unprotected WiFi router over here."

"So what do we do?"

George began to unpack the metal suitcase he had carried in. "For starters, we'll just hope to get lucky. I've brought a TEMPEST scanner kit along with me, and maybe it will turn out our target is less careful than he or she should be. Even so, from this location I'm only going to be able to monitor adjacent apartment on this floor and the one's immediately above and below it."

"'TEMPEST'? What does that mean?" Marla asked.

"Well, Marla, the funny thing is that nobody knows what the acronym stands for; that's apparently classified. And actually, you don't hear too much about this kind of technology anymore – not like you used to, back in the Cold War days of spooks and espionage. With everything running over the Internet now, TEMPEST is pretty passé. Now we just try and intercept information it in the cloud, or plant a keystroke logger on the target's own computer."

Marla sniffed. "Thanks. That was very informative. But completely unenlightening."

"Sorry, Marla. Basically, TEMPEST is a term that applies to tech-niques that let you pick up data that equipment such as computers and printers are handling without having to directly intercept it at all. Sometimes we might listen for mechanical noises that we can match to the actions of individual computer keys, and in other situations we'd try and pick up the electromagnetic emanations that, say, a computer monitor might give off while someone was using it. That's what I'm going to try to do here."

"Of course, that assumes that the person of interest isn't using lead shielding, or generating the electromagnetic or acoustic equivalent of "white noise" to obliterate or neutralize what I'll be looking for. But what the hell, we've got to start somewhere."

Marla thought for a moment. "So because you're not actually tapping a phone line we don't need a warrant?"

Instead of answering, George began humming loudly to himself. Marla took the hint, and let it go at that.

Carl was only half listening to them as he wandered around the kitchen, looking at the clutter that had been Frank's everyday life. He noticed something familiar on the counter and picked it up.

"So what happened to Devil Dog?" he asked Marla, holding up a leather collar for her to see.

Marla snorted. "Lily? My father got Mrs. Foomjoy across the hall to take care of her before he left. And don't be silly. Lily's completely harmless."

"So you say," Carl said as he looked at the collar. A rabies shot tag dangled from a split ring, and behind that, a thick silvery disk. Lily's name was engraved on it, along with Frank's name. What a geek, Carl thought. Instead of a phone number, the tag bore Frank's email address.

Idly, Carl rubbed the tag between his fingers, and thought he felt the back surface dimple at his touch. He turned the tag over and pressed the back again. Yes, it flexed slightly – he wasn't holding a solid metal tag at all. He realized that it was also thicker than he would have expected.

"Say, George, do you have a really, really fine screwdriver in your bag of tricks?"

"Of course." He handed one over that was the size found in an eyeglass repair kit.

Carl sat down at the kitchen table and placed the tag on edge. Marla got up and stood behind him to see what he was doing.

"What's so interesting about Lily's collar?"

"Not the collar – the dog tag. I'll let you know in a minute." Carl pursed his lips, wiggling the screwdriver back and forth. Finally he succeeded in wedging the sharp point of the screwdriver into an almost imperceptible line that circled the outer edge of the disk. With a twist of the screwdriver, he popped the two halves apart.

"Aha! Now what have we here?"

Probing carefully with the screwdriver, Carl found that the tag had a chamber inside containing what looked very much like the workings of a digital watch, complete with battery. He also saw that the back cover of the tag was an extremely thin disk of dark metal – just like the diaphragm you would find in a telephone. Stuck to the middle of the side facing inwards was a small metal and plastic structure, which was connected to the electronic device by a thin wire.

George had joined Marla now at Carl's elbow, and was watching intently. "Marla, do you know where that name tag came from?"

Marla picked up the collar, noting the fancy tooling and red lacing that ornamented it.

"It must have been a gift from Mrs. Foomjoy, across the hall. My grandmother would never have bought something this gaudy, and gosh knows my father wouldn't have spent a nickel on anything for Lily he didn't have to."

"That's that, then," George said, beginning to repack his equipment case. "We've got our hacker."

"But how? And what's that electronic thing inside Lily's tag?"

"Wireless microphone and transmitter," Carl answered, as he reassembled the tiny device. "With an antenna and battery that small, it couldn't have much range. So all roads lead to the apartment across the hall."

0000 0001 0010 0011 0100 0011 0010 0001 0000

President Rawlings scanned the faces around the table as he entered the Situation Room. Yes, the core members of the National Security Council were already seated. He nodded to all as he sat down and got down to business.

"General Hayes, thank you for joining us again. Please bring us up to date."

"Of course, Mr. President." General Hayes stepped to the easel in the corner of the room. No one to flip charts for him this time; today's event was for the inner circle only.

Hayes reached into the large portfolio leaning against the wall and pulled out a wide aerial photo. The title at the top read "Demilitarized Zone plus 30 Kilometers North." A zigzagging double red line crossed the bottom of the image, and above it, dozens of triangles, circles and squares had been applied. Some of the geometric shapes were red, others black.

"The purpose of this first satellite image is to show changes in troop deployments along the DMZ over the past five days. The black symbols mark the previous positions of significant North Korean forces. The more numerous red ones indicate North Korean positions as of 1800 local time today. The meanings of the symbols are as follows: each triangle represents one full division, each square represents one tank corps, and each circle represents one air combat wing."

"Two changes are immediately apparent: not only are there significantly more forces of each type now within thirty kilometers of the DMZ than five days ago, but they are also much closer to the line. The only forces of any magnitude not within three kilometers of the 38th parallel are positioned to guard known North Korean command and control positions. Not shown but included in your briefing package are the locations of numerous missile and anti-aircraft batteries that have been repositioned to the front lines."

The General placed another photo on top of the first.

"In this version of the same photo we have removed the black symbols, and added a new set of markings in green. As you will note, these symbols are grouped in wedges. Each wedge is pointed at one of the areas of greatest troop concentration indicated in red. These green symbols represent divisions of the Red Guard."

"Good God, General," the Vice President interjected. "If those symbols indicate divisions, there must be over a million Red Guards within a few miles of the DMZ!"

"Actually, sir, we calculate the number to be closer to 1,250,000. They've been pouring into the area every night for the past three days, and continue to do so."

There was a stunned silence. The President spoke at last.

"General, is there any precedent for a troop concentration of this size along the DMZ?"

"I'm afraid not, sir. While it's true that the game plan is familiar, the magnitude and composition of the forces massing just over the border are unprecedented. In particular, we have never seen such a concentration of Red Guards along the DMZ, or indeed anywhere, since the truce was signed over fifty years ago."

"And what is the status of the two new, long-range missiles we have been watching?"

"Sir, we assume that they are now fully operational, except for loading liquid fuel. We have not yet detected any lox venting from the missiles, so we assume that fueling has not yet commenced."

"Thank you, General, you may be seated. I expect we will have additional questions, but you've already adequately illustrated the reason I've convened this meeting."

Hayes retreated to his seat, grateful to be only a spectator of the decision making to follow.

The President spoke again, this time to the Council. Hayes thought that his voice had suddenly become a bit unsteady.

"As you can see, we are faced with a fast-evolving situation without parallel since the Cuban Missile Crisis. And I draw that comparison advisedly. As you know, a disaster of unimaginable consequences was averted back then only by the calm judgment displayed by President Kennedy and his most trusted advisors. As we discuss our next moves, I would like each of you to keep their example in mind."

As the Secretary of State spoke up to support the President, Hayes discretely scanned the faces around the table, trying to gauge their reaction to the President's statement. . There seemed to be two camps: those that seemed relieved to hear the President's words, and those with frowns on their faces. The darkest frown of all was on the face of the Vice President.

No surprise there, Hayes reflected. Henry Chaseman was as extreme a hawk as you were likely to find, and as strange a running mate match from that perspective for the dovish president as one could imagine. Moreover, Chaseman and Rawlings had become bitter rivals during the year running up to the primaries, badly splitting the party in the process. Only with great difficulty, after Rawlings had sewn up the nomination for the top spot, had party elders persuaded him to invite his rival to become his running mate in an attempt to reunite the party.

Not that it made much difference to the two men involved. It was an open secret on the Hill that there had been no real reconciliation between them. No one doubted that the inevitable impotence of being Vice President chafed at Chaseman's ego mightily.

Hayes turned to listen to the Secretary of Defense. But as soon as she was done, the Vice President jumped in.

"I'm sorry, Mr. President, but I must emphatically disagree. Of course it's politically correct to talk about what great judgment Jack Kennedy showed back in 1962, but that's only because we don't know how things would have turned out if he'd given General LeMay permission to launch a preemptive strike – or even simply led the Russians to believe he intended to."

"At that time, we had the Soviet Union out-nuked three to one, and they knew it. They weren't attacking us – they were testing us. Now think what the world could have been like if we'd drawn a line in the sand instead of playing cat-and-mouse at sea. We could have forced the Russians to the table to disarm them then and there, and saved twenty-five years of Cold War uncertainty and sacrifice. We might even have avoided the Viet Nam war."

Hayes saw that while some advisors looked uneasy, others were listening to the Vice President with approval.

"I say this is the time to call North Korea's bluff. What are we waiting for? For Kim Jong-Il or his son to build twenty-five more nukes and then try a stunt like this again? We all know our missile defense system is crap. We'd be lucky to knock one out of three of their missiles out of the air if they ever launched a real attack. Is *that* what we're waiting for?"

"And even if I conceded to you your point about the Cuban Missile Crisis, there's no way we can have any kind of semi-rational negotiation with these lunatic North Koreans. Kennedy had Khrushchev to exchange signals with, but we're stuck with Kim Jong-Il- or whatever other maniac is really running the show over there right now."

The Secretary of State broke in. "But what about the missiles? We already know North Korea has successfully tested atomic bombs. What if they have been able to make them small enough to deliver with these missiles?"

Chaseman shot back: "And what if they haven't? Should we wait until they have, or act now while we can?"

"But let's say that I concede this point as well. Why should we think the North have any better luck with these new missiles than they've had with their old ones? The only question in my mind is whether they'll make it off the launch pad without exploding."

"But mark my words – we can't rely on their poor engineering skills to protect us forever. Soon enough, the North Koreans will get the bugs out, and then what? How long will it be before they have dozens of capable, nuclear-tipped intercontinental missiles pointed at us? One year? Two?"

No one responded, so Chaseman pressed his attack.

"So I say the hell with moderation! I say it's time to strike back, and strike back decisively while we can still afford to do so. If Kim Jong-Il fires those missiles at us, I say we fire ours right back, missile for missile."

Chaseman paused a moment for effect, and then added quietly but decisively, "And I say we arm ours with nuclear warheads as well."

There was a gasp from more than one member of the Council. The Secretary of State spoke first.

"Are you serious?"

"Of course I'm serious! The only reason we've never had to use nukes since 1945 is because we used them back then. Unfortunately, it seems like the lesson is getting stale. Maybe it takes a mushroom cloud in the news every fifty or sixty years to keep madmen like the North Koreans and the Iranians in line. And I'd a damn sight rather see that mushroom cloud over Pyongyang than Washington!"

With that, Chaseman folded his arms and leaned back.

Hayes saw that the Vice President's forceful logic had connected with many of his listeners. Like the rest, he turned to hear what the President would say in response.

But Rawlings said nothing, because even as they watched, the President of the United States began slumping slowly down into his chair, his mouth slightly open, and his eyes staring blankly into space.

0000 0001 0010 0011 0100 0011 0010 0001 0000

26

Just a Simple Walk in the Woods

TWO CAN PLAY the same game, Baldwin thought with a smile. Maybe this inter-agency database has something going for it after all.

"Do we have any equipment within range of Eureka, Nevada?" the CIA Director spoke into his intercom.

"Yes, sir. We've got units at our New Mexico test facility. We can send them in above commercial air traffic and then give you approximately five hours over target."

"That will be more than I'll need. I want two ready to go as soon as you can: one for the mission, and the second as backup. Can you get me on target by first light tomorrow?"

There was a pause this time. Baldwin heard computer keys clicking softly in the background.

"Not quite, sir. But I think I can guarantee target video a few minutes after sunrise."

"That will do. I'll also want a real time voice link to the remote pilot. And be sure I've got the video link at least fifteen minutes before arrival."

"Yes, sir. That should be about 9:55 your time. Will anyone else need access besides you and the pilot, sir?"

"No. Make sure no one else has privileges. And be sure the archival footage is coded for my eyes only as well. Thanks." Baldwin all but turned off the intercom with a flourish. It felt good to be directly managing a field operation again. Just like the old days.

0000 0001 0010 0011 0100 0011 0010 0001 0000

FBI agent Ralph Johnson was jolting his way up a Jeep track winding its way up an anonymous Nevada mountain ridge. Next to him, another agent held a large satellite photo in his lap. Whenever the track forked, he compared it to the topographic map displaying on the GPS unit on the four wheel drive vehicle's dashboard and called the turn.

"So how much further, Jeff?"

"Half mile – maybe less. He should be somewhere in that pass you see ahead and to the right."

"Okay. This would have been a whole lot easier if we could have had Bart Thatcher on board. Guy knows this terrain like the back of his hand. But I couldn't get through to him."

"Who's Thatcher?"

"Retired agent that hangs out in Rachel."

"Rachel? The hick town north of Area 351? Why the hell would anyone want to retire to Rachel?"

"Well, he's not married; not sure if he ever was. Probably likes to hunt. Plus, we pay him to keep his ear to the ground. It's not easy telling the UFO crazies from the people we seriously want to keep out of Area 51, and after a career in the field he's got a knack for that."

"He's kind of a strange old guy, too, which is just as well – he blends right in with the type of loners and odd balls you'd expect to end up in a God forsaken place like Rachel. And it's easy money for him, since there's only one place in town to rent a room or eat. All he has to do is drop by for a beer every night like he probably would anyway and chat up whoever is new in town. If he ties up with someone we might want to know about, he lets us know and keeps an eye on them for us."

"Well, better him than me. I'll stick with Vegas."

"Maybe that's where he is – blowing off some steam. Anyway, let's walk from here so we can check things out before this guy sees us."

The plan was no more complicated than the situation demanded. They would pose as bow hunters, and their baggy camouflage clothes would conceal their Kevlar vests and side arms. They wouldn't look particularly threatening arriving on foot, and the huge pines would still provide plenty of cover to duck behind if things got tricky.

Likely enough all they'd have to do would be to knock on the camper door, and then handcuff Frank before he knew what had hit him. Adversego's file didn't indicate any violent tendencies, or that he owned a gun, or even knew how to use one, for that matter. They had checked back through the half dozen satellite photos that happened to have been taken of the area over the last two months, and had found no evidence that more than one person had been in the clearing since Frank had arrived. How hard could this be?

Walking through the widely spaced pines, it became obvious that the only way they wouldn't be seen from a distance would be if Frank just wasn't keeping a watch out for strangers. But then again, why would he be? Odds were, he hadn't seen a soul since he arrived on the scene. Soon, they caught a glimpse of a white truck ahead, with what appeared to be broad, blue wings spreading out from its roof. They stopped and pulled out their binoculars.

"Geez, will you look at that?" the younger man asked. "What kind of crazy crap does he have on top of that thing?"

"Solar arrays. We saw them in the satellite photos. Makes sense, given how long he's been up here. But it looks like he could fly to the moon with that many, doesn't it?" There wasn't much else besides the camper to be seen in the clearing – just a folding chair and a fire ring.

Ralph returned his binoculars to their case, and started moving.

"So that's that. Let's walk straight up to the camper like we're lost and need directions."

They started walking again, trying to carry their compound bows in a way that looked natural but could be easily seen from a distance. About 75 yards from the camper, the solar arrays began to slowly rotate. A minute later, they stopped at right angles to the two agents; they stopped, too.

"Now what's that all about?" Jeff asked uneasily.

"I dunno, but let's start walking again. Act natural and keep talking to me like we're chatting about nothing in particular."

But they had only gone a few steps before the array went into motion once again, this time swiveling its thirty feet of solar panels from horizontal to vertical, until they faced the agents broadside. Ralph and Jeff stopped once again.

"Ralph, I don't know about you, but this is creeping me out. What the hell is he up to?"

"I don't know, but we've got a job to do. Get walking." But only two steps later, the camper's engine roared threateningly to life.

Once more they stood stock still, watching as the camper began to slowly turn until it was pointing straight at them, the solar array remaining pointed at them all the while. The younger man felt like a first-time toreador in a bullfighting ring, watching his nemesis pawing the dust before mowing him down.

And now, a rhythmically repetitive, vaguely unsettling symphonic work began to play from speakers on the camper that they had not noticed before.

"*Shit!* What's he planning to do, run us down?"

"Easy, Jeff. It looks like he only raises the ante when we move closer, so let's just stand here for a minute."

"Hello!" Ralph called out. The headlights of the camper flashed on, but there was no other reply.

The agents exchanged tense glances, and then Ralph yelled again. "Say - can you tell us where we are? We're lost." The emergency lights on the camper began flashing angrily.

The men stepped backwards involuntarily. "Shhhh!" Jeff hissed at his boss. "I think you're just making him mad."

But how could they tell? Adversego had propped one of those shiny silver reflectors up against the windshield that people use to keep the sun from heating up a vehicle's interior. Or was r it bullet-proof armor? Jeff wondered . A slit about two inches high and ten inches wide pierced whatever it was right where the driver's eyes should be, but even with their binoculars the agents couldn't see through into the darkened interior.

As Ralph lowered his binoculars, the engine revved menacingly, and the camper began to inch forward.

To Jeff's relief, Ralph called out again. This time, he said, "Okay, okay, we get the point. We're leaving."

"That's it," Ralph said quietly to his partner. "I've had enough. Let's just back up slowly and get the hell out of here. It's time to call in the SWAT team."

0000 0001 0010 0011 0100 0011 0010 0001 0000

Carl slipped the master key into the door across the hall from Frank's apartment and entered, followed by Marla and George. Outside, Bert and Ernie covered the ends of the block, ready to raise the alarm if either spotted Mrs. Foomjoy returning from her shopping.

Once inside, the trio made a quick circuit of the modest, one bedroom apartment. Aside from a remarkable penchant for tacky decorating and a

morbidly obese corgi snoring on the floor of the bedroom, it was unremarkable. More to the point, the flat was totally devoid of any sign of
technology more advanced than a VCR – and the clock on that item
was blinking "12:00."

"Okay, no surprises. We'll have to look a bit more closely."

George placed his case of TEMPEST equipment on a coffee table
in the living room and opened the lid while Carl peered into closets.

But Marla continued to stand in the middle of the living room with
a puzzled look on her face. "There's something not quite right here."

"No kidding," George replied, scanning the vases of ugly artificial
flowers, frilly curtains, and slip covers. "This takes the banality of evil
to a whole new level."

"No – that's not what I'm talking about. This apartment should be
a mirror image of my father's across the hall, but something's different,
and I can't tell what it is." Marla turned slowly around and then pointed
to a large china cabinet.

"That's it – there should be a closet behind that piece of furniture."

"Excellent – gold star for you! Carl, help me move this monster."

They moved to either side of the breakfront, looking for hand holds
and not finding much to work with. But as soon as they started to grap-
ple with the cabinet, they found that they could push it aside very easily.

George knelt down and peered under the cabinet. "Huh – look at
that. The feet are a couple of millimeters off the floor, and there are
wheels just behind them." He stood up and they rolled the cabinet away
from the wall, exposing a locked closet door.

Happily, the same master key they had used to gain entrance to the
apartment did the trick, and the door swung open. Inside, a single deep
shelf spanned the closet at desk height. Above it were narrower ones,
packed with a miscellany of electronic gear, cables and assorted
junk. Most importantly, in the center of the desk stood a large flat
screen display, and next to it a high-end computer.

"Piece of cake," George said. "I'll have the hard drive copied and
back in the box in no time. She'll never know we touched it."

0000 0001 0010 0011 0100 0011 0010 0001 0000

In the cold pre-dawn darkness, three blacked out, camouflaged military
vehicles labored their way up the same Jeep trail in Nevada that Ralph
Johnson had driven the afternoon before. A driver with night vision
goggles sat behind the wheel of each.

Two were trucks carrying a SWAT team of FBI professionals trained and equipped to handle anything. The third was a Hummer, in which rode Ralph Johnson and the Las Vegas Bureau Chief of the FBI. When they reached the last fork in the road before the pass, they halted and their occupants disembarked.

Ralph and the Bureau Chief watched as the team members donned their equipment and the commander gave his quiet instructions. Then they melted into the darkness, fanning out to assume their positions surrounding the clearing and wait for the rising sun.

The Bureau Chief looked at his watch, and then at the pale glow that was only just beginning to show in the east. "Hell of a cold morning. Let's get back in the Hummer and turn on the heat."

Back inside, the Bureau Chief turned on the cab light, pulled out a sheaf of papers and began reading, leaving Ralph to stare out the window in silence. The sun was close to rising before the quiet was broken by an alarm going off on the Chief's cell phone.

"That's about all this is good for out here. Mind if I borrow your satellite phone?"

The question was of course hypothetical. The Bureau Chief outranked Johnson by multiple pay grades.

"Of course not, sir."

The Chief put on a headset, dialed a number and waited.

"Bureau Chief Burke for Mr. McInnerney. He's expecting my call."

Ralph Johnson's eyebrows rose involuntarily. Was the Bureau Chief really reporting directly to the head of the FBI about the operation they were about to launch? This guy Adversego must be a hell of a lot more important than Johnson had assumed.

"Hello, sir. Yes, everyone's in position. We're initiating contact in half an hour. Yes, I'll call back when we're about to engage."

Burke rang off and said, "Let's go."

Johnson led the way up the Jeep trail. When they were almost in sight of the camper they met the SWAT team commander. He led them off the track to the east and then began to circle to the left so that the sun, when it rose, would be at their backs. Frank would have to stare straight into it to see them, once the action began. Scrambling up a bank, they reached a camouflaged metal shield with a small one-way window that had been set up between two trees.

"This should stop anything that he's likely to have on board, but when in doubt, get behind a tree. He'd need a howitzer to get through one of those, and I rather doubt he does. It's 0704. At 0710, we'll engage." And then he was gone.

Ralph scanned the scene ahead with professional interest. Just as it should, the clearing and the surrounding woods looked exactly as they had the day before, despite the fact that 12 heavily armed operatives were now within 100 yards of the camper. Each agent had been assigned a specific task to execute – four to blow out the camper's tires, one to take out the windshield of the cab with rubber bullets, another to fire a teargas canister through the gap immediately after. The other six, wearing gas masks, would rush in and drag their target, coughing and bewildered, out of his bunk. It would all be over in the wink of a copiously weeping eye.

Burke dialed the satellite phone again and McInnerney's assistant put him through.

"We're about to engage, sir."

"Remember Burke – under no circumstances is Adversego to be injured. It's not him we want, it's who he can lead us to. I want any computer equipment, too – undamaged."

"Of course, sir. I've made sure that's clear to everyone."

"Good. Now I want you to give me everything that happens as it happens."

Just then, the sun began to lift above the horizon. Burke peered out through the thick window. This wouldn't do, he thought. He was looking mostly at the back of the camper and wouldn't be able to see most of what was about to happen. McInnerney wouldn't like that. Burke looked down at his watch. Just enough time to swing wide and get behind another tree before the action started.

Without sharing his intention with Johnson, the Bureau Chief darted out from behind the shield, running across the fall line of the mountain rather than swinging down hill and then up again, as the SWAT team commander had been careful to do.

He hadn't gone twenty feet, though, before the solar arrays on the camper came to life and started to rotate in his direction. By the time he reached his destination tree, they were locked on his position.

"Stand down! Stand down!" The SWAT team commander barked into his headset microphone.

Damn it, he thought, that idiot desk jockey had ruined everything. Two minutes more and the operation would have been all over, and now what? How were they to know where Frank was in the vehicle now? If he was in the cab, they might kill him when they took the windshield out, even using rubber bullets. All their careful planning had now gone by the boards. He'd have to improvise now, and fast.

"What's going on?" McInnerney said impatiently.

Burke broke into a sweat, peering out from behind his tree. "It seems that Adversego knows we're here."

"How the hell did that happen?"

Burke decided he'd ignore that question and follow McInnerney's earlier command to provide real-time commentary.

"The SWAT team commander has just stepped into the open. It looks like he's going to call for Adversego to surrender."

Back behind the shield, Johnson watched a familiar sequence begin to unfold as the team commander moved slowly forward: first the solar arrays locked on him. Then they swiveled to the broadside position. Next, the camper's headlights came on.

Coming to a halt, the team commander yelled towards the camper. "You're surrounded, Adversego. Look around you."

Burke picked up his commentary again. "The twelve operatives just stepped out from behind their trees, sir, all in full battle dress and with rifles aimed at the camper."

But the only response was the roar of the camper's engine as it came to life. Then its emergency lights began to flash.

"Can you see Adversego?"

"No – all of the windows are covered."

"There's no way you're getting out of here, Adversego. Give yourself up before you get hurt," the commander yelled.

The camper was now turning away from Burke and towards the commander.

"Adversego's turning his camper towards the commander!"

The SWAT team leader spoke quietly to his team through his microphone. "Hold your fire; if I give the order, take out the tires and give the engine area everything you've got, but don't touch the cab or the camper. If I can get Adversego to show his face, though, don't wait for an order – take out the windows farthest from him and give him the gas, inside and out. Got it?" Twelve voices confirmed.

"Now what? What's happening?" McInnerney barked impatiently.

"I don't know; I think the commander was giving orders to his team; now he's yelling again."

"Give it up, Adversego. You can't escape. Even if you get by us, you won't go far; we've got forces covering the entire area."

The commander waited, wishing the last part was actually true. But nothing happened. He called towards the camper again. "Frank, I'm just going to walk slowly towards you so we can talk, okay? Nothing else right now, just talk."

"He's trying to get closer and see if he can get Adversego to respond."

The commander took one slow step forward, and then another. But there was no response.

"Adversego is letting him get closer."

The commander took a third step, and then a fourth. Soon, he was only forty feet from the cab.

"Good choice, Frank. That's playing it smart. Now I'm just going to…"

But that was as close as the commander got, because many things began happening at once; so many that it was only later that Burke was able to sort them out.

The chaos began with the camper suddenly lurching forward, throttle wide open in first gear and engine roaring as it red-lined.

At the same instant, music began insanely blaring at ear-piercing volume from the speakers mounted on the camper, almost drowning out the commander's screamed command of "fire" as he dove out of the path of the accelerating truck. But none of the rifleman shot at first for fear of hitting him.

"*What's that? What's that?*" McInnerney yelled into Burke's ear as he heard the sounds of gunfire in the background.

"I think it's Wagner's "Ride of the Valkyries" Burke yelled back into McInnerney's ear.

"No, you idiot! What's *happening?*"

The camper was well beyond the cordon of operatives now, racing downhill to the east. Now it was the SWAT team that was looking straight into the rising sun, hoping at best to pick off a rear tire as the camper careened down the mountainside.

It was just then that CIA Director Baldwin, staring at a video screen on his desk far away, spoke a single quiet word of command into his speaker phone.

"Fire."

0000 0001 0010 0011 0100 0011 0010 0001 0000

Burke had been shouting "He's getting away! He's getting away!" into his earpiece when a giant, invisible hand raised him up, and then threw him down to the ground. Now his head was spinning. Were those pine needles he felt against his cheek? What had happened?

Dazed, he raised his head weakly. What looked like the remnants of a giant fireball were dissipating above from where the camper had been just a few moments ago. He wished the cloud would disappear entirely, so he could see where the camper was headed now. Then he began hearing noises. They must be coming from the objects that were landing around him. A shoe. A spoon. Pieces of paper were fluttering away in the wind, and the sun was glinting on the small pieces of what looked like metal falling gently around him like spring rain.

Burke stood up, shaking. Now he could see the blackened, burning wreckage of the camper; a single axle tilted up at a crazy angle with a charred tire still attached.

He became aware that McInnerney was still screaming "What happened? What happened?" in his ear, so he removed the wireless earpiece and dropped it into his pocket as he stumbled towards the wreckage of the camper. Suddenly, everything was peaceful and still, except for a small, even, far away sound. He stopped and looked up, and then nodded his head slowly.

A Predator drone heading back to base, of course. A Hellfire air to ground missile almost certainly. It all made perfect sense.

Burke replaced his earpiece. It was time he reported in.

"It's all over," he said, and then switched the earpiece off for good.

0000 0001 0010 0011 0100 0011 0010 0001 0000

27

Is this the Person to Whom I am Speaking?

FBI DIRECTOR FRANCIS X. McInnerney pressed the intercom button on his speakerphone.

"Yes, Mary?"

"Mr. Baldwin for you, sir."

McInnerney gave a gasp that began with astonishment and ended with rage. Baldwin was calling *him* after nuking an FBI target less than an hour ago? He punched the phone ferociously with his index finger and cut loose.

"What the *hell* do you think you're doing Baldwin, interfering with an FBI operation on American soil? You're so far over the line I'm going to get your head handed to you if it's the last thing I do!"

"Dear me, Francis. Why, I've just been sitting here at my desk, wondering why you haven't called. I thought for certain you'd want to thank me for the invaluable support the CIA gave you today in your hour of greatest – not to mention most inept – need. And now you're yelling at me! Why, I'm *shocked!*"

"Can the crap, Baldwin. You had no right to interrupt an FBI operation in process and you know it!

"Tut, Tut! "In process," Fran? That's not the way it looked to me. I was watching the live video feed from our drone, and I saw Adversego break through your perimeter and make a clean escape. And goodness, that camper was *traveling!* All your people were running around like ants, and their vehicles were a good mile away. Why, as I understood it, your nearest backup personnel were all the way back in Las Vegas!"

"The way we saw it, your operation was over, and Adversego was fair game. If we hadn't intervened, he would have gotten away for certain. Now, that wouldn't have made the FBI look good at all, would it?"

No, it wouldn't, McInnerney had to admit - to himself. His men had figured that picking up a computer geek in a camper would be a cake walk. And they'd been wrong. For all he knew, Adversego might have had something else up his sleeve, like a getaway car parked a few miles away. If he'd switched vehicles and abandoned the camper, how would the FBI have picked up his trail again?

"I thought not," Baldwin continued sweetly. "So why don't we just chalk this one up to a splendid case of inter-agency cooperation on a matter of vital national security importance? That makes for a much nicer story, don't you think? I'll have one of my people contact one of yours, and we can harmonize our reports accordingly."

McInnerney fumed in silence, not yet trusting himself to respond.

"Excellent! I'm glad we've got a deal."

Baldwin knew he should leave well enough alone. But he couldn't resist lobbing one last grenade into the FBI Director's foxhole.

"Oh - I almost forgot. I'm sending you a copy of our Predator video – it should make a great training tool to help your people avoid screwing up so badly in the...."

It was five minutes before the FBI Director felt sufficiently composed to ask his secretary to replace the speakerphone that lay in pieces on his desk.

0000 0001 0010 0011 0100 0011 0010 0001 0000

Frank burst out laughing as he watched the chaos unfold once again on his laptop.

"You just can't get enough of that video feed from your clearing, can you?" his father asked.

"You know, I really can't. Every time I see the look on that SWAT team commander's face as he vaults out of the way of the Avenger, I just lose it. Maybe we could start a TV show called 'America's Funniest Home Security Videos'?"

"Yeah, well, there may be some explaining to do down the line about that part."

"True. But we wouldn't have been 600 miles away before they moved in if I hadn't had a lot of time to kill over the last couple of months. That, and the extra sensors I found in the camper's tool kit to play around with. I've got to say that I'm going to miss the old Avenger, though. And I wonder what made the video go dead like that?"

Outside, the Great Plains rolled endlessly past, with nothing to see but more of the same. Things had had been peaceful twenty-four hours earlier, too, when Frank first noticed a plume of dust crossing the valley below. That changed immediately when what had been a black dot at the head of the plume grew into his father's ancient Land Rover, tearing up the Jeep's tracks to his clearing.

"Time to move out, Frank – now!" his father had called out even as he slammed the door. "The FBI's on the way, and we've only got a few hours' lead."

"The FBI? How did that happen?"

"No clue – all I know is that I got a message asking me to be part of an operation up in this pass. Either your friends at the CIA aren't your friends after all, or the FBI's going rogue behind their back. Which wouldn't be the first time. Either way, it's time you got the hell out of here, and not in that camper, either."

Damn, Frank thought. It must have been that call from Marla – he should never have let his guard down after being so careful for so long.

"How much can your Rover hold? There's a lot of electronic gear I'm going to need, and there's other stuff it wouldn't be smart to leave behind."

"More than enough, but let's get moving, or it won't matter."

Frank smiled. "Oh, I'm not too worried about that. I think we're going to have all the time we need."

―0000― ―0001― ―0010― ―0011― 0100 ―0011― ―0010― ―0001― ―0000―

Cummings wondered what lay behind the urgent text message from Marla: "Mt me frnt Air Spce Msm 10." That was all. He could see her now up ahead now, and she didn't look happy.

When he was a few steps away, she saw him and walked rapidly towards, and then right past him.

"Whoa, girl! I thought you wanted me to meet you here?"

"Quiet!" she hissed. "Walk a step behind me and just listen."

Well, this was different. Carl adjusted his pace and fell in behind as she headed towards the street, and then flagged a cab.

"What do you know about a SWAT team trying to capture my father?" she asked urgently.

Carl skipped a step in surprise. "Nothing! Nothing at all, I swear it!"

"Well, find out."

With that, Marla slammed the door of the cab and left him standing at the curb.

0000 0001 0010 0011 0100 0011 0010 0001 0000

"Mr. Marchand for you, sir."

John Foster Baldwin looked at the phone warily.

"Gwen, please ask him what it's about."

After a pause she was back. "He says it's urgent news about the Alexandria Project."

Hmm. Depending on what Marchand might or might not yet know, this could be awkward. Better to find out sooner rather than later, though.

"Alright, then, Gwen. Please put him through."

"Good morning George, good to hear from you. What's the news?"

"Actually, sir, that's what I was calling to ask you. I've learned through Adversego's daughter that a SWAT team tried to take him out yesterday. Luckily, he got away, but unless we have a mighty good explanation, we're not going to have further access to him."

Adversego was alive! Baldwin thought quickly – so he must not have been in the camper after all. Baldwin suddenly felt a bit queasy – who was it he had blown away, then?

"Yes, George, that's right. I owe you an apology for not telling you sooner, but things were happening very quickly."

"You mean we *did* try to capture him?"

"No, no, of course not – nothing of the kind. It seems that our friends at the FBI, however, decided to get into the act. Luckily, I got wind of their plans just in time. I put a high altitude Predator over the clearing immediately."

Now what should he say? Did George know how the operation had turned out? If so, how would he explain that? Then he had a sudden flash of inspiration.

"We saw Frank get away before the FBI arrived, so just as the SWAT team made their move, we took the camper out with a Hellfire missile before they could realize he wasn't inside."

George was startled. "How will you explain that to the FBI?"

Baldwin was starting to feel in control again. "No need to worry about me, George. You don't get to sit at a desk like this without learning how to be quick on your feet."

0000 0001 0010 0011 0100 0011 0010 0001 0000

Frank and his father were nearing Des Moines, Iowa, when Frank turned off his phone. Now that he was off his mountain and back on the move, it seemed safe to communicate again with Marla, using disposable phones. And he was hungry for news.

Frank turned to his father. "So here's the party line. According to Cummings, the FBI was trying to make the CIA look bad by hauling me in. Since the CIA knew I was a security expert working for the Library of Congress and had dropped out of sight after being questioned, they could not only win points by hauling me in, but could claim the CIA was asleep at the switch. Should I believe that?"

His father gave a laugh. "Hell yes! Or anyway, Hell maybe. Some things never change. It makes perfect sense, with Congress and the press bashing both agencies for not getting to the bottom of the security breaches. I'm not saying I'm crossing this one off the list yet, but it's not crazy on its face."

Frank looked out the window and let that sink in. He decided he felt better about his own security and a lot less worse for his country's. Then he remembered the rest of the conversation.

"Oh – and there's other big news – Marla and Cummings have found an operative that really is part of the ring that's behind the breaches. Turns out it was a neighbor of mine all along. But they don't know yet who she's working for."

"Well, that's good news, as far as it goes. Now what?"

Frank mulled that over. What indeed? Then he did what he always did when his mental wheels needed lubricating.

"Well, let's review what we do and don't know. What we do know, or at least think we know, is that the booksellers weren't behind anything except the LoC breach. That means whoever is behind the other attacks probably adopted the old guys' story about exposing the vulnerability of the Internet infrastructure as a cover for whatever they're really up to."

"That means we've got two problems to solve: who's behind the breaches, and what it is they're trying to pull off? We can try and tackle one problem before the other, or both at once."

"Sounds right. So which will it be?"

Frank watched the bare fields roll by. The fact was, he didn't know where to begin on either one. "Well, that's the question, isn't it? What do you think?"

His father chuckled.

"What's so funny?"

"Happens it does that a choice must you make."

"Oh, for Pete's sake! You're not planning on going Yoda on me again, are you?"

"Happens it does that your best thinking you do when Yoda I go on you."

"Alright, alright." Frank sighed. After all, his father was right. So which problem should he tackle first? He stared blankly out the window as the news came on the radio, distracting him from his thoughts.

"Acting President Henry Chaseman issued a tough warning today to the North Koreans today, informing them that any act of provocation would be met with an immediate and disproportionate response from the United States."

Frank jerked to attention.

"Turn that up!"

His father did as requested, a surprised look on his face.

Chaseman's warning came in response to yesterday's saber-rattling statement by North Korean General Chan Bach Choy. In that statement, the General announced that the rogue regime would tolerate no restrictions on its nuclear and missile development and deployment activities, and that the previously announced test firing of two new intercontinental missiles would proceed as planned.

The rapid exchange of escalating messages has raised tensions to the highest level between the two nations since the armistice was signed, more than fifty years ago.

Meanwhile, American allies are urging calm, especially while President Rawlings remains in critical condition in the coronary intensive care unit of Walter Reed Hospital.

Frank reached over and clicked the radio off.

"Well, now I know who we're up against."

"All ears am I."

"It's the North Koreans. Ever since I laid eyes on her, my neighbor has reminded me of Kim Jong-Il."

"Well, that's certainly convincing evidence. Are you sure she's even North Korean?"

"Actually, I don't know. I mean, I don't have any proof." He paused. "Actually, she always said she was Chinese."

The car drove onward, but Frank offered nothing further.

"True it is that a North Korean a Chinese is not."

"Okay, okay, but still, maybe she really is North Korean. Wouldn't she hide that, if she truly was up to no good? And what if there is a connection between the security breaches and what's going on now internationally? The North Koreans can't possibly beat us militarily, at least outside their borders, but security attacks are another thing. If I was an enemy with limited resources that wanted to bring the war home against a much larger opponent, that's where I'd focus."

His father gave a shrug. "Okay. Suppose let us that right you are. Many types of attacks can there be. But launch which one, will they?"

Frank thought out loud. "I don't know. But our next step should be to get all the data together that we've got and then look for a pattern or discrepancy – anything that might provide a clue and point us in the right direction."

"Pull off the highway the next time you see a shopping mall; I want to find a Radio Shack and get a splitter outlet for your cigarette lighter. And if your battery's old, let's get a new one, because I'm going to be running a lot of equipment off it."

0000 0001 0010 0011 0100 0011 0010 0001 0000

Baldwin stared at his speakerphone. George Marchand was asking him to stick his neck out, and that was something Baldwin made a point of never doing.

It didn't bother him that Marchand was asking for permission to send Adversego a dump of the hard drive of the computer he had copied. Or even that Marchand wanted to provide the CIA's complete database of networks the Alexandria Project had hacked as well. He could justify that easily, since if Frank really was the bad guy he would already have access to the same information. But Marchand was also asking permission not to log any of his actions into the Homeland Security database.

That made obvious sense, because otherwise the FBI would learn that Adversego was alive, and that would never do. But it would also be a violation of Homeland Security rules, and they both knew it.

There was only one way he could safely give that kind of permission, and luckily for him Marchand was trusting or foolish enough –either way the man was clearly a fool – to seek verbal rather than written permission. If Marchand's actions later came to light, they couldn't be denied. But Baldwin's words could.

"Permission granted, George. Let me know if it gets us anywhere."

0000 0001 0010 0011 0100 0011 0010 0001 0000

High in the mountains of Nevada, FBI Agent Ralph Johnson was overseeing the painstaking forensic examination of the wreckage of the Solar Avenger. Behind him, a support crew was setting up lights powered by a portable generator. As night fell, wisps of fog wafted up from the damp ground and hissed against the lenses of the blinding klieg lights. Above the barely visible horizon far away, a three quarter moon began to rise. Johnson gave an involuntary shiver, realizing that the temperature was likely to drop even lower.

They would need to work quickly. Bureau Chief Burke had made it abundantly clear that the Director of the FBI expected to find a preliminary report on his desk the next morning.

Burke had also left him with no doubt that they had better find out who had tipped Adversego off, or they'd both be looking for new jobs.

0000 0001 0010 0011 0100 0011 0010 0001 0000

213

28

Here's to the Company!

F RANK, SR. SWUNG his ancient Land Rover back onto the highway, a server humming in the back and Frank, Jr. tapping away in the front on his laptop. Power and connector cables snaked between the two seats.

"I've only got a wireless AirCard to work with, but if we're lucky I'll have Foomjoy's entire hard drive replicated by the time we cross the Mississippi. I've already got the list of hacked sites from the CIA, so let's see what that shows."

Frank pored over the data as they drove eastward into the night. There seemed to be no order or pattern to the 192 sites that had been attacked to date. Every type of host had been hit – newspapers, universities, retailers, government sites, non-profits – you name it. After the first few high profile targets, the most obvious conclusion seemed to be that the victims had been chosen at random.

What to make of that?

Randomness would be consistent with the goal of raising concerns over security, since it would make everyone feel vulnerable and therefore get everyone screaming for a fix. But who would care about raising security concerns enough to risk going to jail for easily twenty years? Not your average geek hacker, anyway.

Not a security company, either. That would only showcase how inadequate their current products were. And no career cyber-criminal would have a motive, since the panic was making everyone beef up their security. A foreign enemy would want to keep you vulnerable, too. So who *would* gain anything from exposing how vulnerable current networks were?

It just had to be a cover for something else – one of those 192 sites must be the real target. But how to figure out which one it was?

He realized his father had been whistling for a while now, and the tune he had just started rang a distant bell.

"What's that song?"

"Oh, just an old Irish drinking song. It's called, 'Oh, Dear, What Can the Matter Be?' I'm surprised you recognize it."

Frank was, too. Then the answer came to him.

"Remember when we took the cross-country camping trip all those years ago? The drive took forever, and you sang all these great old songs to keep me from getting bored."

His father smiled, remembering. "Right you are. Your generation doesn't know what a good song is – and doesn't spend any time singing, either. Back when I was young, we did a lot of singing – in the army, in school, in a whole lot of bars – you name it. Sentimental songs, nonsense songs, sly songs – there was a lot of great music back then, and everybody knew the words, too."

"So how did that 'What Can the Matter Be?' song go? Do you still remember the words?"

"Which words? It's an old song, with lots of different versions. Let's see if I can still remember the one that I was probably singing back then...."

He sang half to himself for a few lines, but then picked up confidence as the words came back to him:

Oh Dear, What can the matter be?
Seven old ladies locked in a lavat'ry.
They were there from Sunday to Saturday.
Nobody knew they were there.

"That's the song!" Frank laughed, "But the only verse I remember any of is the one about the lady who forgot her nickel."

"Well, you'll have to wait a few verses before she gets her turn." He started singing again.

The first was a lady named Eleanor Humphrey.
Who sat herself down just to make herself comfy.
And when she got up she could not get her bum free.
And nobody knew she was there.

Frank smiled, but this wasn't solving anything. He tried to focus again on the puzzle that had been challenging him for weeks. If the public attacks were just a cover, what were they a cover for?

The next to come in was dear Mrs. Mason
The stalls were all full so she pissed in the basin
And that is the water that I washed my face in
And nobody knew she was there.

He made a face at that verse, just as he had when he was 13.

The third old lady was Amelia Garpickle;
Her urge was sincere, her reaction was fickle.
She vaulted the door; she'd forgotten her nickel,
And nobody knew she was there.

That was his favorite verse! He tried to block the verses out, but eventually gave it up and listened to his father finish out the song:

The sixth old lady was Emily Clancy;
She went there 'cause something tickled her
   fancy,
But when she got there it was ants in her pantsy
And nobody knew she was there.
The seventh was the Bishop of Chichester's daughter
She went in to pass some superfluous water
She pulled on the chain and the rising tide caught her
And nobody knew she was there.
The janitor arrived in the early morning.
He opened the door without any warning,
The seven old ladies their seats were adorning,
And nobody knew they were there.

His father repeated the last line, drawing out the syllables with gusto:

And no-bo-dy knew they were t-h-e-e-r-e!

"THAT'S IT!" Frank screamed, slamming both hands down on the dash board.

"JEE-sus, Mary and Joseph!" his father yelled back as the car swerved. "You almost made me run off the road. What's the hell's the matter with you!"

"That's what they're up to!"

"Who? The janitor? Or the little old ladies?"

"Not them, the hackers! I know what they're up to!"

"Wonderful! *Great!* That's terrific! Now please share your revelation in a calm, quiet voice, if you please, so I can focus on driving safely at 70 miles an hour."

"Okay - sorry. Only I've been going crazy for weeks trying to figure out what the real strategy behind the public attacks has been, and now I've got it!"

"So what is it? And what made it come to you just then?"

"The last line of your song – it took seven verses and the finale, but there it was, staring me in the face, the way it has been all along: 'Nobody knew they were there!'"

"You see, the site they really wanted to hit will be a site where they didn't leave the Alexandria Project attack screen! I've been assuming their target was a single site on the long list of sites we know were hit, with the rest intended to make it impossible to tell which was the real target. But now it occurs to me that's not the case at all – I'm betting *all 192* sites were camouflage – the whole public campaign must have been launched to divert everyone's attention from a site we would never guess had been compromised at all!"

His father had been listening closely at first, but now he put on an aloof, impassive face as he drove. "Okay, but nowhere does your theory lead us yet."

"Do you really have to do that? Anyway, I'm hoping it does. If Mrs. Foomjoy's hard drive has a record of all the sites the real bad guys have attacked, all we have to do is match it up against the CIA's list. I'll bet there will be one site, or maybe a few sites, that aren't on the CIA's list at all. If I'm right, we'll know we've found what they were really after!"

"Proud of you Yoda is. But point out he must that know you will only what site the real target was, and not after what the evil ones seek."

Frank grimaced. "That was even worse than usual. Do you think in Yoda-speak or something?"

"Actually, no. Matter of fact, it kind of makes my brain hurt."

"Yeah, well, don't feel obligated on my account."

Frank harrumphed to himself. He deserved a little more credit for his revelation, didn't he? After all, this was his first real progress in weeks. Assuming, of course, that he was right.

0000 0001 0010 0011 0100 0011 0010 0001 0000

George Marchand was relieved after speaking with the CIA Director. Being free of the requirement to log his reports into the joint Homeland Security database not only meant the FBI wouldn't learn anything more from him, but that the CIA Director wouldn't, either. Not for a while, anyway, and that was going to be important.

He was in a tough spot, he reflected. The story Baldwin had fed him didn't hang together, and Baldwin probably realized that by now, too. If Baldwin had learned that the FBI was on its way to capture Adversego, couldn't he have sent someone to warn Frank in person faster than he could send a drone from who knows where? And what could he have hoped to accomplish with a Predator anyway?

Worse yet, how could Baldwin have justified sending an armed drone aloft on an operation in the U.S.? What if it had crashed, as they sometimes did? How would he have explained that? It just didn't make sense. The only rational conclusion was that Baldwin had been desperate to take Frank out before the FBI could capture him.

If that was true, it didn't leave George with many options within the line of duty to help Frank. He'd been trying to think of a second one all day, and so far had failed miserably.

Nothing to be done, then, but get on with it, and hope that he still had a job when the dust settled. He picked up the phone and called Marla.

"Hi Marla, it's George."

"Hey George! It's nice to speak to you somewhere other than in a dark alley."

He smiled. "That's what I thought, too. How about dinner tonight? After all, you're my goddaughter and I can't remember the last time we got together."

0000 0001 0010 0011 0100 0011 0010 0001 0000

About 7:30 AM, Frank saw the bridge in the distance he'd been waiting for. He'd slept through half the night before taking over the wheel from his father, and now it was time to turn it back over to him. He pulled into a rest area and shook his father by the shoulder.

"Time to earn your keep, old man. We've reached the Mississippi."

His father groaned as he stepped stiffly out of the Land Rover.

"You know, sleeping in a car sucked when I was half your age. Don't you have any respect for your elders?"

Frank ignored him as he pulled his laptop out of the back of the Land Rover and refreshed the screen. Good – the download was complete. He climbed into the passenger seat and began exploring the disk directory. Ten minutes later, he found what he was looking for.

"Got it! Give me five minutes and we'll see whether I'm on to something or not."

Frank set up the comparison between the CIA's list sites they knew to have been hacked by the Alexandria Project, and the record of hacked sites he had extracted from the copy of Mrs. Foomjoy's hard drive. He held his breath, gently pressed the Enter key, and watched the percentage numbers spin as first one database and then the other was loaded, and then again as the comparison ran.

"*Yes!* There's exactly one new site!"

"Good fishing! What did you catch?"

Frank looked at the Web address and replied in a puzzled voice.

"A U.S. Geologic Survey database?"

0000 0001 0010 0011 0100 0011 0010 0001 0000

George found Marla waiting for him inside the door of an Italian restaurant not far from the Capitol. He hadn't seen her dressed for an evening out before, and he was struck by what an attractive and self-assured young woman she had become.

"Well hello, George. Did you remember to bring your skeleton keys?"

He laughed as the maitre'd ushered them to a quiet table near the back of the restaurant and held her chair.

George sat down, and suddenly felt self-conscious, sitting along with someone half his age at a candle-lit table. Marla smiled at him and he cleared his throat.

"You know, I never have an opportunity to say it with Carl always around, but you've grown up to be quite an impressive young lady."

"Thanks. And I didn't get a chance to say how much I appreciate all you've done for my father over the years." She looked down as she spread her napkin in her lap. "I never realized it at the time, but you really helped him turn his life around. He's shared a lot of things with me in the last few months that I never knew before."

George cleared his throat again. "Well, perhaps that's not a bad transition to what I wanted to tell you this evening. You see, there's one more thing you never knew."

"Oh? What's that?"

"Marla, if I share some things with you I shouldn't, can I trust you completely to keep them to yourself?"

"You know, I can't seem to talk to anyone for more than five minutes anymore without running into that question. Do you think it's something about the way I wear my hair?"

She laughed, but George didn't. "I'm sorry. I didn't mean to be flip. Of course you can, George. Please go on."

"Marla, did it strike you as a bit odd that the CIA would tap a library IT director to help out on a covert operation?"

Marla stared at him. "George! Are you telling me that you're a spook, too? *You?*"

He looked slightly hurt. "I'm too dull and boring to be an agent, is that it?"

"No, no – I'm sorry. It's just that I've known you since I was a kid, and I've never looked at you that way – why, you're the last person in the world I'd expect to be a CIA agent." She paused. "Well, I mean, I guess that's the idea, though, isn't it?"

"Yes, as a matter of fact, it is."

"My, my," Marla said, shaking her head from side to side. "It's going to take me a minute or two to get my brain around this. I wonder who else I know that's leading a double life? Or maybe I should wonder who isn't?" She looked sideways at the approaching waiter with mock suspicion.

"Something to drink? A bottle of wine perhaps?"

George looked at Marla.

She laughed. "Yes, I guess I could use a drink! Wine would be perfect – I don't know exactly what I'm ordering yet, but something white will be fine with me."

George looked at the wine menu. "We'll have the '03 Prosecco – hard to go too far wrong with that."

They studied their menus and ordered when the waiter returned with the wine in a bucket of ice.

When he left, Marla raised her glass. "So here's to the Company!"

"Here's to the Company," George repeated, but with less enthusiasm than he might have a few days before.

They put their glasses down, and Marla spoke again. "You know, this is really a little awkward. I don't know why you're telling me this, or what I can ask you and what I can't, so why don't I just listen."

"Thanks, and you're right – I can't go into a lot of detail. Suffice it to say that I've been part of the CIA for a long time, that working for the Library of Congress is my cover, and that I'm very much involved in the Alexandria Project investigation. That's really all you need to know."

Marla suddenly giggled. She put her napkin to her mouth.

"I'm sorry. It just occurred to me that you might be Carl's boss. It's going to be really hard for me not to ask you to tell me embarrassing things about him."

George smiled. "By my observation, Carl is quite capable of embarrassing himself without any help from me. But seriously, Marla, he's very reliable, and he actually does know what he's doing, even if he is too self important by half for his own good. And if I wasn't sure you would be completely safe under his protection, I would have assigned somebody else to watch out for you instead."

"I am sorry," she said again. "That was out of line." Then she giggled again. "Still, if anything really good should occur to you...."

"Moving on," George said as the waiter brought their appetizers and refilled their wine glasses.

They exchanged small talk , and then George became serious again.

"Marla, here's what I really wanted to talk to you about. I'm worried about Frank. He's done very well taking care of himself so far, but I think we need to get him into a safe house for awhile. Now that he's on the run again I'm worried that the FBI is eventually going to spot him. We can't let that happen. Will you help convince him to take cover again if I provide an appropriate location?"

"Can't you just tell the FBI to chill? Don't you guys ever talk to each other?"

"Yes and no. First and foremost, you have to understand that the U.S. is the FBI's turf – not the CIA's. By law, we can't do much on U.S. soil, and especially not involving U.S. citizens. Our ability to protect Frank is very limited, and right now, the FBI thinks it might be quite convenient for them to hang your father out to dry."

Marla put down her fork.

"You realize, George, that it's going to be difficult for me to convince my father to trust the CIA after the FBI came for him, even if I tell him that you're with the CIA. How does he know that someone else at the CIA didn't tip the FBI off?"

George paused, and then said quietly. "When I said, "safe house," I didn't necessarily mean a CIA safe house."

Marla stared at him. "You mean the CIA did tip the FBI off?"

"I can't know for sure one way or the other. Actually, I don't think they did. But that may be beside the point."

Marla frowned. "George, with all due respect, you're not making much sense."

"I know," he said uncomfortably. Marla raised her eyebrows and waited.

George took a deep breath and then leaned forward.

"Let me lead into this gently. Let's say I'm going to give you some good news, and then I'm going to give you some bad news."

"Okay. I've set my wine glass down on the table and folded my hands neatly in my lap. Do I look composed?"

"Yes, you do. So the good news is that at least for now, the FBI thinks your father's dead."

Marla's eyebrows went up again. "Okay. And that would be why?"

"Well, that brings us to the bad news. It seems that the Director of the CIA blew up your father's camper with a Hellfire missile. And I don't know for sure that he knew your father wasn't in it."

Marla stared at him, and then stood up abruptly. "You're going to have to excuse me."

George watched as she strode off to the rest room. He stared moodily down at the table while the waiter cleared their appetizers and brought the entrees. Now what?

It was almost five minutes before Marla returned. George stood up to hold her chair, but she motioned him to sit back down. She spread her napkin in her lap once more, took a sip of wine, and then looked across the table.

"You know, that wasn't the most persuasive bit of information you could have provided to convince my father to trust you."

"Of course it wasn't. But it was also true. And it *should* convince him how high the stakes are that people are playing for here."

"Granted. But it'll take more than that to convince him."

"You name it, and if it's anything I can do, I will."

"Good! That's the right answer." Looking around to make sure that no one was watching, Marla reached into her purse and then handed him a small slip of paper.

"What's this?"

"That's the address of a database at a U.S.G.S. website. I called my father while I was in the lady's room to bring him up to date. He wants you to get him the password and full rights to access the information at that website."

He looked down at the slip of paper and then placed it carefully in his pocket. "And then?"

"And then I'll see what I can do about bringing my father 'in from the cold.'"

She raised her glass and smiled. "Did I say that right?"

0000 0001 0010 0011 0100 0011 0010 0001 0000

Not far away, Francis X. McInnerney was dining alone. After bungling the capture of Adversego, his people in Las Vegas had come through for him. And a good thing for them they had.

He sipped his celebratory glass of The Macallan, 30-year-old scotch and reflected on the news Johnson had delivered to him. It seems that there was no trace of any human remains to be found in the wreckage of the camper. Baldwin may have thought he'd put one over on McInnerney, but the missile had struck the rear of the vehicle, leaving the engine and more than almost half of the cab more or less intact. Johnson had found parts of a video camera in the grill of the camper. He was almost 100% sure the vehicle had charged his men under remote control.

Johnson had also assigned someone to review all the details in the joint Agency database about Adversego's family and friends, and then ran it against the FBI's own master database of information. When he did, he found a surprising connection. It seemed that Frank's long lost father was actually a retired FBI agent living in Nevada under the name Bart Thatcher. And also that Thatcher hadn't been seen or heard from since Johnson unknowingly left him a voicemail seeking help in capturing Frank.

Thatcher's relation to Frank, of course, would never find its way back into the joint agency database. All the CIA would find there was the fact that every FBI agent and state trooper in the country was looking for an old heap of a Land Rover, light green, with Nevada plates, VEK 452, driven by someone named Bart Thatcher and carrying another person of interest. Upon capture, they were to be brought immediately to the nearest FBI field office.

McInnerney bet he'd be showing that bastard Baldwin who was boss within 24 hours. He swirled his scotch meditatively in his glass, and then with a smirk raised it in a silent toast: Here's to the Company!

0000 0001 0010 0011 0100 0011 0010 0001 0000

29

A Car Chase is the Sincerest Form of Flattery

"WHAT DO YOU mean that website doesn't exist? I'm looking at its log-in screen right now."

George Marchand was on the phone with the director of IT services at the U.S. Geological Survey.

"No it doesn't George. You know what I'm saying."

"I know you're saying you know something you're not telling me."

"No, George. You know I'm saying I know something I *can't* tell you. C'mon, be reasonable."

"Okay, have it your way. Then how about giving me a user ID and a password that don't exist for this website that doesn't exist?"

Bill Fine sighed. He'd known Marchand for years through inter-agency IT meetings and liked him. But he didn't like him enough to end up fired or in jail.

"George, you know I can't do that, either."

Marchand waited, but Fine was silent. "So, is that it?" He mentally crossed his fingers and waited.

Finally, he heard a sigh at the other end, and then Fine began to speak again. "It should be. But as I recall, you were granted the highest level access to a variety of sites last week in connection with an inter-agency interoperability/security pilot that will start next week. Maybe you should take a look at the list of sites that will be part of the pilot. Gotta go."

Well, how about that. So he had. George opened the locked cabinet in the corner of his office and removed a thick envelope. Sure enough, the USGS would be part of the pilot. He sorted through the contents until he found another sealed envelope. In it was a set of log in instructions and two security tokens.

0000 0001 0010 0011 0100 0011 0010 0001 0000

"Second token number entered? Okay, one last time, hit enter." Then the phone line went dead.

Frank pressed the Enter key, and a moment later he was inside the USGS site that didn't exist. But what was it he was looking at?

A database, it seemed. And a big one, too. It must have hundreds of millions of individual data cells. He opened one up at random and found a pair of numbers, ending in the letter "W." He checked a few other cells, and saw that each one ended in an either an "E" or a "W."

"What do E and W have in common?" he asked his father.

"Well, throw in N and S, and you've got the four points of the compass."

Of course – that must be it. These were geographic coordinates – latitude and longitude. And extremely precise ones at that. Instead of reflecting just degrees and minutes - 38° 53' N, 77° 02' W - in the traditional presentation – each pair of coordinates was much more exact, displaying in decimal form to six significant digits. The number in the cell he'd last opened looked like this:

42.495372N-70.858922W

Then he noticed something else that was strange. The last digit in the longitude number had just changed from 2 to 3. This wasn't a simple, static database-of information at all – it was an enormous dynamic data warehouse that was updating in real time. What was *that* all about?

Frank tabbed and copied the number for future reference, and then began browsing through the administrative functions of the database. He found a field marked "search" and another marked "report," so he pasted the coordinates he'd copied into the "report field." He hit enter, and saw the following:

Abbot Hall, Marblehead, Mass.

Well, that was pretty accurate, he had to admit. There was a drop down menu next to the "Report" field, so he clicked on it and saw a number of options, including a field he could fill in to determine the distance between coordinates and place names. He pasted in the coordinates he had just copied, and typed "Washington, D.C." into the "distance from" field. Hitting "Enter," he saw:

$$296.47524$$

That must be a direct line distance in miles. Not too useful for driving. Perhaps for air travel?

"So what did you find?" his father asked.

"Give me another minute." He didn't want to spend any more time on the site than absolutely necessary. Since this whole mad saga had begun, he hadn't done anything illegal, no matter what the FBI might think. Given that the USGS had supplied the log in information he was using he might not even be breaking the law now. But once he started downloading anything from the site, he'd have to be violating who knows how many laws. This had better end well.

He finished setting up the download and initiated the transfer. Then he turned back to his father.

"It looks like a database of geo-coordinates. Hundreds of millions of them. What do you make of that?"

"Well, at the degree and minute level, there's only so many coordinates you could have – you've only got 360 degrees of latitude and longitude to work with, and 60 minutes per degree. So they must be calculating locations a lot finer than that."

"That's right," his son confirmed.

"So let me see... as I recall, a minute of latitude is 1.15 miles, and a minute of longitude can be a lot less than that, since longitudinal lines converge at the poles. When you get down to a 60th of a minute – a second of latitude or longitude - you're talking about a maximum of maybe 100 feet. So if you're looking at hundreds of millions of coordinates, you're probably looking at a database of coordinates accurate to within a few feet."

Frank nodded. "You're right. And there's another thing you should know. The database isn't static; it's live. The last digit of one of the numbers changed as I was looking at it. I guess GPS satellites must have a margin for error."

His father shook his head. "Nope. That doesn't make sense. Sure, the satellites would have a margin of error, but the earth's surface doesn't. There's no sense changing coordinates around for places that aren't actually moving. What you'd want to do would be to set up your database software to average out the data downloaded from, say, a half dozen orbits and then fix the numbers for good. There's got to be another explanation."

They mulled that one over for a while but got nowhere.

"Okay, so let's try another tack," Frank, Sr. suggested. "What's so special about this particular database of geographical coordinates? I've got one loaded in this GPS unit on my dashboard, and it's almost as accurate as the one you just found. If we could figure that out, we'd probably know why it's been hacked."

"Well, I can think of a few reasons," his son replied. "First, even if the data isn't more accurate, it looks like they wanted this set to be a whole lot more secure. That way they wouldn't have to worry about any of the data being corrupted or tampered with. Second, they might have wanted to be sure that it was available when they needed it, so whoever has access to this particular database may have a hardened link in to it. That way they can get to it when they need it, and not have it jammed in transit. Both of those factors suggest a military use."

"Makes sense so far."

"The really intriguing part, though, is the dynamic aspect. The military can afford to include high density data storage in whatever they want, so why do they need to have remote access to a database of geo-coordinates at all? It must be because this one is changing, rather than fixed in memory, like the one in your GPS."

"So we're back to the same question, right? Why is it changing, and why does it matter"

"Right." Frank mused for awhile before he spoke again. "But how about this: if you're going somewhere, you not only need to know the coordinates of where you're going, but also the coordinates of where you are. Otherwise, you can't calculate what direction to go in, or how far you need to go to get there. Maybe this has something to do with where you are, and not your destination."

But his father disagreed. "That's not sounding right to me. That's what the GPS satellites are for. Wherever you are, you just lock on to them, and your GPS unit calculates your location by triangulation, using the length of time it takes the signals to reach you from three different satellites. Let's use my GPS again for comparison: the only thing it's using its internal database for is to display streets and such after the satellites let it figure out where it is. So as long as you've got the satellites, you're only using your coordinates for reference."

"Maybe that's the key then. When might you need to know your location when the satellites *weren't* available?"

"Well, they could be shot down. But there are twenty-four of them, and only a very few countries on Earth have the ability to shoot one down. I suppose you could jam them, at least in theory. But if someone tried to I assume we could pinpoint the source of the signal, and then take it out. Any way you look at it, if anyone tried to shoot down or jam the GPS satellite system, I have to believe we'd be in the middle of an all-out nuclear war."

"Okay, so let's say that's the case. Let's assume this database has something to do with nuclear defense capabilities. That sounds plausible – it's high enough stakes to justify all the hullabaloo the bad guys have engaged in to keep us from focusing on it, right?"

But this time his father didn't answer. Instead, he was looking intently at his rear-view mirror.

0000 0001 0010 0011 0100 0011 0010 0001 0000

Vice President Chaseman rose to welcome the Secretary of State into the Oval Office.

"Good to see you, Jim. Have a seat."

As he walked in, Linda Rauschenberg tried to see as much of the Oval Office as she could without seeming obvious. She thought that it was remarkably poor form for Chaseman to be sitting at the President's desk at all. At least Chaseman hadn't replaced the President's pictures on the wall with his own – yet. Rauschenberg hoped the President would be back in command, albeit from his hospital bed, within a couple of days. Thank God his quadruple bypass surgery had gone well.

"Good to see you too, sir. I assume the topic is North Korea?"

"Pretty safe bet, given that they've commenced fueling those damn missiles. Anyway, the answer is yes. More specifically, I'd like you to alert our closest allies of the steps the United States will take if North Korea launches those rockets."

"Steps, Mr. President? I wasn't aware that you had already reached consensus with the National Security Counsel and the Joint Chiefs of Staff on an appropriate course of action?"

Chaseman gave a tight smile and leaned back.

"That's right, Linda, I haven't. And I don't plan to, either."

"Excuse me, sir?"

"Tell me what section of the Constitution requires that kind of pow-wow? As I recall, the Joint Chiefs of Staff and the Security Counsel didn't exist until the Founding Fathers were long gone."

"But, sir…."

"Don't "But, sir!" me! You know that Rawlings was worried about having a heart attack or stroke. I may have my differences with him on other matters, but he did the right thing on this one."

"As soon as he took office, he had the required letters drawn up to convey the powers of Acting President to me immediately in case he was ever incapacitated. Those letters have been delivered to the Speaker of the House and the Speaker Pro Tem of the Senate and can't be revoked except by the President himself."

"Until he does, I'm the Commander-in-Chief, and I'm determined to act in that capacity. Now listen carefully."

Rauschenberg sat straight up in his chair, alarmed over what she might hear next.

"Here's what you are going to say to the allies: if even one North Korean missile enters U.S. air space, we will immediately deliver, through a means of our choosing, one strategic nuclear weapon over Pyongyang and then trigger that device. If a second missile reaches our airspace, we will deliver a second warhead to a second North Korean target, which will remain unnamed. That device will be triggered as well."

Rauschenberg said nothing. This was not only nuclear madness, but a terrible strategy as well – why commit ourselves to a confrontation where the other guy might not blink first?

"I assume that you have heard me accurately, so I will continue. You will deliver this message personally by secure telephone to the British, the Russians, the Japanese, and the Chinese."

"The Chinese, sir? Not the Germans or the Canadians or the French?"

"Are the Germans or the Canadians or the French likely to contact Jong-Il?"

"No sir, I should think not."

"Do you expect the Chinese will?"

"Yes sir, of course they will."

"Good. Then I assume you understand my plan. You'd better get started. We may have as little as twelve hours to work with."

Rauschenberg started to say, "But, sir!" again and caught herself just in time. "You're assuming that if the North Korean's get word of our plans that they'll back down?"

"That's right."

"But what if they don't believe us? What if they call our bluff?"

"Of course they'll believe us! If we delivered such a threat and didn't follow through on it the credibility of our nuclear deterrent forces would be destroyed forever! Even Jong-Il isn't crazy enough to miss that. If he knows we won't back down, then he'll have to. And he'll stay backed down, assuming he can hang on to power after being humiliated in front of his generals. I'm assuming he won't, which is the second part of the plan."

Rauschenberg couldn't think of another word to start with this time. "But sir – a *nuclear* weapon? The whole world will condemn us! You'll have the blood of millions of innocent people on your hands!"

"I believe I covered that point thoroughly during our last Security Council meeting, Linda. The nuclear taboo has served its purpose. I'm prepared to move on."

The Secretary tried to think quickly; what else could she say that might cause Chaseman to abandon his reckless strategy? Personally, she was unwilling to bet that there was anything that Kim Jong-Il wasn't crazy enough to do, and short of a refusal by the military to obey orders, there was no way to stop Chaseman from following through on his plan. But what General would refuse a direct order from the Commander-in-Chief while a possibly nuclear armed missile was headed towards the U.S.? She tried the last argument she could think of.

"Assuming this works, sir, and the North Koreans back down, what will happen the next time? Unless we're willing to make the same threat every time someone takes us to the wall, we'll have destroyed the credibility of our nuclear deterrence capability anyway. President Rawlings may be back in charge again as soon as the day after tomorrow, and you know very well that he would never want to follow such a policy if there was an alternative. Do you really want to tie his hands that way?"

Rauschenberg's last hope evaporated as she listened to his own words. She realized he already knew what Chaseman's answer would be. The Acting President might be a reckless gambler, but he was clearly a shrewd strategist.

"You're absolutely right! Before his unfortunate medical episode, Rawlings never would have pursued such a strategy. But by the time he comes back, he'll have no choice. When you're only an Acting President, Madame Secretary, you have to work fast."

0000 0001 0010 0011 0100 0011 0010 0001 0000

Frank looked over at his father. "What's up?"

"We've got company. See that black Lincoln Town Car up ahead? You'll notice that it's slowed down so cars will start passing it. Up until a few minutes ago, it was staying exactly five cars ahead of us. Don't be obvious about it, but look behind us and you'll see a gray Ford Crown Victoria slowly moving up on us."

"How can you be sure they're after us?"

"Fifteen minutes ago a State Trooper was coming up fast in the passing lane, until he noticed us. Then he started coasting, and when he pulled level, he looked in my direction. After getting a good view of me, he took off."

"Well, so what? Maybe he's never seen an old Land Rover before?"

"No, that's not it. I'm afraid the FBI has figured out you're not dead – yet – and also put two and two together about our family ties. After all, I did disappear at the same time you did. I was just thinking that they may have put out an All-points bulletin for an old geezer in an ancient, light-green Land Rover when the Town Car and the Victoria showed up. That clinches it."

"Why didn't the Trooper just pull us over?"

"I'm betting the FBI is taking no chances this time. If the Trooper had picked us up, the word might get out. But if the FBI does the job, the CIA will never know we've been grabbed."

"Here's what you're watching: in a couple of minutes, the Town Car will be directly ahead of us. Once there's a long space between the Victoria and any cars behind it, the driver will move up in the passing lane till he's right next to me, going the same speed. Once we're boxed in, the guy riding shotgun in the Victoria will show his ID to me through his window. After that, he'll start to drift right and slow down. We'll have no choice but to do the same – the guy ahead won't be shy about braking till our bumpers touch, if he has to, and then start applying his brakes."

"Then what happens?"

"Once they've got us stopped on the shoulder, they'll pop us into one of the cars, and leave ours where it is. All very inconspicuous when you do it right and the target doesn't do anything stupid. They'll know that I'll know they're heavily armed, and more than willing to use what they're carrying, so they'll be betting I won't do anything stupid. Now let me concentrate."

Frank watched nervously as his father pulled into the passing lane and slowly passed the car in front of them, and then another. As he did, the black Town Car up ahead pulled into the passing lane as well to maintain position, and the gray Crown Victoria behind quit moving closer. Not long after the Land Rover returned to the right hand lane, the gray car behind them started creeping forward again. As soon as it

231

did, his father again entered the passing lane, and once more the FBI cars kept step.

The third time Frank's father moved to the left, he stayed in the passing lane for quite awhile, not returning to the right hand lane until only two vehicles – the black Town Car and a random Honda sedan – separated the Land Rover from two tractor trailers that were just starting the climb up a long upgrade that stretched ahead. Soon, the gray Crown Victoria was directly behind the Land Rover.

By then, the big rigs were starting to lose speed, and the Honda entered the passing lane ahead. Frank's father and their shadows promptly followed. What was he up to, Frank wondered?

He didn't have long to wait to find out. When they were even with the gap between the trucks a few moments later, his father made his move. Without warning, he threw the wheel sharply to the right, shot through the narrow gap between the two trucks and continued across the breakdown lane. As he did, he slammed on the brakes and manhandled the skidding vehicle down the grassy slope beside the highway, barely avoiding flipping the vehicle in the process. Just moments after he had begun the maneuver, they had crossed the strip of grass and were hurtling through the six-foot high weeds of an abandoned farm. By the time the two FBI cars got clear of the tractor trailers, it seemed as if the Rover had simply disappeared off the face of the earth.

Frank had been thrown forward against his seat belt and then from side to side as the car rocked and swerved its way off the highway and into the field. His father was still driving as fast as the vintage Land Rover could handle without flying apart when Frank realized he was holding his breath. He exhaled explosively and turned shakily to his father. "You skipped the part about becoming a wheel man for the Mafia when you brought me up to date."

His father was looking pretty pleased. "What's the use of having an off-road vehicle if you don't go off-road every now and then?"

Soon they were driving more slowly, bumping over the remnant furrows of what must have been a cornfield only a year or two before; here and there, tall, dry cornstalks stood, sprouted from kernels that had escaped the farmer's last harvest. Like the enormous weeds that surrounded them, the cornstalks disappeared under the front bumper of the Land Rover and then struggled half-upright once more after they passed.

Fifty yards later, they happened upon a new but deserted road. Frank, Sr. glanced up at the sun, and turned away from it, heading east. As they drove on, other empty roads crossed their own. Street signs marked the silent intersections of what they realized must be a housing development gone bust during the recession.

"Ha!" Frank's father snorted: "'Cheney Way!' And there's 'Rumsfeld Road.' Looks like this couldn't have happened to a nicer developer."

They continued for another few minutes along the curving road, heading east as much as possible as they sought a way out of the enormous field of weeds, lanes, and cul-de-sacs. Just before crossing Bush Boulevard, though, the black Town Car suddenly shot across just ahead of them, its driver slamming on the brakes as soon as he saw them. Frank, Sr. reciprocated by downshifting and flooring the already much-abused Land Rover.

"Damn! That didn't take long enough. They'll be all over us in no time – this thing isn't built for speed. Hold on."

Frank did very much as he was told as the Land Rover's over-revved engine roared and they hurtled forwards. But in no time, the black Town Car was closing in on them fast. As the cross streets flickered by, they saw that the gray Crown Victoria was now racing along on a road parallel to their own as well. This was beginning to feel familiar.

Frank's father swore, and then he grabbed his son by the arm. "Here – drive."

"*What!!?*" Frank screamed, as he grabbed the wheel and jabbed at the gas pedal with his left foot. But his father was already half out of the car, standing on the driver's seat and craning his head around several feet above the roof of the cab. Frank clenched the wheel with both hands, trying to keep the car from swerving as he perched half way between the driver and passenger seats.

"Got it," his father said as he slid back into the driver's seat, pushing Frank out of the way. Just before he reached the next intersection, his father slammed on the brakes and cornered onto the cross street on two wheels, fishtailing madly in the process.

"Where are we going now?" Frank asked, eye's wide as he looked back over his shoulder to see how long it would take the Town Car to follow.

"Generally or specifically?" his father asked, hunched over the wheel. Frank could already see the Town Car closing in on them once again.

"How about specifically?"

"No clue."

"Okay, *okay* – generally then?

"Not too sure on that one, either, but I'll know it when we get there. For starters, it's some woods I saw over this way. Town Cars and

Crown Vics don't get along with woods too well, but this Land Rover's pretty friendly with them."

Frank turned to look behind again, and saw the head and shoulders of someone sticking up through the sun roof of the Town Car. To his horror, he realized the agent was aiming a gun at the Land Rover.

Frank whipped around. "They're about to start shooting at us!"

He was relieved to see trees now, rising straight ahead above the weeds and cornstalks. But the black Town Car was only a few car lengths behind.

Swooping around a curve, Frank braced himself for what he assumed would be another sharp turn onto a road paralleling the tree line – assuming there was one there, instead of a cul-de-sac. And then he saw it – the gray Crown Victoria, stopped broadside dead ahead, blocking their path. An FBI agent stood at either end, handgun drawn and aimed in their direction.

"Duck!" his father yelled, simultaneously throwing himself down and to the right while throwing the wheel in the same direction. Frank heard the zing of bullets clipping the rear of the car as they hurtled off the road and once again into the weeds.

Corncobs and weed stalks flew in every direction as his father struggled with the wheel. But from behind came the highly satisfying sounds of rending metal as Town Car and Crown Victoria briefly became one, and then dissolved into an impressive array of flying metal and glass, some of which began to fall down around them.

Breathing heavily, his father steered onto a road that did indeed run between the weeds and the woods. He drove more slowly now, and scanned the woods to the side. Only this time he didn't look pleased with the dramatic escape he'd just pulled off.

"We've got to get out of here. Even if there aren't any more cars on our tail right now, they'll probably have a helicopter on the way when one of those guys radios in."

A few minutes later, Frank., Sr. saw what he was looking for – a small, shallow stream running in a culvert under the road. He slowed to a crawl when he reached it, and gingerly turned the vehicle off the road and into the stream. Putting the car in neutral, he jumped out and dragged a large branch a few times over the grass where they had turned off the road until their tire tracks had largely disappeared.

"Hopefully they won't notice we left the road here." He climbed back in and began guiding the Rover down the gently flowing stream, working it over the rocks and branches that littered the stream bed. After a few hundred yards, a grassy woods road approached from the left and began running along the stream. His father turned upon on to it, and they continued onward, more or less heading southeast.

With their windows rolled down and the sounds of birds in their ears, things had become eerily peaceful as they bumped their way slowly along. Overhead, the new leaves of spring largely blocked them from aerial view.

Frank was still tense, though. He couldn't help himself from looking back over his shoulder.

"Now what?" he asked.

"Well, that's it for real roads for awhile. They know where they last saw us, so every cop in Maryland is going to be on the lookout for us. Why don't you fire up your laptop and log onto Google Earth? We need to figure out where we are, and where we should head to next."

Frank did so and zeroed in on their approximate location. "Where are we?"

His father glanced at his GPS and gave him the coordinates. "Isn't there a long park that comes into D.C. from the north?" he asked.

"You mean Rock Creek?"

"That sounds right. Let me know where it goes."

"Found it. The stream that runs through it empties into the Potomac just west of the White House."

"Good. Now follow it back the other way. How far does it go?"

"It looks like the park links into a green corridor that winds generally north for miles – well beyond the Beltway."

"That'll do. Any chance this stream goes anywhere near it?"

Frank dragged the image around on his laptop, watching the coordinates change and comparing them to their position.

"Matter of fact, we're less than half a mile away from the greenway now. Once we intersect, it will be woods and fields all the way into town. There should be enough fire lines, service roads, and park lanes to get us all the way there. We'll have to cross a real road from time to time, but we shouldn't have to travel on one."

"Then the way is clear," his father said. "Now hand me a beer – I've earned it."

They continued on their winding way until they saw a bridge ahead where a secondary road crossed the stream. As they drew closer, they saw that open fields lay just past the bridge, stretching away to the north and south, bordered by trees on both sides.

Frank, Sr. drove the Land Rover under the bridge and stopped on a sandbank. "Nobody's going to see us down here. Better wait for dark before we go any further."

Frank got out of the vehicle and stretched gratefully. Then he noticed a young boy, maybe eleven years old, looking at them from beside the stream about thirty yards ahead. Frank nodded in the boy's direction to his father as he got out of the driver's seat.

His father studied on the situation for a moment, and then ambled over to the lad and smiled. "Howdy, son. Fish'n?"

The boy hesitated, and then said, "No, mister. Just hanging out and skip'n stones."

Frank's father nodded approvingly. The boy continued to stare.

"How come you're driving your car in the creek, mister?" the boy finally asked.

Frank, Sr.'s. face turned serious at the question. He pointed off over the boy's head, and the boy turned to see that a full moon had just started to rise out of the trees. Puzzled, he turned back to Frank, Sr.

"Werewolves can't stand water."

The boy's eyes grew round as the rising moon. Then he scampered over the bank of the stream and disappeared.

0000 0001 0010 0011 0100 0011 0010 0001 0000

30

The Death Defying, Incredibly Exciting, Final !

"MARLA, IF THE FBI has spotted him, we've got to get him someplace safe – maybe somewhere in West Virginia if he's already back east. Where is he now?"

"I don't know for sure. I just know he's headed into town."

"Into *Washington?* Is he out of his mind?"

"He figures D.C. is the last place the FBI will look for him - they won't believe he could get past them."

Washington! If Frank carried that line of reasoning far enough, he'd probably head for his own apartment!

"Listen, Marla – tell him this. There's a service entrance off 2nd Street behind the Library of Congress. Just inside there's an unmarked door he's probably never noticed before. That door leads to a bunkroom, kitchen, and workroom the CIA uses for classified test bed work on the LoC system. Our people put in week-long shifts there a couple times a year so LoC staff don't see them coming and going without a good explanation. I could meet Frank there and let him in without anyone noticing. He'd have the place to himself, and all the secret technical facilities, too, using my password. What more could he want?"

"I'll see what I can do."

0000 0001 0010 0011 0100 0011 0010 0001 0000

"So what do you think?" Frank asked his father.

"Well, the FBI knows what we both look like, so any time we're any-where in public someone could spot us and turn us in. We can't rent a motel room without showing ID. Stands to reason they'll be watching out for Marla as well, so we can't ask her to book something for us. So that means we can't hole up anywhere without risk."

"And we can't head back to the boonies, either, because this rig sticks out like a beach ball at a bowling alley. You can bet they'll have an alert out to all the rental car companies, so no dice on a new set of wheels. We could hotwire a car, but stealing isn't my style. Anyway, we could still get caught once the owner reported the car missing. And it goes without saying they're not going to let you pull off that bus station trick a second time. Way I see it, we don't have a whole lot of choice."

Frank agreed. "I guess that's it, then. I'll let Marla know we'll meet George tomorrow morning."

"Tell her 7:30 – we'll be less noticeable in rush hour traffic than we would be at the crack of dawn."

Frank, Sr. stepped out from under the bridge to watch the moon as it rose while his son contacted Marla. Out of habit, he started to orient himself. The full moon had risen, of course, directly opposite where the sun had set. At this time of year, that would be about south-southwest, so he was looking north-northeast. If he was really good at this, he could likely determine his course more easily by the moon than he could with a compass, since he wouldn't have to compensate for....

He turned and walked rapidly back under the bridge. "I think I've got it. Or at least the point about the numbers changing. You see, if you're relying on compass readings instead of, say, star sights or a GPS to estab-lish position, you have to compensate for the fact that magnetic north isn't in the same place as true north. Unless the magnetic north pole happens to be exactly between you and true north, you've always got to add or sub-tract something to what your compass says to find true north."

"So? I can see why that would matter if you were moving, because the amount you'd have to compensate would change, but locations don't move. Why would you have to change the numbers of the coor-dinates themselves?"

"You wouldn't, at least not necessarily. But there's another thing that changes, and that's the location of the magnetic north pole itself – it's wandering around all the time, maybe because there are currents that move around in the molten core of the earth. So if you were navigating by gyrocompass, you'd always need to know exactly where magnetic north was at that time or you couldn't adjust for it."

"So a database of coordinates you carried on board would grow more and more imprecise over time, unless you knew where north was?"

"Right. Unfortunately, you can't predict the future movement of the magnetic north pole reliably, so you can't build an adjustment into the database software, either. The next day, magnetic north might just decide to head off in a whole different direction, and instead of adjusting for error, you'd be compounding it."

"But that still doesn't make sense," Frank objected. "You wouldn't need a very powerful computer to change all of the coordinates on its own. All it would need would be the new location of magnetic north, and then the software could take it from there. I could write that routine in fifteen minutes."

And indeed that seemed like a dead end once more.

"Hmm. Good point." His father sounded disappointed. "Oh well, time to get moving anyway."

They got back in the Land Rover. Soon, they were driving again, lights out, across the broad, moonlit meadows.

Frank, Sr. turned the radio on, and browsed around the channels.

"Doesn't your generation listen to any music that isn't crap?"

"Uh, my generation doesn't listen to this crap, either. Why don't you try NPR?"

His father explored the left hand of the dial, and found the right channel. But instead of the usual Saturday night fare – music or *A Prairie Home Companion* – two of the weekend news anchors were speaking about foreign affairs.

For those of you that may have just tuned in, that was White House Press Secretary Tom Falconer we were listening to, reading a brief statement about the rapidly escalating crisis with North Korea. Falconer is now leaving the West Wing Press Room, so it looks like there won't be an opportunity to ask questions.

Thanks, Melinda. As we just heard, Acting President Henry Chaseman has placed U.S. troops in South Korea on the highest state of alert, following the statement by North Korea's General Chun Bach Choy that any effort by the West to interfere with the North's current military buildup will be met with a nuclear response.

"Holy Shit!" Frank's father exclaimed, turning the radio up.

The Press Secretary also announced that the U.S. is keeping all of its options open - including a nuclear response if the North attacks the U.S. Melinda, what do we know at this point about the two missiles we've been talking about all week?

Well, Brian, GNN reported an hour ago that it has obtained satellite photos that seem to indicate that North Korea has begun fueling them.

Thanks, Melinda. Let's go now to retired Air Force General Brent Kingston. Can you hear me, General?

Yes, Brian. Good to be back on the show.

Thank you, it's always great to have you here. Now can you tell us, General, about how long it would take the North to make these missiles operational once fueling has commenced?

Well, we know that the new Taepodong 3 missile is a combination solid fuel/liquid fuel launch vehicle, and we have a pretty accurate idea of its dimensions. While we can't be sure of the exact fuel mixture they're using, which affects the ratio of liquid oxygen to liquid propellant to some degree, we can make a pretty good guess – say ten to twelve hours.

So General – that would mean that these missiles could be launch-ready as early as tomorrow morning sometime?

That's right, Brian.

Frank, Sr. whistled softly, and clicked off the radio.

"I wish to hell we'd whipped them for good when I was over there during the war. I've never liked this guy Chaseman, but I agree we've got to draw a line in the sand with them before it's too late. The question, of course, is how?"

"Do you figure the North Koreans could really hit Washington?"

"I don't know. It would be a great circle route over the arctic, which makes it harder for me to visualize the distance. Why don't you check your fancy new database and find out?"

Why not indeed? Frank opened the database he'd downloaded, and then the administrative page with the search function. He typed "Pyongyang" into the "report" function and saw a pair of coordinates display. Then he opened the drop down menu and typed "Washington, D.C." into the "distance from" data field. When he clicked Enter, the display read:

0.0000

"So what did you find out?"

"That I must have done something wrong." He repeated the sequence, and got the same result.

"I don't understand. I'm getting an answer that can't be right."

"Well, what do the coordinates for Pyongyang say?"

Frank went back a step and read them out:

$$38.902431N - 77.016553W$$

"The longitude anyway has got to be wrong" his father said. "Try punching that into my GPS and see what you get."

Frank reached across and typed the numbers into the GPS unit, and then hit the Enter key.

Slowly the Land Rover drifted to a halt as father and son gazed at the map on the small screen of the GPS unit, and in particular at the location of the cursor that blinked on and off, on and off, on and off.

It was dead center on the dome of the Capitol Building.

0000 0001 0010 0011 0100 0011 0010 0001 0000

"General Hayes, sir."

Acting President Chaseman looked at his intercom, and then up at Ken Sanford, his Chief of Staff.

"What the hell does he want?"

"I expect he's come to escort you to the War Room, sir. I understand it's going to take close to half an hour before we arrive and get settled in, and things may start happening very quickly not long after that."

"Why not the Secret Service?"

"In time of war, sir, the military assumes equal responsibility for the President's safety."

Chaseman was beginning to sweat profusely. The North Koreans had decided not to play the role that he had assigned to them. And the President was still unconscious, recovering from his quadruple bypass operation.

"Okay, show him in."

Brigadier General Fletcher Hayes wasted no time. He began speaking respectfully but forcefully from the doorway to the Oval Office.

"Good morning, sir. I've come to escort you to the War Room. Would you please follow me?"

Chaseman and Sanford followed silently down the hall of the West Wing, and then down the stairs that led to the White House kitchen.

The Acting President tried a joke to mask his anxiety. "I suppose you'll be taking us next through a secret door in the back of the meat freezer?"

Hayes didn't laugh. "Hardly necessary, sir. Placing the entrance in the kitchen was a matter of necessity. The White House doesn't always lend itself well to modern modifications. Would you please press your right thumb on this pad please, sir?" Chaseman did as requested.

Hayes swung the steel door open, and then led them down several more flights of stairs. At the bottom they found a golf cart with an enlisted man sitting stiffly in the driver's seat. Hayes joined the driver up front while Chaseman and Sanford climbed in behind. Ahead, a cramped tunnel barely six feet high and periodically lit by single, bare light bulbs extended off into the distance as far as they could see.

"Sorry for the musty smell, sir. This tunnel was opened in 1950, not long after the first Soviet nuclear test. Except for occasional maintenance inspections, it's been closed up since the Cold War ended."

My God, Chaseman thought as the cart accelerated into the void ahead. What have I gotten myself into?

0000 0001 0010 0011 0100 0011 0010 0001 0000

General Chan Bach Choy and President Kim Lang-Dong spoke quietly in the back of the blacked-out limousine. On the other side of the thick glass divider, the driver wore night-vision goggles in order to thread his way slowly along the narrow mountain road.

"What do you think this Acting President Chaseman will do? Will he in fact bomb Pyongyang?" he President asked.

"I believe he will *try* to bomb Pyongyang – but he will fail," the General replied.

The President was not comforted by the General's assurance. "How can you be so sure that we will succeed with our missiles and they will fail with theirs? This has troubled me greatly for some time."

"Do not underestimate the military, my friend. You must leave this in my charge and trust that it will be as I have promised. As soon as the missiles are ready, they will be fired. Approximately twenty minutes later, Washington and another city that will surprise you will be destroyed. There will be utter chaos in the enemy's ranks, and in that chaos, I will give the order for our troops to attack across the border. Seoul will be ours before nightfall."

President Lang-Dong peered into the darkness, his brow furrowed. Despite the General's words, he was very happy not to be in Pyongyang.

The driver turned off the road and stopped in front of what appeared to be a shepherd's stone cottage perched on the steep side of the mountain. The driver opened their door, and then rapped on the door of the cottage. A red light shone on them briefly as a peep slot in the door opened and closed, and then the door itself swung open.

They stepped into a darkened chamber, and then were shown by a guard through a second door. In the well-lit room beyond, they found the Dear Leader and all of his sons sitting around a table. Behind them, a half dozen heavily armed men stood at attention. These were members not of the military, but of Kim Jong-Il's intensely loyal corps of personal bodyguards. Each had been born and raised in the same humble village where the Dear Leader himself had grown up, as had his father before him. General Bach Choy always felt uneasy around them. He wasn't used to men that couldn't be bought or blackmailed.

As soon as they entered the room, Jong-Il spoke. "Is all in readiness, General?"

"Indeed it is, Dear Leader. The fueling process is proceeding perfectly. It will be complete in fifteen minutes, and then the flight readiness tests will commence. When complete, the ten minute countdown will begin."

"Thank you, General." Jong-Il looked uncertain, as if waiting for someone to tell him what should happen next.

The General cleared his throat. "Perhaps you should give the launch order now, Dear Leader, to fire as soon as the missiles are ready. That way you can make your way down into the bunker without further delay. Despite all our precautions, we can never know for sure that the enemy has not discovered your location. It would be best if you were safely underground well before the missiles are launched."

"Yes," Jong-Il agreed. "Yes, that would be wise."

"If I may, sir?" Jong-Il nodded, and General Bach Choy stepped forward. He picked up the telephone that lay on the table in front of the Dear Leader, pressed a button, and spoke a few words.

"Lieutenant Grid-lee, I will hand the phone now to the Dear Leader, who will give you the final order."

Bach Choy handed the phone to Kim Jong-Il. In a surprisingly strong voice, he spoke into the phone: "You may fire when ready, Grid-lee."

The General nodded approvingly. "That was very memorable, sir."

General Bach Choy looked out of the corner of his eye at Jong-Il's eldest son as he replaced the phone in its cradle. "You really should be going now, Dear Leader. We will remain in constant communication with you as the launch and the offensive unfold."

Jong-Il rose unsteadily to his feet, and General Bach Choy and President Lang-Dong turned to go. And then the Dear Leader's eldest son spoke.

"Father, the General and the President have performed their roles so well, it does not seem right to leave them vulnerable to harm. Who knows what will happen even moments from now, and the communications from the bunker are excellent. Why not invite them to share it with us?"

The two men froze, each afraid to look at the other.

Jong-Il nodded. "Yes, you are quite right. If they are with us, I can stay in closer contact with what is happening on the battlefield. My leadership will be essential, of course, to the success of this enterprise. Gentlemen, I must ask you to accept my personal hospitality. Follow us now into the bunker."

The General and the President turned slowly to see the wicked smile on the face of Kim Jong-Il's eldest son. As the Dear Leader stepped through the door of the elevator beyond, his hulking body guards stepped behind the President and the General, blocking the door through which they had entered.

"After you," their nemesis said, gesturing towards the open elevator.

As if in a dream, they walked slowly forward. What else they could do?

0000 0001 0010 0011 0100 0011 0010 0001 0000

Frank, Sr. wore a grim expression as he drove south through Rock Creek Park, still driving overland. Indeed, it was impossible to do otherwise, because the park lane he paralleled, like every other road in Washington, was choked with cars trying to evacuate the city. People stared at them as they drove in the opposite direction, wondering whether the father and son were crazy, or perhaps knew something they didn't and wished they did.

"You've got to get through to someone, damn it!" Frank was yelling into his phone.

"Believe me, I've tried. And I'll keep trying," George Marchand replied. "At this point, you might as well keep heading for the Library – we're moving the most precious items down into the bomb shelter now. There's room for the full staff down there, if we need to duck and cover."

Frank dialed Marla next.

"Where are you?"

"We're already outside the Library. We arrived early, in case you did, too. Things didn't start getting really crazy until we were almost here."

"Call George – tell him to let you in right now! We should be there soon."

The scene became increasingly bizarre as they reached the Potomac. Along the river, everything was deserted and peaceful. But on the roads above, horns blared constantly as people maneuvered frantically for position in their efforts to escape.

Frank turned on the radio. The Civil Defense broadcaster was periodically breaking in on all channels, but it was clear that the authorities had little of use to say. The announcer simply repeated the same message each time.

This is not a test. Repeat: this is not a test.

While there is no immediate danger, the city has been placed on high alert, and the possibility of a nuclear attack cannot be discounted. In the event that the threat escalates, an announcement will be made immediately. If an attack is launched, sirens will sound across the city. Repeat: sirens will sound across the city.

All residents are advised to remain calm. If you have a vehicle and decide to leave Washington, be sure you have a full tank of gas and take sufficient food and water with you to last several days. If you have a home emergency kit, be sure to take that along as well.

"Fat lot of good that will do you!" Frank, Sr. said with a snort. "Same crap as we used to hear back in the '60s."

Please be advised that traffic leaving the city is extremely heavy and may come to a halt. Inbound lanes on many major arteries have been converted for use by outbound traffic. Use extreme caution and do not enter any normally inbound lane unless there is an officer directing traffic into that lane.

In the event that you are informed that an attack is imminent, if you are driving, stop immediately and seek shelter, below ground if possible. If shelter is not available, attempt to get under your car. If you are at home, go to your basement immediately. If you do not have a basement....

Frank, Sr. switched off the radio. "How long?"

"Till we get to the Library or till we're fried?"

"I'd prefer Door Number One."

"Not long," Frank said, as they sped up the grass of the Mall, thumping over the curbs of the deserted cross streets. "But then what?"

~~0000~~ ~~0001~~ ~~0010~~ ~~0011~~ 0100 ~~0011~~ ~~0010~~ ~~0001~~ ~~0000~~

General Hayes escorted Acting President Chaseman into the War Room. Some of the members of the Joint Chiefs of Staff and the National Security Council were already seated; others were standing in twos and threes, speaking quietly.

Around the periphery, technicians wearing headsets sat at terminals controlling the enormous LED displays that encircled the room and periodically flashed from one informational display to the next.

As the General led Chaseman to the head of the table that curved around the room, those standing moved to their seats, and the room grew quiet. By the time Chaseman sat down, a circle of stares, not all of them supportive, confronted him.

What was the script for a scene like this he wondered? Gratefully, he saw the Chairman of the Joint Chiefs rise from his seat.

"Sir, permit me to update you on the situation. It appears that North Korea's ground forces reached their final deployment positions by midnight last night, local time. We've seen no further advances since then, but activity on the ground is intense and may indicate final preparations for an attack at any moment across the DMZ. South Korea's deployment is not as far advanced, with approximately 25% of its forces still moving into position. This is hampering our own final preparations as well. Consequently, almost 20% of our ground forces are still in transit.

The General paused, and Chaseman wondered what he was expected to say. Clearing his constricted throat, he tried this: "General, what do you estimate the final proportions on both sides will be?"

"Sir, only about 405,000 out of South Korea's 522,000 army personnel are field troops. Of those, approximately 380,000 are combat ready and either in, or approaching, position. Of our 28,500 troops in theater, approximately 19,000 are war fighters, but only 12,000 have been deployed to the DMZ. The rest are needed to protect our bases and other U.S. interests in the event of open hostilities. That means that our combined forces on the DMZ will be less than 400,000 once all are in position.

"And for the North?"

"Almost 3 million, sir, but as you know, only a third are regular army. And the Red Guards are equipped primarily with light weapons."

Still, Chaseman thought, those numbers were overwhelming. And while much of the North's mechanized forces were not state of the art, many of South Korea's tanks and artillery were locally manufactured as well; some were even surplus Russian tanks purchased after the collapse of the Soviet Union.

"What do we have in the air?"

"Better than on the ground, but not as much as we'd like; things moved much too quickly for us to get an additional carrier group into the Pacific. Only one of our three B-52 Stratofortress wings is in range for turn-around missions. With three million targets on the other side of the DMZ, we could use everything we've got, but one wing is all we'll have to work with. That means 22 aircraft. We've divided them into three rotating task forces. The first is already airborne."

"We're better positioned with our B-1s, but we've only got sixty-six operational, not all of which are based and can be maintained within practical range. Count on forty-two being available. Again, we can bring more in using extra crew and multiple in-air refuelings, but it's difficult to sustain a long campaign on that basis. We've divided the ready wings into three task forces once again, with one plane in each carrying nuclear weapons in addition to conventional ordinance."

"Finally, we have the B-2's, but we don't see them playing a significant role here, given the magnitude of the challenge. The Navy's Tomahawk missiles, on the other hand, will provide crucial support. And, of course, we've got overwhelming superiority with our land and submarine based nuclear missiles."

The General paused before continuing. "For your nuclear contingency plan, we would recommend using our U.S. based ICBMs. The North will have no defenses against them, and we rate their delivery reliability in excess of 99%."

My God, thought Chaseman. That meant that if he gave the order, it would be 99% certain that millions of people would die by his hand as assuredly as if he were to personally hold a gun to their heads. Could this truly be happening? He forced himself to continue.

"What is the status of their missiles?"

"The North Koreans completed fueling their two long range missiles approximately thirty minutes ago. Operational readiness could be achieved in as little as five minutes, but twenty-five minutes is a more likely figure."

"What probability do you assign to their ability to reach their targets?"

The General paused again. "Sir, we have almost no way to estimate that accurately. The North has never successfully completed a test firing of the Taepodong 2. But they did achieve successful first and second stage ignition in their most recent test – only the third stage failed. As a result, we cannot safely assume that neither missile will reach the lower 48 states, even if it does not reach its final designated target. Whether or not it reaches its intended destination, we should assume that the warhead would be set to automatically detonate at an altitude that would guarantee substantial casualties if it happens to be over a populated area."

"And how do you rate the possibility of our intercepting one or both missiles?"

"As you know, sir, our only defenses nominally capable of intercepting an ICBM are eleven ground based Midcourse Defense missiles. Fortunately, they are all deployed in Alaska. We assume that the North Korean missiles will have only the most primitive deception capabilities, if any at all. That said, our interception and kill capabilities remain questionable at best. If the North has no ability to camouflage its attack, we assign less than a 34% possibility that we will be able to intercept either missile. If they are capable of deploying even basic deception techniques, our assigned probability of interception drops to less than 11%."

The General looked up at a large digital monitor on the wall.

"Sir, it is now less than one minute to earliest potential attack capability."

0000 0001 0010 0011 0100 0011 0010 0001 0000

"There's George – in that doorway over there. Pull in between that construction dumpster and the building."

Frank, Sr. crossed the curb and squeezed the Land Rover out of sight. They ran for the open door, Frank clutching his laptop under his arm. Moments later, Marla was hugging her father, oblivious to all around.

When she disengaged, Marla turned to the old man accompanying her father.

"And you must be, uh, my grandfather."

Frank cut her off. "Sorry, Marla, but you'll have to save that for later – if there is a 'later.' We've got to figure out how to stop our government from incinerating us."

"What do you mean, "incinerate us?""

For the first time, Frank noticed Carl Cummings standing behind Marla. "'Incinerate us,' as in detonate a nuclear weapon overhead, maybe within the hour."

Marla stared. "Yes," Frank continued as they hustled into the building. "I feel like an idiot. I spent the last two weeks trying to make the answer ten times more complicated than it was. I'd been assuming that the database the North was hacking was being uploaded in its entirety for some important military use. It wasn't until we discovered by accident that they'd swapped the coordinates for Pyongyang with those for Washington, D.C. that it hit me – the database must hold the coordinates that our nuclear forces draw on for targeting. So unless we can get through to the War Room, our government may be about to nuke itself, and us along with it."

"We can't do that," George interjected. "I've tried everything. All communications are in locked down mode. I don't have clearance to reach anyone who has clearance to reach anyone in there."

There was silence. Then Marla spoke.

"Dad, maybe whatever we plan to launch at North Korea hasn't been programmed yet. Couldn't you just fix any coordinates the North changed?"

"That's good thinking. Unfortunately, I already thought of it, and there are two problems. First, I've only got viewing privileges to the database, and I haven't been able to hack my way into the edit function. But even if I did, there's the second issue. If Chaseman decides to bomb a second target, there's no way for me to know what that target would be – and there are lots of possibilities."

George broke in. "But you could do a search to find every coordinate with a latitude and longitude that fell within the United States."

Frank shook his head wearily. "I thought of that, too, and guess what? I didn't find another one. But what if they changed the coordinates for a military base in North Korea to a city like Moscow? Needless to say, there are hundreds of thousands of Russian coordinates in the database already, and since the location names are highly encrypted, I can't just search for North Korean locations with coordinates outside the national boundaries. Think about it - what could be better for North Korea than setting off a nuclear war between the U.S. and Russia?"

Frank sat down and looked at them despairingly. "I've been wracking my brain ever since the database answer hit me. I just can't figure out a way to stop them from targeting those missiles."

"Then figure out a way you must to make them stop themselves," his father said quietly.

"It's too late," Frank said miserably, slumped in his chair. "Somebody in the Air Force could be opening up the database right now to access the targeting information and send it to the missiles, and there's no way to stop them."

Suddenly, Frank's eyes widened. He yanked the chain off his neck with one hand and grabbed his laptop with the other. A moment later, he had inserted the thumb drive into its slot in the side of the laptop.

~~0000~~ ~~0001~~ ~~0010~~ ~~0011~~ 0100 ~~0011~~ ~~0010~~ ~~0001~~ ~~0000~~

"Two minutes till expected launch capability."

Chaseman looked up sharply when the unsettling robotic voice spoke from the speakers mounted around the War Room.

"Sir, have you made your targeting decisions?" the Chairman of the Joint Chiefs of Staff inquired.

Who should he choose to destroy? Chaseman thought desperately. Another city of starving, innocent North Koreans? Of course not. But what of Pyongyang and its three and a quarter million inhabitants? He had already committed to obliterating them. Could he let the North Koreans and the Iraqis and, hell, the Russians, too, know that he had only been bluffing?

Steady yourself, he thought. The missiles hadn't been launched yet. They couldn't really be that.... But his thoughts were interrupted by the unfeeling voice from the speakers.

"Missile one is away."

Hayes thought that he saw Chaseman flinch. Everyone else in the War Room seemed to freeze; those around the table looked intently at Chaseman, while those at the terminals strained to hear what he might say.

"Missile two is away."

"Sir, we must have your targeting decision immediately."

Chaseman made up his mind. "The second target will be your first priority military target."

"Target two is military one," an officer standing behind the General repeated into his headset.

"And target one, sir?"

Chaseman gave the only answer he could, and then realized that no one had been able to hear him. He took a deep breath, and tried again.

"Pyongyang."

Hayes watched the ashen-faced Acting President turn away from the table to look at the display screens, locking on the one tracking the North Korean missiles as they moved across a glowing map. The two flashing blips were already well outside the outline of North Korea.

"Second stage separation successfully completed for both missiles."

Hayes noticed that a cluster of technicians had gathered around one of the terminals that lined the walls of the room, underneath the huge display screens. Something must be wrong. But what? One of the technicians broke away and summoned the officer who had relayed the targeting command.

But Chaseman was oblivious to everything that was happening on the floor of the War Room. His eyes were pinned to the missile trajectory map and the inexorable progress of the cold, white blips, hoping that one or both missiles would malfunction as so many had before. The missiles had traveled far enough now that their trajectories to target could be projected with thin, glowing lines. He saw that those lines ended at Washington and New York.

"Time to targets: eighteen minutes."

"Issue Civil Defense alerts for Washington and New York," the General barked, looking for the officer who had been at his side just a few minutes before.

"Send the alerts, damn it!" he yelled when he spotted him across the room, huddled over a terminal with the technicians.

It would be bedlam up above, Hayes thought. There hadn't been a civil defense drill in decades; how many cities even had air raid sirens anymore? What could anyone do, anyway?

"One minute to anti-missile launch."

Chaseman was standing now, hunched forward with his hands gripping the back of his chair as he stared at the tracking screen. The resolution on the tracking screen abruptly increased a hundred fold, and he could see that the two North Korean missiles, their trajectories now more widely separated, were traveling along what must be the coast of Siberia.

"Third stage separation successfully completed for both missiles."

Suddenly, the image of first one missile, and then the second, began to shimmer.

"What's that?" Chaseman called over his shoulder.

"Camouflage, sir. When they blew the bolts for third stage separation, they must have expelled additional material – probably metallic chaff - to confuse the radar on our interceptors."

"Time to interception: three minutes.

Time to targets: twelve minutes"

A new blip appeared now, this one at the opposite edge of the screen. And then another, higher up. Soon the trajectories of eleven anti-missile rockets were splayed across the screen, each intersecting at a different point along the tracks of the North Korean missiles. All were converging rapidly on their targets.

But even as Chaseman watched, the blips representing the North Korean missiles began to expand until they became glowing clouds of light. And the lines indicating their trajectories were now spreading cones of light projecting forward.

"What's going on?" Chaseman demanded.

"We're seeing what our missiles are 'seeing,'" the General replied. "The clouds of light represent the perimeter of the field of camouflage, and the cones indicate the range of possibilities for the trajectory of the actual missile."

Chaseman clenched the back of his chair back as the first defensive missile blip entered the glowing circle one of the North Korean rockets.

"Anti-missile one has missed target."

Except for the cold, robotic voice from the speakers, the War Room was silent as the same, fruitless *pas-de-deux* played out over and over again in real life over the Bering Sea, and symbolically on the wall above them. One by one, the U.S. missiles entered the glowing clouds, either disappearing for good, or reemerging on the other side, only to be destroyed by their controllers. All the while, the shimmering clouds of the Korean missiles moved inexorably onwards, eventually coalescing once more into blips as their clouds of chaff became too diffuse to register on radar.

Why should he be surprised? Chaseman asked himself bitterly. We always knew they wouldn't work.

"Missiles have entered U.S. airspace."

This was it, then, he asked himself. Did he have the guts to make good on his threats? If so, he had no choice but to give the order to fire, before even knowing whether the North Korean missiles would find their targets or not. It was time to face up to the hideous historical role he had assigned himself to play.

"Sir!"

Chaseman turned blankly and looked to the Chairman of the Joint Chiefs. He realized the General had already been speaking earnestly to him for some time.

"Sir, we are unable to obtain the targeting information to program the ICBMs!"

Distraught as he was, Chaseman couldn't believe his ears. "Well, then enter the coordinates manually, damn it! Don't we keep an atlas in the War Room?"

"We can't, sir. For security reasons, we can't program the missiles directly. All we can do is instruct the database to transmit the encrypted target codes directly to the missile."

"Well, then do it, man!" Chaseman roared.

"We can't, sir. It's been hacked. We can't get through to the administrative functions of the database to start the targeting sequence."

"Time to targets: six minutes."

Now Chaseman's fears had been replaced with rage – how could he allow two American cities to be destroyed without retaliating?

"I want to see what you're looking at!" Chaseman roared. "Put it up on a screen!"

A harried technician bent over his terminal and typed furiously while Chaseman fidgeted. Suddenly, one of the huge LED screens lit up with a new image.

Chaseman's eyes widened. It seemed as if he was looking at flames. But the fire soon began to die away. As it did, a new image began to emerge. As he watched in growing confusion, the image resolved itself into a tall building, perhaps some sort of lighthouse. Underneath, there was a line of text, but in characters he couldn't read.

"What's it say?" He asked in amazement.

For the first time, the Director of the CIA spoke up.

"It says, 'Thank you for your contribution to the Alexandria Project,' sir."

With a sudden sense of relief, the Acting President wondered whether perhaps he was in fact in some insane dream. Something like this couldn't really be happening when the world was on the verge of Armageddon. The relentless robotic voice jolted him back to reality.

"Time to targets: four minutes."

What now? he wondered. Had he just been spared from committing genocide? Or was he about to allow millions of Americans to die without raising a finger in response? He decided he couldn't sit idly by.

"General, how soon can one of the B-1s with a nuclear weapon be over Pyongyang?"

"Missile two is no longer tracked."

Chaseman whirled around. One of the two trajectories lines on the screen had come to an end over Ontario.

"Missile one is no longer tracked."

As he watched, the last blip blinked for the final time over Lake Superior.

The War Room erupted into cheers. Chaseman extended a shaking arm behind him and groped for his chair. Finding it, he slowly sat down, still gazing at the brightly gleaming, and now still, map on the giant screen. He thought that he had never seen anything so beautiful in all his life.

~~0000 0001 0010 0011~~ 0100 ~~0011 0010 0001 0000~~

Epilogue

PRESIDENT RAWLINGS LOOKED up from his breakfast of indigestible hospital food and broke into a smile. Standing in the doorway of his room was the old friend he had appointed as his Director of National Intelligence.

"Ad! Great to see you! Come in and sit down. Better yet, wrap some of this crap up in your handkerchief and smuggle it out so I can pretend I ate my breakfast."

Adlai Stevenson Harrison walked in and pulled a seat up to the President's bedside.

"Wonderful to see you looking like your old self again, sir. I hope you know you gave us all quite a scare there for a while."

"Oh really! And for how long was that?"

"From the moment you passed out until," Harrison looked down at his watch, "exactly eighteen minutes ago. That's when your Presidential powers were restored."

Rawlings chuckled. "Yes, I understand that Henry made the most of his little adventure in the Oval Office."

"You have no idea. We survived the experience, but it turns out it was much closer than we expected at the time."

"Indeed. But first, tell me – what's the latest on the North Koreans?"

"It's the damnedest thing, sir. After everyone got done high-fiving each other in the War Room when the missiles fell short, someone remembered to check in on the situation on the ground. We expected to find that the North had already sent a million men across the DMZ but none of them had moved an inch."

"It was eerie – and it's stayed eerie. Nobody budged all day that day, or the next, either. Last night, the Red Guards started to just melt away, and today regular army units have been leaving their positions in what seems like a totally random fashion. It's as if suddenly there's nobody in charge. As you might expect, there are all kinds of wild rumors flying around in the intelligence community."

"Do we know anything more about the missiles they launched?"

"Yes, and that's just as strange. We've located the wreckage of one of them, and there was no warhead – not even conventional explosives! We've had planes with sensors criss-crossing Canadian airspace ever since the missiles disappeared from radar, and haven't found a trace of radiation anywhere. The North Koreans must have been trying to keep weight to a minimum – putting all their money on getting as close as possible to their targets in order to make sure we would launch our own rockets."

"Well I'll be damned. So it was nothing but a ruse the whole time. But if they never crossed the DMZ, what was the ruse for?"

"We still think it was an attempt to keep us from supporting South Korea when the North invaded, but assume that something must have gone wrong at the last minute. We're just guessing, but our current hypothesis is that there was some sort of shakeup at the top. Maybe some new power group used the failure of the missile ploy as an excuse to finally toss Jong-Il and his son over the side while they had the opportunity. Or maybe when we didn't blow up Washington and Moscow, they lost their nerve. We may never know for sure."

"Whatever happened, though, we think the in-fighting must still be continuing. Bach Choy hasn't been seen in days, and no one new has spoken yet for the regime. But there has been one interesting development."

"What's that?"

"We received a feeler from the Chinese through our embassy in Beijing. It seems that they were as unnerved by this whole escapade as we were. They want to broker some sort of final settlement between the North, the South, and the U.S. They're signaling that they'll even support us on taking away the North's nukes."

There was a knock at the door.

"Excuse me, Mr. President," a Secret Service agent said. "Mr. Chaseman to see you, sir. Should I ask him to wait?"

Harrison looked to see how his friend would react. To his surprise, Rawlings was looking down at his hands, brow furrowed and a wry smile on his face.

"I should be leaving anyway, sir," Harrison said. "I expect that you'll have a lot to say to Henry."

"Perhaps not as much as you'd think, Ad. Would things have turned out any better if I'd been sitting in the Oval Office that day? Maybe not. Given how well things ended up, perhaps nobody should be sorry I didn't have to find out. I know I'm not! There but for the grace of God, Ad. There but for the grace of God!"

Rawlings turned to the agent. "Please send Mr. Chaseman in."

Harrison stepped aside as the agent ushered a worried looking (once again) Vice President into Rawlings hospital room. He could only try to imagine the feeling of relief that Chaseman must be feeling as the President gave him a warm welcome.

—0000— 0001— 0010— 0011— 0100 —0011— 0010— 0001— 0000—

CIA Director John Foster Baldwin smiled smugly as he read the report on his desk. It told how the CIA, acting through his direct report, George Marchand, had provided safe haven to Frank Adversego, Jr., thus preventing the FBI, acting on the direct orders of Francis X. McInnerney, from capturing him in the nation's hour of greatest need for his unfettered assistance. Had the CIA not thwarted the FBI's incompetent plans, the report concluded, "the results would have been too horrifying to imagine." He would be sure that a copy was hand-delivered to Congressman Steele.

Baldwin's intercom buzzed.

"Yes, Gwen."

"A letter I think you should see, Mr. Baldwin. May I bring it in?"

"Fine, fine," he said, leaning back in his chair and savoring the closing lines of the report one more time.

His administrative assistant came through the door with a strange look on her face, and handed him a letter. "This arrived this morning, addressed to you in your personal, rather than your official, capacity. It's from an attorney in Las Vegas."

Las Vegas? When had he last been in Las Vegas?

He began to read:

LAW OFFICES OF ARNOLD PORTER, ESQ.
322 Freemont Street, Las Vegas, NV

June 23, 2012

Mr. John Foster Baldwin
CIA Headquarters
McLean, Virginia 22101

Dear Mr. Baldwin,

I represent Mr. Earl Jukes, until recently the owner of a MountainTamer XV-BS four wheel drive expedition vehicle. It is my understanding that Mr. Jukes' vehicle was destroyed by a Predator-launched Hellfire missile, in direct violation of multiple Federal laws relating to the use of such ordinance on U.S. soil other than on government-owned training and test ranges.

It is also my understanding that Mr. Jukes' property was destroyed on your personal orders, in clear violation of restrictions imposed by Congress on the powers of the CIA.

Finally, it is my understanding that Mr. Juke's had invested more than $400,000 in the camper. This amount comprises the original purchase price of the MountainTamer and the costs of the extensive modifications made to the vehicle by my client. Due to its one of a kind nature, the value of Mr. Jukes' unique vehicle was of course higher. Far, far higher, in Mr. Jukes' opinion.

Please be informed that Mr. Jukes intends to bring suit in Federal Court in Las Vegas against you personally for full restitution. He also intends to contact his Congressman, the Hon. Titus Steele, to request a full investigation into your conduct.

However, should you wish to make immediate and full restitution, my client would be willing to settle this matter privately.

I look forward to hearing from you at your earliest convenience....

0000 0001 0010 0011 0100 0011 0010 0001 0000

Chad Derwent put down his newspaper and turned to Sanjay. "You know, it's just like the old days – the two of us sharing an office."

Sanjay broke into a grin. "Yes, except that this is a 400 square foot penthouse office with a view of Silicon Valley instead of a shoebox in a basement."

Life was good indeed. iBalls.com's partnership with The Pangloss Game Company was flourishing. The *iBallZapper!* games had been so profitable that they'd even put together a modest investment fund with Archie and his silent partner, Frank Adversego. No ridiculous VC-type flyers on nonsense business plans, though. They only put their money into pragmatic concepts with proven market appeal and immediate revenue potential.

Investing had turned out to be fun, too, especially when you could get someone else to do all the grunt work. They'd hired a real venture capitalist to do that part – someone who'd been forced out by his own partners after he'd made a laughing stock of their fund.

"So Sanjay, ready to look at business plans?" Chad asked.

"Sure – why not – as long as it's my turn to tell our former VC, 'You just don't get it, do you? I mean, you really, *REALLY* don't get investing at all!"

They had a good laugh over that one. And then Sanjay called Josh Peabody in.

0000 0001 0010 0011 0100 0011 0010 0001 0000

Frank, Sr. wheeled the old Land Rover off the Beltway and began to head west. It would be good to get back to the desert. But of course it had been wonderful to reconnect with his son, too. He wondered whether Frank really would join him during his vacation next year. The West seemed to have gotten under his skin, just as it had his father's so many years before. He was even talking about getting a Mountain-Tamer of his own.

After much hesitation, Frank, Sr. had dropped in on Doreen. She was getting kind of foggy now, but that had made it easier. She only remembered their few good times now, such as they had been – all of the hard edges on her old feelings seemed to have melted away with time and the onset of old age. He doubted he'd visit again, but the sense of closure was welcome after so many years.

And that granddaughter of his was a pistol! He wished he'd had a chance to get to know her as she was growing up, but better late than never. He was looking forward to that.

0000 0001 0010 0011 0100 0011 0010 0001 0000

Carl felt light-headed. The evening had gone far better than he had dared hope. The restaurant was perfect, and Marla looked ravishing. He'd been on his best behavior all evening, and didn't think that he'd stuck his foot in his mouth even once. Across the candlelit table, he thought he caught a gleam of real interest in her eyes. Perhaps....

Marla herself was surprised. Carl was being gracious, funny, and sometimes even self-deprecating. She marveled that she could actually find his company enjoyable, now that all of the tensions and events of the last months were behind them. And she had to admit that he was much more handsome now than he had been as a grad student – and even then he had caught her eye. Don't lose your head, girl, she told herself.

But the cocktails and a bottle of champagne were taking effect. The candlelight and the opportunity to relive and laugh over their shared adventures combined to make it an increasingly magic evening. When at last it was time to go, Carl, ever the perfect gentleman, held her chair, and then her coat. In no time at all, it seemed, they were standing at the door of her apartment in the magical moonlight of a soft, spring evening in Washington, redolent with the scent of cherry blossoms.

Carl looked down into her eyes with an urgent look in his own, and she sensed that he was about to say something. She put a single finger to his lips and uttered a barely audible, "Shhhh!"

"No, don't say anything at all," she said softly. She turned and unlocked her door. Then, she turned back, and stepped forward until her body barely touched his. Slowly, she tilted her head back in the soft moonlight as her eyes drifted shut. "There's something I've wanted to give you for so long now," she whispered.

Carl's heart leapt into his throat.

And then he was leaping backwards, his hand rising involuntarily to the cheek that Marla had just slapped with all her might.

"What was that for?!" he cried in astonishment.

"That was for the 'C' you gave me on my final exam, you bastard!"
She slammed the door in his face.

0000 0001 0010 0011 0100 0011 0010 0001 0000

Frank turned the light on in the limousine and unfolded the letter in his pocket. The gold seal on the Presidential stationary glinted as he held it up to read it once again – a personal letter, signed by the President himself, expressing his gratitude for the role that Frank had performed in cracking the secrets of the real parties behind The Alexandria Project and averting a nuclear holocaust. It invited him to become a charter member of a new Presidential Cybersecurity Advisory Committee as well.

As he returned the letter to its envelope, he reflected that he could never have imagined an ending such as this while the strange kaleidoscope of events that had taken over his life had been unfolding. Learning (or so he thought) that he was under suspicion; his melodramatic, but successful, escape in the department store; the long bus trip and even longer sojourn in the Solar Avenger, perched high above the desert valley floor in Nevada; the unexpected reunion with his father; the long return and increasing frustration at his inability to penetrate the mystery whose resolution seemed always to be just beyond his grasp. Already, these scenes were beginning to seem unreal and vaporous, like mirages that might shimmer into nothingness with the rising of the sun.

The car slowed, and once again he was looking at his down-at-the-heels apartment building, in his run-down neighborhood. The rain that had begun falling as he was leaving the White House had grown stronger as they drove across the District, and now the very heavens above seemed to have opened. He returned the envelope to the safety of the breast pocket of the only suit he owned.

Here was the driver now, opening his door and holding an enormous umbrella over his head. Self-consciously, he allowed the driver to walk him to the front door of the building, and stepped inside without catching a drop. How his life had changed! Would it ever be the same again?

And then he was standing before his own front door once again. He put his key in the lock, turned it, and then silently, thankfully, swung open the door and turned on the light.

Instantly, an ear-splitting din erupted. There was Lilly, paws planted firmly on the ground, her leash in a heap in front of her. Of course. Mrs. Foomjoy had disappeared the day before the crisis with North Korea had reached its climax, and Marla had rescued a very hungry dog from her apartment just that morning.

Frank tried to step past the dog to get an umbrella, but Lilly snarled and would have none of it. Outside the thunder crashed, as Frank sighed and attached the leash. Yes, he still had a plastic bag in his raincoat pocket.

As he stepped out of the apartment and into the rain, Frank smiled a small, ironic smile to himself. He might have a letter of thanks from the President of the United States in his pocket, but he still had to pick up after Lilly, one bag at a time.

0000 0001 0010 0011 0100 0011 0010 0001 0000